GREAT LIVES

Medicine

Medicine
GREAT LIVES

Robert H. Curtis, M.D.

Charles Scribner's Sons · New York

Maxwell Macmillan Canada · Toronto
Maxwell Macmillan International
New York · Oxford · Singapore · Sydney

Charles Scribner's Sons Books for Young Readers
Macmillan Publishing Company · 866 Third Avenue, New York, NY 10022

Maxwell Macmillan Canada, Inc.
1200 Eglinton Avenue East, Suite 200, Don Mills, Ontario M3C 3N1

Macmillan Publishing Company is part of the
Maxwell Communication Group of Companies.

First edition 10 9 8 7 6 5 4 3 2 1
Printed in the United States of America

Library of Congress Cataloging-in-Publication Data
Curtis, Robert H.
Great lives: medicine / Robert H. Curtis. — 1st ed.
p. cm. Includes bibliographical references and index.
Summary: Short biographies of more than thirty men and women who excelled in the field of medical science. Includes Hippocrates, Harvey, Ehrlich, Roentgen, Blackwell, Freud, and Salk.
ISBN 0-684-19321-3
1. Physicians—Biography—Juvenile literature.
2. Medical scientists—Biography—Juvenile literature.
[1. Physicians. 2. Scientists.] I. Title.
R134.C87 1992 610'.92'2—dc20 92-5387

This book is dedicated with love to my wife, Joan, our children, Judy, Joel, Debbie, and Pam, their husbands and wives, Kent, Maria, Chuck, and Al, and to our grandchildren, Jeremy, Jordan, Samantha, Alexander, Elise, Max, and Amelia.

It is dedicated as well to the finest editor any author could wish for, Clare Costello.

Contents

Foreword

In this book the lives of many scientists who have contributed to the world of medicine are described. Although the author has chosen these investigators, quite probably there are thousands who are equally deserving of recognition. It is important to remember that in scientific research, the person receiving credit for his or her work always relies on the contributions of many others, either colleagues or researchers from the recent or distant past. Scientific research is a cooperative venture, and progress in the field is made over a very broad and deep foundation. Like the top of a submerged iceberg, or the top acrobat of a human pyramid, the heroes and heroines in this book would be nonexistent without the support of the base.

Galileo said, "Science is measurement." You, the reader, are contributing to science from the day of your birth, when you add to knowledge of vital statistics and continue to contribute, if only by being a measurable part of a community. Thus all of us—those being measured, those measuring, and those doing both—are in the business of contributing to science.

PART I

Ancient Medicine

Hippocrates

460? B.C. – 370? B.C. Greek physician; father of the scientific study of medicine

The ancient Greeks contributed immensely to the civilization of our world. They excelled in music, the arts, and architecture—and perhaps the greatest gift they gave to us was the idea of democracy, government by the people.

Another important contribution made by the ancient Greeks was the gift of scientific medicine. The man responsible for the foundation of medicine as we know it today was Hippocrates. He was born on the Greek island of Cos around 460 B.C. and lived a long life, dying around 370 B.C. Not much is known about him, but accounts of his accomplishments were written by a few contemporaries, notably Plato and Aristotle. Socrates lived at the same time as Hippocrates, and some claim that the socratic method of teaching (questioning students in order to make them think) was inspired by Hippocrates.

Hippocrates has been known throughout history as the "father of medicine," but what did he do to deserve this title? Not much was known about medicine in ancient times, and many beliefs of the ancients have, as knowledge progresses, disappeared. For example, Hippocrates believed that the body was composed of four "elements"—fire, air, earth, and water. He and his followers suggested that these four components of nonliving matter combined into "qualities" of warm-moist (fire and water), cold-dry (earth and air), warm-dry (fire and air), and cold-moist (earth and water). When these combined qualities entered the

An eighteenth-century French engraving presents the universally accepted image of Hippocrates. *National Library of Medicine, Bethesda, Maryland.*

body, the Greeks believed, they became the "humors"—blood, black bile, yellow bile, and phlegm. Probably the Greeks had observed these body fluids while treating battlefield injuries and illnesses.

The Greeks believed that the humors had to be in harmonious balance for a person to be healthy. Hippocrates, being the first to make the connection between the brain and emotions, said that the overheating of the brain from too much bile resulted in terror and fear, causing the face to flush; overcooling of the brain from too much phlegm resulted in anxiety and grief. (Actually, the concept of the four elements of body composition isn't too far off base. Our bodies are composed largely of water, our lungs are filled with air, our bones are made from calcium and phosphorus derived from the earth, and the burning of foodstuffs [metabolism] is a type of fire. But all that aside, the phlegm theory was incorrect.)

Hippocrates retains his stature today as the "father of medicine" for other reasons. He founded a medical school (the Coan school named after his native island), and he told the world for the first time that medical cures were not accomplished by the use of the supernatural. Instead he insisted that disease occurred when the body was out of harmony with nature and that to cure disease, one had to repair the imbalance. He believed that every disease had a natural cause and that cures could be accomplished by observing the patient's symptoms and recording those observations. He and his school placed much emphasis on caring for the patient and paying attention to the patient's welfare rather than concentrating on some interesting disease process; today much of this philosophy could be applied with great benefit.

To understand what a departure Hippocratic medicine was from the usual healing attempts of that time, one has to look at the treatment given at Aesculapian shrines. Healing power was believed to be held by Aesculapius, the mythical god who was the grandson of Zeus and the son of Apollo. These Aesculapian shrines were somewhat like health spas, located on beautiful hills near mineral springs. Robed priests slowly sang prayers and told of the miraculous cures achieved by the power of Aesculapius and two of his children, daughters Hygeia and Panacea. Most often the patient, sleeping in the temple, would have a vision in a dream, which the priests would interpret to prescribe the proper treatment. Often the therapy consisted of diet, exercise, or simple suggestion that an instant cure would take place. Since most ill people will recover by themselves, the suggested therapy usually worked, but if the treatment failed, the blame was placed on the sick person rather than on the shrine and its priests.

Nobody denies today that positive thinking is helpful in curing all disease, no matter how serious. Hippocratic teaching included such positive encouragement to the patient as well as the first scientific observations of disease and the first *rational* approach to it.

The Hippocratic Collection—or, as it is known, the Hippocratic Corpus—consists of approximately sixty treatises on various aspects of medicine. Most of them were written between 430 B.C. and 330 B.C., many while Hippocrates was heading his school. (The only known author is Polybus, Hippocrates' son-in-law, who wrote "The Nature of Man.") They cover many subjects—general pathology (description of the disease process), pathology of specific diseases, diagnosis, prognosis (the physician's estimate on the eventual outcome of the patient's disease), treatment, physiology, embryology, gynecology, surgery, medical ethics, and several other subjects. We know that they were written by different authors because opinions often contradict one another and also because of the time span involved. Attention to the patient, however, and emphasis on natural rather than supernatural causes of disease are consistent features of all of the treatises. They all stem from the basic teachings of Hippocrates. It is interesting to see how many of the Greek words of the Corpus are used in medical terminology today. We have nephritis from *nephrós* ("kidney"); hepatitis from *hepar* ("liver"); pleuritis from *pleurá* ("rib" or "side"); arthritis from *árthron* ("joint"), and many others.

In ancient times there was no profession of medicine as we know it today. Anyone could claim to heal the sick. Probably Hippocrates was taught medicine by his father, since apprenticeship to a reputable physician was the method of teaching most used. Although Hippocrates was not the first physician, his school set exceptional scientific and ethical standards and formed the basis for the present profession of medicine.

The Hippocratic Corpus was new and therefore unique. Knowledge of this Greek medicine spread throughout the ancient world, especially among the Arabs. Rhazes, who died in 925, Avicenna, who lived in the eleventh century, and the greatest of all, the twelfth-century Averroës, were familiar with the works of Hippocrates. Even in the seventeenth century, those great scientists Sydenham of England and Boerhaave of Holland acknowledged their debt to Hippocrates.

In a nineteenth-century print, after a painting by the German artist Henry Schopin, Hippocrates refuses all pleas to leave Greece and go to the Persian court. *Brown Brothers.*

The most valuable legacy of the Hippocratic school (besides its scientific emphasis) is the code of ethics included in its oath. The Hippocratic oath (in ancient times taken by students just starting to study in the Hippocratic school) now is repeated at graduation by a number of present-day medical schools. The oath was written in the spirit of Hippocrates' teachings, but its author probably was not Hippocrates himself. There are so many translations of the oath that it is impossible to tell which is the authentic one, but they all say essentially the same thing. This is from the Lloyd edition of *Hippocratic Writings:*

I swear by Apollo the healer, by Aesculapius, by Health and all the powers of healing, and call to witness all the gods and goddesses that I may keep this Oath and Promise to the best of my ability and judgement.

I will pay the same respect to my master in the Science as to my parents and share my life with him and pay all my debts to him. I will regard his sons as my brothers and teach them the Science, if they desire to learn it, without fee or contract. I will hand on precepts, lectures and all other learning to my sons, to those of my master and to those pupils duly apprenticed and sworn, and to none other.

I will use my power to help the sick to the best of my ability and judgement; I will abstain from harming or wronging any man by it.

I will not give a fatal draught to anyone if I am asked, nor will I suggest any such thing. Neither will I give a woman means to procure an abortion.

I will be chaste and religious in my life and in my practice.

I will not cut, even for the stone, but I will leave such procedures to the practitioners of that craft.

Whenever I go into a house, I will go to help the sick and never with the intention of doing harm or injury. I will not abuse my position to indulge in sexual contacts with the bodies of women or of men, whether they be freemen or slaves.

Whatever I see or hear, professionally or privately, which ought not to be divulged, I will keep secret and tell no one.

If, therefore, I observe this Oath and do not violate it, may I prosper in my profession, earning good repute among all men for all time. If I transgress and forswear this Oath, may my lot be otherwise.

Two things are obvious about the oath. First, it was taken for granted that only men practiced medicine, and so it remained for centuries. Second, the oath itself is divided into two sections. The first is simply a formula for the practical way to conduct a medical career; the second part and the one that is remembered today is the code of ethics prescribed. One of the most important precepts in the oath is clearly stated in the treatise "Epidemics"—"to help, or at least to do no harm."

Thus Hippocrates and his school began the scientific study of medicine. Approximately five hundred years later, a physician, also of Greek parentage, came to dominate the world of medicine so completely that for the next fifteen hundred years it was dangerous if not impossible to challenge his medical thoughts. His name was Galen.

Galen

A.D. 130? – A.D. 200? Most famous early physician; contributor to knowledge of anatomy and physiology

One of the most famous and controversial physicians of all time was born in Pergamum about A.D. 130. His name was Galen, and Pergamum in those days was part of the Roman Empire. (Today that city is named Bergama and is in Turkey.)

Galen was the son of Greek parents. His father, Nicon, was an architect, seemingly of gentle disposition, and Galen misrepresented himself as having the same sweet qualities as his father. (The Greek name *Galenos* means "calm, or "serene.") Galen didn't care much for his mother, comparing her with the wife of Socrates. Here's Galen's own description of his parents:

> It was my good fortune to have a father who was perfectly calm, just, serviceable and devoted; my mother on the contrary was so irascible that she sometimes bit her maids; she was always babbling and quarreling with my father, as did Xanthippe with Socrates.

Galen eventually became one of the most prolific writers of all times. Since most physicians after Hippocrates' era failed to record their observations, it isn't clear how much of the Galen writings represent original work, but it is known that many brilliant contributions to the knowledge of anatomy and physiology were those of Galen himself. According to medical historian George Sarton, the most complete translation of Galen's writings was the Greek-Latin Carolus G. Kühn edition published from 1821 to 1833 in Leipzig; it consists of twenty-two thick volumes, which could keep anyone absorbed for years.

Included are autobiographical notes (some of the earliest autobiographical writings in history) and Galen's self-written index of all his work, the first bibliography in world literature.

As a young man, he lived on his father's farm just outside of Pergamum, so it is clear that Galen's father was a farmer as well as an architect. There was a famous shrine to Aesculapius, the god of healing, at Pergamum. Both Galen's father and Galen himself were influenced by it. Galen's later religious views were unique and largely responsible for his long reign of authority on all things medical, a reign of some fifteen hundred years. Galen himself was not modest about his knowledge, and those who lived after him kept his legend alive and added to it. So there were several factors—religion, Galen's dogmatic certainty, his literary output, and his disciples—which kept the name of Galen sacred for so long.

Galen's father, Nicon, was determined that his son get a first-rate education, especially after Nicon had what he believed to be a divinely inspired dream that his son should become a physician. Young Galen was sent to study all through the eastern regions of the Roman Empire, visiting even the medical school at Alexandria. He studied the four leading philosophical systems (Plato's, Aristotle's, the Stoic, and the Epicurean) and later the six medical sects (the ancient Hippocratic, dogmatic, and empirical sects, and the "modern" methodist, pneumatic, and eclectic) in order to develop his own philosophy of life and of medicine.

In connection with the books Galen must have used in his studies, it is fascinating to note that a rivalry concerning their respective libraries existed between the Egyptian city of Alexandria and Galen's home city of Pergamum. Manuscripts were written on material derived from the Egyptian plant papyrus, but because of the rivalry, an Egyptian ruler named Ptolemy tried to sabotage the Pergamum library by forbidding the export of papyrus. Consequently there was invented in Pergamum a new kind of writing material derived from animal skins; this became known as *pergamena charta*, "parchment." Sarton points out that "a far reaching consequence of that discovery was the development of the codex, or book, instead of the volumen, or roll; papyrus lent itself better to the roll shape, parchment to the book shape."

Galen began his medical studies of anatomy in Pergamum where he remained for four years; later he studied in Smyrna (now Izmir in Turkey), Corinth in Greece, and Alexandria. By this time, he was an accomplished anatomist. Dissection of human bodies was frowned upon, although Galen had certainly seen the inside of human bodies during the years 158–161 when he was physician to the gladiators at Pergamum. Gladiatorial battles in coliseums were held to amuse the masses, but they were cruel contests, often ending in death. The wounds sustained from swords, spears, tridents, and weighted boxing gloves were deep, and while treating these unfortunate gladiators, Galen must have had an opportunity to see some human anatomy. His dissections, however, were confined to animals, and his observations often led him to conclude incorrectly that human anatomy was the same. He dissected dogs, goats, pigs, and his favorite species, because it closely resembled man, the Barbary ape. (He did, however, acquire expert knowledge of human bones; he had examined a few skeletons and accurately described each component bone.)

Galen's religious beliefs also led him astray. Though he was part pagan, he adopted the monotheistic idea of the small Hebrew and Christian sects in the places he lived. He had practically no knowledge of the details of their worship, but he did believe in the existence of one and only one major God, and he felt that everything in the universe had been created by God according to a master plan. Every anatomical structure had been predetermined by God, he reasoned, and God could do no wrong. In scientific investigation, the object is to observe dispassionately and not to alter observations to fit preconceived theories. Galen's effort to prove that all human structure and function was the direct work of God, while excluding the possibility of evolution, made him popular with theologians and helped to ensure his exclusive dominance for a millennium and a half.

Galen believed that all blood was manufactured daily from food intake and that nutrition was supplied by blood moving up and down in the veins. He was the first to state that arteries contained blood; before Galen, it had been believed that they contained air mixed with a vital spirit called *pneuma*. Galen generally believed in pneuma as the dominant vital force, but he still had to explain how blood entered the left side of the heart and moved into the arteries. To do this, he postulated the existence of *pores*, tiny holes in the septum dividing the right side of the heart with its bluish-colored venous blood from the left with its red arterial blood. Until Vesalius, using careful human dissections, forcefully proclaimed that no such pores existed, Galen's explanation was accepted.

Galen had achieved such fame that after he moved to Rome around the

One of the few likenesses of the physician Galen. *Photosearch, Inc.*

year 161, he eventually became physician to the great Roman emperor Marcus Aurelius and also to two later emperors, Commodus and Septimius Severus.

Galen, despite handicaps of arrogance and incorrect reasoning, made several unique medical discoveries. He showed how the muscles of the body work in harmony and observed that the muscles of the diaphragm and thorax are responsible for expansion of the chest and consequent filling of the lungs with air. He cut the spinal cord of animals at various levels and showed that the resulting paralysis depended on which nerves were transected. By studying the nerves of the larynx, he showed that the voice emanates from that organ rather than from the heart as had been previously believed. He proved, moreover, that speech comes from the brain and not from the heart, since the nerves originate in the brain.

One of Galen's interesting cases, in which he anticipated Freud, was that of a woman whose pulse became irregular whenever she was told that a dancer, Pylades, was to perform. On three previous days, her heartbeat and therefore her pulse had not reacted when the names of other performers were mentioned. Galen described his diagnosis:

> On the fourth evening, I kept very careful watch when it was announced that Pylades was dancing, and I noticed that the pulse was very much disturbed. Thus I found out that the woman was in love with Pylades, and by careful watch on the succeeding days my discovery was confirmed.

But probably Galen's greatest contribution to medicine came from his writing. His works were widely read, and he charted a scientific, even though partially erroneous, method of studying anatomy and medicine itself. What seems sad is that this brilliant man abandoned the scientific experimental method he had established almost as frequently as he stuck to it.

During his later years when Rome became the scene of continuous turmoil, Galen turned to the peaceful setting of southern Italy. He died at age seventy at the end of the century, probably in Sicily. His impact was, and remains, enormous.

PART II

The Beginnings of Modern Medicine

Ambroise Paré

1510–1590 French surgeon; developer of the art and technique of gentle surgery

It is difficult to believe that surgery, that specialty of medicine today responsible for saving so many lives, once was a despised profession. In the sixteenth century in France major physicians did not work at all with their hands but relied on books written in Greek and Latin. Second to the physicians were the surgeons. Theoretically, they were in a better position than the lowest on the totem pole, the barber-surgeons. Yet in reality, the barber-surgeons were the ones who performed venesections (removing blood from veins) and cupping (a method of drawing blood to the surface by suctioning air out of glass cups to form a vacuum); probably neither of these procedures was valuable, but they gave hands-on experience and also provided an income. The surgeons, naturally, were jealous, and the erudite physicians were content to remain above it all.

Into this guildlike barber-surgeon group was born, in 1510, Ambroise Paré, the man who would elevate surgery to a respectable art and science. His father was an ordinary barber and valet, but his older brother was a master barber-surgeon.

Ambroise Paré became a barber-surgeon, too, probably helped by his brother. Later he was apprenticed to another barber-surgeon. Apprentices often weren't treated very well; their teachers didn't want them to learn enough to become competitors. Paré was apprenticed for only a short time when he received an appointment as resident surgeon at Hôtel-Dieu, the

Portrait of Ambroise Paré, engraved by W. Holl. *Photosearch, Inc.*

only public hospital in Paris. He gained much experience there and left in 1536 to begin a career as a military surgeon.

In those days a military surgeon was not a member of a medical corps attached to a military unit such as a regiment or battalion; he was the personal doctor of some military man, usually a nobleman. Paré's first patron was Maréchal de Montejan, whom he accompanied to Turin, Italy, to which city King Francis I had sent an invasion force. Here Paré made the first of two great discoveries, discoveries that would make the treating of wounds far less painful than previously had been the case. Gunpowder only recently had been used in warfare, and those treating gunshot wounds were unfamiliar with the best way to treat these often devastating injuries. What was commonly believed was that gunshot wounds were poisonous. As a result, the usual treatment was to cauterize the wounds with boiling oil, an agonizing ordeal for the wounded man. But during one particular battle Paré couldn't find any oil. Here in his own words is what happened. (The translations from Paré's *Apologie* written in French were done about 1580 by an English surgeon, George Baker.)

I wanted [lacked] oyle, and was constrained in steed thereof, to apply a digestive of yolkes of eggs, oyle of Roses, and Turpentine. In the night I could not sleepe in quiet, fearing some default in not cauterizing, that I should finde those to whom I had not used the burning oyle dead impoysoned; which made me rise very early to visit them, where beyond my expectation I found those to whom I had applyed my digestive medicine, to feele little paine, and their wounds without inflammation or tumor [swelling], having rested well in the night: the others to whom was used the sayd burning oyle, I found them feverish with great paine and tumour about the edges of their wounds. And then I resolved with myselfe never so cruelly, to burne poore men wounded with gunshot.

Probably it was not Paré's innovative treatment but rather his written description of this experience that changed the history of surgery.

Paré's second important contribution was the use of a ligature to tie off bleeding arteries and veins after amputations or wounds inflicted in battle. Prior to Paré, bleeding vessels were cauterized with red-hot instruments, which procedure, in pre-anesthesia days, was extremely painful. Ligature had been used in ancient times but abandoned. Paré's own battlefield experience led him to revert to these gentler methods of treatment. He cites experience as the most important teacher and points out that learning surgery from textbooks alone is useless. In the amputation of a leg, he advised cutting off all gangre-

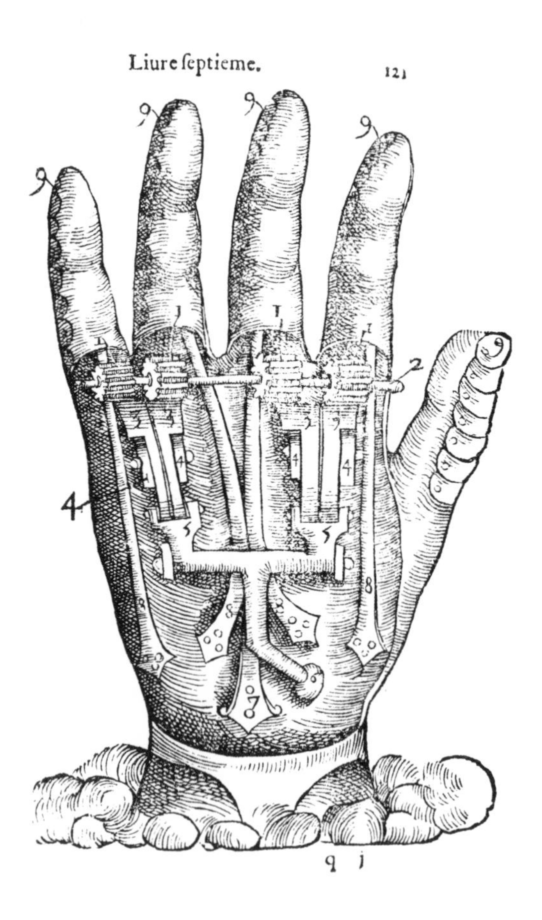

Illustration of an "iron" (artificial) hand. From Paré's *Ten Books of Surgery*, 1564. *National Library of Medicine, Bethesda, Maryland. Photograph by Rudy Vetter.*

nous tissue but as little of the healthy part of the injured leg as possible in order that a wooden leg might be fitted effectively.

Paré personally made excellent prostheses, wooden legs and the like. He treated many different kinds of illnesses and described them in his writings. Hernias, fractures, dislocations, obstetrical techniques, and surgical removal of bladder stones were among the subjects he addressed.

Paré was married twice, in 1541 to Jeanne Mazelin and in 1574 to Jacqueline Rousselet. He fathered nine children (four daughters and five sons); all five boys died in infancy. He himself died in 1590, at the age of eighty, having spent the greatest part of his life, from 1536 until his death, in the field as a military surgeon. During this period he made his greatest contributions to surgery, and he also served as physician to four kings of France: Henry II, Francis II, Charles IX, and Henry III.

During all of his career, Paré never lost his compassion and always remained modest. His most quoted statement was made after a successful operation. *"Je le pansay, Dieu le guarit."* ("I dressed him, God cured him.") Some of his surgical aphorisms also show his philosophy. For example:

> "Raison n'a que voir ny chercher
> Là où l'on peut du doigt toucher."

This means: "Reason cannot see or search as the finger can by touch."

Again he valued personal experience and observation, which qualities are the cornerstones of his surgical approach. Paré was a good and kind man who many authorities consider to be the "father of surgery."

Andreas Vesalius

1514–1564 Belgian physician; author / illustrator of the first accurate textbook on human anatomy

The Renaissance (a French word meaning "rebirth") began in Italy and had its greatest impact from the middle of the fourteenth century through the sixteenth century. Actually this rebirth of scientific and artistic culture extended well beyond the sixteenth century, spreading from Italy to all of Europe. It was as if Europe had suddenly awakened from the hibernation of the Middle Ages; the exuberance of this awakened freedom led to all sorts of discoveries in different fields, precisely because the human mind was now permitted to function freely.

Andreas Vesalius lived during a time when dissection of human corpses was permitted or, in places where not permitted, at least overlooked by the authorities. Vesalius, taking full advantage of this freedom, eventually was able to correct the many errors of the anatomist Galen.

During the several centuries of rule by the Roman Empire, the epoch in which Galen had lived, Latin literature, art, and architecture flourished; respect for the bodies of the dead, however, by religious doctrine and also by law, made dissection of human bodies impossible. Galen had had to rely on the dissection of animals. His conclusions had never been questioned and had been considered almost sacred for fifteen hundred years. Now a youthful Vesalius, who began his studies believing in the accuracy of Galen, would steer medicine in a different and truer direction.

Vesalius was born in Brussels, Belgium, of a distinguished family. The family name, Witing, was changed to

Vesalius (meaning "from Wesel"), since Wesel was the family's town of origin. Andreas Vesalius's great-grandfather was a physician who became head of the medical school at Belgium's University of Louvain. His grandfather was physician to the archduke Maximilian of the Netherlands, and his father became an apothecary, serving as pharmacist to the imperial family of the Holy Roman Empire. Even with the family medical background, Vesalius's own independent thinking must have played a large role in his choice of profession; at an early age, he became interested in the internal structure of animals and performed dissections on them.

According to Charles D. O'Malley, whose text on Vesalius is the richest and most thorough on Vesalius's life, not much is known of his childhood. At age fifteen he entered the University of Louvain. He graduated in 1533 with the degree of Master of Arts, and having decided on a medical career, he entered the medical school of the University of Paris. There he began to have doubts about the way anatomy was taught. One professor performed practically no dissection. Another, Jacobus Sylvius, was such an ardent Galenist that when what he found during dissection differed from what Galen had written, he made the preposterous statement that the structure of the human body had changed since Galen's time; he simply could not bring himself to accept the obvious fact that Galen often was wrong. Vesalius, nevertheless, liked and respected Sylvius, although writing in 1546, Vesalius made it clear that he had really taught himself anatomy.

I don't know if Sylvius paid any attention to the remark in my books . . . that is, that I have worked without the help of a teacher, since perhaps he believes that I learned anatomy from him, he who still maintains that Galen is always right. Sylvius, whom I shall respect as long as I live, always started the course by reading the books *On the use of parts* to us, but when he reached the middle of the first book, the anatomical part, he announced that this was too difficult for us, just beginning our studies, to follow, and that it would be troublesome for him and for us.

Despite the lack of anatomical instruction, Vesalius achieved great skill in this field because he always dissected independently. By early 1536 he was asked by fellow students and even by teachers to conduct dissections. In that year, however, war had broken out between France and the Holy Roman Empire (Germany, Burgundy, the Low Countries, Spain, and northern Italy). France had invaded northern Italy, and Charles V, emperor of the Holy Roman

Empire, had retaliated by invading France from the north and from the south. Since Vesalius was Belgian, in Paris his status was that of an enemy alien, and so he returned to Louvain.

While still studying at the medical school in Louvain in 1537, Vesalius published his first book, *A Paraphrase of the Ninth Book of Rhazes.* This work, probably his thesis for the degree of Bachelor of Medicine, was an attempt to unify anatomical terminology. Vesalius replaced obscure Arabic terms with Latin and Greek words, thus making the Rhazes volume easier for European physicians to understand. This desire to make anatomy clear and accurate heralded Vesalius's famous book, *Fabrica,* that followed only six years later.

It was at this time that Vesalius made an important decision. He realized that the Most Serene Republic of Venice, a city-state, was a leader in the Renaissance. Here Titian and other great artists lived and worked, and at the famous University of Padua (near to and governed by Venice), academic freedom flourished. Students from all over Europe were attracted to this freedom, and so Vesalius came to Padua.

Medical historian Arturo Castiglioni, in an address commemorating the fourth centenary of the publication of Vesalius's *Fabrica,* described the graduation ceremony.

On the morning of the fifth day of December, 1537, a solemn assembly was gathered in the sumptuous hall of the bishop's palace at Padua. The vicar of the Pope, the professors and members of the college of Doctors in their gorgeous gowns were present, and Francesco Frigimelica, prior of the College, after stressing in a flourishing, Latin discourse the merits of Andreas Vesalius, of Brussels, who in previous examinations had furnished ample proof of his proficiency in medicine, conferred upon him the degree of Laureate Doctor of Medicine.

Merit, Vesalius had in abundance; immediately following his graduation, the university appointed him professor of surgery and anatomy. There may be other instances of a student becoming a professor immediately following his graduation, but if they exist, they are indeed rare. Vesalius, however, was no beginner in his specialty. He had studied for years in Belgium, in France, and now in Italy. And with all his experience, he recognized the deficiencies in the way anatomy was taught. Here is his description of that teaching:

The detestable procedure now in vogue is that one man has to carry out the dissection of the human body, while another gives a description of the parts. The lecturers are perched up aloft in a pulpit, like jackdaws, and with a notable air of disdain, they drone out information about facts they never approach at first hand, but which they merely commit to memory from the books of others, or of which they have descriptions before their eyes; the dissectors are so ignorant that they are unable to explain the dissections to the onlookers, and botch what ought to be exhibited in accordance with the instruction of the physician, who never applies his hand to the dissection and steers the ship out of the manual, as the saying goes. Thus, everything is wrongly taught, days are wasted in absurd questions and in the confusion less is offered to the student than a butcher in his stall could teach the doctor.

Obviously Vesalius was forthright in his opinions, but his criticism wasn't empty bombast; it was based on intelligent personal experience. He emphasized what again and again we hear from the great investigators: In the study of science, there is no substitute for careful direct observation.

Vesalius began his teaching dissections in December 1537. He usually managed to have a supply of corpses on hand but would dissect animals if human cadavers were unavailable. And unlike the description above, he didn't sit high up "in a pulpit" tonelessly reciting; instead he was down at the table personally dissecting and demonstrating what he wanted the students to learn. Aided by a skeleton, he first would sketch the outline of the bones on the surface of the skin of the cadaver and then begin his dissection.

His classes were more than popular; over five hundred students and doctors attended the dissections, which lasted as long as three weeks, comprised of morning and afternoon sessions. He fascinated the students with a demonstration that women and men have the same number of ribs. (It had been widely accepted, because of the biblical story of Eve's creation from one of Adam's ribs, that men had one less of these structures than did women.)

At the request of his students he made various anatomical drawings. Finding them useful in the teaching sessions, in 1538 he published the *Anatomicae Tabulae,* six large drawings of the arterial and venous systems and of the nerves of the body. Three of the drawings were done by Vesalius himself, while the other three were drawn by his countryman John Stephen Calcar, a pupil of Titian's and an excellent artist in his own right. These tables supplanted older, inaccurate anatomical drawings. Then Vesalius was asked by a Venetian printer to edit a new edition of Galen's books of anatomy. As he studied the text, he realized that Galen had made many errors. With remarkable insight, Vesalius realized why this had happened: Galen had never dissected a human corpse. "He was cheated by his monkeys," Vesalius concluded, "and in the manifold divergence of the human body from that of the monkeys,

Frontispiece of the first edition of Andreas Vesalius's *De Humani Corporis Fabrica*, 1543. *National Library of Medicine, Bethesda, Maryland.*

had hardly noticed anything except in the fingers and the bend of the knee." Moreover, Galen's work contained no illustrations.

Vesalius was now certain of what he probably had suspected earlier: No accurate textbook of human anatomy existed. Encouraged by friends and students, he set out to correct every mistake he had found, and for three years (1539–1542) he worked on his manuscript. In 1543 his masterpiece was published in Basel, Switzerland, by the printer Johannes Oporinus. Titled *De Humani Corporis Fabrica* ("On the Structure of the Human Body"), it consisted of seven books bound into a single volume, beautifully illustrated. It should be noted that there is much uncertainty about who did the illustrations for the *Fabrica*, but Calcar probably was one of the artists, as was Vesalius himself. Possibly the anatomical drawing of Leonardo da Vinci had some influence on Vesalius's illustrations, but in any case, medical historians consider them unique.

Known generally as simply the *Fabrica*, Vesalius's book begins with a long, flattering dedication to Emperor Charles V. This type of dedication was not unusual for someone who eventually wanted a position in the ruler's household. In the preface, he explains that he is departing from Galen's views:

> For I am not unaware how the medical profession . . . are wont to be upset when in more than two hundred instances, in the conduct of the single course of anatomy I now conduct in the schools, they see that Galen has failed to give a true description of the interrelation, use, and function of the parts of man . . . [Translation from B. Farrington in *Proceedings of the Royal Society of Medicine*, 25, 1932.]

Book I describes the bones, Book II the muscles, Book III the blood vessels, Book IV the nervous system, Book V the abdominal internal organs and the reproductive system, Book VI the heart and lungs, and Book VII the brain. Some parts are more accurate than others. The bones and muscles, for example, are almost flawlessly presented. The most famous drawings are those of the "muscle men," depicting men in motion, all skin from the neck down having been removed and only the muscular structure illustrated. Most of the errors in other sections probably resulted from decomposition of the corpses Vesalius was dissecting. When he dissected, he was racing against time because there was no way of preserving the body and rapid decomposition made the determination of certain structures very difficult.

Here for the first time was an anatomy book beautifully and quite accu-

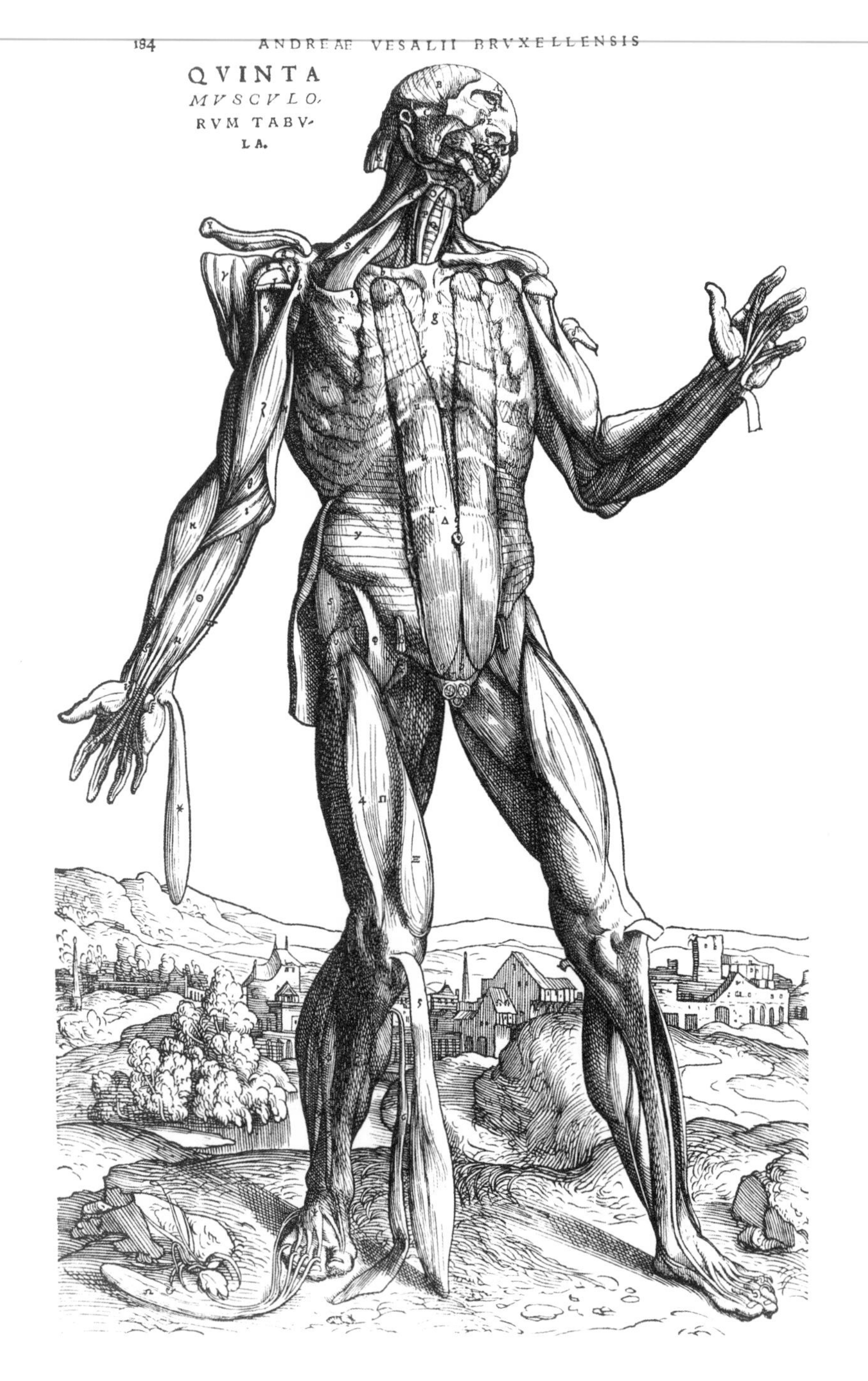

Vesalius's fifth "muscle man." *National Library of Medicine, Bethesda, Maryland.*

rately illustrated. It was important to the study of physiology (function) as well as anatomy. Vesalius did not know that blood circulated, and he accepted Galen's concept, but he could find none of the pores in the septum of the heart postulated by Galen and doubted their existence. Vesalius also questioned the view popularized by Aristotle declaring the heart to be the source of thought and emotion; Vesalius correctly stated that the brain was the organ responsible. The importance of anatomy as it relates to the physiology of these anatomical structures is apparent. When an accurate description of a muscle, for instance, is available, it becomes much easier to understand how that muscle works. In this way, Vesalius corrected inaccuracies in physiology as well as in anatomy.

After he wrote the *Fabrica*, Vesalius published a summary of it, which he titled the *Epitome*. It is a brief anatomy, intended either for students just beginning anatomy or for artists.

It is difficult to comprehend that all of this work was accomplished by a man not yet thirty years old. Sadly, though, the publication of his masterpiece was the culmination of his scientific work. In 1544 Vesalius sought and received an appointment as physician to Charles V, but he became bored with the life at court and missed the active days at Padua. Charles V was an amiable man but a very difficult patient. Furthermore, there was much jealousy among the other court physicians, many of whom were dedicated followers of Galen. Vesalius had just married, however, and a daughter was born the following year, so he needed the security of a well-paying position. Later he became the physician to Philip II, the son of Charles V, under whose rule the Spanish Armada was sent to invade England. But Vesalius became even unhappier and now found his life in Spain intolerable. He tried to leave the court, but his resignation was refused.

His work had brought him fame, but as happens so often to those who upset traditional ways of thinking, he had acquired enemies as well. He was vilified by those disagreeing with him and called a heretic and a grave robber. Some of his most severe critics were his former teachers.

Vesalius had responded sharply to his critics in earlier times, but after the publication of the *Fabrica*, he was always restrained in answering attacks against him. When Fallopio, his successor at Padua, died, Vesalius was offered his previous anatomy professorship. He therefore made a pilgrimage to Jerusalem, probably not intending to come back to Madrid. The pilgrimage offered an opportunity for him to escape from

Spain and then go to Padua. But on the stormy voyage to Italy, he became ill and was put ashore on the Greek island of Zante (now Zakinthos). According to the most reliable account of what happened, written by one Pietro Bizzari, Vesalius developed a fever and because of fear of contagion was left unattended. A Venetian goldsmith who had arrived on the island a short time before Vesalius learned about the latter's illness and tried unsuccessfully to get medical assistance for him. Bizzari reported:

The worthy goldsmith did not fail to do for Vesalius after his death, what he had been unable to do for him alive. With great difficulty, he gained permission of the islanders to bury him, and with his own hands prepared the grave and buried the body so that it might not remain as food and nourishment for wild beasts.

The lonely death of Vesalius was almost a metaphor for his work. Alone, he had successfully challenged a millennium and a half of incorrect thought, and alone he had set anatomy on a reliable course.

William Harvey

1578–1657 English anatomist; discoverer of the workings of the circulatory system

On April 1, 1578, William Harvey, destined to become one of the most famous physicians of all time, was born in Folkestone, a seaport in Kent, England. His father, Thomas Harvey, was a successful merchant who later became mayor of Folkestone. Throughout Thomas Harvey's life, he comfortably supported his family of seven sons, of whom William was the oldest, and two daughters. Another daughter had died when she was only eleven.

William Harvey, reaching manhood, entered Caius College, one of the colleges of Cambridge University, from which he graduated in 1597. He received his medical education from the famed University of Padua, located in the northeastern part of Italy. (Galileo was among the professors who taught there.)

What was Harvey like? The only contemporary sketch of him was written by one John Aubrey.

> He was, as all the rest of the brothers, very cholerique; and in his young days wore a dagger (as the fashion then was, nay I remember my old schoolemaster, old Mr. Latimer, at 70, wore a dudgeon, with a knife, and bodkin . . . which I suppose was the common fashion in their young days), but this Dr. would be apt to draw out his dagger upon every slight occasion.
>
> He was not tall, but of the lowest stature, round faced, olivaster complexion; little eie [eyes], round, very black, full of spirit; his haire was black as a raven, but quite white 20 yeares before he dyed.

Although apparently impetuous, Harvey knew what he wanted and conveyed this sense of purpose to his fellow students at the University of Padua. He was serious, he was organized, and he was intelligent. He combined these qualities, forging them into a bearing of directed concentration. This young man, William Harvey, would accomplish what he wished to.

Padua was somewhat different from other universities, and what made it different was its international character. Here were enrolled students from the many nations of Europe—Spaniards and Russians, Italians and Frenchmen, Germans and Britons. From everywhere some ten thousand of them came to Padua to study and learn. And what also was different was that the students here ran the university. They were very active in its administration, whereas in the English universities, the faculty had the entire say. At Padua each national group of students elected one of their own to serve as its representative, and in 1602 Harvey had, for the third consecutive year, been chosen by the English to be *consiliarius* to represent them. This gesture of confidence from his fellows must have gratified Harvey.

The center of medical education was a steep, five-tiered amphitheater used by the lecturers to demonstrate the fundamentals of anatomy. As the dissection of a body began, more than two hundred students were in attendance, leaning over the railways of the various circular viewing areas. They stared down at a stone room, with a stone table in the center. Lying stretched out on the table was a cadaver. The pallid body, illuminated by eight candelabras, supplemented by lamps held by students, created an eerie sight, particularly for those watching the demonstration for the first time. The prominent lecturer during Harvey's time at Padua was Fabricius, professor of anatomy at the university. He would cut into the body, explaining as he progressed about the skin, muscles, blood vessels, and nerves. Later he would dissect the body cavities, show where various organs were located, and explain the function of each. Harvey watched carefully and took detailed notes during the dissection, which took up the entire day. Undoubtedly he was absorbed by every minute of it and probably vowed to himself that someday he would demonstrate anatomy to students on a cadaver.

Harvey watched and listened as Fabricius, successor to the famed Vesalius, dissected a leg and showed some of its superficial veins. Something the professor said about these veins was wrong, and whether or not Harvey became aware of the mistake at that time is not known; what is confirmed is that many years later Harvey, by experimentation, found out what Fabricius's error was, and Harvey's correction of it proved to be an important link in his theory of circulation.

In April 1602 Harvey was granted his M.D. from Padua. His diploma stated that he had done excellent work "far surpassing the expectations" of all his professors. Armed with the impressive document, he returned to London and began to work as a hospital physician. Besides his hospital work with patients, he continued the anatomical studies that had always interested him. He began to dissect small animals and also to study the workings of the heart by operating on these animals while they were still alive.

The following year two important things happened to William Harvey. In the first place (also related to matters of the heart), he married Elizabeth Browne, daughter of the physician to Queen Elizabeth. Harvey was considered a good match for her, coming as he did from a respected family. The second important event of the year was his official licensure by the College of Physicians. This recognition was granted after three separate oral examination sessions, Harvey performing well in each instance. Three years later he was honored by being elected a fellow of the College of Physicians. The members of this illustrious organization saw the same potential in Harvey that his fellow students at Padua had noted. He became active in the college and enjoyed a close association with it throughout his lifetime.

Harvey's father-in-law died a year after his daughter's marriage. During that interval Dr. Browne had tried unsuccessfully to have Harvey appointed physician to the Tower of London. Had he been awarded the job, Harvey would have taken care of Sir Walter Raleigh among other unfortunates confined to the Tower.

We know very little about Elizabeth Browne Harvey except that she was tall, died sometime between 1645 and 1652, and had a parrot of which she was very fond. Harvey had thought the bird was a male "on account of its skill in talking and singing . . ." until it fell sick one day and died. Harvey, with his customary zeal, performed an autopsy. The bird turned out to be a female.

In 1609 Harvey was appointed physician to St. Bartholomew's Hospital. His duty in this paid job was to take care of the needy patients, and for years the Harveys lived close to the hospital. His responsibilities were not too demanding and allowed time for his anatomy studies. Not only did he continue to dissect various species of animals, but he also became interested in embryology, studying the development of the fertilized egg. He kept detailed notes and invited medical friends to watch his dissections.

Harvey was achieving a reputation as a true scientist, so it was not surprising when the College of Physicians appointed him in 1613 to be one of the censors of that body. Harvey thereby became an examiner, quizzing various candidates who wished to practice, just as he himself had been examined nine years earlier. The censors also checked apothecaries (pharmacists) to see that the medicines they sold met required standards. Further, the censors would question physicians who were considered to be either incompetent or unethical, although there was very little that could be done except to warn the offenders; the college had no legal power.

During the years since his return from Padua, Harvey had from time to time attended the Lumleian lectures. Established by a grant from Lord Lumley, supplemented by a gift from a former president of the College of Physicians, these lectures were given twice weekly throughout the year. In addition, for five continuous days each year, the lecturer would demonstrate the anatomy of one section of the body by public dissection of the corpse of an executed criminal. It took six years to complete the anatomical lectures and dissections, after which the cycle would begin again.

The series had been initiated in 1582, and when Harvey was elected to the position of lecturer, he was only the fourth man to be so honored. The opportunity to dissect and lecture was more important to Harvey than either the honor of his appointment or the generous fee that accompanied it.

Harvey's first lectures were given April 16–18, 1615. He held the post of Lumleian lecturer for the next twenty-eight years. His lecture notes, *Prelectiones*, would become the core of the classic work Harvey would publish in 1628.

No one is certain when the final concept of the circulation of the blood became fixed in Harvey's mind, but the evidence suggests that as early as 1619 he began to point out new ideas in his lectures. He continued to experiment, and each new observation put another hole in the theories of the ancient anatomist Galen. (It had been dangerous to contradict Galen. In 1553 Michael Servetus first described the "lesser circulation"—the circulation of blood through the lungs. For this, his manuscripts tied to his waist, he was burned at the stake by order of John Calvin.)

Harvey often operated on an animal in his laboratory at home. His colleague

An engraving from the portrait of William Harvey by Jansen. *Photosearch, Inc.*

and friend John Argent often would watch. Harvey would explain to him that, like the hearts of humans, dogs' hearts had a right and a left side. The lower two large chambers, the ventricles, both contracted at the same time. Harvey demonstrated how the right ventricle sent blood to the lungs, pushing the blood through a large vein that we know today as the superior vena cava. At the same time the left ventricle pumped blood to all the arteries via the aorta, the largest artery in the body. Harvey explained that in those species without lungs, there was no right side of the heart—only one receiving chamber called an auricle (today called an atrium) and one pumping chamber, the ventricle.

Once Harvey was operating on a lamb, and he opened its left ventricle, allowing blood to spurt out with each heartbeat. After the lamb's body had been emptied of all its blood, Harvey measured the amount. Galen had declared that blood was manufactured daily from the food ingested. Harvey realized that it would be impossible to make that much blood from the daily diet. Galen was wrong, Harvey understood, after repeating this experiment several times. But how was blood manufactured? He didn't know yet.

While Harvey's scientific and political star was rising, the fortunes of his brothers were being made. Finances never interested William Harvey, and fortunately his brother Eliab, a very successful merchant, looked after William's financial affairs. Through his trading with the eastern Mediterranean countries, Eliab had bought coffee. He introduced William to coffee drinking long before it became a popular English pastime with the appearance of coffeehouses. William Harvey loved coffee and drank it copiously. Perhaps that is why he suffered from insomnia. (The caffeine in coffee has a stimulating effect and keeps some people awake.)

Another brother, John, became attached to the court of King James I, and probably through this connection, William Harvey was appointed to be one of the court physicians in 1618. Later he would become the physician and friend of Charles I, the unfortunate monarch who was beheaded at the order of Oliver Cromwell.

The years went by—1622, 1623, 1624—and Harvey continued to see impoverished patients at St. Bartholomew, he continued to lecture, he continued to serve the king, but above all, he continued to experiment. By 1624 he had dissected over eighty species of animals and insects. In most instances, he had experimented with live animals—vivisection—and this work took place before the days of anesthesia.

But he was a driven man. He regretted the pain he caused, but he felt it was important to press on.

Ever since Padua days he had wondered about veins and the valves they contained. His old professor, Fabricius, who had rediscovered these veins first seen by others and then forgotten, mentioned them frequently. Like little doors, Fabricius had said, the valves prevented the blood moving from the heart to the veins in the legs and elsewhere from traveling too rapidly. These valves, Fabricius said, counteracted the forces of gravity.

Later, while Harvey was dissecting a neck vein before the formal Lumleian demonstration began, he opened the vein and closely examined one of its valves. The "little doors" pointed downward rather than upward as in the leg veins. Suddenly a flash of insight gripped Harvey. He at once understood the mistake in interpretation of valve function Fabricius had made during Harvey's Padua student days. If these valves functioned as Fabricius had proclaimed—in order to protect against gravity—the valves would all point the same way, upward. But no, these neck vein valves helped blood to return to the heart. They prevented back flow. Blood flow was *one way*, Harvey reasoned. Blood flowed in a continuous circle, and the heart was the pump that kept the blood moving. The blood returned to the right side of the heart in the veins; then it was pumped to the lungs, where it became red in color, and then it returned to the left side of the heart. Back in the heart, the refreshed (oxygenated) blood was pumped all over the body and returned to the heart again, this time darker in the veins. Harvey realized that somehow the arteries and the veins had to connect, but he didn't know how this happened. Later the Italian anatomist Marcello Malpighi would discover the capillaries, the tiny vessels that connect the arteries and veins, and confirm what Harvey had predicted.

In 1625 and in 1626 his excitement over his discoveries began to infect his colleagues. They marveled at his logic as he placed a ligature, a thin tourniquet, around his arm. He showed them that they could still feel his pulse, so the artery in the arm wasn't compressed. Then he showed them how swollen the veins were because the ligature was tight enough to stop blood flow through them. He pointed out small knots in the veins, which he explained were valves. Blood was being prevented from returning to the heart; his arm above the ligature was flat. He drew the conclusion for them that he had previously reached himself: Blood travels in only one direction. No blood had come down from the heart to fill the veins above the ligature.

After several such demonstrations his friends asked Harvey to write down all of these new findings. They asked him to put everything in book form so the world could learn of his discovery. Finally Harvey gave in and began to write. He knew that he would face the wrath invariably stirred up by any new theory—people prefer the familiar because it is comfortable—but he had the proof. Much of the material was in his lecture notes, and he began to assemble it in logical order. In his book he described heart movements as follows:

> These two motions, one of the ventricles, another of the auricles, take place consecutively, but in such a manner that there is a kind of harmony and rhythm preserved between them, the two concurring in such wise that but one motion is apparent, especially in the warmer blooded animals, in which the movements in question are rapid. Nor is this for any other reason that it is a piece of machinery, in which though one wheel gives motion to another, yet all the wheels seem to move simultaneously; or in that mechanical contrivance which is adapted to firearms, where the trigger being touched, down comes the powder, it is ignited, upon which the flame extends, enters the barrel, causes the explosion, propels the ball, and the mark is attained—all of which incidents, by reason of the celerity with which they happen, seem to take place in the twinkling of an eye.

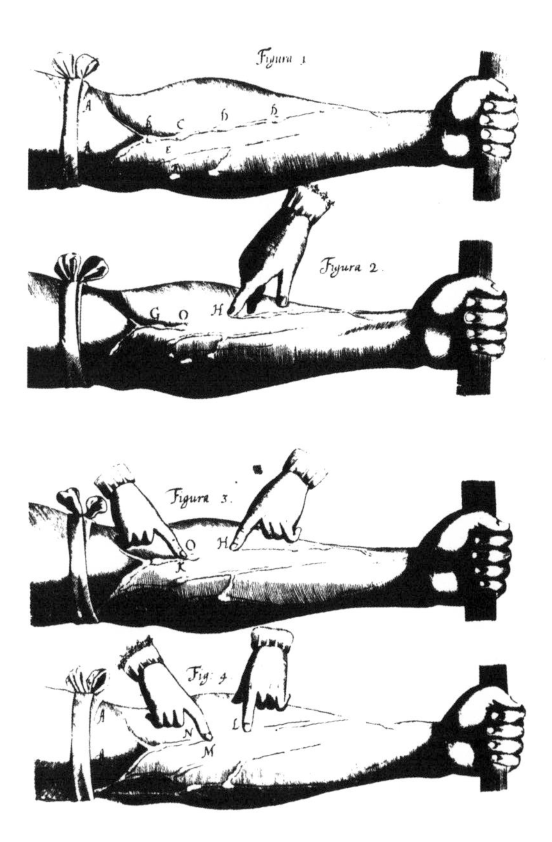

An experiment showing the movement of the blood, an illustration from Harvey's *de Motu Cordis*, 1628. *World Health Organization, Geneva, Switzerland.*

Although Harvey's logic was perfect (and his description of circulation probably the best ever written), his handwriting was terrible, and some minor errors occurred in the printed text. The book was published in 1628. It was titled *Exercitatio Anatomica de Motu Cordis et Sanguinis in Animalibus* ("Anatomical Treatise on the Movement of the Heart and Blood in the Animal"), but it became known to the world simply as *de Motu Cordis*. It is a short book—seventy-two pages divided into seventeen chapters. It was published in Frankfurt by an Englishman named William Fitzer who lived in Germany and had inherited a printing business from his father. Fitzer wanted to save money, so he printed almost all of the books on cheap paper, which soon darkened and crumbled. However, he did print a few copies on good paper. Those copies that still exist today are among the most valuable books in the world.

After publication of the book Harvey had to face the opponents he had foreseen, especially in England, Italy, Germany, and France. He did have supporters in all of those countries, although his warmest enthusiasts lived in Holland, where his doctrine was quickly accepted.

By the time his second and less important book was published in 1651, Harvey finally had received widespread recognition for his discovery.

In 1649 Charles I, the monarch of whom Harvey was so fond, was captured during a civil war. Soon after, largely due to intolerance over his marriage to a Catholic, he was tried and beheaded. The pleasant life Harvey had enjoyed at court was gone, and though he remained a Royalist (he still believed in a monarchy), he was allowed to study and experiment. While he had once traveled widely, now he remained in London. He was seventy years old and suffered severely from gout. But even during his last years, he continued to be active in the affairs of the College of Physicians.

William Harvey died at age seventy-nine of a cerebral hemorrhage, and his remains are in a sarcophagus at Hempstead Church, Essex. He left much of his estate to the College of Physicians to which he had already donated funds for a library. His greatest legacy, the workings of the circulatory system, would revolutionize medicine.

PART III

Drugs

Friedrich Sertürner

1783–1841 German chemist; isolator of the painkiller morphine

Until the nineteenth century surgery was performed without anesthesia. There was opium, of course. Opium, obtained from the juice of the poppy plant, has been used for at least as long as history has been recorded. Effective as it was in relieving pain, its preparations were unreliable and unsafe, and its use frequently resulted in the death of the patient. It was therefore a monumental scientific advance when, in 1803, at the age of twenty, Friedrich Sertürner isolated morphine, the active pain-relieving drug he obtained from an extract of opium.

Sertürner was born near Paderborn in the Westphalia area of Germany on June 19, 1783. At the age of sixteen he was apprenticed to the royal pharmacist, Cramer. There seemed little likelihood that he would make such an outstanding discovery except that young Sertürner was a dedicated student and Cramer an understanding and patient teacher. The apprentice system was, and still is, a widely used method of getting an education by working on the job, under the supervision of an experienced person. It is astounding that only four years after starting his training, Sertürner succeeded in extracting the active principle from the opium plant. This principle, morphine, was the powerful compound that relieved pain; the rest of the opium plant had no such effect. Thus all through those centuries that opium had been used for pain relief, it was really only that part of the plant Sertürner had crystallized that was responsible for its good effects.

Something, then, had been providing pain relief for thousands of years, and it was only during the nineteenth century that the discovery of the pure principle was made.

Until then opium had sometimes been weak and ineffective, doing little or nothing to mitigate pain. At other times an opium preparation had been too strong, resulting in the death of the patient. The essential problem was that the opium preparations were not *standardized.* That is, there was no uniformity to these drugs, so there was no way of telling in advance how strong or how weak they were. The use of opium was a game of chance.

Sertürner studied chemistry from the time he began his apprenticeship, and Cramer allowed him to set up a laboratory in the pharmacy basement. There were a few windows high on the basement walls, but they provided little illumination; therefore he worked by lamplight even during the day and obviously while experimenting at night.

Sertürner began his experiments with opium by soaking it in various alkaline solutions. The most important chemical available for his early pharmacy experiments was ammonia. Acid and alkaline solutions depend on the presence of two kinds of ions (electrically charged atoms). The greater the number of hydrogen ions, the more acid the solution; the more hydroxy ions, the more alkaline the solution. Although we think of acids as causing serious burns, equally serious burns can be caused by strong alkali chemicals like lye. Sertürner used ammonia solutions to alkalinize his extracts and learned that he could precipitate (isolate in the form of solid particles) the active principle of the opium plant. The solution that remained had no narcotic effect. Sertürner repeatedly demonstrated this fact in dogs. It was the precipitated factor that caused drowsiness and pain relief; the rest was inactive. Sertürner not only experimented with animals; he also tested morphine extracts on himself and others and accurately described the physiological changes that occurred with each increase of dosage.

After publishing his results in 1806, Sertürner left Paderborn and moved to Einbeck, where he established his own laboratory. There he continued his work with opium from 1811 to 1817. In 1817 he wrote a paper reporting the details of his method of isolating morphine. A man named Gilbert, the editor of the *Annalen der Physik*, in which journal the paper appeared, seems to have accepted it for publication primarily so he could criticize it, which he did with great vigor. In a footnote Gilbert made several snide suggestions to

Sertürner on how the latter might go about acquiring some knowledge of basic chemistry since Sertürner obviously was entirely wrong. It was in 1817 that Sertürner changed the name of his active principle to *morphine*, after Morpheus, the Greek god of dreams.

When it was announced that a prize for the discovery of morphine was to be given, great controversy arose as to who first had made the discovery. A French pharmacist named Derosne had conducted experiments with opium some fourteen years before Sertürner had been successful in isolating morphine. These experiments were certainly designed to extract the active principle from opium. Unfortunately for Derosne, these extracts were crude and contained almost all the other ingredients of the opium plant as well. Derosne had not obtained the precipitate because he had not alkalinized the extracts. Still many scientists believed that Derosne had been successful in his search for the active principle.

But the matter of who should be given credit was clearly and dramatically settled by the Institut de France in the following manner: In 1817 the renowned French chemist Joseph Gay-Lussac brought Sertürner's name to the attention of the institute. Gay-Lussac actually read a translation of Sertürner's work in the *Annales de Chimie* and noted with surprise that this discovery in Germany had escaped notice in other countries. Following this reading, the institute's scientists voted against their countryman Derosne. The prize of two thousand francs went to Sertürner.

Once the prize was granted, Sertürner's contribution was widely recognized. In that year he was awarded a Ph.D. by the University of Jena, and he was elected to several scientific societies throughout Europe. Sertürner himself published a chemical journal, which he gratefully dedicated to his former teacher and employer, Cramer. In 1921, eighty years after Sertürner's death, a memorial tablet was unveiled in Cramer's pharmacy in Paderborn. In that same year Sertürner's portrait and a picture of his birthplace were printed on German currency.

From 1817 until his death, Sertürner continued his interest in medicine, chemistry, and physics. Correctly he theorized that caustic alkaloids were compounds rather than simple substances. He also suggested that drinking water be boiled to prevent the spread of cholera epidemics, which were exacting a terrible toll. Cholera was proved to be an infectious disease in 1883, and had his suggestion not been ignored, millions of lives could have been saved.

Having so many interests, Sertürner

Friedrich Sertürner, from an 1803 lithograph. *The Bettmann Archive.*

was criticized by colleagues for not concentrating on one field. These gratuitous remarks still managed to upset him. Further, he developed gout, one of the most painful of all diseases; it was only right that his suffering was alleviated by morphine, his own discovery. On February 20, 1841, he was enjoying a cup of tea when he suddenly collapsed and was pronounced dead shortly thereafter.

The isolation of morphine had deep significance that only recently has been sufficiently understood to be appreciated. Unfortunately, today we hear as much about the abuse by addicts of a morphine derivative, heroin, as about morphine's value in medicine.

Many of the drugs known to the ancients were contained in harmless-looking plants. These drugs were made up of powerful chemical compounds, compounds that, when taken in pure form, were capable of causing instant death. These powerful chemicals are now known as alkaloids because they are alkaline compounds, as opposed to acids. Thus the discovery of morphine was in reality a double discovery. Not only was morphine important for its own sake, but just as notable, it was the first alkaloid to be isolated. At that point the stage was set for the development of sixteen other important alkaloids, two from opium and the rest from other plants. This work took place over the next one hundred and three years. Although pure morphine had been isolated in 1803, its makeup was unknown. It was not until 1925 that chemistry had advanced sufficiently to determine the chemical structure of morphine. And in 1952, morphine was synthesized—that is, manufactured in quantity from the elements and compounds that form the substance.

How does morphine act? The exact

mechanism of its action in the central nervous system is a mystery. What is known is that it may have directly opposite effects on certain species. Some forty years ago, a pharmacology professor told a story that illustrates this: A patient who was going to take a train trip from New York to California asked her doctor for something to sedate her cat, who was making the trip with her. The doctor prescribed morphine, unaware that morphine has an opposite effect in cats; it makes them extremely excitable. Three weeks later the patient returned, her face and arms scratched and bleeding. "Doctor," she said, "I want to thank you for giving me the sedative. I can imagine what that cat would have been like if I hadn't given her the morphine." We can imagine, too, what might have happened if Sertürner had decided to test his extract on cats instead of on dogs.

While luck played a role, persistence was the most important factor. Because of his painstaking experimentation, Sertürner was confident that his studies concerning morphine were correct. He was not stopped by the criticism and ridicule of those far better educated and far better established than he was. It is sad that not much has been written about Sertürner since no better drug than morphine for the relief of pain has ever been developed.

Paul Ehrlich

1854–1915 German bacteriologist; founder of chemotherapy

One day when Paul Ehrlich was a young medical student at the University of Breslau, the famed bacteriologist Robert Koch arrived as visiting professor. He demonstrated to the faculty and students the bacterium he had discovered, a bacterium that caused anthrax, a disease deadly to animals and transmittable by contact to man. After completing the demonstration, Koch was led around the laboratories, where Ehrlich was working with various dyes. The physician conducting Koch's tour casually pointed out the absorbed student. "That is little Ehrlich," the Breslau physician told Koch. "He is very good at staining but he will *never* pass his examinations."

Paul Ehrlich *did* pass his examinations and went on to be successful in four fields of science: histology (study of tissues), blood cytology (study of blood cells), immunity, and chemotherapy. He spent ten to fifteen years successively on each of these fields, and in 1908 he shared the Nobel Prize (with Elie Metchnikoff) for his work in immunity. Ehrlich is best known, however, for his researches in founding the field of chemotherapy.

Chemotherapy (the treatment of disease with the use of drugs) had been in use for thousands of years but never on the scientific basis that Ehrlich established. He showed *how* chemotherapy works. (The *chemo* stands for "chemical." Not only drugs but *everything in the world* is comprised of chemicals in various combinations. Our bodies have bones made primarily of calcium and phosphorus, but about 70 percent of the weight of our bodies is made up of the combination of two atoms of hydrogen with one atom of oxygen; this is H_2O, or water.)

We are lucky to know a great deal about Ehrlich, especially his personal life, because his secretary for most of the important years of his scientific life wrote down in shorthand almost every conversation in which Ehrlich participated. Her name was Martha Marquardt, and her book *Paul Ehrlich* is a loving and easy-to-read biography.

Ehrlich was born in Silesia, an eastern region of Germany. His birthplace was Strehlen (today Strzelin, Poland), and there he attended elementary and high schools. While young (and forever after), he loved Latin and mathematics and did well in those subjects. He detested examinations, although he managed to pass his worst subjects, particularly German composition. Ehrlich attended several colleges and eventually received his medical degree in 1878 from the University of Leipzig. A professor of medical history wrote the following about Ehrlich's graduation thesis:

> It contains the germ of Ehrlich's entire life-work which culminated in the invention of Salvarsan. . . . It proves that Ehrlich, when leaving the University and before he even became a clinical assistant, was already on the way to becoming the creator of chemotherapy. This long-lost graduation thesis undoubtedly belongs to the classical, epoch-making works of medical world literature.

In this thesis (in which he described his discovery of a new type of blood cell he called a *mast* cell), Ehrlich stressed the importance of staining tissues with aniline dyes derived from coal tar. This adherence of drugs to tissue is the basis of chemotherapy. Besides the mast cell (which helps the body in infection), eventually Ehrlich discovered five other blood cell types and named them; these names remain in use today. He is considered the founder of modern hematology (the study of blood).

After graduation Ehrlich became a senior house physician at the Charité Hospital in Berlin under the direction of Professor Friedrich von Frerichs. He remained there for almost ten years, but after Frerichs, who was extremely kind to Ehrlich, suddenly died, everything changed. Frerichs's successor, Professor Carl Gerhardt, was a rigid man who insisted that Ehrlich do clinical work (bedside treatment of patients) only and stop his research. Although highly skilled in diagnosis (identifying an illness by history and physical examination), Ehrlich believed that research to discover the cause and treatment of illness was the best way to help patients. In making his various dyes, he became a self-taught chemist.

Ehrlich, who had just married Hedwig Pincus, became ill from all this stress (possibly with tuberculosis) and with his young wife went to Egypt, where he remained for two years, completely recovering his health. Of the unhappy period after Frerichs's death, Ehrlich later wrote:

When I felt so miserable and forsaken during the time with Gerhardt, I often stood before the cupboard in which my collection of dyes was stored and said to myself: "These here are my friends which will not desert me."

His chemicals never did desert him, but while he usually was consumed with research, he always had time for his human friends, and they were many because Ehrlich was gregarious, exciting, and compassionate. He gave money to whomever asked him for it and never investigated if the money really was needed. And he continued this practice all of his life, even during times when his finances were low. At times he also was the typical absentminded professor. Ms. Marquardt relates an incident told to her by Sir Henry Dale, the distinguished British Nobel Laureate. Sir Henry was talking to Ehrlich when another visitor arrived. The scene went like this:

Ehrlich had offered, as was always his first impulse, his precious imported cigars to a visitor, who declined, however, saying that he didn't smoke. Ehrlich went on talking animatedly, and presently renewed the offer:

"A cigar, Herr Kollege?"

"No thank you, I do not smoke!" repeated the visitor.

"Oh, you do not smoke!" said Ehrlich, quite astonished. "Then may I offer you a glass of wine?" (This in spite of the fact that he never kept wine at the Institute.)

"No, thank you very much," said the visitor. "I happen to be a teetotaller."

"Perhaps a glass of water then?"

"Yes, please, a glass of water," said the visitor, anxious to please Ehrlich and not refuse again.

"Kadereit!" Ehrlich at once called out, having opened the door a crack, and then went on talking to the visitor.

When Kadereit came running, Ehrlich muttered, half to himself:

"Now what was it I wanted to ask Kadereit?"

The visitor, reminding him, said: "A glass of water for me, Herr Geheimrat."

"Oh yes, a glass of water for you," said Ehrlich. But when Kadereit brought the glass of mineral water on a little tray, Ehrlich absent-mindedly took it, put it on the floor beside him, and began to drink from it now and then as he continued his voluble exposition to the visitor. This went on until, with the glass of water finished, he noticed that the visitor was not smoking, and again reached for and offered the box of cigars.

In 1890 Robert Koch was appointed director of the new Institute for Infectious Diseases in Berlin and invited Ehrlich to become a member of the laboratory. Ehrlich accepted with pleasure and remained in Berlin for six years. During that time he worked with Emil von Behring, who had discovered that the blood of animals that had become infected with various diseases contained substances called antibodies. These antibodies, when injected into humans, could protect them from the diseases.

Bacteria that are foreign to our bodies contain substances called antigens. These are complex molecules, usually proteins. Our bodies recognize our own tissues, but when foreign substances invade (bacteria, poisons, and so forth), our bodies make antibodies, which become instant soldiers and fight the foreign invaders. The resulting war is called an immune response. When the foreign invader is a poison, or carries one, the poison is called a toxin, and the antibody made to fight it is called an antitoxin. (The words *antigen, antibody,* and *receptor,* all part of today's immunology vocabulary, were coined by Ehrlich.)

When we borrow antibodies made by other species but which still protect us, we get a kind of protection called passive immunity, which lasts only a short time. Our own antibodies, however, provide long, usually lifelong, protection. Behring developed an antitoxin for the deadly disease diphtheria by using the blood of horses that had been injected with the diphtheria bacterium. He was helped immensely in this work by Ehrlich, whose research resulted in a greatly increased amount of antitoxin (often over one hundred times) from the injected horses and who also standardized the serum. Standardizing ensures that the exact strength of each serum dose is known. Otherwise the serum could be too weak to be effective or so strong that it would be dangerous to give to humans. (When asked how it was so easy for him repeatedly to give a horse the great number of injections needed to obtain strong antitoxin serum, Ehrlich responded: "One must love the horse . . . and ask him!")

Behring was grateful but greedy, and through the ruse of promising to get Ehrlich a laboratory of his own, he was able to make a huge profit from the manufacture of diphtheria toxin while claiming to be unable to obtain for Ehrlich the latter's only wish—his own research institute. After that their relationship cooled, and Ehrlich never forgave the injustice.

But Ehrlich's dream did come true.

His creativity was recognized by the Prussian government, and in 1896 he was appointed to head the State Institute for Serum Research at Steglitz, a suburb of Berlin. The institute was soon transferred to better facilities at Frankfurt. Ehrlich remained in Frankfurt until his death, accomplishing much significant work in that city.

At Steglitz he formulated his ideas on immunity, which would win him the Nobel Prize in 1908. Here he developed his famous *side-chain* theory, which later was proved to be correct; essentially the theory postulates that antibodies grow little extensions, like arms, when invaders are present. These "arms" (receptors) grab the invaders. The foreign invader's antigen structures resemble keys that fit into a lock; the antibody receptor structures are the specific lock.

Often receptors are produced in such amounts that they break free of the antibodies and attack invaders by themselves, locking into them and thus immobilizing them. Ehrlich termed antibodies with their side chains "Magic Bullets which find their target by themselves. Hence, their astonishingly specific effect . . ."

We can imagine him—a kindly but demanding laboratory director—always enveloped in cigar smoke, talking excitedly and sprinkling his explanations with favorite Latin and German phrases: *wissen Sie . . . verstehen Sie* ("you know, you understand"), *eo ipso* ("by that fact alone"), or *re vera* ("in truth"). He would work with his test tubes and Bunsen burners—he never used elaborate equipment—as some visitor talked on; yet he was able to absorb all that the visitor had told him and repeat the conversation exactly. He frequently told visitors that scientific achievement resulted from the four Gs: *geld* ("money"), *geduld* ("patience"), *geschick* ("cunning"), and *glück* ("luck"). Daily he would write notes (called "blocks") to his many assistants, giving them their research assignments for the following day. When instructions he considered important were not strictly carried out, he would explode. But such outbursts happened infrequently; nobody wanted to be the recipient of his rare but intense wrath.

Ehrlich's personal study was a mess. He would pile manuscripts, medical and chemical articles, books, and so forth everywhere, especially on a sofa. When he was seated, they towered high above him. When some important official was to visit, the sofa had to be cleared, but after a while, it became impossible. The sofa, with everything on top of it, had won the battle.

After winning the Nobel Prize Ehrlich began a series of studies that even-

Paul Ehrlich in his study.

tually brought him the most fame. There are certain diseases not caused by bacteria, diseases such as sleeping sickness and malaria and syphilis, which are caused by tiny animals, protozoa and other infectious agents. These diseases didn't respond to "magic bullets," which by themselves went straight to the bacterial invaders and destroyed them. So there was a need for what Ehrlich called chemotherapy. "In chemotherapy," said Ehrlich, "we can never count on such complete success and must therefore concentrate all our powers and abilities on making the aim as accurate as we can contrive, so as to strike at the parasites as hard and the body cells as lightly as possible. . . . We must learn to aim, learn to aim with chemical substances."

In 1904 trypan red, one of the dyes Ehrlich had made, proved effective against African sleeping sickness (trypanosomiasis), and in 1910 Ehrlich made an even more extraordinary discovery.

The cause of syphilis, a devastating venereal disease, had been discovered

Paul Ehrlich in his laboratory. *The Bettmann Archive.*

by Fritz Schaudinn and Erich Hoffmann in 1905. The organism causing syphilis was a corkscrewlike bacterium called a spirochete. The following year Hoffmann made an unexpected visit to Ehrlich's laboratory, seeking a drug that might be effective against syphilis. Although Ehrlich had synthesized hundreds of new drugs, which he had bottled and labeled by number, none proved effective against syphilis. A year after Hoffmann's visit, Ehrlich's 606th drug, an arsenical, was synthesized. Ehrlich's assistant declared, however, that it had no clinical use; therefore the bottle labeled 606 was put on a shelf crowded with other preparations.

Then a wonderful thing happened. The great scientist Shibasaburo Kitasato, working then in Tokyo, previously had sent his best student to work with Ehrlich. In the spring of 1909 he sent a second student, young Dr. Sahachiro Hata, to Frankfurt. Hata had found a way to produce syphilis in rabbits, and it was thought that he might be able to help Ehrlich in the search for a cure. One day Hata reported to Ehrlich that

606, the arsenical drug that Ehrlich's assistant had shelved as useless two years earlier, was an effective treatment for syphilis. Ehrlich walked up and down the room, talking excitedly to himself: "I *always* had a strong feeling—have been convinced for two years—*that 606 must be good!*"

After many animal and human tests for safety, a momentous announcement was made to the world. On April 19, 1910, Ehrlich spoke at Wiesbaden at the Congress for Internal Medicine. He related Hata's careful experiments and told of the first human treatments successfully using 606 to cure relapsing fever and syphilis. A better name for the drug had to be found. Its chemical name (dioxy-diamino-arseno-benzene-dihydrochloride) had forty letters and was difficult to pronounce; therefore a new name was chosen: Salvarsan.

The speech at Wiesbaden caused a sensation. Until the end of his life, Ehrlich was visited by a stream of physicians and patients, all inquiring about Salvarsan. Later another drug, Neo-Salvarsan, was developed in the lab. Although less effective than Salvarsan, it was easier to work with. Today penicillin and newer antibiotics have supplanted the arsenicals in the treatment of syphilis.

Ehrlich's last years were happy. Although he loved playing with his five grandchildren, his absorption with research never ceased. He would illustrate his chemical theories by making drawings on whatever was handy with whatever was handy. Once on a train, he explained his side-chain theory by crossing his legs and using a red crayon to draw diagrams on the sole of his shoe! He didn't like to leave his home in Frankfurt; his wife's piano playing and his two daughters and granddaughters kept him amused. He did consent to lecture in London and in the United States, but such lectures and medical conferences were exceptions. He died suddenly at the age of sixty-one of a stroke. Like so many, he would have contributed even more had he lived longer.

Chemotherapy, defined as the treatment of disease by chemical agents, is widely used today in the treatment of cancer. It has been highly successful in the treatment of childhood leukemias and several other diseases, which only forty years ago were incurable. Immunology, another field to which Ehrlich contributed heavily, is currently much in the forefront in the treatment of many diseases including cancer. Compassion, linked with compulsive research until the right answers are obtained, can be a wonderful combination. Ehrlich proved that.

William T. G. Morton

1819–1868 American dentist; discoverer of ether, the first effective anesthetic

The discovery of the use of ether as an inhalation anesthetic was one of the greatest contributions to mankind ever. It completely eliminated pain from surgery, pain that prior to its use had been excruciating. In the saddest irony of all, it brought much pain to its discoverers. The lives of three of the four men involved in what later was known as the Ether Controversy were essentially ruined by a desire to receive full credit for the discovery.

There is no doubt that the man responsible for the first surgical demonstration of ether, followed by world acceptance, was a Boston dentist, William T. G. Morton. It is impossible to know, however, who first thought of the use of inhalation anesthesia. The controversy over the discovery involves a paranoid physician-chemist, Charles T. Jackson, who, while playing a role in Morton's use of ether, never thought of its value as a surgical pain reliever or ever used it as such. Yet Jackson, more than any other by his claims to be the discoverer, ruined much of Morton's life and was responsible for a great man dying impoverished.

The story of inhalation anesthesia probably begins with pneumatic medicine, a form of medical practice that featured the breathing of various gases, a treatment that was supposed to be a panacea for all ailments. Actually the procedure cured nothing but did allow doctors to study the effects of inhaling gases. Most of this "medicine" was practiced at the Pneumatic Medical Institution in England, founded by one Dr.

Thomas Beddoes. (One of his chief collaborators there was James Watt, inventor of the steam engine, who designed much of the equipment.)

Beddoes hired a brilliant young scientist, Humphry Davy, to serve as superintendent of the institution. In 1800 Davy published a book on his experiments with breathing nitrous oxide, a gas discovered almost thirty years earlier. Davy had frequently inhaled the gas, and earlier, when he worked as an apprentice to a Penzance physician, he would giggle uncontrollably, which annoyed both the patients who were reciting complaints to him as well as the doctor to whom Davy was apprenticed, who didn't know the cause of his employee's hilarity. Davy named nitrous oxide laughing gas and noted that it "appears capable of destroying physical pain" and might have use as a surgical anesthetic. (In later years Davy became eccentric and unpleasant. He had a brilliant young assistant, Michael Faraday, whom he tried to turn into a valet during a continental vacation. Later he tried unsuccessfully to keep Faraday, whose experiments on the effect of electricity on gases were an important step in the development of X ray, from membership in the Royal Society.)

Davy's observations on the possible use of nitrous oxide in surgery were promptly forgotten, but as a result of pneumatic researches, it became known in America that the inhalation of gases could produce pleasurable effects. A new fad was started in the early 1800s—ether frolics, or jags—which quickly gained popularity. Parties, usually of college students, took place where guests breathed ether and became hilarious, dancing and laughing. No one could have suspected that because of these ether frolics, effective inhalation anesthesia finally would emerge.

The first man to use inhalation anesthesia was probably the most tragic figure in its history. Horace Wells was a Hartford, Connecticut, dentist who began practice in 1836 at the age of twenty-one and two years later wrote a well-received book on diseases of the teeth. In 1841 William T. G. Morton came to Hartford to study dentistry under Wells, and in October 1843, the two young men joined forces and opened an office in Boston. They hoped to increase their failing practice with their invention of an improved method of making false teeth and inserted an advertisement in the *Boston* that began: "Messrs. Wells and Morton, Dentists, No. 19 Tremont Row, are determined to make their valuable invention . . . known and appreciated in the shortest time possible. . . ."

The advertisement promised that patients would pay nothing except the cost of materials. In this way they hoped to establish a reputation and eventually make money from the project. The practice continued to fail, however, and Wells became discouraged and returned to Hartford to resume practice alone.

Wells knew of Davy's experiments with nitrous oxide, so it was natural that on December 10, 1844, he was in the audience at a demonstration of the effects of laughing gas. On this evening the demonstrator, Gardner Q. Colton, used the gas on a volunteer, Samuel A. Cooley. Under the gas's influence, Cooley cavorted on the stage, to the amusement of the audience, and then ran into a bench and banged his shins. Wells, sitting next to Cooley, noted that the latter's shins were bloody from the accident. When Cooley commented that not only did he not remember anything about hitting the bench but that he *felt no pain,* Wells immediately saw the possibility of using the gas for eliminating the pain of tooth extraction. He stayed on that night and convinced Colton to bring a bag of the gas to his office the next day.

On December 11, 1844, Colton administered gas to Wells while a fellow dentist, Dr. Riggs, extracted a molar painlessly. Years later Colton wrote:

This was the FIRST operation performed in modern anesthesia, and was the forerunner of all the other anesthetics. Beyond all question, this discovery had its birth in the brain of Dr. Horace Wells! I can only claim for myself that I was the occasion of the discovery, having given the gas for the first operation with an anesthetic.

Earlier that year, in May, William Morton had married Elizabeth Whitman and was practicing dentistry while studying chemistry with Dr. Charles Jackson. (Morton intended to become a physician and actually attended Harvard Medical School for two years before dropping out.) Now his former partner, Wells, who had written to Morton about his successful use of nitrous oxide, came to Boston and enlisted Morton's help in getting permission to demonstrate the use of nitrous oxide in a surgical operation.

Dr. John Collins Warren, professor of anatomy and America's most prominent surgeon, agreed. After an amputation case was canceled, Wells consented to demonstrate the use of the gas for painless extraction. First he lectured to the Harvard medical students about nitrous oxide and then came the fateful demonstration on a volunteer. Assuring the gathered students and physicians that the patient would feel no pain, he administered the gas but removed the gas bag too soon. As Wells yanked out the tooth, the patient screamed, and from the audience of fellow medical students came laughs, yells, hisses, and boos. These echoed through the amphitheater and continued to echo in the brain of Horace Wells. He left Boston in disgrace, gave up his practice, tried several other professions including touring as an ornithology lecturer, and maintained for the rest of his life (not without merit) that he was the discoverer of anesthesia. After opening a dental office in New York, he began to experiment with chloroform and inhaled it to relieve his depression. On January 21, 1848, while under its effects, he threw some acid at a passing woman and was arrested. In Tombs Prison, he wrote a sad farewell:

To my dear Wife. I feel that I am fast becoming a deranged man, or I would desist from this act. I cannot live and keep my reason, and on this account God will forgive the deed. I can say no more. Farewell, H.

Four days after his arrest he committed suicide by slashing his thigh after chloroforming himself to ease the pain. As for nitrous oxide itself, it is used in dentistry but is *not* a complete anesthetic and can never be used alone for surgical procedures.

(Ether, which is made by mixing acid and alcohol, was first used in a surgical operation by a doctor from Jefferson, Georgia, Crawford W. Long [1815–1878]. Long, familiar with ether from the frolics he had participated in while still a medical student, put the drug to use on March 30, 1842. He painlessly removed two neck tumors from a patient, James M. Venable, inducing unconsciousness by having the patient inhale from a towel saturated with ether and draped over his face. Long reported that the charge for the operation was "merely nominal, $2.00, Ether, 25¢." He performed several other minor operations after this but unfortunately neglected to publish his results until 1849, well after ether use already was widespread. Although in 1852 Long's friends appealed to Congress to gain recognition of priority, this gentle man never took an active interest in getting credit and lived a happy life.)

Dr. William Morton, still practicing dentistry in 1844 and studying chemistry under Dr. Charles Jackson, was becoming aware of Jackson's mental imbalance. At the dinner table one night, for example, Jackson became infuriated when the paper reported the invention of the telegraph by Samuel F. B. Morse. Jackson claimed this invention (as well as several others like gunpowder) was his. Jackson was, however, an intelligent scientist and continued to contribute to Morton's study of

An engraving from a portrait of William T. G. Morton. *Mary Evans Picture Library, London.*

ether. He prepared "toothache drops" of chloric ether to ease dentistry pain; Morton used these successfully, and although chloric ether is not effective enough to be used to pull teeth, its effect in easing pain stimulated him to search for a way to use ether to exert a more generalized effect. He purchased chemistry books and began, probably in the fall of 1844, to experiment with chloric ether. Unfortunately Morton kept no record of these experiments, which continued all through 1845 and became more promising in the spring of 1846.

Morton became ill during the summer of 1846 and spent the time experimenting while recovering at his home in West Needham, about thirty miles from Boston. He etherized insects, goldfish, his dog, and finally himself. Now he became obsessed with the potential of ether use and temporarily turned his practice over to a neighbor dentist, Dr. Hayden, while he continued to experiment. Morton always was secretive about his work, hoping to profit immensely if eventually he became successful with his ether work.

Something, however, was not completely satisfactory about these experiments; the dental assistants whom Morton anesthetized often became more excited than subdued. Results were inconsistent, and finally Morton was forced to consult Charles Jackson. Morton didn't tell Jackson the real reason for his visit but tricked Jackson into a long discussion about ether. He learned two important facts: If Morton wanted to try ether for extractions, he should purchase *sulfuric ether*, and a glass flask would be better for administering ether than a rubber bag. Probably Jackson thought of ether as having a stupefying effect on the patient rather than eliminating pain. If the idea of using sulfuric ether for anesthesia had occurred to Jackson, as a licensed physician he certainly would have experimented with it and arranged, as Morton did shortly thereafter, for a public demonstration.

Morton rushed from Jackson's house to Burnett's Pharmacy, where he bought some pure sulfuric ether. Then he sat down in the dental chair in his office and anesthetized himself:

> I shut myself up in my room, seated myself in the operating chair and commenced inhaling. . . . I then saturated my handkerchief and inhaled from that. I looked at my watch and soon lost consciousness. As I recovered, I felt a numbness in my limbs with a sensation like a nightmare, and would have given the world for someone to come and rouse me. I thought for a moment that I should die in that state, and the world would only pity or ridicule my folly. . . . Gradually, I regained power over my limbs and

full consciousness. I immediately looked at my watch and found I had been insensible between seven and eight minutes.

It was a brave experiment and one sufficient to prove that sulfuric ether would work in a surgical operation. Morton told his neighbor, Dr. Hayden, what had happened. At nine that evening, their conversation was interrupted by the doorbell. A music teacher, Eben Frost, was in agony from an infected tooth. Morton, with Hayden observing, convinced the patient that ether was preferable to the mesmerism (hypnosis) that Frost had requested. Morton proceeded to extract the bicuspid tooth painlessly. Frost signed a glowing letter, witnessed by Hayden, and a brief news item about the occurrence appeared in the *Boston Daily Journal* the following day. The item mentioned that the extraction was painless because the patient "was put into a kind of sleep, by inhaling a preparation. . . ." A well-known Harvard physician, Dr. Henry Bigelow, came to Morton's office and convinced Morton that a public demonstration was necessary. Bigelow suggested that Morton see John Collins Warren, the same surgeon who had allowed Wells his day in the amphitheater.

Morton presented his case to a gaunt and reserved Dr. Warren on the fourth or fifth of October. Warren, the most renowned surgeon in America, was nearing seventy, and he had yearned to find something that would relieve patients of the appalling pain they had to endure during surgery. That is why he had given Wells a chance and why he now courageously agreed to allow Morton to administer anesthesia. Dr. Warren would bear the overall responsibility for the operation, and he was now ready to risk his established reputation on the promise offered by a comparatively unknown dentist whose experience thus far had been confined to extractions.

On Wednesday, October 14, 1846, Morton received the following letter from Dr. C. F. Heywood, house surgeon of the Massachusetts General Hospital:

Dear Sir,
I write at the request of Dr. John Collins Warren to invite you to be present Friday morning, October 16, at ten o'clock at the hospital to administer to a patient who is then to be operated upon, the preparation you have invented to diminish the sensibility to pain.

Dr. Warren, remembering his promise to Morton, had asked his patient, a young printer named Gilbert Abbott, if he would be willing to defer for a few days the procedure to remove a vascular tumor from his neck. Something new that might lessen the pain of the operation would be tried if Abbott would consent, which he did immediately; he had dreaded the prospect of the pain.

Morton awoke at dawn on Friday, October 16, after a few hours of fitful sleep, and hurried to an instrument maker named Chamberlain. He explained the urgency of further repairs to the ether inhaler and watched with despair as Chamberlain methodically and slowly worked on the apparatus. Eben Frost, whose tooth had been extracted under ether, was with him because Morton thought that reassurance to the patient from Frost would help. Morton panicked as the clock struck ten, realizing that it was unlikely that he would get a second chance for a demonstration. A few minutes later Morton wrested the equipment from Chamberlain and began a desperate jog toward Massachusetts General Hospital a few blocks away. Holding the glass inhaler in his hands and the ether bottle in his pocket, Morton rushed to reach the fourth floor of the hospital and his appointment with destiny.

In the meantime, pale young Abbott had been wheeled into the surgical amphitheater and placed on the operating table. He noticed the hubbub in the filled room, all seats taken because news of the demonstration had been widely circulated. Now a distinguished group of faculty and other physicians sat in their frock coats to witness this occurrence. Dr. Warren announced that a test would be conducted for which "the astounding claim has been made that it would render the person operated upon free from pain."

The tension grew as moments ticked by. Finally Dr. Warren picked up his surgical knife and walked to the operating chair. It was now 10:15 A.M. After glancing at the door, Dr. Warren turned to the audience and announced that since Dr. Morton had failed to appear, "I presume he is otherwise engaged." Then, at the moment Warren sat down, ready to start the operation, Morton, breathless from his race against time, entered through a side door, Frost in tow. Warren, mystified by the late arrival, said to Morton, "Well, sir, your patient is ready."

Morton and Frost quickly walked to Abbott's side, and as Morton took the patient's hand and explained what would happen, Eben Frost reassured Abbott that the procedure would, as promised, be painless. Then Morton began to administer the ether. He placed a sponge in the glass inhaler and poured the ether onto it. (The ether was disguised by some perfume so as not to reveal the "secret.") With the patient's mouth open, a mouthpiece was inserted. Then his nostrils were held closed, and Abbott was asked to inhale deeply through his mouth. Approximately three minutes later Morton was satisfied that his patient was unconscious. "Your patient is ready, doctor," he announced to Warren, an announcement that is still made by anesthetists today.

Warren began the surgery, and we can only imagine his surprise and excitement as his incisions resulted in silence instead of the dreaded screams hitherto heard in all surgical amphitheaters and operating rooms. He completed the operation quickly, and as soon as Abbott regained consciousness, Warren asked him whether he had suffered pain. Once convinced that what he had witnessed *was* a method that did indeed prevent the patient from feeling pain, he turned to the audience and made that famous announcement: "Gentlemen, this is no humbug."

This was the highest authority speaking. Here was no fakery, quackery, or charlatanism. This discovery was both real and wonderful. With the imprimatur of Warren, the essence of integrity, the news now could be transmitted. America was ready to offer the world a most humane gift.

Two weeks after the hospital had resumed etherization, Dr. Oliver Wendell Holmes, Harvard professor, author and father of the famous Supreme Court justice, wrote to Morton:

Boston, November 21, 1846

Dear Morton:—

My Dear Sir,—Everybody wants to have a hand in the great discovery. All I will do is give you a hint or two as to names, or the name to be applied to the state produced, and to the agent.

The state should, I think be called anesthesia. This signifies insensibility. . . . The adjective will be anesthetic. . . .

I would have a name pretty soon, and consult some accomplished scholar, such as President Everett, or Dr. Bigelow, Sr., before fixing the terms which will be repeated by the tongues of every civilized race of mankind. You could mention these words which I suggest for their consideration; but there may be others more appropriate and agreeable.

Yours respectfully,
O. W. HOLMES

Since no better names were suggested, anesthesia and anesthetic are the words in use today. Later, during the battle between Morton and Jackson as to who should receive credit for the invention, Holmes was asked his opinion. "It should go," he replied humorously, "to 'e(i)ther.' "

Considering that word of this new discovery had to be transmitted by steamers, it was amazing how quickly ether was in use all over the world.

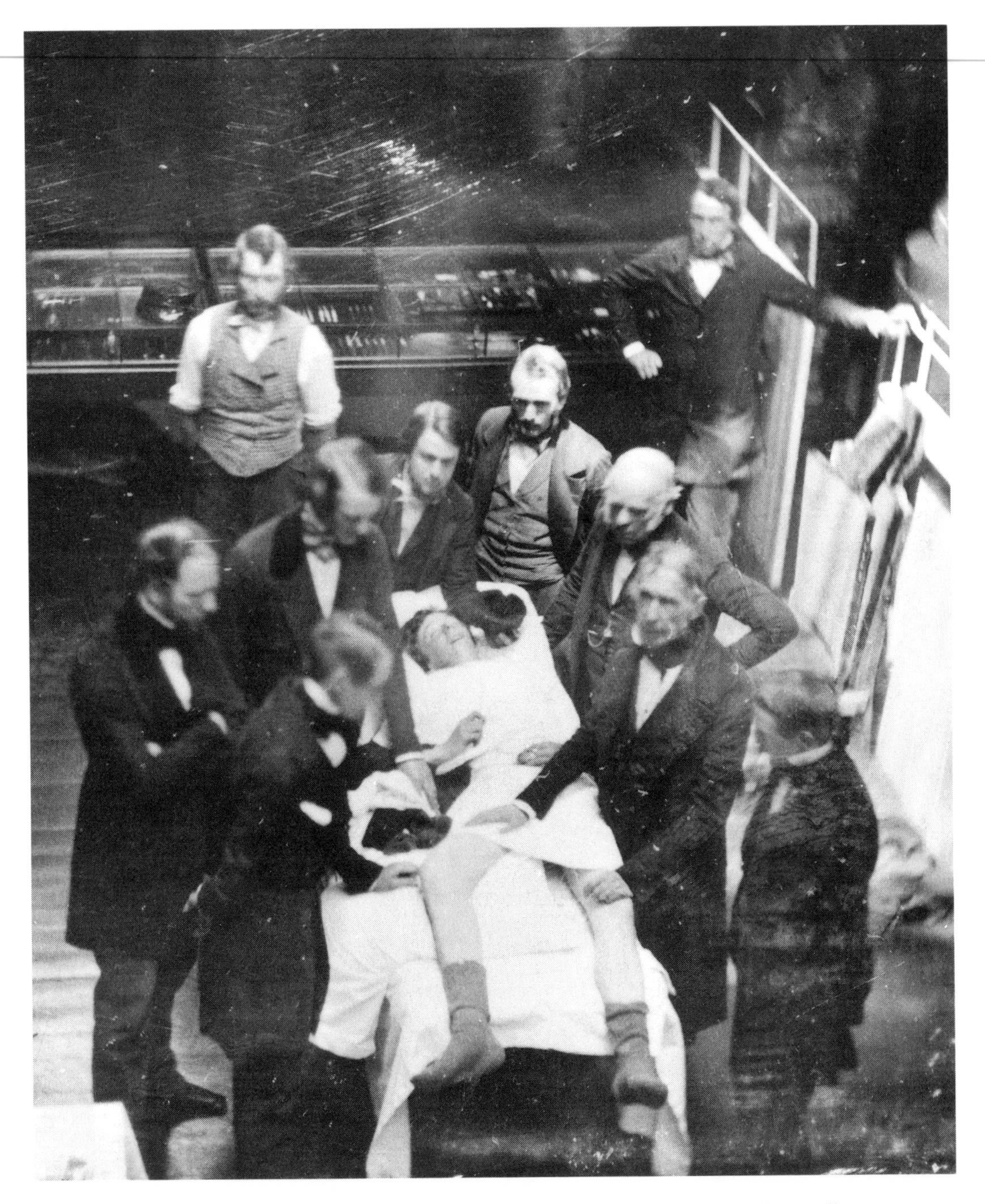

This early daguerreotype shows (*right, his hands on the patient*) Dr. John Collins Warren, cofounder and chief surgeon of Massachusetts General Hospital, and other surgeons surrounding an anesthetized patient. *Massachusetts General Hospital, Boston, Massachusetts.*

At the University of London in December 1846, ether was used for a painless amputation by the famed surgeon Robert Liston. After realizing that the patient wasn't even aware that the leg was off, Liston exclaimed: "This Yankee dodge, gentlemen, beats mesmerism hollow." Ether was used in France in 1846, and by 1847 ether was in use in countries as far away as China and Russia.

Morton tried to keep his substance a secret, to patent its use under the name Letheon, and to charge steeply for its use, but he failed in all efforts. The new surgical chief at Massachusetts General Hospital refused to allow the use until the nature of the substance was revealed. Morton relented, donated an inhaler, and revealed that he had used sulfuric ether. The English simply ignored the patenting fees, saying they were illegal, and the United States quickly followed suit.

Supporters of Morton's claim included the prominent physicians at Massachusetts General Hospital. They tried to obtain scientific recognition for Morton and a large honorarium from Congress. An impartial commission at the hospital (most of whose members knew Jackson far better than they did Morton), ruled almost unanimously that Morton was the discoverer. However, vicious letters from Jackson, not only to Congress but to all parts of the world, claimed credit, even going so far as to suggest that he had sent Morton as his agent to give the demonstration at Massachusetts General.

Morton, obsessed as was Jackson with fighting for his cause, gave up anesthesiology, making three trips to Washington to plead his cause. (During the Civil War, he did administer anesthesia to wounded men in Grant's army.) The Ether Controversy dragged on year after year, with proponents of deceased Horace Wells, friends of Crawford Long, Morton, and Jackson all contending for the prize of recognition and financial reward. Sir Francis Darwin, the son of Charles Darwin, stated a rule that can always be applied: "In science, the credit goes to the man who convinces the world, not to the man to whom the idea first occurs."

On a hot July day Morton was so upset by a Jackson pamphlet that he traveled to New York to file suit. Driving through Central Park, his wife by his side, he suffered a massive stroke and died on the afternoon of July 15, 1868.

A memorial monument marks his grave in Mount Auburn Cemetery near Boston. The inscription on the stone, written by Dr. Jacob Bigelow, reads as follows:

WILLIAM T. G. MORTON

Born August 9, 1819 Died July 15, 1868
Erected by the citizens of Boston
Inventor and Revealer of Anesthetic Inhalation
Before whom in all time surgery was agony
By whom pain in surgery was averted and annulled
Since whom science has control of pain

Crawford Long, who never became personally involved in the Ether Controversy, died in 1878 while attending a woman in childbirth. Jackson became increasingly incited and disturbed by the fact that with each passing year, and despite his own continuous and vitriolic campaign, the credit for the discovery was more and more recognized as belonging to Morton. The breaking point for Jackson, in retrospect a tragic though malignant figure, occurred on a July day five years after Morton's death. He wandered to Morton's grave at Mount Auburn and, upon reading the inscription, became psychotic and had to be carried off to McLean Asylum. He died there seven years later in 1880. Now the last of the claimants for the discovery of anesthesia was gone, and history alone would sort out the complex events.

Frederick G. Banting

1891–1941 Canadian orthopedic surgeon; discoverer of insulin

On a farm near Alliston, in the province of Ontario, Canada, a boy was born in 1891 who before the age of thirty would, with the assistance of a twenty-three-year-old medical student, isolate the hormone insulin. The discovery, which medical authorities had predicted could never be made, has saved the lives of millions of people suffering from the disease diabetes mellitus, more commonly known as sugar diabetes. *Diabetes* is derived from the Greek *diabētēs* ("passing through") and the Latin *mellitus* ("sweet as honey"). This disease results in the passing of excessive quantities of sugar-filled urine. (There exists a different and far rarer disease, diabetes insipidus, where large quantities of urine also are excreted, but here the urine is sugar-free, and the cause of the disease is a defect in the posterior portion of the pituitary gland. When people mention diabetes, almost always they're referring to sugar diabetes.)

A farm in a sparsely populated area—Canada's concentration of people per square mile is approximately one-tenth that of the United States—hardly was the birthplace one would expect of a great medical scientist. And his birthplace might have been still more remote. Frederick Banting's father wanted to move his family to the unsettled wilderness of the Canadian West. Had he done so, it is almost certain that Fred, his youngest child, never would have had the opportunity to go to college and medical school. Luckily William and his wife, Margaret, stayed put on that farm, approximately fifty miles north of Toronto, the city that was home to Canada's largest university.

William Banting wanted his son to become a minister, but Fred felt that he might want a medical career. Perhaps the death from diabetes of a fourteen-year-old girl who was his friend had some influence on his decision. At any rate, his father did not discourage him, and one year after young Banting entered Victoria College in Toronto, he enrolled in the University of Toronto Medical School. He entered the Meds Seventeen class, which meant that after five years of study, he would graduate in 1917. Lithe and muscular from farm work, dark haired and very shy, Banting was stubborn, completely honest, and fiercely independent. These qualities later would allow him to persevere in his experiments under the most trying conditions imaginable.

In Toronto he found rooms in the home of a widow, Catherine O'Neil, who became a lifelong friend; she acted as a second mother to him and on a few occasions gave him advice that saved his career. While Banting was in medical school World War I began, following the assassination of Austrian Archduke Ferdinand—there was a complex system of alliances—and Canada as a member of the British Commonwealth was at war with Germany. During that year, even though he was still a medical student, Banting was given special permission to perform an emergency tonsillectomy because most of the doctors were overseas. He nervously read his surgery book and then walked into the operating room and did the procedure excellently.

When Banting graduated from medical school he joined the Canadian Army Medical Corps as a lieutenant. Eventually he was sent overseas to England, where, during his spare time, he began to collect beautiful pieces of rare china. Then his unit was sent to France, where the fighting was bloody and almost unceasing. He would operate for hours without rest. On September 28, 1918, in the midst of a violent battle at Cambrai, a large piece of shrapnel penetrated Banting's right forearm, puncturing an artery. He was ordered to return to the rear, but since he was the only doctor present, seventeen hours later he was still dressing wounds. Ordered to get into an ambulance that would drive him to the rear lines, Banting lost consciousness on the way from loss of blood.

Later, at a hospital in Buxton, England, a young physician who happened to be a lieutenant told him that the arm was infected with gas gangrene and would have to be amputated. Banting had saved the limbs of several soldiers who otherwise would have had arms or legs cut off, and now Captain Banting—he had been promoted and awarded the Military Cross—refused to have his arm amputated and ordered the lieutenant to get out. What good would one arm be to an aspiring orthopedic surgeon? In time, the arm healed, though a deep scar remained.

When the war was over, Banting returned to Toronto and worked for a year at the Hospital for Sick Children. There he successfully repaired clubfeet, curved spines, and other childhood orthopedic problems. He was wonderfully kind to these young patients, who adored Uncle Doctor Fred.

In Toronto he was fortunate to work with Professor C. L. Starr. Of Professor Starr he wrote:

> It is impossible to describe in words what he gave to me, but I know of no man of whom it may be more truly said, "What you are speaks so loudly that I cannot hear what you say." I always got encouragement and inspiration from Dr. Starr and never left his presence without feeling stronger and better able to carry on. He was an idealist and unconsciously imparted this idealism to those who were associated with him. I recall at least a dozen outstanding surgeons who owe much of their success, both in practice and Research, to the influence of the late Dr. Starr.

It was time, Banting decided, to earn some money, although actually money was one thing that had never really interested him as long as he had enough to purchase research equipment. He bought a beat-up old Ford and drove to London, Ontario, that province's second largest city. A loan from his father provided the down payment on a house. On the lawn he put up a wooden sign that read: DR. F. G. BANTING.

Banting would have liked a flourishing orthopedic practice, but instead he chain-smoked and waited for some patients to appear. One finally did after twenty-eight days had passed; his total income for the month was around ten dollars. To supplement this tiny income, he secured a teaching job at the University of Western Ontario, becoming a favorite instructor of the students. In his spare time, he began a hobby that he enjoyed as long as he lived; he bought an easel, brushes, and other equipment and began to paint. He particularly enjoyed painting landscapes and became accomplished at this recreation.

Then one evening a marvelous thing happened. Here Banting describes it:

> Important ideas often come as strange coincidences: for example, on the night of October 30, 1920, I was preparing a lecture on the Physiology of the Pancreas, during the early part of the evening. It occurred to me that there was a possibility that it was the external secretion of the

pancreas which destroyed the internal during the process of extraction. Before retiring, I read an article by Moses Barron describing the damage produced in the pancreas by the obstruction of the duct by gallstones. This article pointed out that similar damage could be produced by tying the pancreatic ducts.

It can be assumed that Banting had done much reading about all the previous work concerning the pancreas; he prepared his lectures with great care and thoroughness. He knew that the pancreas is an organ situated deep in the abdomen behind the stomach. It has two functions. It produces digestive enzymes that break down proteins and fat. These secretions empty into the intestine through a duct and help food get absorbed. The pancreas also has clusters of cells that look like small islands. These cells, scattered throughout the organ, produce a hormone that goes directly into the bloodstream, making the pancreas, in effect, a ductless gland as well. In 1895 this hormone was referred to as "hormone X" by Sir William Osler, who predicted that someday someone would isolate it and use it to treat diabetes. Many investigators spoke of hormone X, although few of them felt it even existed, including the famous professor of physiology at the University of Toronto, J. J. R. Macleod, who had written in his textbook that there was no proof of an internal secretion from the pancreas.

The islands that produce this hormone were noted in 1869 by a medical student named Paul Langerhans. These clusters of cells, so different from the main body of pancreatic cells, became known as the Islands of Langerhans. In the pancreas these islands were not destroyed or damaged by the acini (grapelike) portion that produced the digestive enzymes. But when the island tissue was mixed with the digestive tissue, the latter destroyed the former. Thus in 1889 two famous investigators, Von Mering and Minkowski, had removed the pancreases of dogs, who all proceeded to die in diabetic coma within three weeks. They attempted to prevent these deaths by injecting an extract made from the pancreas of an ox, but the experiment failed for the above reason—the mixture effect.

Barron's article set Banting's mind on fire. Here was a way to destroy most of the pancreas while leaving the islands intact. From these islands an extract of hormone X could be obtained and a treatment for dreaded diabetes would be a strong possibility. Unable to sleep that evening because of the excitement produced by the article, Banting went to his notebook and wrote the following immortal words. "Ligate the pancreatic ducts of dogs. Wait six or eight weeks for degeneration. Remove the residue and extract."

His associates at the University of Western Ontario were enthusiastic about Banting's research idea but advised him to apply to Professor Macleod for research facilities and funds, since Macleod was the authority. Accordingly, in November 1920, Banting, after being granted an interview, drove to Toronto in his old Ford, probably wondering what the famous Scottish professor was like, since Banting had graduated two years before Macleod arrived.

It didn't take him long to find out. Macleod deprecated Banting's ideas. When all sorts of better men had tried to get such an extract, what made this bumpkin orthopedic surgeon think he could succeed? The answer was no. No research facilities would be made available. Banting had a second interview during the Christmas holidays and again was turned down, but Banting's persistence paid off. Learning that Macleod would vacation in Scotland in the summer and his labs therefore would be empty, Banting again made his request to the professor. Macleod, annoyed, decided to let this upstart make a fool of himself. He told Banting that after the school term ended in May 1921, he could have the use of a small laboratory, ten dogs, and a bright medical student who knew biochemistry.

The following day, twenty-one-year-old Charles Best came to Macleod's office to hear Banting's plan. Blond, tall, the well-groomed son of a physician, Best's appearance was almost the opposite of his prospective partner. Reluctant at first, Charley Best remembered a favorite aunt who had died of diabetes. As Banting revealed his experimental plans, Best was somehow impressed. Whether it was Banting's honesty, enthusiasm, or logical plan that sold Best on working with him is not known, but he agreed to become a member of this team of two. There would be no stipend for either investigator.

Their experiments began on May 16, 1921, when Banting tied off the pancreatic ducts of several dogs. Early experiments were unsuccessful, and they needed more dogs but had no money to purchase them. Best, who died in 1978, recalled:

> Suggestions have been made by poorly informed authors that dogs were appropriated from the street with very little ceremony. This is not true, but there were occasions when we made a tour through various parts of the city and bargained with owners of animals. They were paid by funds which we took from our own pockets. This money may have come from the sale of Banting's automobile. Neither of us received a stipend during the summer of 1921 and for a time I used funds which he loaned me. A part of this

money certainly came from the sale of his Ford car.

Best also remembered Banting's affection for his experimental dogs, whom he trained to put out their paws when blood samples were needed. Anesthesia was always used during surgical procedures.

July 27, 1921, was a steaming hot day. A week earlier, Banting had removed the entire pancreas from a dog that now lay on a table dying from diabetes. On a second table, Best placed a duct-tied dog. Banting, sweating profusely from the heat plus nervous expectation, opened its abdominal cavity, extracted its pancreas, and handed the gland to Best. Since the Islands of Langerhans were intact because of the prior surgery, Best, using some ice and preservative fluids, prepared an extract of these islands, filled a syringe with this extract, and handed the syringe to Banting. Banting injected the extract into the dying dog. After Best drew another sample of blood, the two investigators waited nervously. Soon Banting saw signs of life in the dog, now emerging from its coma. Its eyes were brighter, and it began to wag its tail. At the same time, Best told Banting that the last blood sample had been almost normal; the blood sugar had dropped from its high diabetic levels. These two unlikely candidates for greatness had found hormone X. Diabetes could be cured.

It soon became obvious that insulin acted for just a short time. The dog that had recovered died. A better supply of insulin than dog pancreases was needed.

Macleod was skeptical about the research when he returned from Scotland, saying that far more work was needed to prove that Banting and Best had been correct, and that while they could continue to use the lab, no money would be forthcoming. But Professor Velyien Henderson came forward to help Banting remain at Toronto by offering him a paying job in the Department of Pharmacology. Eventually large supplies of iletin, as hormone X was now called, were obtained from slaughterhouses. After Banting and Best had saved the lives of several dogs and kept them alive, Macleod relented. He hired J. B. Collip to help purify the extract and insisted that it henceforth be called insulin from the Latin *insula*, meaning "island," a name easier to pronounce and first coined years earlier by de Meyer of Belgium and Shafer of Edinburgh. Both of these men, and Sir William Osler as well, had predicted that the isolation of this substance would one day control diabetes.

In diabetes the essential problem is the handling of carbohydrates. Instead of glucose being converted into glyco-

Frederick Banting and Charles Best in 1921 with the dog that was the subject of their experimentation. *World Health Organization, Geneva, Switzerland.*

gen (a complex carbohydrate) with the help of insulin, high amounts of glucose remain in the bloodstream, which results in a high blood glucose (sugar) and much glucose excreted from the blood into the urine. The extra glucose in the urine pulls in water, which results in passing large quantities of sugary urine and therefore depletion of body water (dehydration). Because of the lack of carbohydrate calories, fats are burned to supply needed energy to the body. Instead of supplying adequate nutrition for the body, this burning of fats results in an acid condition known as acidosis, which in turn leads to coma and death.

On January 11, 1922, in Toronto General Hospital, a fourteen-year-old boy, Leonard Thompson, was dying of diabetes. He weighed sixty-five pounds, and his breath smelled of acetone. First Banting and Best, uncertain of the proper amount of insulin to use on a human, injected themselves several times to insure its safety; there were no serious consequences—only some red skin welts. Then they began to inject the boy. By the end of two weeks, he was bright and alert. The first human had been saved from a disease that had been known as a killer of mankind since ancient Egyptian times.

Banting and Best talked to various groups in Toronto, but the first important meeting where the momentous discovery was given to the world was held at Atlantic City, New Jersey; the occasion was the annual meeting of the Association of American Physicians. Banting's address, a stumbling affair since he was a poor public speaker, was followed by the smooth and dramatic presentation of Professor Macleod. This talk was followed by tremendous applause, and the audience inferred that it was really Macleod who had made the discovery and that Banting and Best were only a couple of lab assistants. Professor Macleod did nothing to dispel this falsehood. (Perhaps he believed in the German philosophy that the head of a department should receive all the credit for work done in that department even though that chief had played little or no role in the discovery.)

Not one cent of profit from insulin was made by the investigators. All patents were turned over without charge to the University of Toronto. (In 1921 Banting still had not been able to repay the four thousand dollars his father had lent him.)

By the end of 1922 the Connaught Laboratories of the University of Toronto and the Eli Lilly pharmaceutical company, using pancreases of various species (e.g., porcine), had developed large-scale facilities for the production of insulin. By 1923 insulin was available in large quantities, enough to be placed on general sale in pharmacies throughout the world. Now the disease whose diagnosis only a few years earlier had been a death warrant was controllable. (It was soon discovered that the disease is more complex than had been originally believed and that other hormones such as the anterior pituitary are involved. Also, much research is being done on the long-term complications developed by some diabetics, such as circulatory problems. But insulin, which must be injected, or oral insulin substitutes still are required for treatment. Today there is also available an insulin having the exact structure of human insulin.)

In 1923 it was announced from Stockholm that the Nobel Prize in medicine and physiology was to be awarded to Doctors Macleod and Banting for being the "codiscoverers" of insulin. Banting was furious because Best's name was omitted and because Macleod had had very little to do with the experimental success. At first Banting wanted to refuse the prize, but associates talked him into accepting it. He did so only after the order of names was changed to Banting and Macleod and because he felt that he could not refuse this honor to his country. He was hurt and upset, however. While Charles Best was addressing a medical meeting at Harvard, Banting sent a telegram to Dr. Elliot Joslin, the chairman of the meeting and a leading diabetologist, requesting Joslin to read it aloud. The telegram read:

AT ANY MEETING OR DINNER PLEASE READ FOLLOWING: I ASCRIBE TO BEST EQUAL SHARE IN THE DISCOVERY. HURT THAT HE IS NOT SO ACKNOWLEDGED BY NOBEL TRUSTEES. WILL SHARE WITH HIM.

BANTING

Banting's announcement that he was sharing his half of the prize with Charles Best must have embarrassed Macleod, who immediately decided to share his cash award with J. B. Collip, M.D. Actually, Collip had done marvelous work in purifying the extracts. Collip and Banting became close friends. But Collip liked Macleod, and Banting's hostility toward Macleod so annoyed him that one day he threatened to stop all further experiments with Banting and start to produce insulin independently. Banting, furious, landed a haymaker, and Collip lay, dazed and confused, on the laboratory floor.

History, however, did include Banting's young helper; when the discovery of insulin is discussed or written about, the names mentioned are always Banting and Best.

Despite Banting's desperate efforts to avoid the limelight, he was an international hero, and he discovered that the obscurity he desired was impossible. Honors came from everywhere, including a knighthood in 1934, but the most fulfilling of all was the creation by his alma mater, the University of Toronto, of the Banting and Best Department of Medical Research, with Banting receiving its professorship at a salary of six thousand dollars a year.

Banting continued with various research projects, such as supervising the work on preventing silicosis, a disease affecting the lungs of miners.

In June of 1939 he married Henrietta Ball and at last achieved marital happiness, his first marriage having ended in divorce in 1925.

By 1938 Banting had seen that World War II was imminent. He had always hated the Nazis and their anti-Semitism, but most of all, he wanted to help in preparing Canada for the coming conflict. He enlisted simply as Major Banting shortly before Canada declared war. On a mission to bring improved flying suits to England, his plane crashed in Newfoundland on February 21, 1941. One of his former researchers, Dr. E. J. King, reported the following to the British medical journal *Lancet* in its April 26, 1941, issue:

> Sir—Details of the death of Sir Frederick Banting are only now beginning to reach England from Canada; from these it is apparent that he died as generously as he had lived. He was not immediately killed by the impact of the crashing plane but lived for some hours; his first act was to attend to the injuries of the pilot. Characteristically he refused to have any attention paid to his own wounds, and insisted on dressing those of Pilot Mackie, who then set out to look for help. Banting then seems to have dragged himself from the plane and to have lain down on some pine boughs which the airplane had torn from the trees skirting the frozen lake on which the attempt had been made to land. There, with his overcoat pulled over him against the bitter cold, the pilot found him later—dead.

The letter continues, telling of Banting's breadth, modesty, and compassion. Losing someone of his caliber at age forty-nine was a terrible blow to the scientific world.

Probably it is best to end this chapter with a few of Banting's observations on medical research.

> Research men are born, not made. The research man is fundamentally inquisitive—not about things that everybody knows, but about things which nobody knows. The child starts out in life with an inquisitive mind but the average child is satisfied and contented by the answer given by an adult. The child soon loses that inquisitive quality if he is suppressed. As a child grows older, it is not always in his best interests to answer his

questions, but he should be encouraged to answer them himself as far as possible. In 1923 I visited the City of Washington and had the pleasure of meeting an eminent physician of that city. He told me that every Saturday morning, he took his two boys, of 6 and 8 years, for a walk. On one occasion, the two boys plied their Daddy with questions until he became displeased and told them that they should not ask so many foolish questions, but that they must think before asking. When they arrived at the zoo they went to see the lions and after some time the older boy asked "Which is the daddy lion?" His father told him that it was the one with the mane. On thinking it over, the child said, "I don't think you're quite right about that, Daddy. Mother's hair is longer than yours." I would like to follow the career of that child, for he has the making of a research man. His answer also involved a fundamental principle in Research—the challenge of authority. He did not accept without due consideration the explanation given to him.

Alexander Fleming (1881–1955)
Howard W. Florey (1898–1968)
Ernst Boris Chain (1906–1979)

Discoverers and producers of penicillin

Possibly no drug in history has saved as many lives as has penicillin. As is the case with most scientific discoveries, luck, patience, and skill played important roles first in the recognition and later in the production of penicillin.

The man who brought penicillin to world recognition was a Scot, Alexander Fleming. Even in primitive society, molds (fungus growths) were known to have therapeutic value. John Tyndall, a Victorian scientist, noted in 1876 that he had found "dormant Bacteria, the cause of their quiescence . . . the blanket of penicillium." Still it was Fleming's experiments that started the process that brought penicillin to its place on the world stage.

But the penicillin story involves two other men, Howard Florey and Ernst Chain. They are responsible for definitively showing the therapeutic power of the drug and also for starting its production; their Oxford laboratories produced small amounts at first and then larger amounts. Later, spurred on by World War II and the enormous help of the American government and its pharmaceutical industries, huge quantities of penicillin were produced. In 1945 Florey and Chain shared with Fleming the Nobel Prize in medicine and physiology.

Alexander Fleming was born in 1881 on a farm in Lochfield, Ayrshire, Scotland, leased by his father, Hugh, whose first marriage yielded four living children. His second marriage yielded four more, of which brood Alec (as he was called) was the third child. Alec enjoyed farm life, fishing, and, with the help of a brother, snaring rabbits with his bare hands. "We unconsciously learned a great deal about nature, most of which is missed by a towndweller," he later recalled. The farm life also enhanced his powers of observation.

While still a boy, he was running around the corner of a wall when he collided with another boy. The accident left him with the upper part of his nose flattened—a boxer's nose—but despite this he remained handsome. Since education was so important to the Scots, after some early schooling Alec left the farm at age thirteen and a half and traveled to London to live with his brother Tom, an ophthalmologist. A few months later four Fleming boys were living in the house on Marylebone Road, and the housekeeper was their sister Mary. It was 1895, the height of Queen Victoria's reign; the underground (subway) was run by steam, and every ten minutes the house shook as a train rumbled by. Alec and his younger brother Robert explored the city atop horse-drawn buses. They rarely spoke except to point out to one another some unusual sight like the Tower of London. (Years later Ernst Chain, who shared the Nobel Prize with Fleming and Florey, commented on Fleming's reticence: "He was a man of few words who found it difficult to express himself, but he gave the impression of a warmhearted person though he did everything to appear unemotional and aloof.")

For a time Alec worked as an office clerk for a shipping firm. Although he didn't enjoy the job, he later felt that the practical experience gained was valuable to his scientific career. At age twenty he received an inheritance from an uncle and was advised by his physician brother to study medicine. In 1902 aided by an academic scholarship, he enrolled in St. Mary's Hospital because the medical school had a good water-polo team and Fleming was an excellent swimmer. (At the time there were twelve medical schools in London, all loosely under the jurisdiction of the University of London.) An outstanding student as well as a hard worker, he won all the academic prizes, graduating in 1908. At the same time he passed the surgical exams with honor and became a Fellow of the Royal College of Surgeons (FRCS). However, he decided against a surgical career, opting to work with germs too small to see with the naked eye, each called a microbe, a word coined in 1877 by Charles Sédillot.

Soon he joined the Inoculation Department of St. Mary's under the tutelage of famed Sir Almroth Wright, his former bacteriology professor. The laboratory, which would be directed by Wright for forty-five years, had an excellent shooting team, and since Alec was a good shot, he was a welcome addition to the team. Many years later, when lecturing to medical students, Fleming told them:

> You should know even at this stage of your career that there is far more to medicine than mere bookwork. You have to know men and you have to know human nature. There is no better way to learn about human nature than by indulging in sports, more especially in team-sports.

Sir Almroth, an intimate of British aristocracy, many of whom were his patients, was a brilliant Irishman, one of the first to use typhoid vaccine on humans. Among his close friends was George Bernard Shaw, who once said to him: "You handle a pen as well as I do." Once Shaw asked Wright what would happen if only a limited supply of some medication was available. Sir Almroth replied that in such an instance, it would be necessary to decide whose life was worth saving. Shaw saw the drama in this situation, which resulted in his play *The Doctor's Dilemma.* Wright was the obvious model for the play's hero, Sir Colenso Ridgeon. Sir Almroth never was distant to his students, and biographer André Maurois reported about a French visitor to St. Mary's:

> [He] was astonished to see Fleming, solemn faced and dexterous, go up to Wright while the latter was holding forth and, without a word, prick the august finger so as to get a drop of blood which he needed for control purposes, while Wright went on talking without paying the least attention to this rite.

Wright's primary interest was immunology. He never believed in chemotherapy and so was unhappy with Fleming's faith in the effectiveness of the drug penicillin. (Today chemotherapy usually refers to drugs used to treat cancer, but actually it means all drugs used to treat disease.) However, years later Wright was proud enough of his student to notify the *London Times* that Fleming was responsible for the success of penicillin. (The Oxford group, not mentioned in Wright's letter, understandably was upset. The rivalry of scientists is just as strong as that of any other group.)

At 2 A.M. Fleming was usually at work in the lab. A short man with blue eyes and a cigarette always dangling from his mouth, he was a favorite of students who could drop in at that hour to have a beer with their teacher.

When World War I was declared, Fleming served as a medical officer with the British army and was sent to France. In 1915, while on leave, he married Sarah McElroy, a trained nurse from

Sir Alexander Fleming at work in his laboratory. *Brown Brothers.*

Dublin. Always called Sareen, she was a lovely wife. (When she died in 1949, Flem, as he was called then, was devastated.)

Soon he was back in France dealing with serious wounds from artillery explosions; he quickly realized that dead tissue was a good culture medium for infection and advised surgeons to cut away this tissue, a process now called debridement. He also found that although Lister's work was completely valid, strong antiseptics used in *deep* war wounds actually promoted bacterial growth—especially gas gangrene—and he recommended saline solutions for irrigation. (Several physicians felt that although his later penicillin discovery overshadowed everything Fleming accomplished, still his studies of strong antiseptics remained his most ingenious and perfect experiments.) Fleming's war work was complicated by the 1918 influenza pandemic (worldwide epidemic). No one knew what caused the disease. The influenza virus wasn't identified until 1933, and the young soldiers either recovered by themselves or died of pneumonia. Trying to help soldiers who were flu victims and those with gas gangrene wounds kept Fleming exhausted until the war ended.

After the war he worked with an enzyme called lysozyme. He noted that some of his nasal mucus, which he added to a Petri dish when he had a cold, actually lysed (dissolved) some of the bacteria. (A Petri dish is a circular glass container filled with media like agar on which bacterial colonies are grown.) He also found that lysozyme was present in tears and in even higher concentrations in egg whites. Although the lysed bacteria were not virulent, still Fleming felt that it was possible that a stronger substance might be found someday.

That "someday" happened dramatically during the month of September 1928. Fleming, unlike other investigators, often saved cultures for a long time. Everyone hated contamination, but on this particular day a contaminant on one of the Petri dishes suddenly interested Fleming. He had been growing the very virulent staphylococci bacteria in preparation for a book chapter he was writing. What caught his attention was that, on the dish, the yellow-golden staphylococci colonies previously present had become transparent. "That's funny," Fleming remarked to a colleague as he studied the dish. A little later he told a visiting Canadian Rhodes scholar: "You think yourself a clever fellow; explain this one."

What had killed these bacteria was a greenish mold that Fleming identified as *Penicillium rubrum.* (Later the American mycologist Dr. Charles Thom correctly identified the mold as *Penicillium notatum.*) Apparently a spore from the mold had blown in through a window or had been blown to Fleming's lab from a lab on a floor below and grown into the furry mold. Fleming named the liquid that came from the mold and that was the active principle *penicillin,* a name that has lived on in history. Penicillin is an antibiotic, a word coined in 1941 by Selman Waksman, the discoverer of streptomycin. An antibiotic is a living substance that fights other, dangerous living substances.

Fleming's penicillium mold, even greatly diluted, continued to kill staphylococci, and when injected full strength into mice and rabbits, it proved to be nontoxic. However, penicillin was almost impossible to produce, except in very small quantities. It was unstable and seemed to just disappear, even under the eyes of the chemists Fleming enlisted to help find the secret of production. Finally Fleming became discouraged and gave up on the idea of any large-scale therapeutic use of penicillin. Even so, he published his experimental studies in the June 1929 issue of *The British Journal of Experimental Pathology*. In the article he cited penicillin's lack of toxicity and suggested "that it may be an efficient antiseptic for application to, or injection into, areas infected with penicillin-sensitive microbes."

Some ten years later the scene would shift to Oxford, where Howard W. Florey, the Sir William Dunn Professor of Pathology, had by 1936 assembled the team that would produce penicillin, purify it, and give it to the world.

Howard Florey was born on September 24, 1898, in Adelaide, Australia. The only son of Bertha and Joseph Florey, he attended the finest primary schools and eventually was educated in medicine, graduating from Adelaide University Medical School with the highest grades. Florey later commented: "I don't know why I turned to medicine but, at the time, it just seemed a very natural thing for me to do." (His sister Hilda became one of Australia's first women doctors.) A great athlete as well—his sports were tennis, football, cricket, and swimming—he graduated in 1922 and traveled to Oxford as Australia's Rhodes scholar. Florey had two outstanding characteristics: he spoke honestly but bluntly, and no matter how far ahead he was in a tennis match, he remained a ruthless competitor through the last point. (His father, who once had been a successful industrialist, was possibly defrauded by his accountant and died penniless. Howard Florey had to pay for his passage to England by being the ship's doctor.)

At beautiful Magdalen College, Oxford University, Florey was uncharacteristically shy. At first he made few acquaintances, which often was the case for an outsider. But soon he met John Fulton, an American Rhodes scholar, and they became close friends. Later Fulton would house Florey's children in his home in New Haven during World War II and also be of great help in finding the right contacts to get penicillin mass-produced in America. In time Florey made other friends and soon felt thoroughly at ease.

An interview in March 1923 with the great neurologist Sir Charles Sherrington really was the beginning of Florey's anti-microbial career. Sir Charles was impressed by the young man and invited him to work in his department. Subsequently he frequently was invited to the Sherrington home, where he sat in chairs that had been used by Darwin, Lister, Ehrlich, and many other great men of science. Sir Charles, president of the Royal Society, was a power in British science, and having Florey as a sort of protégé greatly benefited the young student. "Always remember," Sherrington would remind his students, "the more intelligent the question you ask of Mother Nature, the more intelligible will be her reply."

Florey made outstanding grades, and at age twenty-five and two years out of medical school, he was told by Sherrington that the new field of experimental pathology was an exciting one and that a position in it had opened at Caius College in Cambridge. Aided by a scholarship, Florey accepted; within eleven years he would return to Oxford as professor of pathology. During that last summer before going to Cambridge, he joined an expedition to the Arctic, acting as medical officer. His biographer Lennard Bickel reports:

> Soon afterwards, a senior academic from Adelaide called on him at Caius and, informing him that Adelaide had advertised a post for a lectureship in physiology, said that this had been done in the hope and expectation that Florey would apply. Florey took the remark as a rebuke. Flushing with anger, he asked his visitor, "Then why the hell didn't you ask me?"
>
> His caller was taken aback and replied loftily that this was not a practice followed by the University in South Australia.
>
> "More's the pity," Florey replied, and then showed the man out. Tact never was one of Florey's strong points.

At Cambridge, like Fleming, he was always seen with a cigarette dangling from his mouth. This young man with spectacles was admired for his integrity. He could be ruthless but often kind; he often shouted down opponents, although he never praised himself. And he used only surnames in addressing not only acquaintances but also friends. In short, he was a complex man.

While at Adelaide, he had met Ethel Reed, a medical student in one of the lower classes. She was just finishing her sixth year of medical school when he wrote to her, proposing marriage. She came to Cambridge, where they were wed on October 19, 1926. The marriage was not a happy one since Florey never was able to communicate his inner feelings to his family. (Before the marriage Florey was offered a Rockefeller grant and worked at Pennsylvania State University with A. Newton Richards, another American who later would prove of great value in the penicillin story.)

At Cambridge Florey heard for the first time of Fleming's work with lysozyme, and this interested him because of the possibility that it could fight bacteria. He began experiments and for many years continued to work with the substance, finding it in the mucus secreted by the colon; he understood that lysozyme served as a natural protection for the body.

Florey traveled to Spain and worked briefly with the great histologist Ramón y Cajal, learning to stain bacteria. The Floreys' love for Spain was reflected in the name of their first child, a daughter, Paquita.

Next Florey was appointed professor of pathology at Sheffield University, remaining four years in this smoky, industrial setting. During the Sheffield years Ethel gave birth to their son, Charles, completing the family.

Finally, in 1935 Florey's greatest dream was satisfied; he returned to Oxford as professor of pathology and began to assemble a superb staff. He realized that he needed a biochemist and traveled to Cambridge to talk to Professor Sir Frederick Gowland Hopkins, the "father of British biochemistry." Hopkins, who had learned of Ernst Chain from the great J. B. S. Haldane, recommended to Florey this twenty-nine-year-old German-born chemist. This young man was destined to share with Fleming and Florey the 1945 Nobel Prize. Chain later wrote: "The whole of my career in England is really due to Haldane."

Ernst Boris Chain was born in Berlin on June 19, 1906, of Russian-German parentage. He was a piano virtuoso, at one time considering becoming a professional musician. Ernst's father died when he was thirteen, and the family, originally middle class, found themselves poor. Ernst's mother took in boarders to make ends meet. Chain graduated from Friedrich Wilhelm University in 1930 with a degree in chemistry and physiology. For a time he worked in the chemistry department at the Charité Hospital, where he earned a Ph.D.

Chain, with mustache and hair reminiscent of Albert Einstein, had left Berlin in 1933, when he no longer could continue his enzyme work under the Nazis. (He expected that Hitler's regime would last only six months, and so his mother and his young sister, Hedwig, remained in Germany; as Jews both were executed in the Theresienstadt concentration camp.) In 1936, a year after he had been hired by Florey, he met his future wife and colleague, Anne Beloff. Their happy marriage in 1948 eventually produced three children, all of whom are enjoying exciting careers.

At Florey's suggestion Chain began reading through the literature to see what programs might be valuable for the laboratory. Chain found three subjects in which his training would be helpful; Florey later said: "Eventually Chain proposed, and I agreed to go along with it, that we should make a thorough investigation of antibacterial substances. That is why we looked at penicillin."

While reviewing the literature, Chain had come upon Fleming's original 1929 article on penicillin. He felt at once that under the proper conditions this drug could be produced and that cold temperature would be of vital importance in the process. This idea led to one of the critical steps in penicillin production, freeze-drying, a process in which the liquid is frozen and water is then removed. Immediately after reading the Fleming article, something clicked in Chain's mind. He knew that a colleague was working with molds, and he crossed a corridor to find her.

> I asked her if she knew the strain of the mould and if, by any chance, it was penicillin notatum. She looked surprised and then said "yes" it was, and that she had been using it for some time in the bacteriology lab. . . . I was astounded at my luck in finding the very mould about which I had been reading, here, in the same building, right under our very noses.

The colleague, one Miss Campbell-Renton, gave Chain a sample and told him that it had been obtained from Fleming by Florey's predecessor. Chain further contributed to the lab's penicillin success when he suggested to Florey that he ask Dr. Norman Heatley, an outstanding chemist, to join the lab; soon Heatley became a member of the team, which included, among several distinguished investigators, one Dr. Margaret Jennings. (Dr. Jennings remained Florey's colleague for thirty years, and he married her in 1967 after the death, in 1966, of his first wife, Ethel.)

During the first months of Florey and Chain's association, they learned about a new drug, Prontosil, which had been developed in Germany by Gerhard Domagk. Following Ehrlich's lead, Domagk had run a whole series of azo (nitrogen) dyes through bacterial tests to see if any would be effective. Developed in secrecy, the drug proved powerful and in 1932 successfully cured mice infected with streptococci. Later Domagk used it to cure his own daughter of a serious infection.

Domagk published his results in 1935. A year later Professor and Madame Trefouels at the Pasteur Institute found that it was only one portion of Prontosil, the sulfanilamide portion, that was effective; the azo, or dye, part of Prontosil had no effect against bacteria. This Pasteur Institute research, when added to Domagk's discovery, introduced the sulfonamides to the world. (Gerhard Domagk was forced by the Nazis to decline the Nobel Prize awarded to him in 1939 for his discovery and use of Prontosil.)

As valuable as the sulfa drugs were and are, sometimes there were serious side effects, and the drug wasn't active against certain virulent bacteria. Penicillin still had a future!

In 1939 Hitler invaded Poland. En-

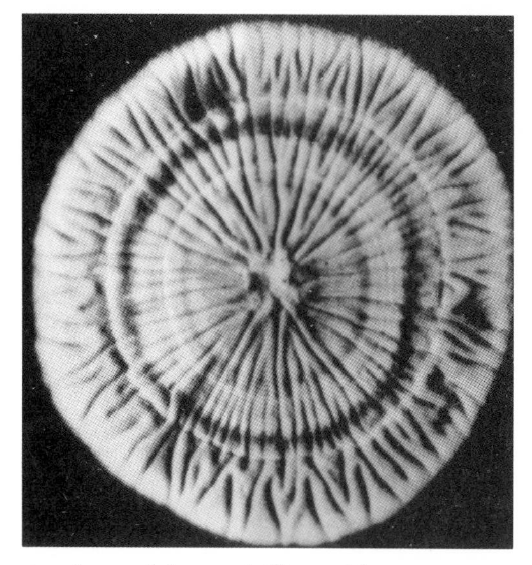

A colony of the penicillin mold.

gland, finally realizing that appeasement was useless, declared war on Germany. Despite the bombings (in 1940 Fleming's London house was destroyed, and he barely escaped being killed), work in the Oxford lab continued. Florey, his mind set at ease when he sent his children to America to live with the Fulton family, assigned Chain and Heatley, and later Professor Edward Abraham, to the biochemical studies of extraction and purification of penicillin. He himself would do the biological investigations and also be in charge of raising badly needed funds. Actually, although some financial help came from England despite war demands, it was Chain who assured the completion of the penicillin research; his suggestion to Florey to ask the Rockfeller Foundation for funds resulted in a very generous grant. The broth that nurtured the penicillium mold produced yellow droplets, which contained the penicillin. The addition of Brewer's yeast increased the yield, and finally, with the use of freeze-drying, a small amount of brown powder was obtained. (The essentials of penicillin production ultimately would be: 1. fermentation; 2. extraction and purification; and 3. drying of penicillin and putting it into ampules.)

On Tuesday, March 19, 1940, Chain dissolved eighty milligrams of the precious brown powder in water and walked downstairs to ask Dr. J. M. Barnes, working on some other project, to inject the solution into the abdominal cavities of two mice. Barnes complied, and Chain intently watched hour after hour, looking for any signs of toxicity, such as staggering. None occurred, and penicillin was declared safe. (This historic day was also a lucky one; later it was discovered that only 1 percent of the brown powder was penicillin; the other 99 percent was comprised of impurities that fortunately were not toxic. Otherwise the entire project might have been abandoned.)

On May 10, Winston Churchill became prime minister of Great Britain, and two weeks later English troops in Dunkirk, France, were encircled; they were miraculously saved, primarily by a fleet of small privately owned power boats. When on June 6, 1944 (four years later)—D day—many of those same troops landed on the shores of Normandy, the ships that carried them were plentifully supplied with ampules of purified penicillin. That was how fast the commercial production of penicillin, certainly hastened by the necessities of treating the war-wounded, progressed. (Actually penicillin turned out not to be a brown powder at all; it was made up of beautiful, pure white crystals.)

The war did away with weekends in Florey's lab; every day was a working day. In May 1940 fifty milligrams of brown powder, one week's production by the lab staff, was used in a critical biological test, using eight mice; all had been injected with virulent streptococci, but only half of the group received penicillin. By the following morning all of the penicillin-treated mice were alive; the other four were dead.

Howard W. Florey injecting penicillin into a mouse. *Reportagebild, Sweden.*

When Florey said that it "seems like a miracle," Chain replied: "Of course it does. It *is* a miracle." But Florey wanted more production and told Heatley that he wanted to move on to human tests. "Remember," he told the chemist, "a man is 3,000 times as big as a mouse." But first, more mouse trials were successfully performed, and the findings were written up and sent to the esteemed British medical journal *Lancet*. Titled *Penicillin as a Chemotherapeutic Agent*, the article's authors were listed alphabetically—Chain, Florey, Gardner, Heatley, Jennings, Orr-Ewing, and Sanders. The editor buried the two-page article on page 226 of the August 24, 1940, issue. Fleming visited the Oxford lab a few days after reading the *Lancet* article but said very little and surprisingly offered no praise whatsoever.

The Oxford team realized that the only hope for mass production of penicillin lay in America. Both Florey and Heatley, anticipating a trip to the United States when they received permission to go, made plans for the safe arrival of the drug. Heatley rubbed penicillium spores into the pockets of a suit, and Florey rubbed the mold on the lining of his raincoat; they made certain that neither article of clothing would be dry-cleaned in the meantime.

Heatley increased production by making several drives to a factory at Stoke-on-Trent, eventually accumulating six hundred rectangular clay pots for growing the mold. Then "Oxford Penicillin girls" worked in an icy, refrigerated room, wearing wool coats and warm gloves; their efforts greatly increased the yield. Finally enough extract was ready for human testing. After two trials on patients, both of whom had high temperatures, Dr. Abraham found and eliminated the toxic factor that had caused the rise in temperature.

On February 12, 1941, a trial was begun on a dying policeman, Albert Alexander. The case had been brought to her husband's attention by Dr. Ethel Florey, working at Radcliffe Infirmary. Sulfonamides had been ineffective, and Alexander remained overwhelmed with *Staphlococcus aureus* infection; he had abscesses all over his body, and surgeons had had to remove his infected right eye. Penicillin was injected intravenously every few hours, and all his urine was sent by bicycle to the Oxford lab to have any penicillin extracted from it.

Alexander's improvement was miraculous, but on the fifth day of treatment, the penicillin supply was exhausted. His infection started up again, and he died a month after treatment had been started. Florey was downhearted but made the decision to treat only children where smaller doses would be used. Within weeks several children were treated effectively.

The first injection of penicillin was made in the United States on October 15, 1940, at Columbia University's Presbyterian Medical Center. It was given by Dr. Martin Dawson to a patient with subacute bacterial endocarditis (a heart valve infection). The patient died, but there were no toxic effects from the penicillin.

Florey and Heatley finally obtained permission for the trip to the United States. They left Oxford on June 26, 1941, Florey carrying a briefcase containing written data, penicillium molds, and some penicillin extract wrapped in cotton wool. (Florey's raincoat and Heatley's suit, both previously rubbed with spores, weren't needed.) The possibility of being shot down en route by

German aircraft was a real one; the secret trip was made by air, stopping in Lisbon for a few days and then flying to America on a KLM plane.

A description of the mass production of penicillin would require a book in itself. Dr. A. Newton Richards, Florey's old friend, was of great help, but probably the most important factor leading to success was the presence in a government lab in Peoria, Illinois, of Dr. Robert D. Coghill. He devised the process of deep-submerged culture of the mold. Coghill also found that the addition of lactose to a product called corn-steep liquor, which was derived from maize and often used in Midwest fermentation, increased the yield tenfold. Searches for stronger penicillium molds began, and one Peoria woman, who acquired the name Moldy Mary, brought in a rotten cantaloupe that eventually became famous. The mold growing on it, after treatment with X rays and other agents, proved to be extremely powerful.

Florey's trip across the United States was productive. Soon American pharmaceutical companies were producing penicillin in huge fermentation vats. Florey gave special credit to three of them—Merck, Pfizer, and Squibb.

On December 7, 1945, the Nobel Prize in medicine and physiology was awarded to Fleming, Florey, and Chain. Fleming and Florey were knighted in 1944 and Chain in 1969. But despite the multiple honors each received, the Nobel Prize remained their most important scientific award.

All three investigators remained intellectually active up to the times of their deaths. Fleming was working in his laboratory the day before he died on Friday, March 11, 1955. His ashes rest in a crypt in St. Paul's Cathedral. Although the three prizewinners traveled all over the world to give conferences and receive honors, it was Fleming who seemed to flourish in the spotlight. This essentially shy man basically liked people, and eventually he overcame his earlier reticence and spoke with ease and confidence. However, both Florey and Chain felt that Fleming was receiving too much credit for the penicillin triumph.

Chain left Oxford in 1948 to set up a biochemistry lab at the Istituto Superiore di Sanità in Rome. He remained there until 1964, when he returned to England to become director of the new biochemistry department at Imperial College. In his later years, and loving southern Ireland, he purchased a home at Mulranny, County Mayo, where, in August 1979, he died.

Florey remained at Oxford until his death from a heart attack on February 21, 1968. He always had tried to avoid the limelight, but fame forced him to remain visible and in the forefront of

The Queen Mother, Elizabeth, with Ernst and Anne Chain and their children at the opening of the new biochemistry department at Imperial College in 1965. From *The Life of Ernst Chain,* by Ronald Clark. New York: St. Martin's Press, 1985.

new developments. He was president of the Royal Society for five years, and among other honors, he was named chancellor of Australian National University. He and his team had a second major triumph with the mold Cephalosporium, a cousin of penicillium. Florey's associates, Abraham and Newton, after six years of work, developed Cephalosporin C, a powerful new antibiotic that led to a complete family of drugs effective against virulent bacteria.

Regardless of all the differences between them, these three men, along with hundreds of coworkers, created a miracle for the world. Newer, powerful antibiotics are developed each year, but Fleming, Florey, and Chain will remain always as participants in one of the most exciting chapters of medical history.

PART IV

Medical Devices

René T. H. Laënnec

1781–1826 French physician; inventor of the stethoscope

Born in France on February 17, 1781, René Théophile Hyacinthe Laënnec was destined to make several vitally important contributions to medicine during his short life span of forty-five years. Undoubtedly, the most valuable of these was his role in establishing the importance of diagnosis in medicine. A disease rarely can be be treated correctly unless it is diagnosed (identified) correctly. Laënnec's stethoscope, along with the art of auscultation that resulted from it, played a central role in diagnosis. (The word *auscultation* is derived from Latin and means "to listen carefully"; *stethoscope* is derived from two Greek words—*stethos*, meaning "chest," and *scope*, meaning "to examine." Laënnec was the first to add the words *stethoscope* and *auscultation* to international language.)

Laënnec had a difficult childhood. His mother, Michelle, died (probably of tuberculosis) when he was six, leaving him temporarily in the care of a father, Théophile-Marie, who never was much help to his three children. It isn't clear exactly what Théophile-Marie did. Supposedly, he was a lieutenant in the Admiralty in the Brittany seacoast town of Quimper, where his children were born; mostly, however, he had minor political appointments, which he would lose and regain. He had a flair for writing poetry. He was always tightfisted, and when small sums were needed by his sons for their education, he sent the money reluctantly.

René, the oldest child, his brother, Michaud, and his sister, Marie-Anne, all were sent away by their widower father at an early age. Marie-Anne was sent to be raised by an aunt, but the boys were lucky in that their father sent them to live with his brother, Guillaume Laënnec, a distinguished physician. Guillaume Laënnec lived in Nantes, a Brittany city southeast of Quimper. He cared deeply for both nephews, and it was he who convinced René to study medicine. Michaud, a year younger than his brother, studied law and became an accomplished attorney. René was only seven years old in 1788, when he came to live with his uncle. One year later the French Revolution with its Reign of Terror and other excesses began. Nantes was not spared, and a guillotine was installed in the Place de Bouffay; Guillaume Laënnec's home overlooked that plaza, and we can only imagine the horror that the three small boys (René, Michaud, and Guillaume's young son, Christophe) witnessed during those years.

At least three thousand citizens of Nantes were executed, and despite Guillaume's efforts to keep the boys in the back of the house and away from the windows, they saw at least fifty heads fall into the guillotine's basket. In addition, mob bloodthirstiness demanded faster killing than was possible by guillotine, so drownings and shootings were added to speed up the carnage. In 1795 General Napoléon Bonaparte effected a peace of sorts. During that same year, fourteen-year-old René began medical studies at the University of Nantes.

Although of frail constitution, René drove himself constantly to acquire knowledge. As with most educated youths of those times, he was skilled in many fields; he played the flute well, he was competent at art and dancing, and he was an enthusiastic hiker and swimmer. At his uncle's urging, he traveled to Paris in 1801 to complete his medical education, walking the two hundred miles in ten days.

In Paris he lived in the Latin Quarter with his brother. His principal teacher was Jean-Nicolas Corvisart, one of the two leaders in French medical thought. (The other was Philippe Pinel, who taught at the Salpêtrière Hospital and was the man who freed mental patients from the bondage of chains and leg irons.) Corvisart, who was Napoléon's physician, taught his students at the Charité Hospital to observe closely the physical appearance of the patient and also required them to be present at autopsies. Since many patients had illnesses that were incurable in those days (tuberculosis, for example), it was not unusual to follow a patient for a time on the wards and then to examine his or her organs during a postmortem examination.

Shortly before Laënnec began his

training, bedside teaching had begun at the Charité, and many foreign physicians came to observe the method. One patient to a bed was another innovation of that hospital. Only a few years earlier, several patients of both sexes often were piled into the same bed. A patient falling asleep at night might have to endure the terror of waking up next to one or two corpses.

Xavier Bichat, who was the first to describe tissues, was one of Laënnec's teachers, as were G. Dupuytren and a future colleague, G. L. Bayle. René was an excellent scholar, winning several prizes and publishing articles during the summer of 1802 while still a student. The most important paper, the result of a year's observations, clearly described for the first time the peritoneum, the thin tissue that covers the abdominal organs, and peritonitis, inflammation of the peritoneum, a dangerous condition today known to be caused by infection. During that year also, Laënnec passed a competitive exam and enrolled in the École Pratique, where over a three-year period he studied pathology, chemistry, and surgery. He completed medical school in June 1804, dedicating his graduation thesis to his uncle Guillaume.

Laënnec's periods of illness began during his medical school years. He attributed his attacks of shortness of breath to asthma, denying the possibility that he might be developing early tuberculosis. From time to time, he would take brief vacations in Quimper and its beautiful surroundings; he always returned to Paris refreshed and healthier. He was short in stature (approximately five feet three) with pale skin, high cheekbones, and thin, fine brown hair. Looking very slim but elegant, he continued to be a dynamo, rushing around and always in need of more time for all his activities.

Although Laënnec had thought of returning to Brittany after his graduation, Paris was intellectually too stimulating to leave, and he set up a private practice and taught at several hospitals. By 1807 his practice was successful, he was an editor of medical journals, and he had been elected to several prestigious medical societies. Yet he never had enough political power to obtain a major hospital post, such as a professorship or chief of a service. During all these years before and after graduation, he had described the venereal disease gonorrhea and was the first to describe the malignant skin lesion melanoma. He described and gave a name to a disease primarily of alcoholics, cirrhosis. This refers to the shrunken liver that becomes hard and changes in color from its normal chocolate brown appearance. He took the word from the Greek *kir-*

ros, which means "orange-yellow"; today the disease is called Laennec's cirrhosis.

Along with now-colleague Bayle and Professor Corvisart, Laënnec studied the primary lesion of tuberculosis. Prior to their work, the disease had been called either consumption or phthisis—which means simply "wasting." Henceforth it was termed *tuberculosis*, an acknowledgment that diseases should be known by the anatomical derangements they caused. The tubercle is the body's reaction to a foreign invader—in this case *Mycobacterium tuberculosis*, which microbe had not yet been discovered. Laënnec found that these tubercles, comprised of swollen cells attempting to protect the patient by localizing the disease, could be found all over the body, even in bone. The tubercles grow in an attempt to wall off the invader. Eventually tubercles begin to degenerate at their centers, which softenings end in tuberculous cavities.

Laënnec, who eventually died of tuberculosis, could have contracted the disease in several ways. The infectious nature of TB was not known then, and he might have breathed in the germs during his medical rounds or from his brother, Michaud, who died of tuberculosis in 1810, thus ending a promising law career. Laënnec performed autopsies on TB patients and frequently pricked his finger. Tuberculous germs could have entered his body that way. Finally, a hereditary predisposition might have made him more susceptible to the disease.

Palpation (the use of the hands) in physical diagnosis had been used from earliest times. A physician could, and still can, place his hand under a patient's right rib cage while asking the patient to take a deep breath. If the liver is felt as the diaphragm pushes it down, the liver is known to be enlarged. Sometimes vibrations caused by abnormalities of blood flow can be felt by the examiner's hand; these are called thrills.

In 1761 a Viennese physician named Leopold Auenbrugger introduced a second major aid to physical diagnosis, the art of percussion. Auenbrugger probably learned the technique as a boy while working in his father's inn. By tapping on a barrel of beer, he could tell how much of it remained. A hollow, resonant sound meant air, while a flat, dull sound meant that there was beer where he had tapped. Applying this technique to medicine (placing his middle finger extended on a patient's chest, he would tap against it with the middle finger of the other hand), he was able to distinguish fluid from air, as well as to define the outline of the heart. A physician today learns to become expert in the

A lithograph of Dr. René Laënnec. *Photosearch, Inc.*

feel produced by this tapping and can tell from both this feel and the sound produced whether what lies beneath the skin is gaseous or fluid. Auenbrugger's publication attracted practically no attention until Corvisart read it, translated it, and popularized it, always giving credit to the method's originator.

In 1816 Laënnec finally received some academic recognition. Through the political efforts of a friend, he was appointed physician to the Necker Hospital. This hospital was located on the outskirts of Paris and was far from the best-known hospital, but Laënnec accepted the post. During that same year he invented the stethoscope.

Despite palpation and percussion, it was the stethoscope and the clear auscultation accompanying its use that was by far the most important diagnostic tool to date; its invention really marked the beginning of scientific diagnosis. It is said that Laënnec hit on the idea one day when watching two boys outside the Louvre. One was scratching one end of a beam with a pin while the other was listening at the other end of the beam to the augmented sound. This story may or may not be true, but here is Laënnec's description in his own words. (First it should be noted that direct auscultation—placing one's ear directly on a patient's chest to hear heart or breath sounds—was unsatisfactory. Used from the times of Hippocrates on, it never was very helpful.)

> In 1816 I was consulted by a young woman presenting general symptoms of disease of the heart. Owing to her stoutness little information could be gathered by application of the hand and percussion. The patient's age and sex did not permit me to resort to the kind of examination I have just described (i.e., direct application of the ear to the chest). I recalled a well-known acoustic phenomenon, namely if you place your ear against one end of a wooden beam the scratch of a pin at the other extremity is most distinctly audible. It occurred to me that this physical property might serve a useful purpose in the case with which I was then dealing. Taking a sheaf of paper, I rolled it into a very tight roll, one end of which I placed over the praecordial region, while I put my ear to the other. I was both surprised and gratified at being able to hear the beating of the heart with much greater clearness and distinctness than I had ever done before by direct application of my ear.
>
> I at once saw that this means might become a useful method for studying not only the beating of the heart but likewise all movements capable of producing sounds in the thoracic cavity, and that consequently it might serve for the investigation of respiration. . . .

This discovery was followed by three years of study in the autopsy room. The

The type of wooden stethoscope invented by Dr. Laënnec. The parts of the stethoscope fit together. *Dr. Philip Reichert, New York.*

sounds heard during a patient's illness were later related to abnormalities found after death and could therefore be recognized as coming from a diseased heart valve, for instance, or a tuberculous cavity. It took two thousand years for the invention of this superb method of listening to the heart and lungs to appear. The cylindrical roll of paper was like Laënnec's flute in reverse; the sounds came from the chest of the patient, and Laënnec was the audience listening to them.

On August 15, 1819, Laënnec published his observations in a two-volume work.

At the end of the movie *Casablanca*, actor Claude Rains tells a subordinate to "round up the usual suspects." As with every innovation, the usual suspects—doubters, skeptics and denigrators—were around, but the stethoscope was finally accepted as an ingenious tool for diagnosis.

Laënnec, although he coined the word *stethoscope*, called his tube a cylinder; later he discovered hollowed-out light wood (beech or linden, preferably) was the best medium for sound transmission, and he made many of his cylinders on his own lathe. Modern stethoscopes have evolved from Laënnec's primitive cylinder. Today we use rubber tubing, an earpiece for each ear of the listener, and a bell or diaphragm to be applied to the chest.

Now, at last, honors were heaped on Laënnec. He was named professor of medicine at the Collège de France, and he returned to the Charité to teach. Foreign visitors, as well as his own students and assistants, attended his daily rounds, which, except for talks with patients, were conducted in Latin.

But Laënnec's physical health continued to fail, and his emotional state was hampered by some vicious rumors. In 1822 Mme Jacqueline Argou, a widow he had met some nineteen years earlier, moved into his apartment. The sickly man was seeking companionship, not romance, with a most unattractive woman. However, the rumors persisted, and two years later the couple was married.

Théophile-Marie Laënnec, never a great father, had frequently requested money from both sons once they were professionals. Michaud, to avoid being defrauded, actually had sued Théophile, but they became reconciled before Michaud's death. René, who worshiped and was adored in return by his uncle Guillaume, had a love-hate relationship with his father. When he wrote to some friends about his prospective marriage to Mme Argou, he commented: "My father thought that it was a very good idea, which was my only reason for thinking that it might not be so."

Despite trips to Brittany, Laënnec's health continued to deteriorate with each passing year. After receiving the last rites, the end finally came on August 13, 1826. A few hours before his death he removed his rings, saying: "Because someone would soon have to render me this service, I wish to spare them this painful task."

While today X rays, electrocardiograms, sonograms, and all sorts of other electronic equipment have immeasurably improved diagnostic capabilities, it should never be forgotten that the stethoscope came first. It still is the most widely used bedside instrument for following patients. Most important of all, before there can be adequate treatment, there must be proper diagnosis. This is Laënnec's great legacy to us.

Wilhelm Conrad Roentgen

1845–1923 German physicist; discoverer of X rays

Many inventions important for medical diagnosis have depended on the use of electricity. One example is a machine to record the electrical action of the heart. A Dutch physiologist, Willem Einthoven, devised the electrocardiograph (ECG, or EKG), whose tracings, when abnormal, lead to correct treatment of various heart disorders. He was awarded the Nobel Prize for this invention in 1924. The electroencephalogram (EEG) helps recognize brain lesions.

But a physicist, Wilhelm Roentgen, recognized a diagnostic tool that today probably has the most general and widespread use of any discovery ever made. His observations led to the discovery of X rays, X-ray machines, and their sophisticated descendants.

Wilhelm Roentgen (Röntgen in German) was born on March 27, 1845, in Lennep, Prussia. This small town, located eighteen miles east of the industrial city of Düsseldorf, today houses a Roentgen museum. Wilhelm's father, Friedrich Conrad Roentgen, was a well-to-do Prussian cloth merchant. Wilhelm's mother was a native of Utrecht, Holland. Probably for business reasons, the family moved to Apeldoorn, Holland, when Wilhelm was three years old. He lived a happy childhood, attending grammar and high schools in Apeldoorn. He began his higher education in Utrecht at an agricultural college but was expelled when he refused to give the names of the other boys involved with him in some minor prank. Although he didn't know what he wanted to do, farming was out now, and he considered other alternatives.

At age eighteen he entered Utrecht Technical College. (During the course of his education and later teaching career, he relocated frequently; in all, he was involved with ten colleges and universities—three in Holland, two in Switzerland, and five in Germany.) In 1868 he received his mechanical engineering degree from the Federal Polytechnical College in Zurich, Switzerland. Apparently he now was set for a career in engineering because the following year he received his Ph.D. from the University of Zurich. He might have stayed with engineering but for the advice of a professor whose lectures he had attended. Here, in a 1919 letter, are Roentgen's own words about the matter:

Although I already possessed two diplomas—one as engineer and the other as Dr. Phil., I still could not take the decision to go into engineering, as had been my original plan. At this critical moment I made the acquaintance of a young professor of physics—Kundt—who asked me one day: What do you really want to do in your life? When I answered that I did not know, he replied that I ought to try physics. When I had to admit that it was a subject to which I had hardly as yet paid any attention, he volunteered the opinion that I could quite well make up for that. And so, at the age of twenty-four and more or less already engaged to be married, I began to study and practise physics. I remained faithful to my choice. . . .

Roentgen's friend, August Kundt, went to Würzburg to teach, and Roentgen followed as his assistant, but he had never forgotten the young woman Bertha Ludwig, whom he had met in Zurich and who, besides running an inn, gave lessons in fencing and languages. Roentgen married Bertha in January of 1872, and the couple, childless, lived happily together for fifty years. Roentgen taught at the University of Strasbourg, and then in 1879 he received his first major teaching post as chair of the Department of Physics at the University of Giessen. In 1888 he became professor of physics at the University of Würzburg, the institution where he would discover X rays.

Würzburg was a beautiful town of some fifty thousand residents, situated on the Main River. Its Roman Catholic university had been founded in 1403, and the town retained much of its medieval architecture; especially notable were its tenth century Romanesque cathedral and a long stone bridge spanning the river and adorned with statues of saints. Many of the nearby slopes were vineyards. The entire atmosphere was one of a relaxed college town; the students wore caps of scarlet, green, and blue.

Biographer Otto Glasser tells us that Roentgen became interested in cathode rays in June 1894. Although he had done much original work in other areas of physics and was one of the leading investigators in his profession, from October 1895 on, he devoted himself exclusively to cathode ray experiments. Cathode rays had been discovered by physicist Julius Plücker at Bonn. Essentially, they consist of a stream of electrons discharged from a negative metallic electrode, the cathode, when the cathode is excited by high voltage. A cathode was often located in glass tubes that contained low concentrations of gas. (This partial vacuum was accomplished by evacuating most of the air and other gases.) Then what is called an induction coil produced the high voltage that excited the cathode to release the electrons.

Various physicists, H. Hertz, P. Lenard, and others, had worked with cathode rays and found that the rays could penetrate a thin aluminum window in a glass tube but only traveled beyond the tube for a few inches before they were diffused in the outside air. It was known also that if a screen was coated with barium platinocyanide and held very close to the glass tube, the rays could make the screen light up, or fluoresce.

On the now-famous date of November 8, 1895, Roentgen was working as usual in his laboratory at the Physical Institute, part of the University of Würzburg. He wanted to see if the earlier fluorescence noted by others could be reproduced by the heavier glass Hittorf-Crookes tube and also if this fluorescence could be eliminated if no light from the excited tube could escape.

Accordingly he selected a pear-shaped Hittorf-Crookes glass tube from a rack and covered it entirely with pieces of black cardboard. Then he hooked up an induction coil to produce the high voltage and excite the cathode to release its rays. Biographer Glasser continues the description of Roentgen's discovery of X rays in these words:

> After darkening the room in order to test the opacity of the black paper cover, he started the induction coil and passed a high tension discharge through the tube. To his satisfaction, no light penetrated the cardboard cover.
>
> He was prepared to interrupt the current to set up the screen for the crucial experiment when suddenly, about a yard from the tube, he saw a weak light that shimmered on a little bench he knew was located nearby. It was as though a ray of light or faint spark from the induction coil had been reflected by a mirror. Not believing this to be possible, he passed another series of discharges through the tube, and again the same fluorescence

appeared, this time looking like faint green clouds moving in unison with the fluctuating discharges of the coil. Highly excited, Röntgen lit a match and to his great surprise discovered that the source of the mysterious light was the little barium platinocyanide screen lying on the bench.

Here was the spark of genius. Others had noted fluorescence when working with cathode ray tubes, but none had realized it had been caused by previously undiscovered rays. But Roentgen realized immediately that he had discovered a new type of radiation. He named these rays *X rays;* X in mathematics or physics generally stands for unknown. He was modest; he could have named them Roentgen rays, but that was not his nature. These X rays were produced by the collision of electrons with solid body targets, and a heavy element such as the platinum (on the barium platinocyanide screen) was found to yield far more secondary X rays than a lighter metal, such as aluminum.

Roentgen began concentrated studies on his new phenomenon, wanting to find out the properties of these rays before releasing information about them. Obviously he was not rushing for instant fame. It was not until December 28, 1895, that he released his first historic report on his discovery, titling it "Concerning a New Type of Rays." He presented this paper accompanied by the first medical X ray; it had been taken on December 22, 1895, by Roentgen himself, and it was a photograph of his wife's hand, the bones of which were easily seen as was the less intense soft tissue surrounding them.

H. J. W. Dam, a London correspondent for the American magazine *McClure's*, obtained a rare interview with Roentgen shortly after the discovery. He described what he saw:

Professor Roentgen entered hurriedly, something like an amiable gust of wind. He is a tall, slender, and loose-limbed man, whose whole appearance bespeaks enthusiasm and energy. He wore a dark blue suit, sack coat [a loose-fitting coat], and his dark hair stood straight up from his forehead, as if he were permanently electrified by his own enthusiasm. His eyes are dark and penetrating; and there is no doubt that he much prefers gazing at a Crookes tube to beholding a visitor, visitors at present robbing him of much valued time.

One can't blame Roentgen for preferring to gaze at a tube rather than at this particular correspondent, who, after graciously being given an X-ray demonstration by Roentgen, tried to purchase the "little table on which the first radiograph was made." Roentgen smiled and informed Dam that the table was not for sale. The correspondent then asked Roentgen about his November 8 discovery.

"And what did you think?"

"I did not think, I investigated," Roentgen replied. "I assumed that the effect must have come from the tube, since its character indicated that it could come from nowhere else. I tested it. In a few minutes there was no doubt about it. Rays were coming from the tube which had a luminescent effect upon the paper. I tried it at greater and greater distances, even at two metres."

"What is it?" the reporter asked.

"I don't know," was Roentgen's prompt response.

By December 28, 1895, Roentgen had learned a great deal about X rays. Of extreme importance, he found that photographic emulsions were sensitive to X rays and that in fact all substances were more or less transparent to X rays. He showed, for example, that X rays could pass through glass more easily than through aluminum and through aluminum more easily than through wood. We know that X rays pass through soft tissue more easily than they do through bone. The explanation is that X rays have the shortest wave length (250 million X rays/inch) of all electromagnetic radiation. By contrast, the number of visible light waves per inch is fifty thousand. Since matter is comprised of atoms and molecules and there are crevices between them, smaller waves can pass through. So X rays pass more easily through flesh than through bones; more collisions take place in bones, and the increased secondary X rays that bounce off the bones therefore produce a denser photograph.

On January 6, 1896 (less than two months after the discovery), a physician named Moritz Jastrowitz presented "Roentgen's Experiments with Cathode Rays and Their Application in the Field of Diagnostics" to the Berlin Medical Association. He ended the lecture by stating the many ways in which the new discovery would prove valuable to the medical profession. (Unfortunately the early investigators were unaware of the harmful effects of radiation and worked with bare hands. One of the most prominent of these scientists was Heinrich Albers-Schönberg, who was primarily interested in treating skin diseases, but treated leukemia and sarcoma as well. In 1908 a cancer first appeared on one of his fingers. Despite several later amputations, the cancer continued to spread, and after much suffering he died in 1921.)

Word of the new discovery spread rapidly via the press to all parts of the globe, and Roentgen became famous overnight. Honors from many countries were awarded to him, and he was invited to dine with the kaiser, to whom he gave an X-ray demonstration. But Roentgen was interested in neither honors nor money. He refused to patent his invention, thereby foregoing a huge profit; he preferred a quiet life of teaching and experimentation.

After twelve very happy years at the University of Würzburg, he moved at the request of the government to Munich. There, on April 1, 1900, he became head of the Physical Institute of the Ludwig Maximilian University. One year later, in 1901, when the establishment of Nobel Prizes was initiated, he was awarded the first Nobel Prize in physics. His last years were relaxed, and he frequently found enjoyment in mountain hikes. More often than not, he refused numerous invitations to attend scientific conventions; he was reluctant to express an opinion on any subject on which he had not yet formed a clear picture, labeling premature scientific communications "unlaid eggs." In 1919 he gave up teaching and retired to a village suburb of Munich. Shortly afterward, his beloved wife died; he had devotedly attended her through a lingering illness. On February 10, 1923, Roentgen died of colon cancer at the age of seventy-eight.

Roentgen had performed valuable research on the properties of crystals, on elasticity, on gases, and on electromagnetic rotation of polarized light, but no work of his was more important than his discovery of X rays. Not only did it launch the science of radiology, but his work initiated the electronic era in physics.

Through the years, advances in X-ray technique, such as having the patient swallow the contrast medium barium or administering the barium by enema, have permitted visualization of the entire alimentary tract; also, injections of various liquid chemicals into veins, arteries, or bile ducts have made it possible to see on X rays abnormalities of almost every organ of the body. Soft tissue, however, is not clearly defined.

In 1929 Werner Forssmann, a German surgeon, performed a daring experiment on himself, inserting a catheter into an arm vein and advancing it into his heart. Then he had an X ray taken to confirm that the catheter was in place. Many years later André Cournand, a French physician who became a U.S. citizen, was working in collaboration with Dickinson W. Richards on the study of thoracic diseases at Bellevue Hospital in New York City. Cournand performed the same daring procedure on himself as had Forssmann, inserting the catheter and then actually walking

A photograph of Dr. Roentgen taken in 1906 at the Physical Institute of the Ludwig Maximilian University, Munich. *The Burndy Library, Norwalk, Connecticut.*

across the street to have the confirming X ray taken. These procedures allowed the measurement of blood volumes, oxygenation, and pressures inside the heart, a process called *cardiac catheterization,* which permits exact diagnosis of several kinds of heart disease. For this procedure Forssmann, Cournand, and Richards were awarded the 1956 Nobel Prize in medicine.

CAT scans (*c*omputerized *a*xial *to*mography scans) and MRIs (*m*agnetic *r*esonance *i*maging) were developed during recent years and allow visualization of cross sections of the body, studies that cannot be done with longitudinal X rays. Organs, body fluids, bones, and soft tissues now are easily seen and differentiated.

Not only did X rays become an excellent diagnostic tool, but later they found valuable use in treatment. Radiation therapy today is highly effective against malignant tumors and is frequently employed for other medical conditions.

Antony van Leeuwenhoek

1632–1723 Dutch scientist; developer of the microscope and microscopic studies

Epidemics of infectious diseases have killed millions of people throughout history. One of them, plague, in epidemic form, repeatedly wiped out a large segment of the world's population. (The worst of the plague epidemics, the Black Death of the fourteenth century, killed thirty million people in Europe.) There was of course no lack of theories to explain it. Originally it was believed to be a punishment meted out by God—a way of repaying humankind for its sinfulness. This idea gradually gave way to the general belief that the plague was due to some cosmic disturbance—perhaps a bad wind, or miasma, which blew from the skies and caused death when it touched the earth. Regardless of the general acceptance of an atmospheric cause, in fact blame was fixed on more ready victims than the sky. Religious minorities were persecuted and burned alive, accused of poisoning the wells. People who acted in a "suspicious" manner were tortured until they admitted they were purposely spreading plague; after they had confessed, they were burned at the stake. Dogs, thought to be spreaders of the disease, were clubbed to death, also innocent victims of a terrified populace. In England during the epidemic of 1665–1666, the thought of plague even got into children's games. They sang and danced to:

> Ring a ring a-Roses,
> A pocketful of posies,
> Tishoo, tishoo, we all fall down.

The song was related to the plague. The "Roses" were the red rash, which was an early symptom; the "pocketful of posies" was the scented herbs that were used to sweeten the air; "Tishoo" was the sound of sneezing, another symptom; and when people became very ill, often they suddenly fell down.

Throughout all of those epidemics, plague continued to be a mystery. Today we know that the cause of plague is a microbe—a tiny, tiny germ that cannot be seen without a microscope. The victims of this microbe were rats, who became sick. Then fleas that abandoned the dying rats would carry the microbe to humans. Until Antony van Leeuwenhoek made his famous discovery of microscopic life, it was not known that there were organisms small enough to be invisible to the naked eye. And then two hundred years would pass until the world would know without doubt that these microbes could cause disease.

The germ that causes plague was identified in 1894 independently by Shibasaburo Kitasato, a Japanese physician, and by Alexandre Yersin, a Swiss bacteriologist. It is not uncommon to find scientists working in different places discovering the same thing at the same time. And now there is effective treatment for infection by the plague bacterium.

Today we are experiencing a terrible worldwide epidemic (pandemic) caused by the smallest type of microscopic life, a virus. This epidemic disease is AIDS (*a*cquired *i*mmune *d*eficiency *s*yndrome), and the virus responsible for AIDS is HIV (the *h*uman *i*mmunodeficiency *v*irus). Scientists all over the world are working to find drugs that can slow or cure the disease, and considering the complexity of this virus, they have made great strides. Scientists also are working on various vaccines that can protect people against becoming infected with the virus.

The story of those scientists, past and present, who have studied all kinds of infectious disease is a dramatic one. Let us begin at the beginning, the successful use of the microscope.

No one knows who invented the microscope. It may have been a father and son, the Janssens, or the astronomer Galileo. One thing is certain, however. The man who really made the microscope known and used it to discover a whole new world of minute living beings was a self-trained scientist named Antony van Leeuwenhoek (pronounced Lay′ ven-hook). He was born in 1632 in Delft, Holland, a town about eight miles from Rotterdam.

The year 1632 was an auspicious year for the birth of creative men. In England another squalling infant, Christopher Wren, would grow up to become a noted astronomer as well as the world's greatest architect, and in Spain another baby, Spinoza, would become a famous philosopher. In Delft itself, Jan Vermeer was born in that year, and when that great painter died, it would be Leeuwenhoek who would administer his estate.

Antony van Leeuwenhoek was born into a middle-class family and remained in comfortable circumstances all of his life. At age sixteen, he was sent by his widowed mother to Amsterdam. He worked there as a bookkeeper for a draper, an occupation dealing with the making and selling of cloth. Leeuwenhoek decided to learn the cloth workers' trade; after six weeks, he passed an examination that qualified him as a master of this trade, although this process usually took several years. He undoubtedly used a magnifying glass in examining cloth, and this experience may well have inspired him to use optical equipment to see things invisible to the human eye.

At age twenty-two he returned to Delft and began a haberdashery business. That year he also married Barbara de May, daughter of a draper, who, before her death in 1666, bore him five children. His second child, Maria, in later years took the responsibility of seeing that her father was always well cared for. (Leeuwenhoek remarried in 1671 but again became a widower twenty-three years later.)

When his income increased because of inheritance and revenue from various municipal jobs, he quit the haberdashery trade. Now that he had more free time, he began to practice grinding lenses, and he became an expert. From these lenses he constructed his own microscopes; these were in reality powerful magnifying glasses. Looking at them today, we would never recognize them as microscopes.

Essentially Leeuwenhoek's microscopes were almost rectangular and consisted of two plates made of silver, gold, copper, or bronze, which were compact enough to be held comfortably in one hand. After a small hole was drilled near the top of these plates, a convex lens was fitted into the hole, and then the plates were riveted together. Behind the plates a vertical thumbscrew held the object to be examined, which could be moved from side to side or up and down. A few of his microscopes had holders so tubes of liquids could be viewed. Primitive as they were, Leeuwenhoek's microscopes were powerful; he achieved magnification of up to five hundred times.

The first indication that he was engaged in microscopy came on May 7, 1673, when Regnier de Graaf, an emi-

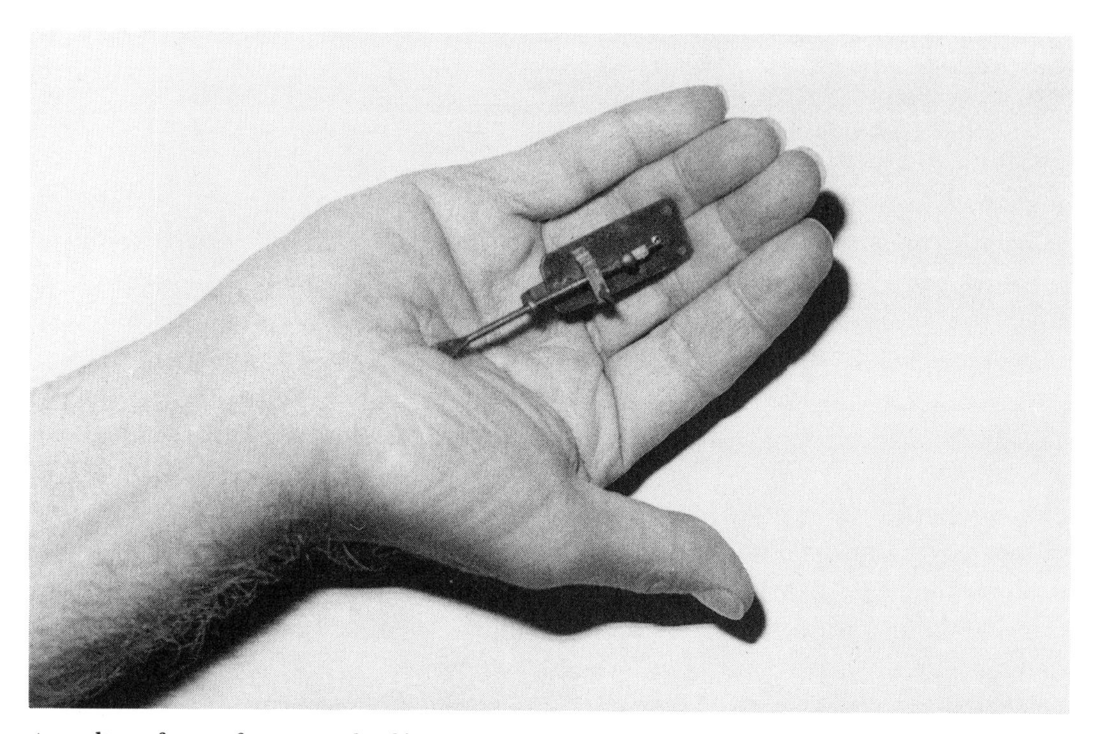

A replica of one of Leeuwenhoek's microscopes, held in the author's hand. *Deborah Curtis Schwartz.*

nent physician of Delft, wrote to the Royal Society in London. "I am writing to tell you that a certain most ingenious person here, named Leeuwenhoek, has devised microscopes which far surpass those we have hitherto seen. . . ." De Graaf went on to say what Leeuwenhoek had observed about the legs of a bee. The members of the society were fascinated and requested more observations. Thus began a correspondence between Leeuwenhoek and the Royal Society that was to last for fifty years. Seven years after Leeuwenhoek's introduction by de Graaf, the Royal Society elected Leeuwenhoek to membership.

Leeuwenhoek bequeathed twenty-six of his microscopes to the Royal Society. One biographer reports that during Leeuwenhoek's lifetime, he made about five hundred and fifty microscopes. Only ten are now in existence. Those willed to the Royal Society disappeared. He used fine rock crystal for his lenses and was proud of his workmanship; however, while generous in showing his work to visitors who came in increasing numbers to see him in Delft, he rarely would let them see his best microscopes. Neither did he want to teach lens grinding as he felt it would "reduce me to a state of slavery."

He measured everything he saw, and the accuracy of these measurements has been confirmed today by modern techniques.

Of all Leeuwenhoek's correspondence sent to the Royal Society and elsewhere, no letter is more famous than that written on October 9, 1676. Here, for the first time, a new world populated by *living microscopic forms* was revealed. This letter describes many observations made during the preceding year. Leeuwenhoek had been collecting rainwater in an open container for study. One day he placed a drop of this ordinary rainwater in a small container. Later he described the scene:

In the year 1675 I discovered very small living creatures in rain water, which had stood but a few days in a new earthen pot glazed blue within. This invited me to view this water with great attention, especially those little animals appearing to me ten thousand times less than those represented by Monsieur Swammerdam, and by him called water fleas, or water lice, which may be perceived in the water with the naked eye.

Here, as he noted, were forms of life ten thousand times smaller than the smallest living creature noted up to that date. Leeuwenhoek had discovered a new universe of life (he called its inhabitants *animalcules*), and in this universe were forms that could make man sick or kill him. In this universe there were also organisms that could produce antibiotics, make vaccines and vitamins, and help man in industry and in research. Moreover, this world of microscopic beings contained microbes that extracted nitrogen from the air, thus insuring crop production and thereby the survival of most species of life. Leeuwenhoek knew none of this as he gazed at his preparations, made his beautiful sketches, and wrote his letter to the Royal Society. While nobody guessed at the implications of his observations, the observations themselves were the subject of a great deal of heated conversation, most of it angry or ridiculing.

At the Royal Society, Robert Hooke, the eminent scientist and microscopist, joined at first in doubting that these were living creatures, but on November 15, 1677, Hooke reported to the Royal Society that Leeuwenhoek was indeed correct. Hooke demonstrated these forms to the group present, and the names of those witnessing the demonstration were recorded. Included was the name of that great architect, Sir Christopher Wren.

Leeuwenhoek was relatively unschooled. "To my sorrow . . . I do not know any tongue but the Nether-Dutch," he wrote. Speaking and writing

An engraving of Antony van Leeuwenhoek. *Mary Evans Picture Library, London.*

Nether-Dutch seems like an adequate skill for a man living in Holland, but in those days it was not the language of scholars. The educated people in the Royal Society, with whom Leeuwenhoek communicated, used Latin and Greek and went back for scientific information to Hippocrates and Galen. Leeuwenhoek's lack of education may have been an advantage because rather than reading other people's work, he did his own. Having the leisure to observe with his microscopes, the brains to reason about what he saw, and fifty years to do both, the result was possibly the most incredible body of work ever produced by an individual.

In his first letter, he described protozoa and bacteria. Throughout the years he would make original observations about spermatozoa, structure of muscle, bone, tooth and nerve, retina, lens of the eye, and in fact almost every tissue in the human body. He made startling discoveries about circulation using the webbing of a frog's foot, fins of fishes, tadpole tails, and other tissues. He and Malpighi completed Harvey's work on the circulation of the blood because each described the capillary system. He examined the tissues of animals as small as fleas and as large as elephants and whales. There was practically nothing—animal, vegetable, or mineral—that evaded his curious eye, and if his reason faltered on occasion, his observations never did. His notes describing microbes living on fleas inspired the English author Jonathan Swift to write a famous quatrain:

So naturalists observe a flea
Has smaller fleas that on him prey;
And these have smaller still to bite 'em;
And so proceed ad infinitum.

Through the years, Leeuwenhoek's reputation grew, but he remained unaffected. He was visited by royalty but was more intrigued by his work than by any adulation he received for it. A description of Peter the Great's visit to Leeuwenhoek was left by the historian Girard van Loon.

The Czar left the Hague in one of those yachts used on the canals, and arriving at Delft invited the celebrated Antony van Leeuwenhoek to call upon him and bring his incomparable microscopes. Van Leeuwenhoek then had the honor of showing his Imperial Majesty, among other things, the circulation of the blood in the tail of the eel. This curious observation and others so pleased the Czar that he spent two hours with van Leeuwenhoek and when he departed, he shook hands with him and thanked him.

Leeuwenhoek lived almost ninety-one years and died without ever having retired from his microscopic studies. He was survived by only one of his six children. Less than thirty-six hours before his death, he was writing a report to the East India Company concerning the possible presence of gold in a specimen of sand they had sent him to examine.

There is an epitaph on his tomb at Delft, but it is neither as eloquent nor as appropriate as the Latin inscription on a medal given to him on the occasion of his election to the Royal Society in 1680. Taken from the writings of Virgil, it reads: "*In tenui labor, at tenuis non gloria.*" This may be translated: "His work was in little things, but not little in glory."

PART V

Infectious Disease

Edward Jenner

1749–1823 English physician; developer of the smallpox vaccine

Long before Antony van Leeuwenhoek showed the existence of a microscopic universe, it was known that some diseases were contagious; they could be passed from one person to another, and those victims of a highly contagious disease were "avoided like the plague." Most people thought disease was spread by a miasma (bad air), but very few guessed that specific infectious agents were the lethal ingredients of the miasma.

The first man to mention and theorize correctly about contagious disease was an Italian physician named Girolamo Fracastoro (whose poem about a young shepherd Syphilus gave the disease syphilis its name). In his book on contagious disease written in 1546, he mentions seeds of infection that "have the faculty of multiplying and propagating rapidly." However, this was only good guesswork and not confirmed until two centuries later, when Pasteur and Koch proved that tiny organisms like those that Leeuwenhoek had observed were the cause of infectious diseases. Some of the largest of these microscopic "germs" were animals called protozoa, and other smaller ones belonged to the plant family—bacteria and fungi. The smallest infectious agents, viruses, were not seen until the most powerful microscopes were developed during this century, but their existence was assumed. (The exact nature of viruses is not known today, but much has been learned about them; debate continues as to whether or not they are living organisms. They certainly have some characteristics of living organisms, such as the ability to reproduce.)

But even if nobody knew *why* some diseases spread rapidly from one person to another, *everybody knew that they did,* and during epidemics of plague, for example, many people kept traveling away from epidemic areas in order to avoid the disease.

Just as it was known earlier that infections could spread from person to person, so it was known that in many diseases one attack could give lifelong protection against the disease. After getting the illness, the person would be immune to it in the future, no matter how closely or how often she or he was exposed to it. Therefore, early attempts were made to prevent the severe form of a disease by giving a person a mild form of it. This process is called immunization. Even today there is no effective treatment for most infectious diseases caused by viruses, so prevention is absolutely essential. Such is the case with polio, and so it was with another fearful viral disease, smallpox.

Smallpox was, and still is, a dreaded disease. Sometimes when it appeared, only a few persons got sick; at other times it would appear in epidemic form, killing and maiming millions. It had been present since ancient times, contributing, along with malaria, to the fall of the Roman Empire. In the middle of the eighteenth century a smallpox epidemic in Russia killed over two million people.

Smallpox attacks mostly the young, although many adults, too, contract the disease. About two weeks after being exposed, an eruption (breakout of the skin) appears. Initially the eruption consists of clear blisters, but soon these become filled with pus and are called pustules. If the patient survives, the pitting (scarring) caused by these pustules is largely confined to the face; often blindness results. Smallpox is transmitted from person to person by contact with a patient or his or her immediate surroundings.

The historian Thomas Macaulay describes the disease in England as follows:

> . . . the smallpox was always present, filling the churchyards with corpses, tormenting with constant fears all whom it had not yet stricken, leaving on those lives it spared the hideous traces of its power, turning the babe into a changeling at which the mother shuddered, and making the eyes and cheeks of the betrothed maiden objects of horror to the lover.

Thus, it is not surprising that attempts were made to prevent the disease. The earliest attempts were made by the ancient Chinese, who would insert dry crusts from a smallpox pustule into the nose of someone they were trying to protect. The results were partially successful. The most commonly used attempt at prevention was called inoculation. This consisted essentially of scratching the skin and placing some material from a smallpox scab on it with the hope that the patient would get a mild form of smallpox and be spared from getting a serious case.

Inoculation was used all over the world, but not on any regular basis because it was dangerous and uncomfortable. The introduction of inoculation into Europe resulted from the efforts of Lady Mary Wortley Montagu, wife of the British ambassador to Turkey. In 1721 she had herself and her infant son "ingrafted," as inoculation was called in Turkey. Upon her return home to England, she was influential in popularizing inoculation. King George I had the procedure tried first on seven condemned prisoners, one of whom was an eighteen-year-old girl. Their lives were spared as a result of their participation in the experiment. None of the seven died from smallpox, so inoculation gained popularity, although setbacks occurred from time to time. In Ireland and Scotland, however, deaths occurred with the first few inoculations, so the procedure made little headway in those countries.

In 1757 an untrained Englishman, Robert Sutton, calling himself a physician, announced that he had devised a safer method of inoculation. The main feature of his technique was to use a smaller amount of smallpox material, inserting it barely under the skin, not drawing blood. (Some prior inoculators actually put smallpox material into the veins of those being inoculated.) Sutton and his two sons kept their method as secret as possible for commercial reasons, finally teaching it to others in exchange for a share in the profits of the pupils who used his system. Although Sutton was greedy, his safer method was a definite improvement over earlier ones.

The physician who gained most from the Sutton technique was Dr. Thomas Dimsdale of London. He inoculated several European monarchs and was invited to Russia by Catherine the Great to introduce the method into that country. Dimsdale was made a baron of Russia and given a personal fortune for his efforts.

Inoculation was not popular for a time in America until Benjamin Franklin wrote a pamphlet in London in 1759 urging its wider adoption in the colonies. He claimed that in London the mortality rate of those inoculated was one patient in 267, whereas one-fourth of those getting natural smallpox died.

However, inoculation presented many serious problems. Successfully inoculated patients developed a mild case of smallpox and still had to be nursed for a while, and it was often difficult to find someone who had had smallpox to do the nursing. As Lady Montagu wrote to her husband in 1721, "I cannot engraft the girl; her nurse has not had the smallpox." Further, since the smallpox virus itself was used for the inoculations, the results were somewhat unpredictable, and often, instead of a mild case, the patient would get a severe and possibly fatal case.

Moreover, a case of smallpox caused by inoculation could spread the disease. We can imagine the pain and outrage when, as the result of smallpox inoculation, the disease appeared in epidemic form in communities that had never before had a case. In one instance a child whose parents owned a shop was inoculated with smallpox. Although the child recovered, seventeen people who had visited the shop contracted smallpox, and eight of them died.

In the town of Berkeley, Gloucestershire, England, on May 17, 1749, Mrs. Stephen Jenner, wife of a minister and herself the daughter of one, gave birth to her third son, Edward. The clergy in England was well to do and ranked high in social circles, so it was into comfortable conditions that Edward Jenner began his life. No one could have guessed that he would make the human condition far more comfortable than he had found it.

Jenner's parents died when he was five, and he was raised by his oldest brother, Stephen, also a minister. Edward was generally a happy, outgoing boy, but he was subject to periods of sadness. Much thought was given by his brothers as to what occupation Edward should follow. Since the local community could support only so many Jenner and in-law clergymen, it was decided that young Edward should become a doctor. Accordingly, when he was only thirteen years old, he was sent to be an apprentice to Daniel Ludlow, a physician practicing in a town fifteen miles from Berkeley. In those days career training began early. (Lord Nelson entered the navy in 1770 when he was only twelve.)

Certainly one significant incident happened during Jenner's apprenticeship. One day a young girl was in the office, and when the neighborhood smallpox scare was mentioned, the girl said she was not fearful of getting smallpox. "I cannot take it, for I have had cowpox."

Jenner never forgot that remark. It started him wondering why the girl was so sure she had nothing to fear. More important, it planted the seed that he, Edward Jenner, would someday see if there was any reason why someone who had had cowpox would not get smallpox.

At age twenty he went to London to continue his medical studies under the great surgeon John Hunter, in whose home he lived. A remarkable friendship developed between the two that lasted until Hunter died. Edward helped Hunter plan and organize his famous medical museum and through this work became interested in natural history. He later made original and important studies on the migration of birds, hibernation of hedgehogs, and nesting habits of cuckoos. This latter work resulted in his election to the Royal Society. In 1771 he turned down an offer to be a naturalist for the second famous voyage of Captain James Cook.

Jenner liked country life, and in 1773 he returned to Berkeley to begin practice. Life was leisurely. He had time to do experimental nature studies for Hunter and to send animal specimens as well as research results to London. He also had time to build, along with his friend the earl of Berkeley, a hydrogen balloon. The unmanned balloon was launched and drifted ten miles, landing near the Kingscote estate. A romance was also launched that day that culminated in the marriage of Katherine Kingscote to Jenner.

The remark about cowpox made by the young patient during Jenner's apprenticeship had never been forgotten. Jenner began to interest himself in what was common knowledge among the milkmaids of the countryside—that cowpox protected against smallpox. In fact, an English farmer named Benjamin Jesty had actually vaccinated his wife and two sons in 1774. Fifteen years later, one of the sons was inoculated with smallpox and had no reaction whatsoever. The vaccination his father had performed had been successful.

The importance of what dairymaids and farmers knew was not evident to the medical community, however. They ignored it while continuing to use inoculation in haphazard fashion. Edward Jenner, because of his genius—and we can only call it that—saw the potential value to the world of such protection. While his colleagues were saying "So what," he was asking himself "Why?" and "How?"

Shortly after starting his practice, he began to study and do research on the subject. He collected cases of patients who had had cowpox and found that they were indeed immune when he tested them with smallpox inoculation. He also found that there were other diseases that looked like cowpox, causing eruptions on the udders of cows. However, these diseases did not create immunity to smallpox as did cowpox. He found that the immunity provided

An engraving of Edward Jenner. *Mary Evans Picture Library, London.*

by cowpox varied, and some strains of the virus were too weak to give lasting protection.

In 1780 Jenner was riding with a friend, William Gardner, when he confided that he had been working on the problem. Gardner asked how the studies were progressing, and Jenner answered that he felt he was on the right track but that one thing worried him: Whenever he brought up the subject of cowpox at the local medical meetings, nobody seemed interested, and he even became afraid to tell anybody that he was investigating the subject. Jenner asked Gardner not to tell anyone of his work with cowpox for fear that he would be ridiculed all over Gloucestershire.

But in London when Jenner told his ideas to John Hunter, he was not ridiculed. "Don't *think*, Jenner, but *try*," had been the latter's advice. Jenner had promised to keep William Gardner informed of any good thing his studies produced, and he was true to his word. In 1796, sixteen years after the horseback ride with his friend, Jenner wrote to Gardner:

> As I promised to let you know how I proceeded in my inquiry into the nature of that singular disease the cowpox, and being fully satisfied how much you feel interested in its success, you will be gratified in hearing that I have at length accomplished what I have so long been waiting for, the passing of the Vaccine Virus from one human being to another by the ordinary mode of inoculation.
>
> A boy of the name of Phipps was inoculated in the arm from the pustule on the hand of a young woman who was infected by her master's cow. Having never seen the disease but in its casual way before; that is, when communicated from the cow to the hand of the milker, I was astonished at the close resemblance of the pustules, in some stages, to the variolous (smallpox) pustules. But now listen to the most delightful part of my story. The boy has since been inoculated for the smallpox which, as I ventured to predict, produced no effect. I shall now pursue my experiments with redoubled ardor.

The date of that historic vaccination was May 14, 1796. The name of the dairymaid with an open wound on her finger who had contracted cowpox when milking a cow was Sarah Nelmes. It was material taken from the lesion on her hand that was used for the vaccination. (Modern smallpox vaccination solutions are obtained from calves who have been given cowpox.)

The following year Jenner sent the results of all his years of experiments to the Royal Society, but his work was returned because it was felt that there was not enough evidence to warrant publication in the Royal Society's journal. Jenner, however, did not feel that he could wait any longer. He had been working on the subject for over twenty years. He decided to publish his results himself at his own expense and in 1798 did so in a book titled *An Inquiry into the Causes and Effects of the* Variolae Vaccinae.

This small book of seventy-five pages, which sounded the death knell for smallpox, went through three editions and was widely translated. In it Jenner described many case histories of immunity to smallpox in those who had acquired cowpox naturally as well as many cases that he, Jenner, had vaccinated with cowpox.

". . . what renders the cowpox so extremely singular, is, that the person who has been thus affected is for ever after secure from the infection of the smallpox," wrote Jenner on page six of his book. He did not know *why* cowpox protected against smallpox. That was in the realm of immunology, a science that would not be born for almost another hundred years. Jenner knew only that cowpox *did* protect, and his crusade changed the face of the earth by preserving the faces of its inhabitants from the ravages of smallpox.

The book was bitterly attacked by many with different views, and Jenner had to come to London for a while to fight for his cause. It seems to be the rule rather than the exception that many learned authorities everywhere resist new ideas. They prefer to cling to something they *know*, even when proved erroneous, rather than give up their crusty viewpoints. This process is just as prevalent in medical science as in other fields of endeavor.

Some of Jenner's critics insisted that those vaccinated would develop the features of a cow. Others tried to claim credit for the discovery. However, within a few years, Jenner had won the battle. Vaccination was used all over the world, and the terror evoked by the very word *smallpox* began to disappear. A friend of Jenner's had named the process *vaccination;* the word was derived from the Latin *vacca,* meaning "cow."

The empress of Russia rightfully was enthusiastic, considering the dreadful eighteenth-century epidemic her country had experienced; she ordered that the first child vaccinated be named Vaccinoff, and this baby received a royal pension for life.

In France Napoléon, who had ordered all of his soldiers to be vaccinated, released an English prisoner at Jenner's written request. "What *that* man asks is not to be refused," the emperor said of Jenner, which is amazing, since England and France were locked in a death struggle at the time.

Although honors and recognition came from everywhere, Jenner remained unaffected by fame. He answered letters, continued his country practice, and vaccinated the poor without charge in a summer house in his

Edward Jenner inoculating his son. *Brown Brothers.*

garden. It is sad to note that despite the honors, he had been forced to defend vaccination so often that he remarked a few days before he died of a stroke in 1823, "I am not surprised that men are not thankful to me; but I wonder that they are not grateful to God for the good which He made me the instrument of conveying to my fellow-creatures."

One letter in particular must have gratified Jenner. It came from a man who recognized early the value of vaccination, taking time from his enormous duties to vaccinate himself, family, and some two hundred friends. This was President Thomas Jefferson, who wrote to Jenner, "You have erased from the calendar of human afflictions one of its greatest. Yours is the comfortable reflection that mankind can never forget that you have lived; future nations will know by history only that the loathsome small-pox has existed. . . ."

Ignaz Phillipp Semmelweis

1818–1865 Hungarian physician who introduced the antiseptic principle into hospital practice

The general hospital of Vienna is known as the Allegemeine Krankenhaus, and beginning in 1844, a young physician started to understand why so many women there were dying in childbirth. The doctor's name was Ignaz Phillipp Semmelweis, and he was a Hungarian, born in Budapest in 1818.

Semmelweis was the fourth of eight children of a grocer. His original purpose in coming to Vienna in 1837 was to study law, but since he found law boring, he switched professions and became a medical student. He spent a year in Vienna, went home for two years to continue his medical studies at the University of Pest, and in 1840 returned to Vienna to complete his medical studies.

Several changes in the administration of the medical school and the hospital had taken place during the two years of Semmelweis's absence. The single change that was to have the greatest effect on his life and on the lives of the pregnant women he was taking care of concerned the two divisions of the Lying-in Hospital, which cared for the impoverished women of Vienna. Before Semmelweis left, medical students and midwives had staffed both divisions equally. Now, on his return, he found a new policy in effect. The authoritarian director of the maternity hospital, Dr. Johann Klein, had ruled that the medical students be taught in the First Division while the midwives received their training in the Second Division.

Obstetrics then was a relatively new field, and most babies were brought into the world by trained women called midwives. There was an important difference in the training of medical students and midwives. The midwives were taught using a model of a woman's pelvis, a mannikin, whereas the medical students were trained by means of dissections on actual bodies (cadavers). After finishing these dissections, the medical students would walk immediately to the wards and, using only soapy water to wash their hands, would proceed to examine those women who were about to give birth or who had just given birth.

A frequent disease of such women was childbed fever, or puerperal fever. The disease had been recognized since ancient times, but it occurred rarely. However, with the advent of hospitals, the disease often appeared in epidemic form. Women who had their babies outside of hospitals were the lucky ones; except for an occasional case, they were spared the disease.

Today the cause of puerperal fever is known. It results from infection of the uterus by the streptococcus microbe, the same organism that causes strep throat, scarlet fever, and several other infectious diseases. The uterus of a woman about to give birth has been stretched and is susceptible to infection. Similarly, the wombs of women who have just given birth are vulnerable to infection; the passage of the placenta (afterbirth) leaves a raw, unprotected area. Germs would be introduced by the dirty hands of examiners, dirty instruments, or contact with dirty sheets. In the uterus, the streptococcus germs would multiply and then travel through the bloodstream, causing septicemia (blood poisoning) and usually death. In those days nobody knew that germs could cause disease. That discovery would be made in 1857 by Louis Pasteur.

In Semmelweis's time, all sorts of theories were propounded concerning the cause of deadly puerperal fever, but no way existed to cure the disease. It was simply accepted as an unfortunate complication of pregnancy. This was the situation that existed when Semmelweis returned to Vienna to complete his medical studies. He graduated in 1844 and received a minor teaching appointment in the First Division of the Lying-in Hospital.

From all accounts Semmelweis walked quickly and was subject to rapid changes of moods. He was known, however, for his consistent and extreme kindness to the women under his care. It was the habit then (as it is now) for the physician to walk the hospital corridors and wards with medical students in tow. Semmelweis and his students would examine women who were be-

Dr. Ignaz Phillipp Semmelweis. *The Bettmann Archive.*

ginning labor, but it must have been discouraging when they would stop at a nearby bed and see a young woman who had had her baby several days earlier. One look would be enough to tell Semmelweis that the patient, who a day earlier had looked healthy and happy, now was marked for death. Her face would be flushed and her pulse extremely rapid. Even while he questioned her, he knew what would happen. In a day or two the hospital priest would be summoned to her bedside to administer the last rites, and then a bell would toll, announcing her death to the terrified other patients.

The bell sounded its sad message much more frequently in the wards of the First Division than it did in the Second. Why? Why? This was the question that plagued Semmelweis. Since it was simply rotation, and thereby chance, that determined which division a woman would be assigned to, why was the death rate so much higher on the First than it was on the Second?

When in March 1847 the exhausted Semmelweis decided to take a vacation trip to Venice, three of his older friends, Professors Karl von Rokitansky, Ferdinand von Hebra, and Joseph Skoda, were relieved. Before he left, he asked the hospital priest if it would be possible to stop the ringing of the bell. He explained that the women were already frightened; they knew, as did much of Vienna, of the high mortality rate in the First Division, and many begged, to no avail, to be admitted to the Second. The priest, unaware and sorry that the bell had caused terror, immediately assured Semmelweis that the practice would stop. So the tolling for death came to an end but not the death toll.

When Semmelweis returned from his vacation, he received a dreadful piece of news. Another friend, Dr. Kolletschka, had just died at age forty-three. The cause of his death was an infected cut finger suffered while he was doing an autopsy. Professor Rokitansky then had the sad duty of performing an autopsy on his colleague. Semmelweis studied the findings: infection had been rampant, involving the blood vessels, lung surfaces, and abdominal cavity, and many distant seeded abscesses had been present. Then in a brilliant flash, Semmelweis realized that Kolletschka's death due to contamination was identical to the deaths, from childbed fever, of women and babies.

With this insight Semmelweis had the answer to the difference between the First and Second divisions. The medical students of the First Division, coming directly from their dissections in pathology, were depositing the poisonous material still clinging to their hands into the bodies of the women they examined. Their hands planted the seeds of infection and became hands of death. Soapy water did not kill the germs.

Semmelweis took immediate steps to combat this procedure. Chlorine had been used as a disinfectant for over twenty years, probably because its strong odor was capable of neutralizing the smells of putrefaction and death. Semmelweis ordered basins of chlorinated lime to be installed in several places in the wards. He had signs posted stating that before examining any patient, hands must first be washed in a basin filled with the chlorinated solution.

The mortality rate in the First Division began to drop. Semmelweis was elated but no more so than the three aforementioned friends, Rokitansky, Hebra, and Skoda, all of whom would later gain lasting fame for their respective contributions to pathology, dermatology, and medical diagnosis. If these three regarded their protégé with pride, there was one powerful man who did not. Professor Johann Klein had reason to resent the new theory of his young assistant. It was Klein who had established the dissection procedure, when he replaced Professor Boër. Boër had used the mannikin to train students, the same method used to train midwives. As a result, it was under Klein's regime that the mortality rate had begun to rise. He refused to believe that Semmelweis's good results were any more than coincidence and interpreted the enthusiasm of other faculty members as interference with his department.

Klein began to undermine Semmelweis in every way possible. His attitude and remarks caused many medical students and nurses to turn against the ideas of this "unstable foreigner." As a result, Semmelweis had to be even more diligent and strict; some students deliberately disregarded the new hand-washing procedure, and whenever this happened, the incidence of childbed fever would again rise.

In 1848, during the European revolt against Austrian oppression, Semmelweis's relationship with Klein deteriorated even more. Most of the Vienna faculty was sympathetic to the idea of more freedom and formed an academic legion. Klein was an archconservative, and when one day he wandered onto the wards of the First Division, he was angered by the sight of Semmelweis dressed in the uniform of the legion. This furthered his determination to get rid of Semmelweis. When the revolution was crushed by the intervention of Russia, Klein's great political power was further increased.

Amazingly, considering the active disapproval and undermining by his chief, Semmelweis's methods worked. In 1846, before chlorine hand washings, the incidence of childbed fever had been 11.4 percent, over one in ten women. By 1848, after the introduction of chloride of lime, the incidence had been reduced to 1.27 percent. Furthermore, for the very first time since 1822, the incidence of childbed fever in the First Division was *lower* than in the Second, or midwife, Division.

Because of this success Semmelweis now found that he had made other powerful enemies besides Klein. Such a situation frequently occurs when people champion new concepts; it happens regularly enough to be called a general rule. Those holding the older ideas are reluctant to discard them and often become defensive and angry toward those proposing something new. In 1843 Dr. Oliver Wendell Holmes, the father of America's most famous jurist and a Harvard University physician and author, stated his belief that puerperal fever was contagious. He advocated the use of chlorine washings, and as a result he was subject to abuse by professors of obstetrics and other practitioners all over the country. Semmelweis knew nothing of Holmes's work, just as later Lister would give antisepsis to the world knowing nothing of Semmelweis's findings. In each instance, the benefactors had two things in common. They knew that infection could be prevented, and they received much abuse for their efforts to combat it. Of these three giants of antisepsis, only Semmelweis was so affected by opposition that he became insane.

Klein finally got his wish. In October 1850 Semmelweis was offered a minor teaching post with humiliating restrictions. He could demonstrate to students only by using a mannikin and could not perform dissection. Previously Klein had prevented Semmelweis from being promoted, but this last offer was, in essence, a vicious demotion. It was too much for Semmelweis, who hurriedly left Vienna and returned to Budapest.

Back in his home city, he was understandably depressed. His parents were dead, many of his brothers who had been revolutionaries were now refugees, and he himself had no job. However, his doctrine at least was known, and he applied for and received an appointment in the Department of Obstetrics at St. Rochus Hospital. This began the happiest period of his life.

The appointment at St. Rochus, although without pay, was important because it allowed Semmelweis to begin private practice and earn badly needed money. It also permitted him to extend his method of preventing infection. An epidemic of childbed fever was raging despite the fact that no examinations were made on the obstetrics ward by medical students. Semmelweis discovered that examinations on women were performed, however, by surgeon-obstetricians whose hands were contaminated. Semmelweis went to work installing his basins filled with chlorinated lime and posting his rules for cleanliness. The mortality rate promptly fell, but as in Vienna, his chief, Professor Birly, was not impressed. Semmelweis's reputation grew, however, and he developed a successful private practice. In 1855 Semmelweis was appointed professor of midwifery at the University of Pest. It was a high honor, but no easy job. Much reorganization of the teaching program was needed, and Semmelweis made the necessary changes.

In 1857 Semmelweis married a woman twenty years his junior. The marriage was a good one, and his young wife accompanied him on his house calls, reading patiently in the coach as her husband attended to his patients. He was happy, and yet the diatribes against him disturbed him more and more. In addition, their first two children, a son and later a daughter, both died in infancy, leaving the Semmelweises heartbroken.

In October 1860, smarting from the attacks of his enemies, Semmelweis published a long and carefully written book, *The Etiology, Concept, and Prophylaxis of Puerperal Fever*. The first part of the book was organized, factual, and brilliant, but the second half revealed how unstable Semmelweis had become. This section consisted of a series of letters written to and answered by him. The letters Semmelweis had received from various professors criticizing his views were rebutted by him in a scathing and emotional tone; as a result, readers became more interested in the printed insults than in the evidence Semmelweis had presented. The scientific impact the book might have produced was lost in the smoke screen of rhetoric.

Semmelweis became more desperate. He began to write letters to professors of obstetrics denouncing his many opponents. One of the most vocal of these was Dr. Friedrich Scanzoni, professor of obstetrics at Prague, to whom Semmelweis wrote directly. "I denounce you before God as a murderer, and the History of Puerperal Fever will not do you an injustice when, for the service of having been the first to oppose my life-saving teaching, it perpetuates your name as a medical Nero."

Despite the joy of having three healthy children following the loss of the first two, Semmelweis became obsessed with the urgency of having his doctrines accepted. He began to stop strangers in the street, who became confused and frightened by his rantings. When he acted irrationally at a faculty meeting, his mental illness could no longer be denied. It was decided to hospitalize him in a Viennese sanitarium headed by Dr. Riedel, an eminent psychiatrist. Semmelweis thought he had been invited to inspect the sanitarium, and when he was forcibly restrained from leaving and placed in a straight jacket, he became delirious. He was not confined for long. A finger injured in Budapest during a surgical operation became infected, and like his friend Kolletschka, Semmelweis was soon dead. The official cause of death was listed as blood poisoning, but the real cause was the deafness of much of the scientific world.

Semmelweis showed that the healing hands of the physician could become instead the hands of death when they spread infection. While his views initially failed to gain worldwide acceptance, still Semmelweis had taught many pupils well. Their application of his discovery saved the lives of countless women while the world waited for Joseph Lister to convince it to adopt the principles of antisepsis.

Joseph Lister

1827–1912 English surgeon; developer and popularizer of use of antisepsis in surgery

One of those sad but frequent historical ironies occurred in 1865, the year that Ignaz Semmelweis died in a sanitarium for the mentally ill. The antiseptic principle for which he had unsuccessfully fought and died was introduced. After a long period of experimentation and struggle, antisepsis was accepted by the world of medicine. The personality of Joseph Lister, the man responsible for the adoption of the antiseptic principle, allowed him to succeed where Semmelweis had partially failed.

Joseph Lister was born into an affluent Quaker family of wine makers. His parents' beautiful home, Upton House, was located in a village near London, which at the time of Lister's birth was a rural area. The community was largely comprised of Quakers, or the Society of Friends, to use the official designation. The sect differed somewhat from other Christian denominations; its manner of austere and simple dress and its unique speech, with the use of *thy*, *thee*, and *thou*, set it apart. Therefore Quakers were more comfortable living close to one another, and this arrangement was also convenient for holding prayer meetings.

Lister's father, Joseph Jackson Lister, was interested in optics as an avocation. He completed the work Leeuwenhoek had started by perfecting the achromatic lens for the compound microscope. This distinguished work resulted in his election to the Royal Society. Joseph Lister's mother had been a teacher, and so his home, filled with classics and science, was stimulating.

Young Joseph enjoyed listening to the guests, often Royal Society members, who would come for evening discussions with his parents.

It was almost certain that young Lister would choose medicine as a career. Professional opportunities for Quakers were limited. Their pacifism ruled out military careers, and their reluctance to take sworn oaths resulted in few of them choosing the legal field. Most Quakers went into business, and their industrious, honest, and disciplined ways were usually rewarded by spiritual and monetary fulfillment.

Lister's early contact with science, however, made every other field seem dull to him. After attending excellent private schools, he entered University College in London. This college was established in self-defense by those minorities—Catholics, Jews, and certain Protestants like Quakers—who were denied admission to Oxford or Cambridge because they did not belong to the Church of England. Derided because of its secular character, it was called the Godless College in Gower Street. Lister remained at University College for nine years, getting his medical degree and becoming a member of the Royal College of Surgeons in the same year, 1852. In that year Lister made an important original observation, which he reported. He was the first to discover that the iris of the eye was made up of two muscles, one to dilate and the other to contract the pupil. (The pupil is simply the hole in the doughnut iris.)

During his training at University Hospital, Lister witnessed in 1846 the kind of operation that revolutionized surgery and deeply increased the need for what would become Lister's major contribution to that field. This operation was an amputation and was unusual because for the first time in England ether was used to anesthetize the patient. Before this, several strong men had been employed to hold down the screaming patient while a surgeon raced through an operation in twenty-eight seconds. Now a new, painless era had arrived, and the need for speed had vanished. This American invention was wonderful for many reasons, but it increased one major hazard. Before anesthesia, surgical operations were infrequent and largely limited to amputations. Now with the patient comfortably asleep, it was safe to undertake new and more complicated operations. As a result, the incidence of surgical infection was greatly increased and resulted in many more patients dying from infection than ever before. Anesthesia was introduced before the germ theory of disease was discovered, so nobody really knew *why* these surgical wounds became infected. It was just taken for granted that infection was a formidable but necessary risk about which nothing could be done. Lister would change all that.

After graduation Lister was faced with the decision of where to go for advanced surgical training. Professor William Sharpey, a respected teacher at University Hospital, suggested to him that he go to Edinburgh to study under Dr. James Syme, a brilliant Scottish surgeon who once had taught in London but had left because of conflicts with other surgeons. Lister followed Sharpey's advice.

Although Lister intended to remain for only a few months with Syme and then return to London, things worked out differently. It would be almost twenty-five years until Lister would return to live in London. His great contribution would be begun and carried out in Scotland, while England, his home, would actually be almost the last place in the world to accept his doctrine. As the saying goes: "A prophet is not without honor, save in his own country."

From the start Syme was attracted to the serious, quiet-spoken young man who had come so highly recommended. In turn, Lister became devoted to the fiery Scot who would teach Lister so much and who would advise him concerning critical decisions the latter would be required to make. Syme provided one nonsurgical joy to Lister—Syme's daughter, Agnes—who in 1856 became Lister's wife. Since the Symes were not Quakers, Lister "married out" of the Society of Friends and was forced to relinquish membership in that church. Despite this action he always remained a Quaker at heart, and the extremely warm and close relationship he enjoyed with his father remained intact. However, he did change his dress to the more fashionable style of the day.

Lister and his bride took a Continental honeymoon, stopping at various medical centers. The most memorable visit during the trip was the time in Vienna. There the Listers were entertained by Professor Rokitansky, the famous pathologist who had been like a father to Ignaz Semmelweis.

Lister, at the time he was married, had already established a reputation. Starting as Syme's assistant in 1853, he had progressively earned more responsibility, and in 1855 Lister gave a course of lectures on surgery and pathology. His manner and his learning so impressed his students that they began to call him Chief, a warm token of their esteem for him. His first student, in fact, recalled that "the general assumption was that he was a great thinker, and he was treated as such by all the men." In addition to teaching, he performed important research on inflammation and blood coagulation and reported these studies to the Edinburgh Medical Society.

Thus it followed that when the position of professor of surgery at the University of Glasgow became vacant, Lister was among the candidates, and after much political maneuvering, he was selected. His father-in-law, Syme, vigorously backed Lister's candidacy, and this support was generous considering how much Syme sacrificed when his most trusted assistant, along with his beloved daughter, moved to Glasgow.

Lister had mixed feelings about leaving Edinburgh. His seven years there had been happy, but he wasn't completely on his own. The powerful figure of Syme was ever present. Probably wondering how he would fare without the loyal support of the great Syme, Lister entered the large city of 390,000 inhabitants and found that he had arrived "home." Here in Glasgow he would find, as in Edinburgh, the warm companionship, love, and respect of colleagues, medical students, and house officers. And here in Glasgow he would begin to eradicate wound infection with antisepsis, the discovery for which the world remembers and honors him.

In 1860 the problem of wound infection was horrendous. About 40 percent of patients who had amputations, for example, died after surgery. Infections in hospitals were rampant and known under the general term *hospitalism.* No one knew what caused these infections, but it was assumed as always that some vague tainting of the oxygen in the hospital air, a miasma, was responsible. The air was indeed tainted, but not by any miasma. It was tainted by deadly microbes floating from one infected wound to find a new home in the space between the stitches of a freshly amputated leg. Here, in the new tissues, these microbes would multiple and often kill by poisoning the blood or by impairing circulation so that tissue death (gangrene) would result.

In 1860 nobody knew what caused wound infection. It was just accepted, and the smell it created was accepted also as that "good old surgical stink." The appearance of pus, that yellowish substance, was thought to be a good sign of healing and called "laudable pus." It was true that those patients who lived long enough for their wounds to ooze pus had a better chance to survive than other patients whose wound infections traveled rapidly inward and who died before pus could appear; actually, pus is the remains of the body's defense cells, the white corpuscles that have died fighting the deadly microbes.

A portrait engraving of Dr. Joseph Lister. *Photosearch, Inc.*

But because microbes still live in this yellow sea, pus itself is a source of infection.

When Lister made rounds, his students would see a man of average height with spreading sideburns in the muttonchop fashion of the day. He spoke with a stammer, so slight that it never interfered with his teaching. His voice was soft, nor did he raise it even under the most trying circumstances. His rounds were informative. For example, he would stop at the bedside of a patient who had recently undergone amputation of a leg. First he would demonstrate the appearance of the purulent wound, and later, away from the patient, he would tell the students that he disagreed with those surgeons who welcomed the appearance of this "laudable" pus. Lister explained that common sense decreed that it would be far better if a wound could heal simply without the always dangerous infection. Then he might ask a student to describe the cardinal symptoms of inflammation and follow with other questions to stimulate thought.

And so it went, year after year, 1860, 1861, 1862, 1863—infections of all sorts—pus in the bloodstream, pyemia; the bright red skin infection, erysipelas; the grayish black infected dying tissue, gangrene. And more often than not, these infections were halted not by the anxious doctors, but by death, always around in the guise of hospitalism.

Then one day in 1865 Dr. Thomas Anderson, professor of chemistry, walked into Lister's office carrying a journal. He told Lister that he was aware of the latter's great interest in the chemistry of putrefaction and asked him to read an article written by Louis Pasteur. Anderson felt Lister might discover something of importance in the article and, at any rate, he would enjoy this beautiful piece of work. The article titled "Researches on Putrefaction" described fermentation that resulted from the action of microbes. These microbes, Pasteur pointed out, came from the air and could multiply in solutions, thereby contaminating them.

Lister read on and found the answer he had been looking for. Here was wound infection explained! It wasn't tainted oxygen in the air that caused wound infection. It was Pasteur's microbes. Kill the microbes and there would be no sepsis, no wound infection. Enforce *antiseptic* principles—prevent the germs from seeding or destroy the germs before they could multiply—but how?

Then Lister remembered that the city of Carlisle in northern England had successfully used a substance, carbolic acid, to get rid of the smell from garbage. He traveled to Carlisle to see the process for himself, and now he understood what carbolic acid did. It rid the air of the smell because it killed the germs that caused garbage to decompose or decay.

Lister returned to Glasgow and asked Professor Anderson to obtain some carbolic acid for him. He now had a plan for using it on the wards of the Glasgow Infirmary. Lister's idea was to use this antiseptic in cases of compound fracture, that serious type of fracture that results in breakage of the skin. Intact skin has the ability to resist infection, but when it is scratched or damaged, microbes gain access and infection results. Compound fractures always became infected, and the mortality rate was chilling.

Therefore we can imagine how excited Lister was when in March of 1865 he first used dressings soaked in carbolic acid on a compound fracture wound; for the first time, the infection that invariably followed such a fracture did not develop. He wrote to his father:

> This is one of my cases at the Infirmary which I am sure will interest thee. . . . Though hardly expecting success, I tried the application of carbolic acid to the wound. . . . Well, it is now eight days since the accident and the patient has been going on exactly as if there were no external wound . . .

Following this first description of antisepsis, Lister continued to treat cases of compound fracture. He improved his dressings, diluting the carbolic acid and mixing it with oil so it would not burn the skin. He trained his assistants carefully in the method and taught them to wash their hands frequently in carbolic acid solutions. Further, he extended the use of the treatment to abscesses.

He reported his excellent results (nine of the eleven compound fractures healed without complications) in the British medical journal *Lancet* in 1867. Then he began to lecture on the subject, his first talk being to the British Medical Association, which met at Dublin. There he stressed that the antiseptic principle could be applied to all forms of surgery.

Lister experimented with, lectured on, and above all taught antisepsis to his assistants and medical students. In 1869 he moved back to Edinburgh as professor of surgery there; he replaced his father-in-law, who had suffered a stroke and who had decided to resign despite partial recovery.

The following year Lister was called to Balmoral, Scotland, for a minor operation on a major patient. Queen Victoria had an abscess in her armpit. Lister opened it and did something that was entirely new in surgery. He inserted a rubber tube to allow drainage of infected material to the outside. Rubber drains are still used today, and it is surprising that a queen was the first experimental subject.

Lister's fame spread, and now doctors from foreign countries came to Edinburgh to listen to him and learn his antiseptic method. At the bedside of a typical surgical patient in the Royal Infirmary, Lister would stand with a group of foreign physicians. Unhurriedly he would softly chat with the patient before cutting the dressing with bandage scissors. Invariably he smelled the dressing, commenting that it smelled "sweet" because the odor of infection was absent. Then he would invite these foreign doctors to confirm the lack of offensive odor, and they had no choice but to comply, each in turn smelling the dressing. Then Lister would mention how frequently, before antisepsis, the germs from one patient's infection would contaminate the wound of the patient in the next bed. He would invite the visiting doctors to watch antiseptic surgery in the operating rooms, where each instrument used would be disinfected with carbolic solutions.

After completing the adult rounds, Lister would enter the children's ward. His compassion for his young patients was legendary. He might approach the bedside of a little girl who was crying because the leg of her precious rag doll had accidentally been torn off. Lister then would sit on the side of the bed and request a needle and thread, while softly promising the young patient that the leg could be repaired. Then the master surgeon would begin to work, meticulously sewing the leg to the doll. After the doll was whole again and the little girl had laughed joyously, Lister would also show his delight. All in a day's work, no less important than his other surgery.

Lister's principle of preventing wound infection was being accepted all over the world. Only in England was his doctrine ignored, and it was probably for this reason that in June 1877 he accepted the chair of surgery at King's College in London. He was leaving a large university where the incoming freshman class averaged one hundred eighty students to take charge of the surgical department of a small medical college whose entering class numbered twenty-five new students. Why? One reason was that London was his home city, but the main reason probably was his strong desire to have antisepsis practiced in England.

Lister was disappointed in his students. They were a different lot from those in Edinburgh. Their main objective was to pass examinations, and Lister's lectures, with wider purpose in mind, were poorly attended. However, London doctors came to listen and were convinced. Gradually England, too, accepted antisepsis.

Honors now came from everywhere. Queen Victoria made Joseph Lister a baronet, and when Sir Joseph Lister became Lord Lister a few years later, the scientific world rejoiced. But probably the honor that touched Lister the most was his being selected to represent medicine and surgery in paying tribute to Louis Pasteur at the latter's seventieth birthday celebration. The ceremony was held at the Sorbonne in Paris in 1892. The two scientists had corresponded since 1874, when Lister wrote to tell Pasteur that he had been able to apply Pasteur's findings in avoiding wound infection; however, they had met only once some years earlier in London. Now Lister came to the platform and delivered a speech of appreciation to Pasteur so eloquent that when Lister finished, Pasteur was moved to rise to his feet and embrace Lister. The audience of twenty-five hundred distinguished guests was treated to one of the most touching gestures of all time.

But Lister's life was terribly shattered when on vacation in Rapallo, Italy, the following year. His wife suddenly developed a shaking chill, and within four days she was dead of pneumonia. His constant companion and helper was gone. Lister was a lonely man, and the joy of recognition was tempered by not having his beloved Agnes by his side to share in the honors accorded him.

Lord Lister participated in debates in the House of Lords on those few occasions when medical topics were discussed, but gradually he retired more and more from public life. He suffered a stroke in 1903, and after that his health deteriorated markedly. Still he lingered on, a frail shell, confined to his room. Finally on February 10, 1912, he died in his sleep. He had almost reached his eighty-fifth birthday.

Two of the greatest contributions to surgery had occurred during Lister's lifetime. The first was the use of anesthesia, which occurred when Lister was a freshman medical student. The second was the development of antisepsis, and for this blessing the world will forever be indebted to Joseph Lister.

Louis Pasteur

1822–1895 French chemist; founder of microbiology

Nobody, including its inventor, Antony van Leeuwenhoek, could have guessed how much the discovery of microscopic life would change the world. However, this discovery *was* momentous, and two pathways of study resulted from it.

The first one involved a controversy concerning spontaneous generation—the theory that somehow these tiny forms of life could all at once develop from nonliving material rather than be the "babies" of other microscopic forms just like themselves. Jan van Helmont, in the sixteenth century, offered a recipe for making mice by placing some dirty rags and some cheese in a vessel. This procedure did not increase the rodent population.

Later, people believed that insects or maggots were born spontaneously from decaying meat. Francesco Redi in 1688 in a scholarly work disproved this. His experiments were simple. He allowed meat to putrefy in a jar but covered the lid of the jar with gauze. Flies attracted by the meat laid their eggs on the gauze, which prevented them from alighting on the meat. These eggs hatched in the larval form, maggots or worms, which then matured into flies.

Since spontaneous generation of visible life had been disproved, now argument developed over microscopic life. Leeuwenhoek himself never believed that the microscopic life he viewed had arisen spontaneously, but the argument raged on, and it was not settled until Louis Pasteur's experiments.

The second pathway of research involved the germ theory of disease. Granted that these tiny animals and plants exist, but were they ever responsible for causing disease? It was not until approximately two hundred years after Leeuwenhoek first saw germs that these two general problems were answered in France by that giant of scientific research, Louis Pasteur. "The most perfect man who has ever entered the Kingdom of Science" was how Sir William Osler characterized gentle, generous, and brilliant Louis Pasteur. In all the years that have passed, there has been no valid reason to contradict the great Osler.

Born on December 27, 1822, at Dôle, France, a year after Napoléon Bonaparte died in exile, Louis Pasteur, during the course of a long career punctuated by shocking physical and emotional blows, would show the living nature of fermentations, would prove that spontaneous generation was a myth, and would begin a new era in immunology. Most important of all, he would make microbiology into an exact science.

Louis, the son of a hardworking tanner, came from a close-knit family. After a family move to Arbois, he attended primary and secondary schools, eventually entering the Royal College of Besançon, where he graduated with a bachelor's degree. Although he was a fine artist, his heart belonged from the first to science, and he was appointed assistant mathematical master at the college. His letters to his sisters stated his primary philosophy: "These three things, will, work, and success, between them fill human existence." Ironically, in 1842 when he won his baccalaureate in science, his diploma read "mediocre" in chemistry. But he wrote his father after this: "Just be patient and trust me. I shall do better as I go on."

In 1843 Pasteur was admitted to the École Normale and attended chemistry lectures by J. B. Dumas at the Sorbonne, lectures that proved inspirational. After receiving his doctorate, he was appointed to the faculty of the École Normale, where he began his famous researches on the form and structure of chemical crystals. These crystallography studies resulted in his appointment as professor of chemistry at the University of Strasbourg. There he immediately fell in love with Marie Laurent, the daughter of the university's rector. He first wrote to the rector:

My father is a tanner at Arbois. My sisters help him in his business and in the house, taking the place of my mother whom we have had the misfortune to lose last May. My family is comfortably off but not rich. . . . As for myself, I have long ago resolved to surrender to my sisters the whole share of the inheritance which would eventually be mine. I have therefore no fortune. All that I possess is good health, good courage and my position in the University. . . . I plan to devote my life to chemical research with—I hope—some degree of success. . . . With these humble assets I beg to submit my suit for your daughter's hand.

The rector turned the letter over to his daughter, who said, "No!" After writing a plea to Marie's mother, Pasteur finally pressed his suit with Marie herself. His persistence won out, and a long and happy marriage resulted.

In 1854 he was appointed to the post of dean of sciences at the new University of Lille, and at the request of a local manufacturer whose son was his pupil, Pasteur began to study the fermentation of beet sugar into alcohol. (Fermentation is a chemical change caused usually by yeasts, a change that results in effervescence, or bubbling.) The manufacturer, Bigo, complained that the alcohol was often contaminated during the fermentation process. Pasteur looked for hours, using the microscope to examine yeasts as well as other microscopic organisms. Suddenly one day in the midst of his observations, an original and brilliant idea occurred to him. *Fermentation was caused by living organisms!* It was the life processes of these yeasts and other microbes that *caused* the fermentation. This concept was revolutionary because all of the foremost chemists of the time, including Justus von Liebig, the leading one, felt that the yeasts found in fermentation had died and were only decomposing chemical substances.

Pasteur disproved the decay theory, although he never was able to convince Liebig. Continuing his work with various ferments (wine, vinegar, beer, milk) through the years, he showed that fermentation was always an active, *living* process caused by microorganisms. He suggested two new major concepts as a result of this study. The first was that some organisms could live with or without the free oxygen of the air. When these organisms caused fermentation, they did so by extracting energy from the organic substance being fermented. (Organic means living, and the composition of organic compounds includes the elements carbon, oxygen, hydrogen, and nitrogen.) Thus yeasts, deep in a fermenting solution of grapes, while living and multiplying in the absence of free air, would change the sugar in the grapes to alcohol.

Pasteur's second concept was that of competitive fermentation; he contended that various other microorganisms contaminating a solution would be competing to make their own ferments. Pasteur first discovered this in 1857 and showed why milk became sour because microorganisms were changing lactose, the sugar of milk, into lactic acid. Here then was the start of scientific microbiology.

Pasteur went on to study ways of encouraging useful fermentation while simultaneously suppressing contamination.

Pasteur, at all times kind and generous, also was a passionate man. He spent most of his life arguing for his views. It did not matter if his opponents never conducted an experiment; Pasteur was so rational that he felt he could, by logic, convince those who had been derailed from the scientific track. Further, he believed his arguments were important roads to truth. Pasteur was unfailingly committed to the truth, so when he decided to settle the issue of spontaneous generation, he had to disregard the urgings of his old professor Dumas to avoid this controversial and unpopular subject. Although he was forced for the rest of his life to argue against advocates of spontaneous generation, he really won the battle in 1860 by devising flasks with S-shaped necks instead of straight necks. In these flasks, he placed organic solutions that, when exposed to air in straight-neck flasks, would become contaminated by air bacteria and become cloudy, even after boiling. However, because of the S-shaped neck, the boiled solutions of these flasks remained sterile and clear because the microbes from the air fell on the curved neck and never reached the bottom of the flask.

Further, Pasteur showed that bacteria floated in the air either freely or attached to dust particles by taking a trip armed with seventy-three sealed flasks containing organic fluids in which bacteria could easily grow. At different places along the way, he opened the flasks and then immediately resealed them. The most dramatic event of the trip occurred when he opened and resealed twenty flasks high in the Alps at Mer de Glace; of the twenty, only one became contaminated with bacteria while those opened at lower altitudes had a much higher rate of contamination. The reason is that bacteria are breathed into air by man or animals and often attach to dust particles; at high altitudes fewer living agents are present to spread bacteria, and less dust is present in rarified air.

From 1865 to 1870 Pasteur, at the request of Professor Dumas, stayed in Alais, France, to work on the epidemic that was ruining the silkworm industry. Pasteur, who initially knew nothing about the silk industry, experimented steadily for five years, finally discovering a way to eradicate the silkworms' disease by grinding up the moths after they had laid their eggs. These eggs were kept until the moth emulsion was examined under the microscope. If the disease agent was present, the eggs the moth had laid were burned. If the moth was disease-free, her eggs could be cultivated and used. By following his methods, the silkworm industry began to prosper once again.

These productive years of 1865–1870 were also years of the most dreadful tragedy for Pasteur, tragedy that first struck six years earlier when his oldest daughter, Jeanne, had died from typhoid fever. His father died in 1865, followed a few months later by Pasteur's youngest daughter, Camille. The next year, his twelve-year-old daughter, Cécile, died, the second of his children taken by typhoid fever.

In June a cabinet minister friend named Duruy, unaware of Pasteur's recent loss, wrote asking about progress on the silkworm studies. Pasteur's answer was touching, allowing but a glimpse of his grief to show:

I hasten to thank you for your kind reminder. My studies have been associated with sorrow; perhaps your charming little daughter, who used to play sometimes at M. Le Verrier's, will remember Cécile Pasteur among the other little girls of her age that she used to meet at the Observatoire. My dear child was coming with her mother to spend Easter holidays with me at Alais, when during a few days' stay at Chambery, she was seized with an attack of typhoid fever, to which she succumbed after two months of painful suffering. I was only able to be with her for a few days, being kept here by my work, and full of deceiving hopes for a happy issue from that terrible disease. I am now wholly wrapped up in my studies, which alone take my thoughts from my deep sorrow.

In 1867 Pasteur discovered flacherie, a second disease of silkworms, whose cure he also found. In that same year Duruy convinced Emperor Napoléon III to have a well-equipped laboratory built for Pasteur adjoining the École Normale. The following year, 1868, Pasteur, not yet forty-six years old, suffered a stroke that caused paralysis of his left side. He recovered after several months, although he had residual damage to his left side for the rest of his life. During his convalescence at the École Normale, he looked out of the window and noticed a solitary workman casually moving a wheelbarrow. All other activity on the new laboratory had stopped. "They are waiting for me to die," thought Pasteur, who then became visibly depressed.

Emperor Napoléon III, hearing of the work stoppage, ordered full-scale resumption of building, and the happy noises of this work speeded Pasteur's

Louis Pasteur at work in his laboratory. *Musée Pasteur, Paris.*

recovery. He was well enough by January 1869 to return to the Cevennes area.

Next his interest turned to the disease called anthrax. At the same time as a brilliant young German doctor named Robert Koch was studying the bacillus (bacterium) that would prove to be the causative agent, Pasteur had turned to study this disease on its home grounds, the farms. In France anthrax was called *charbon*, and its principal victims were sheep, but other animals and humans as well could become infected. Pasteur found the causative agent in the blood of the sick animals and then, over the years, performed ingenious experiments to learn about the disease.

In 1880 Pasteur made a momentous announcement. In addition to his anthrax studies, he had been working on the disease chicken cholera, which was caused by a bacillus. One day, by accident, he injected some hens with an *old* culture instead of a fresh one. Those hens did not get the disease—the microbes in the old culture had been weakened by exposure to oxygen—but more important, the hens were immune to later ingestion of deadly cholera bacilli. Thus Pasteur had discovered the principle of attenuation, or weakening, of deadly strains and found that vaccines could be prepared. This was the most important discovery of his life, and our modern vaccines are based on it. This field of immunology opened by Edward Jenner at the end of the eighteenth century was extended by Pasteur who, out of recognition of Jenner's contribution, also called his process vaccination. It was fortunate that cowpox prevented smallpox, but here Pasteur showed that a weakened strain of microorganism could *itself* protect against the disease it normally caused. He showed that the weakened organism stimulated the host in some way to make protective substances. Thus in 1881 he applied this principle to anthrax, preparing a vaccine against the disease. That the vaccine worked was proved in a daring and dramatic public demonstration. Many of Pasteur's scientific enemies were present on May 5 when the widely publicized experiments were started at Melun in the yard of a Pouilly-le-Fort farm.

Twenty-five sheep, as well as six cows, were vaccinated over a period of several days while the same number of unvaccinated sheep were set aside for the final test on May 31, when an injection normally capable of killing would be given to all of the animals, those vaccinated and those not. Excitement was high on that day as the injections were made without incident. "The twenty-five unvaccinated sheep will all perish," Pasteur had written the previous month. "The twenty-five vaccinated ones will survive."

Pasteur was to view the results of these experiments two days after that final injection. The night of June 1, 1881, was an anxious one for Pasteur. He had received an erroneous report that one of the vaccinated sheep was dying, and he spent a sleepless night.

In the morning Pasteur arrived at the farmyard. He was greeted by applause. Twenty-two unvaccinated sheep were already dead. The other three unvaccinated sheep were dying. But *all of the protected, vaccinated sheep were in perfect health.* Pasteur was a kind man who must have felt much sadness watching the remaining unprotected sheep staggering to their deaths. Yet he realized that these animals provided proof that would save countless others from a similar fate.

This dramatic demonstration was characteristic of Pasteur. He did his experiments painstakingly, and when he was certain that he was correct, he would boldly and vigorously put his beliefs to the test. Let his detractors (and these were many) show him up! He frequently would challenge his critics, but he was never proven wrong by them. He made mistakes in his experiments but recognized them himself. He never published or spoke about a theory until he was certain he had explored all alternative theories.

While he was working on anthrax, Pasteur in 1878 gave a lecture that forecast the future of surgical sterility:

> If I had the honor of being a surgeon, convinced as I am of the dangers caused by the germs of microbes scattered on the surface of every object, particularly in the hospitals, not only would I use absolutely clean instruments, but after cleansing my hands with the greatest care . . . I would make use of bandages, and sponges which had previously been raised to a heat of 130°C., to 150°C.; I would employ water which had been heated to a temperature of 110°C. to 120°C.

Pasteur moved from anthrax to dangerous studies on rabies. This disease is caused by a virus that is the smallest form of microscopic life. Viruses were not visible until the twentieth century, when powerful electron microscopes revealed their presence. However, even though Pasteur could see no rabies germs under his own microscope, he predicted that a "microbe of infinite smallness" would prove to be the cause of this disease.

Rabies occurs in people who are bitten by animals, usually dogs, that are infected with the disease. Untreated, it is fatal to all, animals and humans. The disease formerly was called *hydro-*

phobia, from the word meaning "fear of water." Actually, animals with rabies are not afraid of water itself, but seeing water frightens them because it gives them the desire to swallow, and swallowing is very painful because the disease causes strong throat spasms.

Pasteur and his associate Dr. Pierre Roux realized that the symptoms of the rabid dog came from brain inflammation and that the virus was likely to be found in much greater concentrations in nerve tissue rather than in saliva. Therefore Pasteur prepared vaccines using rabbit spinal cords, based on the same principle he had discovered in the preparation of other vaccines. He used the action of oxygen to weaken the infection he had produced in this spinal cord tissue. Then he protected dogs by giving them immunizations with progressively stronger doses of vaccines made from the rabies-infected spinal cord. Someday he would use his method to save human lives. (As usual Pasteur insisted that animals be anesthetized. He could not bear the thought of any living creature suffering.) He now requested that a commission be appointed to evaluate the ongoing experiments.

But July 6, 1885, changed his plans for continued, careful animal research on rabies vaccine. On that day there was a sudden commotion in the hall and sounds of people rushing about. Pasteur stepped out to see what was disturbing the order in his laboratory. The sight was pitiful. A mother, her eyes red from crying yet wide with fear, stood transfixed for a moment in the presence of the great man. Her little boy, Joseph Meister, age nine, was also crying. He knew that everybody thought he was going to die. Joseph didn't know anything about death, but he knew that he didn't want to stop playing in the Alsatian hills. Right now he just wanted the pain to go away.

When Mme Meister looked at Pasteur, her eyes implored him to help her little boy. Joseph had been attacked by a rabid dog and had been bitten fourteen times. He would have been killed on the spot had not a bricklayer driven the dog off. Mme Meister, having learned of Pasteur's studies, brought the boy to Villeneuve l'Etang. Pasteur's emotion demanded of him that he help, but he was in a quandary because treatment of humans had never been tried and might be fatal. M. Vulpian, a trusted member of the commission, told Pasteur what he already knew. Without treatment Joseph would die, so it was worth taking the risk.

Pasteur began treatments. The plan was to vaccinate young Meister in exactly the same way as he had the dogs. Twelve successive injections would be given, each stronger than the preceding one. As each dose of the vaccine was administered into the boy's side, Pas-

Louis Pasteur surrounded by children who had come to him for vaccine treatment after having been bitten by rabid dogs. *Musée Pasteur, Paris.*

teur began to have nightmares about killing little Joseph. After a while Pasteur became ill and had to entrust the injections to an assistant. He left for the country to try to regain his health. Because of the long incubation period, he felt he had treated the boy in time, and yet he waited for the dreaded message telling of Joseph's death. The message never came. The world rejoiced as Joseph Meister, and many others after him, survived and proved the value of Pasteur's vaccine against this previously incurable virus disease. And how the victims of dog bites began to flock to the laboratory! From Russia, from the United States—all over—they came to be saved and usually were.

(In later years Meister came to work as a gatekeeper at the Pasteur Institute. In 1940, during the German occupation of France, fifty-five years after he had received treatment, Joseph Meister was ordered to open Pasteur's burial crypt. For some unknown reason a German official gave this command, and rather

At a jubilee celebration at the Sorbonne, Paris, on Pasteur's seventieth birthday, Pasteur is escorted by the president of the Republic and greeted with outstretched arms by Dr. Joseph Lister. *Musée Pasteur, Paris.*

than obey, Meister committed suicide.)

Because Pasteur's health began to fail, his last years were spent less in active research than in looking over the shoulders of the many inspired pupils who came to work with him and who made great contributions to science. However, in 1889 Pasteur did discover the cause of childbed fever when he cultured and identified the streptococcus germs. How Ignaz Semmelweis, who struggled to save the lives of its victims, would have cried with relief!

There was sadness and there was happiness in the closing years of Pasteur's life. Of his five children, only a son and a daughter survived him, but there was great satisfaction in having received every scientific honor imaginable. When Pasteur had begun his studies, his laboratory was in an attic. He lived to see the construction of great laboratories for investigation. More important, Pasteur lived to see the marvelous humanitarian application of his researches. His name became part of scientific language, including the word *pasteurization*. Louis Pasteur died peacefully on the afternoon of September 28, 1895. One of his hands held a crucifix; the other rested in that of Mme Pasteur.

Robert Koch

1843–1910 German bacteriologist; convincingly confirmed that germs can cause serious disease

It was a serious young man who, on an April day in 1876, was writing a letter with the precision and earnestness with which the world would come to know him. But the world did not then know him. In fact, practically nobody, even in his own district in Prussia, had ever heard of this industrious country doctor.

The letter was addressed to Ferdinand Cohn, the famous professor of botany at the University of Breslau. (Breslau is now a Polish city named Wroclaw but in those days was part of Prussia.) The thirty-three-year-old letter writer was Dr. Robert Koch of Wollstein. He wrote as follows:

Esteemed Herr Professor: Stimulated by your work on bacteria published in *Contributions to Biology of Plants*, I have, for some time, been at work on investigations of Anthrax, as I was able to secure the necessary material. After many vain attempts, I have finally been successful in discovering the process of development of the bacillus anthracis.

Should you, highly esteemed Herr Professor, be willing to grant my humble request, will you kindly appoint the time when I may come to Breslau. With the highest esteem, Yours respectfully.

Robert Koch had been born into a family of thirteen children and had been raised in Klausthal, Germany. Originally his father had wanted Koch to become a shoemaker, but when finances improved, the boy was allowed to study medicine at the University of Göttingen. As an adolescent he had shown interest in science, roaming the Harz Mountains, magnifying glass in hand, examining plants and watching animals. He had also learned to play the zither and piano, and in addition he became the school chess champion. At Göttingen he had done well, stimulated by his anatomy professor, the famed pathologist F. G. J. Henle, who greatly influenced Koch's later work. In medical school Koch performed original research, graduating with honors.

Koch wanted to become a ship's surgeon because the idea of travel appealed to him. However, love, in the form of a practical fiancée, intervened, and Emmy Fraatz anchored Koch before he could set sail. They were married in 1867 and moved from place to place as Koch tried to eke out a living in private practice. The Kochs were extremely poor, and at one point, in desperation, they almost moved to America to join Robert's brother. However, a wealthy patient had an accident, and the fee collected was sufficient to allow the couple to remain in Germany.

Finally they settled in Wollstein, and Koch acquired a microscope. Like Pasteur, he had become interested in the primarily animal disease anthrax but began to study it in a somewhat different way. He wanted to demonstrate that the rod-shaped organisms he saw under his microscope were the cause of the disease and also to show how the disease was spread. His work in his home laboratory was devoted entirely to studying everything about this germ.

Koch was thorough and he was patient. When he had completed something, no investigative step, no matter how minor, had been omitted. His genius was in these qualities rather than in the brilliant insight of Pasteur, who has been called an "architect" while Koch was referred to as a "builder."

Koch mailed the letter and waited to hear from Dr. Cohn. His work on anthrax had not been part of any paid job. He had begun to satisfy his scientific curiosity in 1872 by fitting in his anthrax studies during spare hours. Naturally attendance to patients superseded his investigations. Finally Koch completed his experiments. The most important thing about them was that, for the first time, proof was obtained that a *specific disease* of animals and man was caused by a *specific microbe.* This premise followed naturally from Pasteur's 1857 work on lactic acid fermentation. Microbes could indeed be villains. There were many new things Koch had done in arriving at this proof. For one thing he had succeeded in growing the anthrax bacillus in pure form in the fluid from a rabbit's eye. Second, he had shown that the rod-shaped microbe could break up into tiny round seeds, or spores. These would be excreted in the meadows by animals dying of anthrax. The spores were tough and heat resistant and could live for several years. Then grazing animals would eat them; they would change form back into rod-shaped bacilli and kill the animals. Finally Koch had experimentally produced anthrax by injecting the germs into animals.

It was certainly possible that Professor Cohn, one of the few people in the world who could understand the value of the work, might decide not to see Koch. A busy professor could easily suspect that nothing of great importance would result from the work of a country doctor in Wollstein. Koch would publish in any event, but Cohn's approval might mean the difference between recognition of his discovery or oblivion.

Usually a stiff, formal man, Koch was elated when at last he received the awaited word that he could come to Breslau. He packed, and taking his notes and drawings with him, he set out on his journey.

Professor Cohn was as surprised as he had been skeptical. His generosity demanded that every investigator, no matter how little known, deserved a hearing. However, what Koch painstakingly demonstrated to him at Breslau was such significant work that Cohn summoned the great pathologist Julius Cohnheim to send a representative to Breslau at once. History was being made! Cohnheim went himself to Breslau, and the two older investigators took Koch as their protégé. Koch remained for a while in Breslau, publishing his studies before returning to Wollstein.

In Breslau he met Karl Weigart and the latter's young cousin, Paul Ehrlich. Both had developed staining techniques in which some infected matter would be spread thinly on a glass slide and then stained with dyes so the bacteria could be seen and identified. Koch borrowed their methods the following year, 1877, to report on preparation, staining, and photographing of bacterial smears. The next year, 1878, he reported on wound infections, showing the presence of grapelike clusters of microbes in surgical infections with pus and small round microbes arranged in long chains that were found in some skin infections. He both excited and pleased his two sponsors, who arranged for him to return to Breslau, where he remained for a time.

Cohn and Cohnheim had obtained some minor paying jobs for Koch, but they were better scientists than businessmen; they didn't realize until it was too late that Koch was not making enough money in Breslau to permit him and Emmy to stay, even though Emmy was taking in laundry to supplement her husband's income. The Kochs were forced to return to Wollstein, where Koch resumed practice and was very successful.

In 1880 Professor Cohnheim secured a position for Koch as a member of Berlin's Imperial Sanitary Commission. It turned out that Koch liked everything about Berlin except its most illustrious scientist, Rudolph Virchow. As the founder of cellular pathology—the microscopic study of diseased tissue—Virchow was at the pinnacle of worldwide fame. It was only natural for Koch to want to show his anthrax studies to Virchow.

As Koch showed the slides to the great man, he described the features of the bacteria, with its spore development. He explained how the bacterium becomes elongated and beaded like an irregular thread and how the beaded structures became spores. Then he explained the life cycle of the spores, their ingestion by grazing animals, and so forth.

After looking for a time through the microscope, Virchow dismissed what he had been shown and dismissed Koch himself, as well. Usually helpful to young scientists, Virchow had, for some unknown reason, taken a dislike to Koch. He said he saw far more interesting things every day and reproved Koch for wasting the master pathologist's time.

Koch must have felt embarrassed and disappointed as he gathered up his demonstration material. After the warmth of the Breslau reception, he had expected some enthusiasm from the great Virchow. Koch left, humiliated and angry, vowing never again to have any dealings with Virchow. He also vowed that a day would come when he would have his revenge.

In Berlin Koch attracted many bright young scientists who wanted to work with him. In time each would make his own contribution to the science of bacteriology. There was Friedrich Löffler who, in 1884, discovered the cause of diphtheria; and there was Kitasato, who five years later would isolate the deadly tetanus bacillus. These and similar discoveries would come as a result of one of Koch's greatest contributions to bacteriology—the development of the gelatin culture method in 1881. After this discovery, various bacteria of disease, according to Koch's own words, fell into his and his pupils' laps "like ripe apples from a tree."

Shortly after Koch had completed his anthrax studies, his wife was busy in the kitchen when she noticed a spot on some food that had been left out. She called this to the attention of her husband. Koch looked at the spot under his microscope and was amazed at what he saw: thousands of bacteria and *all the same kind*. He realized what had

Dr. Robert Koch in his laboratory. *Mary Evans Picture Library, London.*

happened and the importance of it. A microbe that had landed on the food had become trapped. Then it began to divide. What had developed—what the spot represented—was a *pure colony* of bacteria. Now Koch saw that he could grow a pure culture of germs by using a solid nutrient. He began with potato slices. Then he made an important switch. He began to use jelly for his cultures.

The jelly, enriched with beef broth to feed the bacteria, had the advantage of being transparent. Now an investigator could take some infected material and with a platinum needle smear it over some jelly in a plate or tube. In two or three days, pure colonies of the various bacteria present in the material would grow on the jelly and be identified by their appearance. These colonies usually were not very big—about the size of the head of a pin—but each contained thousands of germs. Every germ colony differed from that of others in size, shape, color, and other characteristics. This was the discovery that Koch announced in 1881.

The development of solid growth media stimulated research that would result in one of the most exciting discoveries in medical history. It would pit Koch directly against Virchow.

Nobody knew what caused tuberculosis. What *was* known was that people with the disease would lose weight, cough blood, run fevers, and in most cases die after several years. When these patients were autopsied, their lungs, and sometimes other organs, were filled with tiny granules that had a distinctive appearance under the microscope. Koch's enemy, Virchow, thought that the symptoms of tuberculosis, a disease then known as consumption, phthisis, or the white plague had nothing to do with these lung granules, which he believed represented a different disease.

Koch knew that tuberculosis was an infectious disease. After all, in 1865 Jean Villemin in Paris had succeeded in transmitting the disease to animals, and Cohnheim also had had success in giving the disease to animals. The problem was that nobody had ever seen anything resembling a microbe in any tuberculosis lesion. Patient as always, Koch in 1881 began his methodical search for the microbe he felt certain was somewhere in the tubercles, these lung "granules" of tuberculosis. He prepared thin slices of tissue and stained them with methylene blue, which stain had worked so well to show other bacteria. He looked hour after hour—nothing, no microbes. Yet he was sure they were there. Then he borrowed from Weigert and Ehrlich. He stained his thin smears with methylene blue *this time fortified with potash.* The potash made the solution alkaline, which allowed the tubercle bacilli to be stained bright blue.

Having examined hundreds of slides before, he now looked and looked again. There they were—thin, long, brightly stained blue rods! Right before his eyes were the killers that had been hidden until this instant. Here he was, the first man to see one of the deadliest killers of them all. Now he pledged himself to grow the organism in culture, to experiment. In short, he resolved to do everything that his anatomy professor at Göttingen, F. G. J. Henle, had told him would be required to prove beyond doubt that this microbe caused the disease tuberculosis. He allowed himself one year to complete the work, after which time he would present it publicly.

Koch began at once smearing infected material on his gelatin plates and waiting. Soon the colonies should appear. He told his assistants to watch the plates carefully, explaining that in a few days their experimental group would be the first to see colonies of the white plague. However, after a few weeks had passed, Koch realized that these germs, which had been so hard to see, were equally difficult to culture. Then Koch had another idea. The famed Irish scientist John Tyndall had used blood serum to grow germs. Perhaps Tyndall's method would work better than gelatin.

So Koch used jelled blood serum instead of ordinary gelatin. He promptly forgot that he had borrowed the idea, and this refusal to give due credit was one of Koch's chief defects. He never could admit that his ideas often weren't original nor could he acknowledge the prior work of others. Perhaps the great Virchow had sensed this and was angered by it, making him blind to Koch's extraordinary demonstration. In any case, Koch worked painstakingly, and since most of his work was novel, his experiments usually originated in his own head.

Koch watched his blood serum plates day after day. Apparently this method was working no better than the gelatin had. Five days—nothing; ten days—nothing; two weeks—no growth. Anybody but Koch would have heaved the plates into a wastebasket since all other bacteria had grown out in a few days. But Koch continued to observe the plates. Then, on the twentieth day, Koch entered the laboratory as usual. On the surface of one of the plates there were a few raised, roughened areas. He methodically scraped some of the roughened material onto a glass slide and stained the slide as he had before with methylene blue and potash. Then he placed the slide under a microscope and looked. There they were! Hundreds of the thin blue rods of death! He had succeeded in culturing the tubercle bacillus. (Today tuberculosis microbes are stained with carbolfuchsin, which gives them a red color. Acid fails to decolorize these bacteria, so they are called *acid-fast* bacteria. The recognized name of the microbe is *Mycobacterium tuberculosis.*)

Now that Koch had the organism in pure form, he experimented with increased intensity, determined to meet his own deadline. Then one day throughout Berlin, the physicians and other scientists of that city received a most exciting announcement from the Berlin Physiological Society. The subject to be discussed by Dr. Robert Koch on the evening of March 24, 1882, was "The Etiology of Tuberculosis." Dr. Koch would tell the world what caused tuberculosis. We can easily imagine the excitement in the medical community.

There was a full house on the evening of March 24. All of the important scientists were there, including the great Rudolph Virchow. Everybody knew by this time that he and Dr. Koch were bitter enemies. They knew that Virchow could demolish a theory with the same ruthless speed with which he performed an autopsy. But they knew also that Koch was a careful man; he probably would be able to defend himself better than others who had been unfortunate enough to suffer the sarcastic and crippling remarks of an angered Virchow. Several who were present later described the event.

The buzzing in the room stopped when Koch entered and moved to the lectern. Dignified, bearded, and mustached, wearing a black suit, black bow tie, and gold watch chain, Koch stood for a moment after being introduced. He glanced over the large audience and then began to speak:

> If the number of victims which a disease claims is the measure of its significance, then all diseases, particularly the most dreaded infectious diseases, such as bubonic plague, Asiatic cholera, etc., must rank far behind tuberculosis. . . .

Koch paused, and the audience nodded in assent. Who in the crowd had not experienced the pain of watching a loved one die, of having to stand helplessly as the patient coughed and coughed until death seemed merciful?

Koch continued, beginning by explaining the staining technique and showing a projected slide of the blue killer microbes lined up in the tubercles of the lung itself. He went on to discuss infected material from human beings, cattle, hogs, monkeys, guinea pigs, and chickens. Next he illustrated the blood serum culture techniques. Finally he told how he had experimentally produced the disease by injecting into animals the microbes grown on the culture plates. The disease tuberculosis was produced in every case. The granules in the lungs and other organs were all filled with these microbes, all *caused* by them, experiment after experiment.

What Koch had done was to obtain microbes from humans and animals dying of tuberculosis. He had cultured these germs. Then he had produced the same disease as occurred naturally by injecting the microbes he had cultured. And finally he had recovered the germs again from the animals he had experimentally infected. These were the principles of proof of infectious disease first taught to Koch at Göttingen by Professor Henle. Now on this evening they entered bacteriology's hall of fame as Koch's postulates. His paper was concluded. There was nothing more to say.

For one of the few times in the history of any medical meeting, there was absolute silence. The audience realized it had participated in a great historical event, too important for applause or even cheers. Then all heads turned toward Virchow. If there were any weaknesses in Koch's presentation, it was certain that Virchow would attack. The chairman called for questions. There were none. Virchow sat stonily. His dual theory of tuberculosis had been annihilated.

Koch achieved instant fame all over the world. The following year, in 1883, he traveled to India, where he discovered the microbe that caused cholera, another disease that had killed millions of victims.

Then in 1890 he made the most serious error of his life. He announced a cure for tuberculosis. The product was tuberculin, which is an extract from dead tubercle bacilli. The vaccines against various diseases had always been prepared from weakened strains of the disease agents. Thus it was logical to suppose that this would be true in tuberculosis as well. Koch experimented with guinea pigs and other animals, and indeed the tuberculin appeared to arrest the disease process. However, he made the mistake of not trying the preparation on humans with tuberculosis. Had he done so, he would have seen that what cured guinea pigs did not cure people.

The world was horribly disappointed. A cure for tuberculosis would come as a result of Koch's identification of the tubercle bacillus, but more than half a century would pass before it was announced. (Selman Waksman discovered and produced in 1943 the soil antibiotic streptomycin, the first effective drug to treat tuberculosis. He received the Nobel Prize for this work in 1952.)

Tuberculin does, however, have some diagnostic value today. A small amount of tuberculin injected under the skin of a person will cause inflammation if that person is, or has been, infected with tuberculosis.

For his research in discovering the cause of tuberculosis, Koch was awarded the Nobel Prize in physiology and medicine in 1905.

Koch was sent to Africa in 1902, where he made significant discoveries while studying various tropical diseases, including sleeping sickness. In 1908 he traveled to America accompanied by his second wife.

From the time he first became interested in bacteria, Koch's researches and practice required more and more of his time. He took frequent scientific trips, leaving his first wife, Emmy, and daughter, Gertrude, at home. The Koch domestic life was less than ideal, and the couple decided on a divorce in 1891, when Koch was forty-eight years old. The marriage had lasted twenty-four years, and the parting was amicable.

Approximately two years later Koch was sitting for his portrait when he met an eighteen-year-old student of the artist. This lively and intelligent girl, Hedwig Freiberg, was attracted to the world-renowned scientist. Koch, in turn, fell in love with Hedwig, and the couple were married after a brief but ardent courtship. The dispassionate, methodical Koch suddenly felt like a youth again, proud of his bride. However, the citizens of Klausthal, his birthplace, were so enraged at his marriage to a young woman that they ripped a plaque in his honor from the house in which he had been born.

If Koch's popularity was temporarily dimmed at home, it remained high elsewhere. He was revered all over the world. In Japan he visited his old pupil Kitasato, and in that country a temple was erected in Koch's honor.

He returned home and continued his investigations. Then in April 1910 he began to note symptoms of heart trouble. He rallied for a while and finally was well enough to travel to Baden-Baden, where it was hoped he could rest and recover.

On May 27, 1910, his physician coming to visit found Koch sitting in a chair. He had died peacefully, but the enormous contributions of this country doctor lived on. He was a giant who had taken giant steps toward the conquest of infection.

Charles L. A. Laveran (1845–1922)
Ronald Ross (1857–1932)

Discoverers of the cause of malaria

Malaria, a disease characterized by recurrent chills and fever, probably still is the most prevalent serious infectious illness in the world. Recurrences of the disease are called relapses. It has been estimated that in the middle of the twentieth century, the disease was killing over one million persons each year in India alone; today approximately 500 million people are attacked by malaria every year, but many develop an immunity to the disease and others are cured by drugs, primarily by quinine, its relatives, and newer drugs. In less serious forms of the disease, the attacks of chills and fever get fewer, and eventually the disease disappears spontaneously, leaving its former victims healthy. Malaria was officially eradicated in the United States in the 1940s, although a few cases still occur, usually in people who have come from other places.

Quinine, obtained from the bark of the cinchona tree, which grows in certain parts of South America, actually was the New World's gift to the old. Because it was first sent to Europe by the Jesuit Fathers in South America, who learned of its medicinal use from the Indians of Peru and other countries in the area, it was once called Jesuit bark. Quinine is the chief alkaloid of that bark. A derivative of quinine, quinidine, is used in the treatment of certain disturbances in heart rhythm.

Malaria, although thought of primarily as a disease of hot climates, actually can occur almost everywhere, in temperate climates and even in extremely cold places close to both the North and South poles. Still it is most common in the tropics and for a reason now easily understood; the disease is spread by the bite of a certain genus of mosquito. The climate in the tropics is favorable for the breeding and multiplication of these pesky insects. Water is needed for the completion of the life cycle of mosquitoes; eggs are laid on the surface of water, from which mosquito larvae hatch.

It is interesting to note that what the disease is called gives a completely wrong idea of its cause; Torti, in 1709, gave it the name malaria from *mal aire* ("bad air"). Another name for the disease is also misleading. Malaria was sometimes called paludism (from the Latin *palus*, meaning "swamp," or "marsh"); it was thought that breathing the bad air of these swamps caused the illness. The swamps are not blameless—they are excellent breeding grounds for the mosquitoes—but it is the *bite of an infected mosquito* and not person-to-person-contract, breathing air, or even drinking swamp water that causes the disease.

Malaria was known in ancient times, and Hippocrates described the different varieties of the disease, based on whether the fever recurred daily, every other day, or every third day. It has played an important role throughout history, epidemics of malaria being thought to have contributed to the fall of the Roman Empire.

Although the Nobel Prize for finding the cause of malaria was awarded to two men, Charles Louis Alphonse Laveran in 1907 and Sir Ronald Ross in 1902, as in all scientific discoveries many investigators played important roles. Dr. Jaramillo-Arango, author of *The Conquest of Malaria,* makes the following point:

In medicine, as in science generally, and in fact, in any creative activity, creation is a process of evolution; almost every discovery rests normally upon a former idea, notion or emotion; that is to say, it is inspired by a pre-existing fact. Many a time the stroke of genius manifests itself in being able to explain correctly a phenomenon which others have previously observed—and not always with indifference, often on the contrary, with great interest—thus determining by such an act, which appears so simple once it is known, a complete revolution in the knowledge of that subject.

In the case of malaria, at least ten scientists had "strokes of genius," and Jaramillo-Arango considers that the mosquito-malaria theory rests primarily on four pillars. The first pillar is the understanding (by several men, including Laveran) that the mosquito bite can cause the disease. The second pillar is the discarding of the idea that the disease is caused by poisonous vapors breathed in or inoculated by mosquitoes; a scientist barely remembered, one Louis-Daniel Beauperthuy, working in Venezuela in 1854, was the first to insist that what the mosquitoes injected in their victims was not poison from the marshes but *living germs*.

Beauperthuy declared:

> These insects, which are the torment of the nights in hot countries, introduce under the skin and cellular tissue of man a septic virus which alters the blood and causes general symptoms which sulfate of quinine reduces. . . .

The term *virus* used above simply meant an infectious agent. Actually viruses, the smallest infectious agents, weren't known to exist before the 1930s and 1940s, when they were studied and identified. Many decades after Beauperthuy's contribution, it was proved that the infectious agent of yellow fever was indeed a true virus.

The third pillar of the malaria "house" was created in 1878, when Sir Patrick Manson, known to the world as the "father of tropical medicine," showed (in connection with a different disease, filariasis) that when a mosquito bites a person, the insect can absorb, along with the blood of the infected person, a germ that can cause disease and that it is absolutely necessary for this parasitic germ to live for a time inside the mosquito in order to complete its life cycle.

The fourth and final pillar was supplied by the investigations of the eminent Cuban physician Carlos J. Finlay, whose studies concerned primarily another infectious disease, yellow fever. Finlay was the first to suggest that yellow fever was directly transmitted from the sick to the healthy by the bite of a mosquito.

Both Manson, in his filariasis studies, and Finlay, in his yellow fever studies, were dealing with different genera of mosquitoes from the one, the *Anopheles*, that causes malaria; however, the principle is the same: Mosquito bites sick host—human, bird, and so forth—and later bites and infects healthy host.

The Panama Canal could not have been completed had not epidemics of both yellow fever and malaria been ended by the elimination of the breeding places of these mosquitoes. In an address given by Dr. Finlay to a Cuban medical society in 1898, he described how this could be accomplished:

> Why should not the houses, in yellow fever countries, be provided with mosquito blinds, such are used in the United States as a matter of mere comfort, whereas here it might be a question of life or death? The mosquito larvae might be destroyed in swamps, pools, privies, sinks, street sewers, and other stagnant waters, where they are bred, by a methodical use of permanganate of potassium or other such substances, in order to lessen the abundance of mosquitoes; but the most essential point must be to

Dr. Charles Laveran. *The Nobel Foundation, Stockholm.*

prevent those insects from reaching yellow fever patients, and to secure a proper disinfection for all suspicious discharges, in order to forestall the contamination of the insects.

Because Finlay was so obsessed with these famous ideas of how to prevent mosquito-spread disease, he was often referred to, especially by ladies of high society, as "the mad doctor." But Finlay's remedies were used by Walter Reed and William C. Gorgas to save the Panama Canal.

Despite the many contributors to an important scientific discovery, the Nobel Committee selects only a very few for the Nobel Prize. It is strange that although the contribution of Laveran to the malaria puzzle came years before the work of Ross, he wasn't awarded the prize until five years after Ross.

Charles Laveran was the French physician who discovered the infectious agent of malaria. Born in Paris in 1845, he completed his medical studies at Strasbourg and later joined the staff of Val-de-Grâce School of Military Medicine. Thus he followed in the footsteps of his father, also a surgeon in the military. In 1878 Laveran was assigned to serve in Algeria. This assignment was fortunate for the world because it was there that Laveran made his momentous discovery.

In North Africa malaria had taken a tremendous toll of both the native population and of colonial armies. It was while Laveran was doing postmortem (after-death) examinations of malaria victims that he noted the parasite causing the disease. His discovery came during a time when the knowledge that bacteria were responsible for various diseases was causing an explosion of excitement all over the world. Bacteria are typically one-celled microorganisms that are classified as plants, but what Laveran saw was a one-celled animal called a protozoan (from the Greek *proto*, meaning "first," and *zōion*, meaning "animal"). It was the first recognized instance in which a protozoan caused a disease and was a fundamental element of Manson's "first pillar" in the malaria story.

This later proved to be the malaria parasite, which changes form several times during its life cycle inside the victim, usually man, and inside the mosquito. When the mosquito bites a person with malaria, it sucks in the parasite, which is fertilized and matures in the stomach wall of the mosquito. The fertilized organisms go through various forms and eventually end up as sporozoites that enter the salivary gland of the mosquito. When the mosquito bites an uninfected person, it is these sporozoites that infect the new victim.

Laveran returned to France, remaining in the military and teaching. In 1896 he retired from the army and entered the Pasteur Institute. He devoted the rest of his life to research, establishing the Laboratory of Tropical Diseases there. Besides the Nobel Prize, he was awarded many honors and published over six hundred papers and textbooks. He remained at the Pasteur Institute until his death on May 18, 1922.

The man with whom Laveran shared the Nobel Prize, Sir Ronald Ross, was born in 1857 in India, where his father was a British general stationed in Almora. Ross first saw England when he was sent there to school at the age of eight. He later considered a musical career, wrote voluminously and thought of becoming a writer, and was interested in mathematics and philosophy. His keen mind embraced everything that interested him; he was truly a Renaissance man.

To please his father, who wanted him to have a career in the Indian Medical Service, Ross entered medical school and received his degree in 1879. For a time following his medical school graduation, he was a ship's surgeon on the transatlantic Anchor Line, but in 1881 he passed the required examination for the Indian Medical Service and was sent to Madras. He first became interested in mosquitoes when he was stationed in the interior of southern India. Noticing the relationship between the breeding of mosquitoes and water, he tried to get the breeding places destroyed but met with resistance. One adjutant told him that, since mosquitoes were created for some purpose, it was his duty to bear with them.

It is impossible to understand the almost unbearable difficulties Ross suffered once he began the scientific study of mosquitoes and their relationship to malaria. That scientific interest began on his first furlough to London in 1888. During that leave he met and married Rosa Bloxam; also during that leave Ross studied bacteriology, hoping to apply this knowledge somewhere in India.

Sir Ronald Ross. *Wellcome Institute Library, London.*

But the military service had no interest in Ross's mosquito studies once he returned to India as staff surgeon. He would get deeply involved in some location where malaria was prevalent, and no sooner did he begin to make progress than he was reassigned to a place where there was no malaria.

During a later furlough to London in 1894, this erratic and troubled military surgeon made a wise decision: He sought out the great Sir Patrick Manson, who became his mentor. Manson showed him the malaria parasite discovered by Charles Laveran. Manson had been the first to show that the mosquito could be the carrier of a disease (in his studies, filariasis), and he strongly believed that the mosquito carried the disease to man; but Manson was not aware that it was the bite of the mosquito that injected the parasite.

Often an investigator who contributes mightily to the solution of a scientific problem never gets the credit he or she deserves. Such was the case of Dr. Giovanni Grassi, who studied malaria for years and was the first to recognize that the *Anopheles* genus was responsible for malaria; he also was the first (in 1898) to transmit the disease to humans by allowing female *Anopheles* mosquitoes to bite a volunteer in a Roman hospital. This volunteer, one Mr. Sola, then developed malaria. Grassi never got the Nobel Prize, and he was honored only in Italy, where he was elected a senator.

Ronald Ross, unaware until much later of Grassi's work, returned to India, by now a surgeon-general in the Indian Medical Service. He continued to study the mosquito's relationship to malaria and also maintained an active correspondence with Sir Patrick, who continued to sponsor and encourage him. During his tours in India, Ross himself developed malaria but recovered. Independently he had come to realize that the brown genus of mosquito, the one with spots on its wings that stung with its rear end up in the air (the *Culex* variety sat down while stinging), was the one that caused malaria, and it was the bite of the female that was responsible. The final proof came on a day in Calcutta, when Ross found that the parasite developed into its deadly form inside the stomach of the *Anopheles* mosquito. Ross recalled:

The 20th August 1897—the anniversary of which I always call Mosquito Day—was, I think, a cloudy, dull hot day. I went to the hospital at 7 A.M., examined my patients, and attended to official correspondence; but was much annoyed because my men had failed to bring any more larvae of the dappled-winged mosquitoes, and still more because one of my three remaining *Anopheles* had died during the night and had swelled up with decay. [Ross left his laboratory and later returned.] At about 1 P.M., only one more of the batch [of seven] remained . . . half an hour's labour at least. I was tired, and what was the use? I must have examined the stomachs of a thousand mosquitoes by this time. But the Angel of Fate fortunately laid his hand on my head; and I had scarcely commenced the search again when I saw a clear and almost perfectly circular outline before me of about 12 microns in diameter.

The following day, Ross dissected the seventh and last of the *Anopheles* he had available. He reasoned if it was a form of the parasite he had seen the previous day, it would have grown. And it had. Again he saw the pigmented-filled, circular parasites, twenty-one of them now, and much larger.

That evening Ross wrote a poem of thanksgiving whose last stanza, partly derived from the Bible, reads as follows:

I know that this little thing
A million men will save—
Oh death where is thy sting?
Thy victory oh grave?

Ross continued to experiment, transmitting malaria to caged birds via the bites of *Anopheles* mosquitoes. After receiving news of these experiments from Ross, Sir Patrick Manson announced the results at a meeting in Edinburgh of the British Medical Society. Generously, he gave complete credit to Ronald Ross, ignoring all the help he himself had given to Ross.

Ross's Nobel citation in 1902 read: "For his work on malaria, by which he has shown how it enters the organism and thereby has laid the foundation for successful research on this disease and how to combat it." Ross was knighted in 1911. After a long life of teaching and experimentation, Sir Ronald died peacefully on September 16, 1932.

Elie Metchnikoff

1845–1916 Russian bacteriologist; formulator of the theory of phagocytosis

Elie Metchnikoff was born in a small village on the steppes of Russia near Kharkov on May 16, 1845. He had three older brothers and an older sister. Unwanted by his father, he was nevertheless loved instantly by his mother, Emilia. The father, Ilya Metchnikoff, a nobleman and army officer, actually had few responsibilities in regard to his children, seeing them only in the morning and at bedtime when they would kiss his hand. Serfdom, a kind of slavery, still existed in Russia, and serfs performed all the duties of running a household or an estate. The family had lived originally in St. Petersburg, but after Ilya Metchnikoff had squandered his wife's fortune, the family had moved to Panassovka, where they lived on land inherited from Ilya's father.

Elie was a nervous, energetic child with boundless curiosity. Only music calmed him; he could listen to someone play a musical composition and remain enthralled for hours. Music provided the only harmony of his early life. He had weak eyes, and his parents had been told that crying would be detrimental to his health. Elie soon learned to use his eyes as a weapon, threatening to cry if he didn't get his own way. Despite this practice, he was a warm, affectionate child with strong ethical and humane feelings. He couldn't stand to see someone sick or unhappy or victimized. As he grew older, his greatest happiness came from taking care of family and friends.

From the time that Elie was about eight, it was evident that biology had a special interest for him. He found tremendous excitement in examining all sorts of plants and insects that he came across during his hikes around the Russian countryside. In nature he found the tranquility so lacking in his own temperament.

At age eleven Elie began formal training at the Lycée in Kharkov. He read every book he could obtain, and when he was fifteen, he saw for the first time illustrations of primitive microscopic life. As he viewed amoebas and the like, his course was set; he would devote his life to biology.

Though only a high school student, he obtained permission to take a course in histology (the microscopic study of tissues) at the University of Kharkov. Resolving to produce some original work in the biologic field, Metchnikoff submitted a paper to a Moscow naturalist journal about some microscopic animals named infusoria. The article was accepted. Upon further study, young Metchnikoff found that his conclusions had been wrong, and his elation turned to terror. Luckily his desperate attempt to quash the article before its publication was successful, and he was both relieved and chastened. However, impetuosity remained a lifelong characteristic.

Since the biologic course at Kharkov University was not of the quality Elie desired, he traveled to the University of Würzburg, where he intended to study under a celebrated zoologist. When he arrived, however, he learned that classes would not start for six more weeks, and after several disagreeable incidents involving landlords and Russian students studying in Germany, he returned home. He resumed his studies at the University of Kharkov, completing his course in two years instead of the customary four. He also became interested in Charles Darwin's *On the Origin of Species*. He felt that if he could prove that the laws of evolution applied to certain previously unclassified lower species, this find would further affirm Darwin's theory. He began to study these species, which had characteristics of both plant and animal. In 1864 at age nineteen, in order to better define them, he voyaged to a small island, Heligoland, in the North Sea near Germany. About this time he met Ferdinand Cohn who had been of so much help to Robert Koch. Cohn admired both the brilliance and enthusiasm of Metchnikoff and advised him to work under Rudolf Leuckart at Giessen, Germany.

Leuckart was happy to have Metchnikoff study in his laboratory, and Elie worked on nematodes (roundworms). Leuckart went on vacation, but Metchnikoff stayed on in the laboratory, working steadily on the life cycle of a particular species of roundworm. One day he made a startling discovery. He was studying a hermaphroditic worm, which had both male and female sexual organs and was presumed to be sterile. However, this worm gave birth to a worm that reproduced in the usual fashion. That such a thing could happen was previously completely unknown. When Metchnikoff showed the evidence to Leuckart, the latter was unconvinced at first but with further observation realized that his student was correct. Leuckart was extremely annoyed when he realized that in his absence an important discovery had been made by a student. He promptly ordered a tired Metchnikoff to take a vacation, promising that the results of the new discovery would be published in a joint memoir. Later in Heidelberg, Metchnikoff picked up the *Göttingen News* and read the article describing the discovery. Leuckart had claimed the credit for himself, alluding to Metchnikoff only in a brief sentence. Metchnikoff later learned that this was not unusual behavior for Professor Leuckart. Other investigators told him that Leuckart always claimed credit for others' work. Thus far, publishing had proved disillusioning for the young investigator.

As Metchnikoff studied the lower forms of life, he became very interested in the way they developed before birth. This was the study of embryology, the science that shows the stages through which the fertilized egg passes as it matures until it is ready for birth and an existence independent from its mother. In higher forms—humans, for example—a fertilized egg divides into two cells, which in turn divide forming four cells, and so on. Soon the early embryo is a solid mass of cells called a morula, which evolves into a hollow blastocept. This embryo continues to undergo changes in form that lead to its maturation.

Basically three concentric layers of cells are involved in this process—the outer ectoderm, which forms the skin and nervous system; the inner entoderm, whose cells form the digestive system; and the middle mesoderm, whose cells develop into the blood, muscular system, and the skeleton. In the human the entoderm infolds to form a digestive tract into which food enters through the mouth, is digested, and is pushed along by muscular contractions called peristalsis, ending up as waste excreted by the rectum. Metchnikoff found that the embryological development of lower forms was similar to that of humans. The three basic cell layers are present in invertebrates (lower forms without a backbone) just as they are present in higher forms of life.

Metchnikoff noticed one very unusual difference, however. In some lower animals the entoderm formed a hollow digestive tube, but there were other species such as sponges in which no cavity was formed. However, in all of the lower forms, the cells of the mesoderm had a primitive digestive ability. While the entoderm cells were the primary digestive cells, the mesoderm cells that had the ability to wander *also* had the ability to digest foreign matter. The one-celled amoeba must do its own digestion; it actually engulfs a food particle and absorbs it, but Metchnikoff understandably was fascinated to see the same process in more complex species. A tiny fact clicked in his active brain, was photographed, and stored. At a later date this fact would be retrieved and would form the basis of one of the most exciting concepts in nature. It would initiate the phagocyte theory proving that living things are not helpless against microscopic invaders. These living species, happily including the human breed, can mobilize their own armies of defense. All of this work would come later.

Metchnikoff divided the years beginning with 1867 between travel-study and teaching. He was appointed to the faculty of the University of Odessa, but a dispute with the head of the department made Metchnikoff so uncomfortable that he moved to St. Petersburg, where he was appointed professor of zoology. Between teaching periods, he traveled to Messina (Sicily), Naples, and Moscow before returning to St. Petersburg.

Metchnikoff's kind heart led him naturally into his first marriage. He developed a sore throat and was nursed by a sickly young woman who was a friend of the family. He recovered, but his feeling of obligation remained. He decided to marry the young woman, Ludmilla Fédorovitch, despite the protestations of his mother. Although she had not met Ludmilla, she felt that her son might find a happier marriage. Metchnikoff's letters concerning his fiancée were not the type to fill a mother's heart with joy concerning her prospective daughter-in-law:

You are mistaken in thinking that I did not like Ludmilla Fédorovitch at first. I was not in love with her but we were good friends, and whilst I did not consider her as my feminine ideal, I was sure of her absolutely honest, loyal, and kindly disposition. . . . She is not bad-looking, but that is all. She has fine hair; her complexion is not pretty. She has faults which must seem graver to me than to you, but what is to be done? Fortunately she herself sees them. The greatest of her faults is a too great placidity, a lack of vivacity and initiative; she adapts herself too easily to her surroundings.

He married Ludmilla, who was so weak from tuberculosis at the time of

A portrait of Dr. Elie Metchnikoff. *Musée Pasteur, Paris.*

the wedding that she had to be carried to the church in a chair. Her health improved for a while, but she became ill again, and Metchnikoff had her taken to Madeira. This beautiful island was so filled with invalids that Metchnikoff thought of it as "a flower-decked grave." He returned to his teaching studies, leaving Ludmilla in Madeira. In January 1873, he was notified that his wife was worse and told to come at once. He left Russia immediately and remained with his wife until April of that year when she died.

Metchnikoff was despondent over his sad loss, his worsening eyesight, his terrible financial situation, and his pessimism about a future career. He decided to end his life and swallowed a vial of morphine, which overdose made him nauseated and which he promptly vomited up. He realized that the time for him to die had not arrived.

Within a few months he had returned to his scientific studies. Somehow the pessimism that had characterized the first part of his life began to yield to a more optimistic viewpoint. His scientific observations had something to do with the change in his philosophy. So did his second marriage.

Metchnikoff was once again teaching at the University of Odessa. He found it hard to concentrate on preparing his lectures because the family upstairs with its eight children was so noisy. Finally Metchnikoff decided to complain and climbed the flight of stairs separating him from his tormentors. The father of the family promised that the stamping on the floor would stop. Then when Metchnikoff saw one of the children, Olga, he immediately became infatuated with her. To his delight he learned that she, too, was interested in natural science, so he offered to tutor her. Romance quickly ensued, and in February 1875 Metchnikoff took himself a very young bride. Before the ceremony Olga's brothers and sisters took her for a sleigh ride, realizing that in a few hours she no longer could play as a child. Her wedding gown was the first long dress she had ever worn. (Their exact age difference was never revealed. In her biography of her husband, Olga states nothing more specific than that she was a child bride.)

The marriage was the best thing that happened to Metchnikoff and also to Olga. Their interests were similar and their temperaments complementary. Olga loved her Elie for his irascibility as well as for his warmth. Communication between them was total in an era when husbands often were despotic. Their domestic life was completely happy, but life in Russia was beginning to be difficult for intellectuals. The assassination of Czar Alexander in 1881 resulted in progressively repressive measures. The lack of freedom would later force the Metchnikoffs to leave their native land and become expatriates in France, in which country they would find the love and freedom for which they had been searching.

The phagocyte theory was actually born in Messina, Sicily, in early 1883. Metchnikoff had never forgotten the way the mobile mesodermal cells of lower species could digest foreign material. One day while his family was at a circus, he described the moment of revelation:

I remained alone with my microscope, observing the life in the mobile cells of a transparent star-fish larva, when a new thought suddenly flashed across my brain. It struck me that similar cells might serve in the defense of the organism against intruders. Feeling that there was in this something of surpassing interest, I felt so excited that I began striding up and down the room and even went to the seashore in order to collect my thoughts.

I said to myself that, if my supposition was true, a splinter introduced into the body of a star-fish larva, devoid of blood vessels or of a nervous system, should soon be surrounded by mobile cells as is to be observed in a man who runs a splinter into his finger. This was no sooner said than done.

There was a small garden to our dwelling in which we had a few days previously organized a "Christmas tree" for the children on a little tangerine tree; I fetched from it a few rose thorns and introduced them at once under the skin of some beautiful star-fish larvae as transparent as water.

I was too excited to sleep that night in the expectation of the result of my experiment, and very early the next morning I ascertained that it had fully succeeded.

That experiment formed the basis of the phagocyte theory, to the development of which I devoted the next twenty-five years of my life.

Metchnikoff at once grasped the broader concept. The microbes that had just been discovered to be the cause of certain diseases were like the thorns, foreign invaders. As did the starfish, humans, too, could fight back against these killers. He began to experiment to see if his theory would hold up when higher animals were infected.

The great Rudolph Virchow happened to be visiting Messina at the time. Metchnikoff showed the experiments to the famous pathologist. Metchnikoff, contrary to what had happened to Robert Koch, received tremendous encouragement from Virchow. He pointed out that Metchnikoff's correct theory ran counter to prevailing thought, which was that inflammation was harmful. Actually, an area of infection was red, Virchow declared, because it had become, according to Metchnikoff's experiments, a bloody battleground. Metchnikoff's phagocytes, which their discoverer first called "eating cells," had reached an infected area in great numbers. They did not represent, as the world thought, a way of spreading infection, but were rather a sign of healthy defense. Virchow advised Metchnikoff that there was no doubt that his work would in time be recognized but suggested that he proceed prudently because his theory was so revolutionary. Metchnikoff always remained grateful for Virchow's support.

Another visiting scientist, Kleinenberg, was equally encouraging, but unlike Virchow, he advised Metchnikoff to press his viewpoint and publish. Accordingly, Metchnikoff went to Vienna where Karl Claus, the professor of zoology, requested Metchnikoff to submit his theory for publication in the journal that Claus edited. The article appeared in 1883, and the word *phagocyte* was used for the first time. It was a combination of Greek words meaning "devouring cells."

With the birth of the phagocyte theory, Metchnikoff became a happier man. Somehow his fundamental discovery satisfied a philosophic need. The human body was not merely a mass of protoplasm helplessly awaiting any attack from the outside; rather it was a versatile machine that could mobilize its own army and fight its enemies.

In 1887 the situation in Russia had so deteriorated that the Metchnikoffs decided to leave that country permanently. In Paris Louis Pasteur immediately offered Metchnikoff space in his institute. Before accepting, Metchnikoff decided to visit other centers. After he visited Robert Koch's laboratory in Berlin, he was convinced that the Pasteur Institute was the place for him. In Berlin he was treated coldly by Koch and his associates, who were completely hostile to the concept of phagocytosis. The Metchnikoffs hurried back to Paris and the Pasteur Institute. Finally they had found a home. Everybody, from Pasteur to the youngest assistant at the institute, loved Metchnikoff. It was as if he had been there all his life. He was at once involved as a researcher, a teacher, and a warm friend to the others in the "house," as its members called the institute.

Metchnikoff learned much more about phagocytosis as he continued to study the process. He found that it was not only the white blood corpuscles that could engulf microbes but also certain other cells that were not regular members of the blood army. These other cells were like wandering musketeers coming from a great distance to the battle, attracted to the site of the infection by a chemical stimulus. He also found that all of these phagocytes could pass through the blood vessel walls (a process called diapedesis) and head straight for the bacteria in the tissues.

Metchnikoff was for years able to withstand the attacks of his enemies without losing his composure. He had learned, as everyone must, that there is no such thing as unanimity. No matter how rational, how good, or how proven an idea is, there will always be plenty of skeptics around to denounce it. However, Metchnikoff's theory received a body blow in December 1890 when in Koch's laboratory, Behring and Kitasato announced that the blood serum of animals previously inoculated with tetanus (lockjaw) germs had protective ability. Since this serum was cell free, it was reasoned by the German school that this was the primary way the body defended itself against disease and that the phagocytes played little, if any, role.

Metchnikoff, hair and beard unkempt and pockets bulging with scientific papers, worked furiously at the Pasteur Institute to try and prove that this serum actually was augmented by phagocytes. In this hypothesis he was wrong, but in his argument that phagocytosis and antitoxin protection were related, he was entirely correct. Today we know that both mechanisms, phagocytosis as well as antibodies—the noncellular substances in the blood discovered by Behring and Kitasato—are both important factors in body defense against infection and other disease. Years later, in Amsterdam, Metchnikoff described his studies on phagocytosis to an international congress:

There occurs between these two elements—the microbes which are strangers to us, and the white blood cells which are a part of our body—a veritable struggle for existence. The microbes produce poisons which hinder the activity of the white blood cells and often kill them, as they also kill other elements of our body such as red cells and nerve cells. But it is only in the minority of cases that the white cells lose the battle. Much more often, it is they who bring the victory and eat and destroy inside their own bodies, the pathogenic microbes. It is precisely thanks to this property that the white cells have been given the name of phagocytes, that is to say, "devouring cells."

It all depended on the situation. The earlier surgeons who said that pus was laudable were correct in that pus is comprised of white blood cells that have died fighting microbes. Lord Lister was right in saying that pus is not laudable in wound infections because surgeons can prevent wounds from getting infected in the first place. Metchnikoff certainly agreed with Lister but proved that if infection had *already* occurred, it is good that the body has the ability to fight it, and pus is only a manifestation of this struggle.

In 1908 Metchnikoff because of his

phagocytosis studies received with Paul Ehrlich the Nobel Prize in Stockholm for their independent work in immunity. After the ceremony the Metchnikoffs visited Russia, where they were warmly received by Count and Countess Leo Tolstoy. When the great writer discussed his philosophy of life with Metchnikoff, he was delighted that their views were essentially identical.

Metchnikoff's last years were happy ones, although the symptoms of heart disease, first experienced several years earlier, became more severe. He was cheered, however, by a wonderful celebration of his seventieth birthday at the Pasteur Institute. Emile Roux, the eminent bacteriologist and director of the institute, gave a very touching tribute on that occasion. Among other things, he said:

> Your erudition is so vast and so accurate that it is made use of by the whole house. How many times have I not availed myself of it? One never fears to take advantage of it, for no scientific question ever finds you indifferent. Your ardour warms the indolent and gives confidence to the skeptical. . . . More even than your science, your kindness attracts; who amongst us has not experienced it? I have had a touching proof of it when, many times, you have nursed me as if I were your own child. You are so happy doing good that you even feel gratitude towards those whom you serve. . . .

When he became sicker, Metchnikoff was moved into Louis Pasteur's apartment at the institute. He had always honestly discussed his feelings with his wife. Now he asked her to write his biography after his death. He wanted the world to know him, and he omitted nothing about himself, even if it reflected badly on him. He told Olga repeatedly that he had no fear of death and was prepared for it. His calmness in the midst of several heart seizures showed that his words were not merely bravado.

His wife's hands in his own, Metchnikoff died on July 16, 1916, at the age of seventy-one. He was cremated, and his ashes rest in the library at the Pasteur Institute. His ideas remain intact. He showed us that we are not helpless in the presence of disease. Our bodies can and do fight back fiercely and usually successfully.

At the end of her husband's biography, Olga wrote a tribute to him; the last part goes beyond Metchnikoff and has universal meaning:

> But his beautiful, ardent soul, his audacious and fertile ideas, all that rich inner life which had developed into a harmonious and puissant symphony, all *that* cannot be dead, cannot disappear! The ideas, the influence we give to life must persist, must live; they are the sacred flame which we hand on to others and are eternal.

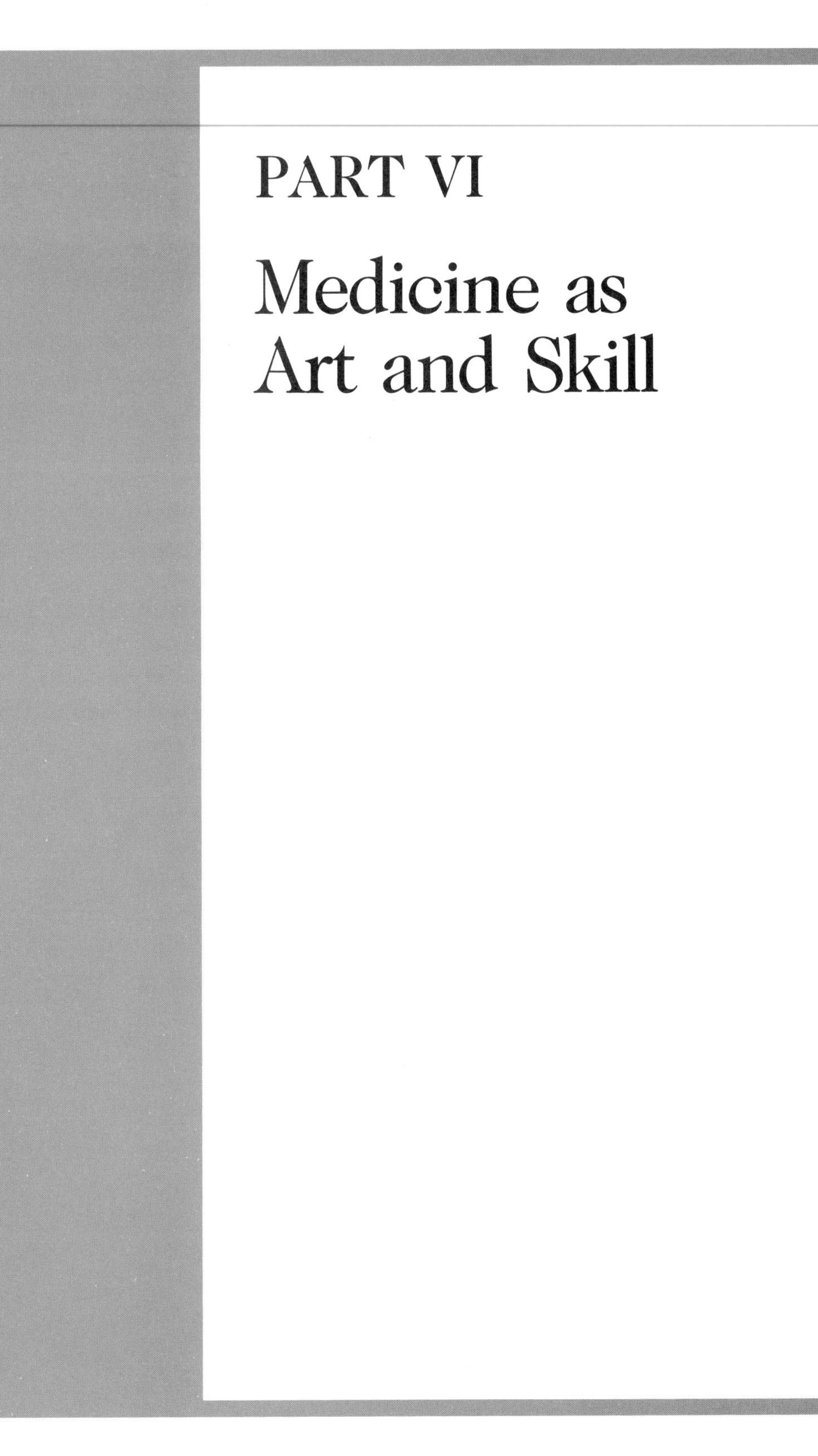

PART VI

Medicine as Art and Skill

Elizabeth Blackwell

1821–1910 First woman to receive a medical degree from an accredited medical college

There were women physicians in ancient times, during the Middle Ages and the Renaissance, and even as late as during Napoléon's reign. In modern times, however, beginning with the early nineteenth century, there were midwives but no women doctors. Women were simply not accepted into medical schools. One woman, Elizabeth Blackwell, a determined and courageous pioneer, changed all that. Because she stuck doggedly to her profession despite appalling abuse and repeated rejection, she greatly influenced the practice of medicine today. We are fortunate that women physicians now constitute a significant proportion of the profession and that their skill and compassion enrich all phases of medicine—practice, teaching, and research.

Elizabeth Blackwell was born on February 3, 1821, in Bristol, England. She came from a large and interesting family. Her father, Samuel, ran a sugar refinery while his wife, Hannah Lane, supervised the large household. Besides the new baby, Elizabeth, there were two older daughters, Anna and Marian. Then there were four of Samuel's sisters who lived with them. Aunt Barbara, the oldest, was a stern disciplinarian who carried around a black book. If the children transgressed in Aunt Bar's eyes, their behavior was noted in the black book, and punishment soon followed. Apparently, Hannah Blackwell was willing to delegate discipline to her forceful sister-in-law. Following Elizabeth's birth five other children were born: Samuel Charles, Henry,

Emily (who was to follow her older sister into the medical profession), Ellen, and John. A ninth child, George Washington (called Washy) was born in America.

Samuel and Hannah had met when they were both teaching Sunday school. Samuel was a dynamo. Not only was he a successful merchant, he was a lay preacher and a dedicated abolitionist. Above all and most important for his daughters, he believed strongly in equal education for women and put his beliefs into action. Latin, mathematics, philosophy, and astronomy were added to the customary study (for young women of that era) of French, embroidery, music, painting, penmanship, and drawing. Later he introduced them to the classical writings of Goethe, Schiller, Carlyle, and the like. Samuel and Hannah Blackwell belonged to the Independent church, a sect whose simplicity and teachings of equality resembled most closely the Quaker faith.

Everything was proceeding happily for the Blackwell family until labor riots began in Bristol. The justified anger of the workingmen exploded! They were poorly paid, worked long hours, and were denied the right to vote. For three days they set fires, looted, and killed to emphasize their desperation. When Samuel Blackwell's refinery was burned to the ground, he decided he had had enough of England. He made the difficult decision to emigrate to America. In the summer of 1832 the family, accompanied by governess Eliza Major, boarded the steamer *Cosmo* and set sail for New York. (The fares for fifteen passengers, plus two servants who stowed away because they wanted to remain with the family, must have put a dent in Samuel's pocketbook.)

The family arrived in October after a seven-and-a-half-week voyage to find a cholera epidemic raging in New York. Eleven-year-old Elizabeth was too fascinated by the new sights and smells of what looked to her like a Dutch village to worry about disease. The family settled for a time in Greenwich Village in lower Manhattan. For outings they visited what were then the villages of Yorkville (the present streets in the East Eighties of New York City) and Harlem farther north. Samuel, who once more entered the sugar refinery business, became a close friend of the abolitionist leader William Lloyd Garrison. Garrison visited the Blackwells frequently. His publication, *The Liberator*, was avidly read by Elizabeth.

Two years later, in 1834, the family moved to Jersey City, but they were not destined to remain long in the spacious Jersey City home; the great national depression of 1837 affected Samuel's sugar business, and he sold the refinery. He was down on his luck and almost broke, but the family pitched in. Anna and Marian took teaching jobs, and the boys quit the private New York school they had been attending. Still Samuel felt he would fare better elsewhere, and he decided to move the family once again. In 1838 they traveled west to Cincinnati, Ohio. (Anna and Marian remained at their teaching jobs in Vermont and New York, respectively.)

Shortly after their arrival Samuel bought a house and leased a sugar refinery, but his usual enthusiasm was gone. He was an ill man, suffering from some vague liver ailment. In early August of 1838 he died at the age of forty-eight. The total family assets were twenty-five dollars, and there were many debts owed for funeral expenses and medical bills. But this unusual family wasted no time on self-pity. They organized a financial recovery. Anna and Marian came to Cincinnati, and everyone helped again. Elizabeth, understanding that education was an important part of the fine legacy her father had left his children, proposed that they start a boarding school for boys ages six through ten. She believed in the progressive education theory of Horace Mann, who had recently returned from Germany with innovative ideas, and she was influenced as well by the way teaching was conducted in the East at Rutgers Female Institute.

The school was a success. Elizabeth's sisters relied on her to maintain order if the boys became boisterous. There was something about Elizabeth's demeanor that demanded respect; it was a quality she exhibited throughout her long lifetime. In appearance she was of less than average height, slight and wiry, her eyes gray-blue in color, and her hair straight, light, and parted in the middle. She was described as plain but did little to make herself attractive, usually wearing somber clothes.

When the boys, who had begun work immediately after their father's death, began to bring in a comfortable income, Elizabeth decided to travel to Kentucky to open a girls' school. Now twenty-three, she reached Henderson, Kentucky, via a trip on the Ohio River and found conditions depressing. The school was satisfactory, but she disliked seeing slaves at work and was outspoken about her disapproval of slavery. This attitude undoubtedly made her unpopular, and she returned to Cincinnati. The family had moved to a pretty suburb called Walnut Hills. There they became acquainted with an abolitionist minister, Lyman Beecher, president of the Lane Theological Seminary. His daughter, Harriet Beecher Stowe, the future author of the classic *Uncle Tom's*

Cabin, was married to one of the seminary professors. She noticed the intellect of the Blackwell girls and invited them to join the Semi-Colon Club, which met weekly to hold fascinating readings and discussions.

It was a fateful visit to a dying woman that gave Elizabeth Blackwell the impetus to study medicine. The woman, Mary Donaldson, noting Elizabeth's intelligence and compassion, suggested a medical career. When Elizabeth discussed this idea with Harriet Beecher Stowe, she was disappointed to hear that her friend thought the idea completely unworkable. But Elizabeth was not a person who ever gave up. With her brother Henry's enthusiastic encouragement, she decided to try for a medical career.

A diary entry at this time showed her state of mind.

At this very time when the medical career was suggested to me I was experiencing an unusually strong struggle between attraction towards a highly educated man with whom I had been intimately thrown, and the distinct perception that his views were too narrow and rigid to allow of any close and ennobling companionship.

I grew indignant with myself, at a struggle that weakened me, and resolved to take a step that I hoped might cut the knot I could not untie, and so recover full mental freedom. I finally made up my mind to medical study. . . .

Firmly resolved not to be distracted by any interest, romantic or otherwise, Elizabeth talked to friends and physicians about her plan to go to medical school. Most of them discouraged her, but the Reverend John Dickson, who had once practiced medicine, needed a music teacher for his parsonage school in Asheville, North Carolina. Reverend Dickson offered to give Elizabeth some medical instruction while she earned money for medical school by teaching music.

Samuel and Henry Blackwell drove their sister in a bumpy coach to her new destination. The first night at the Dicksons, looking out the window, Elizabeth felt disturbed and prayed. Then she seemed to undergo a mystical experience. Much later she described it:

Then suddenly an answer came—a brilliant light of hope and peace instantly filled my soul. At once, I know not how, the terror fled away, my joy came back; a deep conviction came to me that my life was accepted, that I should be helped and guided. A peace as to the rightness of my course settled down upon my mind that was never afterwards destroyed. During the years that followed I suffered many and bitter sorrows; but I have never since been able to doubt that, imperfect and full of shortcomings as my life has been, it has nevertheless been providentially ordered in its main outlines, and has been used in the divine evolution of the race.

Elizabeth's life with Reverend Dickson and his wife was pleasant, but at the end of the year she followed their suggestion that she move to Charleston, where Reverend Dickson's brother, Dr. Samuel H. Dickson, could give her more complete medical instruction. Dr. Dickson was generous with his time and also secured for her a job, again as a music teacher, at a fashionable school enabling her to earn additional money. At Dr. Dickson's suggestion she studied Greek and made rapid progress in that classical language.

Now it was time for Elizabeth to attempt to do what no other woman had previously done—obtain admission to an accredited medical college and graduate from it. In May 1847 she traveled to Philadelphia, the city housing the finest medical schools, which included the University of Pennsylvania and Jefferson Medical College. Every attempt at admission was thwarted. It was even suggested by a distinguished physician, Dr. Joseph Warrington, that Elizabeth disguise herself as a man and go to Paris to study medicine. She would not consider doing such a thing. She applied to *twenty-nine* medical schools and finally in October 1847 was admitted to Geneva College (now Hobart) in New York State. Classes had been under way for three weeks, and she hurried north to her great adventure.

Elizabeth Blackwell didn't know the circumstances of her acceptance. Dr. Warrington had written to urge that Geneva College admit Elizabeth. Not wanting to offend this prominent doctor, the faculty decided on what they thought was an unbeatable ploy. They would ask the students to decide on this unprecedented request. Undoubtedly the students would angrily vote it down, and then the faculty could blame the students for Miss Blackwell's rejection. But the students, mostly as a joke, voted to accept Elizabeth, and the faculty could do nothing but comply.

Accordingly Elizabeth began her life in Geneva, a town at the northwest corner of Lake Seneca near the Canadian border. Initially she was treated rudely by the other guests at the rooming house where she stayed, was looked at as some kind of freak by the town residents, and was the victim of a few jibes from her medical school classmates, 129 in number. But her dignity coupled with her intelligence soon won the admiration of her classmates. In time, the townspeople, although never friendly, took in stride Elizabeth's pursuit of this male profession.

After she had completed the first

term, she returned to Philadelphia and worked at Blockley Almshouse, the oldest hospital in the United States. A combination hospital and poorhouse, Blockley served as her first training ground in clinical medicine. She was assigned to the women's syphilitic department, an experience that resulted in her lifelong fight to prevent venereal disease. Actually she was one of the first advocates of *prevention* of all disease, through sanitation and other measures. Her dedication to prevention today would be considered thoroughly modern.

On January 23, 1849, Elizabeth graduated from Geneva at the top of her class. Henry Blackwell wrote home about his sister's graduation:

> He [Dr. Lee, the dean] pronounced her the leader of her class; stated that she had passed through a thorough course in every department, slighting none; that she had profited to the very utmost by all the advantages of the institution, and by her ladylike and dignified deportment had proved that the strongest intellect and nerve, and the most untiring perseverance were compatible with the softest attributes of feminine delicacy and grace, to all which the students manifested, by decided attempts at applause, their entire concurrence.

(Henry Blackwell married Lucy Stone, an active participant in the women's suffrage movement. In later years their daughter, Alice Stone Blackwell, also involved in the suffrage movement, was a great comfort to Elizabeth.)

Sadly Elizabeth Blackwell was unable to receive any postgraduate training in the United States. She traveled to Paris, stopping off first in London. In Paris the physicians she spoke to regarded her as a midwife and suggested she enter La Maternité, the largest maternity hospital in the world. She swallowed her pride and entered the gloomy hospital in the role of a student midwife. She was housed in a dormitory with sixteen other students. It soon became evident to students and teachers alike that Elizabeth was a font of knowledge, and eventually she was consulted for any medical or maternity problem that arose. She was appalled when an epidemic of puerperal fever struck the wards. She told an intern, Dr. Hippolyte Blot, of the way Dr. Semmelweis in Vienna had prevented this fatal disease. (Elizabeth was attracted to Blot, but once more she refused to allow romance to interfere with her career; they remained good friends.)

On November 4, 1849, Elizabeth accidentally squirted some infected fluid into her eye, and as a result she lost the sight in her left eye. She had hoped to become a surgeon, but this tragic accident made it impossible for her to

Dr. Elizabeth Blackwell, first woman doctor and founder of the New York Infirmary. *New York Infirmary—Beekman Downtown Hospital.*

pursue this specialty. She learned as much as she could at La Maternité and then traveled to England, where her reception was entirely different from that in France.

The famed physician James Paget invited her to become a graduate student at St. Bartholomew's Hospital. There she attended lectures and made ward rounds. Among the lifelong friends she made in England were Lady Noel Byron, widow of the poet, and Florence Nightingale, the founder of modern nursing.

In July 1851 Elizabeth Blackwell returned to New York and began a medical practice at 44 University Place. Her landlady refused to allow her to put up a sign, but she approached Horace Greeley, the editor of the prestigious newspaper the *Tribune*. He consented to print the item she had prepared:

> Miss Elizabeth Blackwell, M.D., has returned to this city from a two years' residence abroad, which she spent at the hospital of La Maternité in Paris, and at St. Bartholomew's Hospital in London. She has opened an office at Number 44, University Place, and is prepared to practice in every department of her profession.

From the moment that item appeared, Elizabeth never lacked for patients. But when she asked to work in one of the city's clinics, its director refused her services. "Found your own!" he told her. Probably much to his displeasure she later followed his orders.

Elizabeth's sister Emily had graduated from Western Reserve, had gone to Europe to study surgery, and was now back trained as a surgeon. In May 1857 the Blackwell sisters, aided by a doctor, Marie Zakrzewska, who had come from Berlin to study medicine in America, founded the New York Infirmary for Women and Children at 64 Bleecker Street. Eight months later training of nurses was instituted in the infirmary. During the Civil War Elizabeth was active in the United States Sanitary Commission and the Women's Central Relief Association, both founded to improve the medical care of wounded soldiers by recruiting qualified women for nursing training. After the war a fifteen-year struggle to found a women's medical college in the infirmary was rewarded by its official opening in November 1868.

The Blackwell sisters also founded the first chair of hygiene, and Elizabeth became its professor. She enjoyed teaching the skills of disease prevention, with emphasis on sanitation. Surprisingly, however, as late as 1898, Elizabeth Blackwell would not accept the findings of Pasteur on rabies nor the work of Koch on cholera. She thought that the results of Semmelweis

The first women medical students at Bellevue Hospital, about 1888. *T. Anthony Caruso.*

proved the "value of research carried on by the use of the comparative method, with absolutely no resort to experiment." She was against any experiments using animals.

The later years of Elizabeth Blackwell's life were spent in England. She maintained her interest in hygiene while practicing in London. Tired of living alone, she had adopted a seven-year-old Irish orphan, Katherine Barry. The adoption proved a blessing for both of them, and Kitty became a loving companion, always referring to Elizabeth as "Doctor." (Later Elizabeth willed her beautiful home in Hastings, England, to Kitty. During the final fifteen years of her life, Kitty returned to the United States and lived with Elizabeth's niece, Alice Stone Blackwell.)

Elizabeth Blackwell died in her sleep on May 31, 1910, at her home, Rock House, in Hastings. She was buried at a favorite place in Scotland, Kilmun on Holy Loch in Argyllshire.

A memorial service was held at the New York Academy of Medicine on January 25, 1911. The words of Dr. William Welch, one of the famous "big four" (Welch, Kelly, Osler, and Halstead) of Johns Hopkins University summarized her place in medical history.

The lives and work of Dr. Elizabeth and Dr. Emily Blackwell have been of great historical significance—how great we hardly realize today to the full extent. The entrance of women into the profession of medicine is an event of importance—not only to the medical profession, but to humanity and to society, and it will always have a place in human history. And whenever the history of women in medicine is written it will begin with the name of Dr. Elizabeth Blackwell, and the year made memorable will be the year 1849, when she received her degree of Doctor of Medicine. Elizabeth was not only the pioneer but, with her sister, also the leader for over fifty years in this very important movement.

Albert Schweitzer

1875–1965 French theologian, musician, missionary physician

One of the most complex, gifted, and humane men was born on January 14, 1875. Albert Schweitzer was born in Alsace, the borderland area between Germany and France. During his ninety years of life, he became a noted theologian, philosopher, musician, and fighter for peace. He also became a physician who established and ran the first African hospital in the jungles of French Equatorial Africa. Probably his fame today rests largely on his work at that hospital in Lambaréné, now located in the independent country of Gabon. Several years ago a European journal polled distinguished scholars, asking them to rank Western civilization's geniuses. Schweitzer was rated third; only Leonardo da Vinci and Goethe were rated higher.

Born in the small town of Kayserberg, Albert Schweitzer spent his boyhood in the village of Günsbach. His father was a Protestant minister.

As a boy he accompanied a friend to shoot birds with slingshots. As they waited for the birds to appear, a church bell announcing Lent rang. It seemed to young Albert to sound a divine warning: "Thou shalt not kill." He purposely startled the birds by waving his arms, insuring their escape, and ran home. "This early influence upon me of the commandment not to kill or to torture other creatures," Schweitzer later wrote, "is the great experience of my childhood and youth." It grew into the central theme of his life—reverence for all created things, living and nonliving.

He was always independent, even

when young. He would argue with his elders if he thought them wrong, something almost unheard of in Prussian Germany. At age ten he was sent to Mülhausen to live with a schoolmaster uncle. Albert studied hard, preparing for careers in both music and the church. He had begun playing the piano at five and also studied the organ. At age nine he substituted for an ill organist at his father's church. Both his grandfather and his father were not only pastors but were interested in organs and organ building. Albert followed their path, becoming expert in playing and repairing organs.

During studies for his confirmation, young Albert questioned some biblical writings, a challenge that annoyed the pastor who was instructing him. His early belief was that the preachings of Jesus were straightforward and pure but had been needlessly complicated by dogma. He persisted in this belief all his life. His religious beliefs paralleled those of the famed Jesuit scholar and scientist Pierre Teilhard de Chardin.

Schweitzer entered the University of Strasbourg in October 1893 to study for a doctorate in theology. He was drafted in the middle of his studies and, during his army period, became interested in philosophy. Eventually he received his Ph.D. in that subject, studying both at the Sorbonne and at the University of Berlin. He returned to Strasbourg, where he received his doctorate in philosophy and theology. (While studying theology, he was given the post of preacher in one of the Strasbourg churches; many of those in the congregation later became supporters of the Schweitzer Hospital.)

Schweitzer joined the Strasbourg faculty in 1902 and a year later was appointed permanent principal of one of the theological colleges. In 1906 his great theological work, *The Quest of the Historical Jesus,* was published. He was already famous by age thirty.

The seed idea for Schweitzer's medical career was planted in 1904, when one evening he picked up a magazine and read an article titled: "The Needs of the Congo Mission." Written by the president of the Paris Missionary Society, it told of the suffering and disease in French Equatorial Africa. From this moment Schweitzer's life goals were charted; he wanted to follow Jesus' teachings, and he felt that action rather than preaching was the way to achieve them. He wanted to help relieve the suffering he had just read about; the best way would be to serve as a doctor at that African mission.

His decision to study medicine stunned not only the Strasbourg theologians but his family and friends as well. How could he cast aside his brilliant achievements in several fields to embark on a new career? Only a young woman, Helene Bresslau, supported his decision. The daughter of the distinguished professor of history who was one of Schweitzer's teachers at the University of Strasbourg, Helene over the course of a ten-year friendship fell in love with Albert Schweitzer. (During that decade, Schweitzer had frequently visited her home to discuss philosophy with her father and her.) When she understood that Schweitzer was determined to go to Africa, she knew that she had to accompany him. She studied nursing, understanding that he would need an assistant. She would have to sacrifice much, but she realized that life without Albert Schweitzer would be intolerable.

He maintained his theological post while attending medical school but was relieved of most of his administrative duties. The medical school course was long and difficult. First he studied anatomy, chemistry, and other basic sciences. After passing an exam, he continued on to the clinical studies—medicine, gynecology, bacteriology, pathology, and pharmacology. His cousin, writer Jean-Paul Sartre, was born in 1906 and always felt close to Schweitzer, calling him Uncle Albert. Schweitzer graduated in 1910, passed the state medical examination in October 1911, and went to Paris to study tropical disease in the spring of 1912. (He paid for expenses involved in all his studies by giving organ concerts. Schweitzer is still considered by classical musicians to be the foremost authority on Bach. Both his extensive writings on Bach and his magnificent recordings of Bach's music, even though performed before the advent of stereo, account for this preeminence.)

On June 18, 1912, Schweitzer married Helene Bresslau. He decided that he needed more knowledge about tropical medicine and studied in Berlin, completing his specialty of tropical medicine in 1913. Now he was ready for Africa.

He asked to set up a hospital under the sponsorship of the Paris Missionary Society, but to his amazement he was turned down. Despite the fact that there was no physician within a thousand miles of the mission at Lambaréné, the society decided that Schweitzer's religious views were too untraditional; the fame he had already achieved hurt rather than helped him. Finally, when he promised not to preach but to serve only in the capacity of physician at no cost to them, the society relented and gave him permission to go.

In the meantime Schweitzer had to ring doorbells to raise money. "The tone of my reception became markedly different when it came out that I was there not as a visitor, but as a beggar," Schweitzer recalled. "Still, the kindness which I experienced on some of these rounds outweighed a hundredfold the humiliations which I had to put up with. . . ."

Schweitzer purchased seventy packing cases filled with medical equipment and supplies. After overseeing their loading on the train, he and Helene traveled on the Easter weekend of 1913 to the seaport of Pauillac. There they boarded a small steamer, *Europe*, and began their life's voyage.

The seas were high, making for a rough trip. During the voyage Schweitzer learned much about the area he would settle, some from experienced European colonials but most from African natives on deck. They told him forcefully that he must wear a helmet at all times during the day because the African sun was deceptive; even on cloudy days, sunstroke resulted from uncovered heads.

The Schweitzers touched Africa for the first time when the ship stopped at Dakar, then headed southward along the lush areas known as the Pepper Coast, the Ivory Coast, the Gold Coast, and the Slave Coast (today comprising the nations of Sierra Leone, Guinea, Ghana, Nigeria, Cameroon, and Gabon).

When they reached Port Gentil at the mouth of the huge Ogowe River, they transferred to a smaller riverboat, which went inland on the Ogowe, a river that roughly parallels the equator. Schweitzer felt overwhelmed by the lush, dense foliage and then noted two monkey tails. "Now the owners of the tails are visible. We are really in Africa." And Africa would be his home for over half a century.

The boat stopped at native villages, and after a few days it stopped at Lambaréné, actually a two-mile-long island in the middle of the river. (The mission itself was located on the hills adjoining one of the riverbanks two miles upstream from the island at a place known as Andende, but Schweitzer's hospital always is described as being located at Lambaréné.) The Schweitzers now transferred once more, this time into native canoes hollowed out of tree trunks. Soon they viewed the white houses of the mission on the slope of the hills they were approaching. They were met by a welcoming party of Africans and mission personnel. That evening the children gave a musical program in honor of the doctor's arrival, which had been eagerly awaited.

Schweitzer was shown the plans for his hospital—the supplies to build it hadn't yet arrived—but he was appalled. The site decided on was at the top of a hill. Patients arriving in litters from the river, as well as supplies, would have to be carried up the hill. Schweitzer showed mission officials how impractical their plans were and finally after a few weeks obtained permission to build the hospital at the foot of the hill near the landing.

The first night Dr. Schweitzer talked to the assembled crowd of natives, many of whom had come from great distances. He spoke in French—a language the Africans who had attended mission schools knew—explaining that his medical supplies hadn't yet arrived. A doctor without his medicine, he told them, was like a fetishman (medicine man) without his charms. He would need three weeks. As the crowd dispersed and the pirogues (canoes) began to carry home those who had come from afar, the Schweitzers could hear drums spreading the news. The drums called him Oganga, the fetishman who was powerless until the next boat arrived with his charms.

The morning after the supplies arrived, sick and injured Africans were waiting at dawn, having arrived during the night. Schweitzer began treating them on the veranda of his house, assisted by Helene. A torrential downpour convinced him, however, that patients would have to be treated in an abandoned chicken coop, the only available structure that didn't leak, until the hospital was built. On August 15, 1913, a patient arrived who was in agony from a strangulated hernia. (This condition, for some reason common among the natives, results in part of the intestine being trapped and its blood supply cut off; death results without emergency surgery.) Dr. Schweitzer knew he had no choice but to operate in the primitive chicken-coop operating room, and he did so successfully. (He declared: "Pain is a more terrible lord of mankind than even death itself.")

The need for prompt construction of a proper hospital was clear. Aside from cases requiring surgery, Schweitzer was faced with serious tropical diseases. Malaria and sleeping sickness were the worst, but dysentery, leprosy, and tropical skin diseases also were abundant. Moreover, the people working in lumber camps frequently were bitten by dangerous animals and snakes.

Supplies finally did arrive—lumber, corrugated iron, and raffia leaves tightly woven into tiles for the roof—and construction began. By January 1914 Schweitzer realized that he would need to alter his original plans. He needed an isolation room for patients with infectious disease, more space to allow forty patient beds instead of the sixteen first planned and used, and more rooms for the attendants. He realized then that the responsibility for constant planning, maintenance, building, and the like would be added to his duties of taking care of the medical problems; he accepted this hard physical, mental, and emotional work without complaint.

Assisted by a native named Joseph, Schweitzer learned much. Joseph advised against treating patients who had been given up as hopeless by the witch doctors, feeling that failures by Schweitzer would ruin the doctor's reputation. But Schweitzer insisted on treating all, and gradually the natives understood that his medicine was more powerful than that of the witch doctors. Schweitzer initially was amazed when the babies of mothers he had just delivered were immediately painted white, and sometimes even the mother herself; Schweitzer asked if they wanted to become white, a thought that induced howls of laughter. The paint was to ward off evil spirits, he was told. White was a dreaded color.

Schweitzer kept records of patients in a ledger and also gave each departing patient a numbered tag to wear around the neck in case he or she needed to return to the hospital. The tags were valued as fetishes against evil spirits tamed by the doctor, and not one was ever lost.

Schweitzer always valued the customs of the Africans, respected their culture, and never attempted to convert them. (Once when a missionary was telling the natives that to become good Christians they must abandon the joys of polygamy, Schweitzer tapped the man on the shoulder and in a whisper asked: "My brother, what makes you so sure that to have more than one wife would be a joy?")

Initially there were two tribes in the area, the Galoas and the Pahouins, although after World War I members of several more tribes drifted to Lambaréné. Schweitzer never forgot that his mission was to relieve their suffering, using science they did not possess. He treated not only natives but also the European missionaries and their families. Once he was asked by the natives the main differences between Europe and Africa. He replied that there were three. First, there were large forest fires in Europe, while in Africa, even during the dry season, moisture prevented fires. Second, in Europe people rowed for pleasure; this practice amazed the natives, whose rowing was for survival and not for pleasure. Third, the natives paid for a wife, and since this dowry was needed, boy babies were not wanted. They found it hard to believe that European men didn't buy their wives.

When World War I broke out, the Schweitzers, Germans in this French

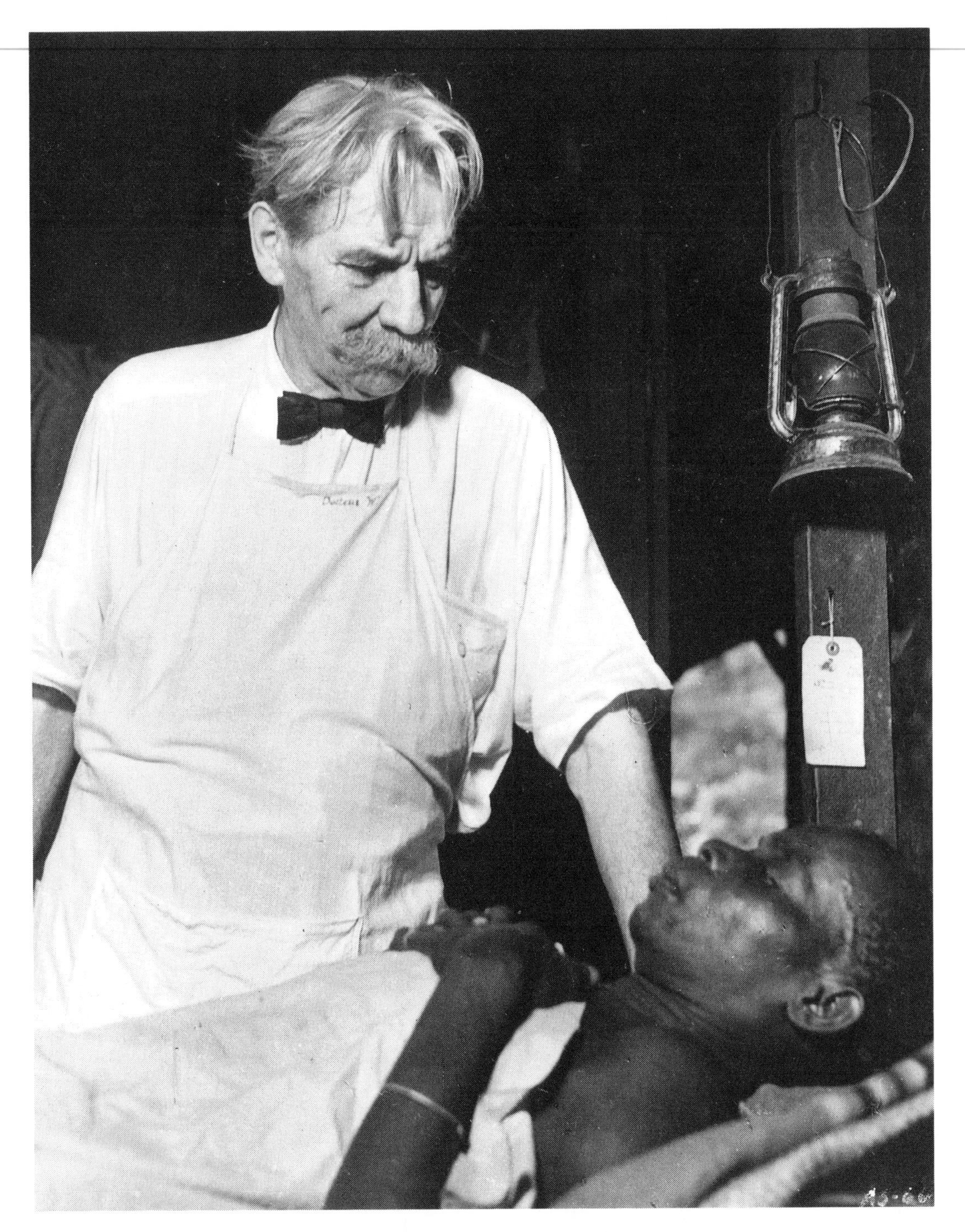

Dr. Schweitzer with a patient in Lambaréné. *Hill and Anderson.*

Dr. Albert Schweitzer with his daughter, Rhena, in Germany in 1923.

colony, were regarded as prisoners of war and were deported to Europe. As they were about to leave, the father superior of the Catholic mission insisted on saying good-bye, pushing aside officials who tried to stop him. "You shall not leave the country," he told them, "without my thanking you for all the good you have done it."

The Schweitzers were interned in France in prison camps. At St.-Remy they were placed in a chilly monastery, which disturbed Schweitzer because it all seemed so familiar to him. He felt he was losing his mind until he remembered a Vincent van Gogh painting he had seen; the monastery, painted by van Gogh, once had served as a mental institution where van Gogh had spent four terrible months before his suicide. After the war Schweitzer went into a serious depression. He learned that his mother had accidentally been trampled to death by German cavalry, but it was really the devastation and savagery of the war as a whole that caused his breakdown. He was helped by the Swiss analyst, Freud disciple Dr. Oscar Pfister, but was helped even more by being invited to lecture at the universities of Uppsala in Sweden and Oxford and Cambridge in England. Several of his books were published. The birth of their daughter, Rhena, on January 14, 1919 (his own birthday), gave Helene and him much joy.

His mental health restored, Schweitzer returned to Lambaréné in April 1924. Helene's health did not permit her to endure the tropical conditions, but she unselfishly convinced her husband to continue with his work in Africa. The hospital was in shambles when he arrived but was rebuilt, and the first registered nurse along with a physician arrived to help him. They were joined in early 1925 by a second physician.

Later a site for a new hospital was agreed on, and Schweitzer decided as well to cut loose from the constraints of the Paris Missionary Society. This break involved fund-raising and much work, but as Schweitzer's fame increased, so did donations. By 1927 the Schweitzer-Bresslau Hospital was completed.

Schweitzer made trips to Europe to see his family, but Africa remained his home. Visitors began to come from all over the world, and more staff arrived to help with the hospital's increasing load. War clouds gathered again as Hitler gained power and began to conquer Europe. Schweitzer forcefully decried Nazi brutality and vowed never to set foot in Germany while Nazism existed. Finally World War II began. Both Charles de Gaulle of the Free French fighting the Vichy puppet regime and Winston Churchill in England promised an end to colonial rule in Africa. Helene returned to Lambaréné in 1941, which was fortunate because many of the staff had had to return to Europe. The hospital was saved that same year when a gift of American supplies arrived just in time.

After the war ended Schweitzer repeatedly spoke out against the proliferation of nuclear weapons. On October 30, 1953, he was awarded the Nobel Peace Prize, the highest among many honors bestowed on him. He was heartened by the signing of the 1962–1963 Geneva nuclear test-ban treaty.

Sorrow began to haunt him as the years passed. Helene died in Switzerland in May 1957 after being ill for several years. He missed the many friends he had lost, but he continued to be active at Lambaréné, serving now as administrator rather than taking care of patients. The hospital that evolved after World War II was actually a third hospital; it was modernized, since funds were now available, and finally it was staffed by an excellent team of physicians and surgeons. Dr. Paul Dudley White, the eminent Harvard cardiologist, declared Schweitzer's work remarkable and said that the hospital's "record over the years is outstanding."

Dr. Albert Schweitzer, though saddened by his losses, enjoyed his four grandchildren and continued to hear from friends like Albert Einstein.

He was over ninety when he died quietly on the evening of September 4, 1965. At the burial service, the vice president (and future president) of the Republic of Gabon gave a eulogy on behalf of the nation that the kind doctor had served so faithfully.

Rudolph Virchow

1821–1902 German pathologist; identifier of the basic unit of life, the cell

At the time Rudolph Virchow was born in Pomerania on October 13, 1821, nobody really knew why people became sick. There were all sorts of theories advocated by numerous schools of medical thought, almost all of them entirely wrong; what Virchow accomplished, among so many other diverse achievements, was to identify the basic unit of life, the cell, and to show that diseases cause changes in the structure and function of these cells. Essentially he proved that the study of disease begins with the study of anatomical and functional changes in the body wrought by that disease.

Virchow's birthplace was in northeast Prussia. That powerful state, whose capital was Berlin, was eventually incorporated into the nation of Germany. In time Otto von Bismarck, the autocratic prime minister of Prussia who had much to do with the formation of the German nation, was to find a formidable enemy in Virchow, whose social consciousness angered Bismarck.

Virchow, the son of a farmer, was a brilliant student, as well as a hard worker. (When he later taught medicine, he performed a four-hour autopsy for his students every Monday morning of his life!) Although he finished at the top of his class, it probably was the influence of an uncle in the military that secured his entrance into the prestigious Friedrich-Wilhems Institut, a medical school designed to produce Prussian military physicians. But while Virchow was militant and always ready to attack fellow scientists when he thought they were wrong, he certainly didn't intend to have a military career, nor did he, although he served with distinction in the Franco-Prussian War of 1870.

Virchow's father wanted him to become a practicing physician and to confine himself to studies at the institute. But young Rudolph had many other interests and angered his father. In self-defense, Virchow began one of his letters home with:

My dear Father,

You state that I am an egoist; that is possible. But you accuse me of having an overweening opinion of myself; that is far from being true. Genuine knowledge is conscious of its ignorance; how much and how painfully do I feel the gaps in my knowledge. It is for this reason that I do not stand still in any branch of science.

Virchow received his M.D. degree in 1842 and entered house staff training at Berlin's Charité Hospital. Soon he was teaching and doing research; as Dr. Sherwin Nuland points out in his scholarly book *Doctors*, before three years had passed since graduation, young Virchow had made two of the three major discoveries for which he is known: the discovery of leukemia in 1845 and the discovery of the way blood clots in the living body. Clots can form within blood vessels (thrombosis), and sometimes parts of these clots break off and travel to block narrower locations in the blood vessel (embolism), thus greatly or entirely cutting off blood flow. Besides describing the processes, he coined the terms *thrombosis* and *embolism*.

Virchow also had his first scientific fight during these years when he attacked a theory of disease propounded by the great Karl von Rokitansky of Vienna. Eventually Rokitansky recognized the error of his theory that a blood disorder was responsible for all disease and admitted that Virchow was correct.

Virchow's reputation was established in 1846 when he was appointed interim prosector. A prosector performs dissections for anatomical demonstrations; these usually are postmortem (after-death) dissections, also called autopsies. This was an important position, and Virchow took the place of a former teacher of his, Frorieps, whose assistant he had become only a few months after finishing medical school. He wrote to his parents the results of achieving fame so early in life:

At a ball, dancing with a young woman, my partner asked, "Have I correctly understood that you are Doctor Virchow?" As I answered, "Yes," she asked again, "V-i-r-c-h-o-w?" Greatly astonished, I again answered affirmatively. Thereupon she said, "Oh then it is certainly your

A portrait of Dr. Rudolph Virchow. *Photosearch, Inc.*

father who gives the lectures of pathological anatomy."

In 1847 Virchow and an associate published the first volume of an anatomical, physiological, and clinical medicine journal that exists to this time; today, instead of its long original name, the journal is entitled *Virchow's Archive.* In the initial issue Virchow stated his idea of what scientific medicine was, an idea that differed considerably from the then current medical thinking.

Virchow was equally concerned with public health and recognized that hazardous environmental conditions could cause disease. He was responsible for many public health improvements. In Berlin, particularly, he designed sewage systems and garbage disposal plans and made certain that its citizens had a clean water supply.

Virchow's interest in public health started early. In 1848 there was an outbreak of typhus in Upper Silesia. The government of the Prussian ruler, Frederick William IV, was pressured by the press to do something about the epidemic. As a result, a commission was formed with Virchow serving as its medical officer. He remained in Silesia for three weeks, and on his return to Berlin, he wrote a report that strongly criticized the government for policies that "kept the peasants of Silesia in a state of moral degradation, personal filth, and indolence." In time he became Europe's leading advocate for social fairness, pointing out the relationship between many diseases and the rotten system of public health that existed. "Physicians are the natural attorneys of the poor," he wrote.

Shortly after Virchow's return from Silesia, the revolutions of 1848 broke out in several countries of Europe. Germany was no exception, and as in other nations, barricades, much like those of the French Revolution, were raised by liberal thinkers in the streets of major cities. The forces of democracy didn't triumph for long, but while they did, Virchow made forceful speeches to large audiences. As a result, he was elected to the new Prussian Diet, but his jibes against the government cost him his medical position, and he was ordered to resign from the Charité. Actually the authorities unknowingly did him a favor. Because his reputation was so great, a specially created chair of pathology was created for him at the University of Würzburg in Bavaria.

Virchow remained in this beautiful and tranquil college town from 1849 through 1856, and there he produced his most important scientific studies. But before leaving for Würzburg, he became engaged to Rose Mayer, the seventeen-year-old daughter of a friend. His marriage proved to be a happy one and produced three sons and three daughters.

While he was at Würzberg, Virchow began his great work on the study of cells. Logical searches for cures depend greatly on the examination of organs, tissues, and cells. (Organs are parts of the body that do particular jobs. The eye is the organ of vision, the ear is the organ of hearing, and so forth.) Organs are made up of tissues, collections of similar cells that work together to perform particular functions. Tissues, in turn, are composed of cells. A cell is the basic unit of life, so small that it can be seen only with a microscope. It is protected by an outer covering called a cell membrane, which fits around it like the skin of an apple. Inside is the cell substance itself, called cytoplasm. Somewhere close to the middle of the cell is the nucleus, or core, which controls the life of the cell. In the nucleus are the chromosomes. Chromosomes contain the genes. The genes carry the "plans"—the inherited characteristics—for how the body will develop.

The first scientist to point out that body changes result in disease was Giovanni Battista Morgagni (1682–1771).

Next, in France, M. F. Xavier Bichat (1771–1802) described tissues, which he called membranes. He declared that the seat of disease lay in these membranes but did not realize that tissues are comprised of cells.

Theodor Schwann in 1839 reported that tissues were comprised of cells, but he did not realize that new cells were the "babies" of parent cells.

Virchow, during his years at Würzburg, became increasingly convinced that cell division was the fundamental process of growth and of life itself. As early as 1852 he was propounding this theory, and in 1855 he stated the famous dictum: *Omnis cellula e cellula* ("Every cell comes from a previously existing cell").

Every time we wash our hands, we destroy thousands of skin cells. But we don't have to worry. The cells of our body continue to divide and make millions of ancestral cells.

The liberal views of Virchow never changed. In 1856, as chairman of the finance committee of the House of Deputies, he thwarted Prime Minister Bismarck's demand for an appropriation to expand the German navy. This action so angered the burly Bismarck, an expert Prussian dueler with sword or pistol, that in a cowardly display he challenged the slight, bearded, bespectacled Virchow to a duel. Virchow thought the possibility of losing one's life in this way ludicrous. He said he would accept the challenge only if it were fought with scalpels. The entire affair was erased by the laughter of Virchow and everyone else except Bismarck.

In that same year the University of Berlin, well aware of Virchow's increasing scientific worth, persuaded him to come back and accept the chair of pathology. At his demand, the university built for him a pathological institute called the Virchow Institute. Upon his triumphant return to Berlin, Virchow delivered a series of lectures, which in 1858 were published as a book titled *Cellular Pathology.* Almost a century later Edward Krumbhaar, an eminent pathologist and historian, wrote:

> This book deserves to be placed with Vesalius' *Fabrica*, Harvey's *De Motu*, and Morgagni's *De Sedibus* . . . as the greatest tetrad of medical books since Hippocrates.

Virchow proclaimed that the only way to advance medicine was through scientific investigation. He declared that the way the cell *acts* (physiology) is more important than how the cell *looks* (pathologic anatomy). As a result of his doctrines, there was rapid advancement in other branches of investigative medicine such as pharmacology, biochemistry, and physiology. Virchow's work made it evident that in a disease like cancer, for example, the patient's first malignant cell was born from a healthy parent cell; this new cancer cell had undergone some change (mutation), and its own children were cancerous. If you want to find out what brings disease to the body, you have to look at the cells. Virchow taught that the body is "a state in which every cell is a citizen. In disease there is a state of civil war, in which the citizens battle because of some outside influence."

(Recently we have learned that it

Dr. Virchow in his study in 1901, the year of his eightieth birthday. *Culver Pictures.*

is not always outside influences that change cells but sometimes genetic defects of the cells themselves, defects that may not show up for years.)

Virchow remained at his post in Berlin for the rest of his life. Primarily he taught, but his interest in related fields including politics never waned. As a member of the city council and later of the Prussian legislature, he brought political as well as scientific pressure to bear on public health problems.

The fields of anthropology and archeology also interested Virchow. He participated in several archeological digs, and in 1878 he accompanied Heinrich Schliemann to Troy, the ancient city discovered by Schliemann a few years earlier.

Virchow also is remembered for his debunking of a dangerous German national myth: that racial purity derived from their mythical ancestors. In 1876 he began a survey of millions of German schoolchildren, and his final results were published in the *Archive of Pathology* in 1886. He found that fewer than a third of the children had the blue eyes, height, and blond hair of their mythical Teutonic ancestors. Hitler, born three years after the completion of the study, eventually tried his best to besmirch Virchow's memory. While Hitler murdered millions of innocent victims, he never could erase the world's awareness of Virchow's contributions to science.

During all of his life, Virchow worked at a hectic pace. Even so, it is almost impossible to realize how much he accomplished during that long lifetime. His eightieth birthday was the occasion for a great international tribute attended by notables from all over the world. He spoke for two hours, without notes, describing the development of medicine.

On January 4, 1902, Virchow jumped off an electric streetcar, fell, and fractured a hip. Later in the year, he reinjured the hip, but this time there were cardiac complications as well. He died on September 5. When thinking about Virchow, we always remember his role in bringing the study of the cell to the forefront; humanity can be grateful to all those ancestors whose cells eventually produced Rudolph Virchow.

Walter Bradford Cannon

1871–1945 American physiologist and teacher

In one of those strange coincidences, the small town of Prairie du Chien, Wisconsin, figured in the lives of two famous physiologists who did extensive experiments on the gastrointestinal tract. The first man was a frontier American army surgeon, William Beaumont, who in the 1820s nursed to health a Canadian hunter whose stomach had a permanent hole in it as a result of an accidental gunshot wound. Later in Prairie du Chien, Beaumont was able to directly observe various changes in the stomach of the often reluctant experimental subject, Alexis St. Martin.

The second physiologist associated with Prairie du Chien was Walter Bradford Cannon, born there on October 19, 1871. His father was Colbert Cannon, a brilliant but peculiar man. His mother, Wilma, a kindly but incessant worrier, died of pneumonia when Walter was ten. On her deathbed she called her son to her bedside to give him a final request. "Walter," she said tenderly to her oldest child, "be good to the world." And Walter throughout his life was indeed good to the world—to his students, his colleagues, his experimental animals, his friends, his research, and the public in general. Colbert Cannon remarried a year and a half later, primarily to get a housekeeper and a caretaker for his children, but his new wife, Caroline Mower, was kind to the children, and they became devoted to her.

Colbert Cannon's ancestor, Samuel Carnahan, had migrated from Ireland to Massachusetts in 1718. Somewhere along the line, Carnahan came to be spelled Cannon because that's how the name was pronounced.

Although Colbert Cannon worked for the railroads all of his life, he really wanted to be either a farmer or a doctor, and he read extensively in both areas. (Without any formal training, he set up a medical office in his home, where he inexpertly treated friends, neighbors, and his unfortunate family.) He had spells of depression, and even though he saw that his moods were affecting Walter and his three younger sisters, he was unable to control these unhappy periods.

Colbert Cannon moved the family to St. Paul, Minnesota, where Walter attended elementary and high schools. Colbert believed in work as well as schooling, so he took young Walter out of school at age fourteen and insisted that his son work as an office clerk for two years. Eventually Walter demanded that he be allowed to finish his high school education.

One thing Walter Cannon later recalled with pleasure was that when he was a boy, his father refused to buy ready-made toys. He gave Walter instruction on how to use tools and then allowed him full use of his own carpenter's tool chest. Later Cannon found the expertise he had acquired as a boy valuable in building laboratory apparatus.

Walter's search for knowledge resulted in some family friction. Young Cannon had learned to think for himself, and although his father was a devout churchgoer, Walter read Thomas Huxley and others whose writings convinced him that the strict Calvinist teachings he had been taught were too arbitrary. He stopped going to church. His father was quite angry with Walter at first but eventually understood why his son needed to have intellectual independence.

Partly aided by a scholarship, Cannon entered Harvard in the fall of 1892 and graduated summa cum laude (the highest scholarship honors) in 1896. While still a Harvard undergraduate, he gave a course in introductory zoology to students at nearby Radcliffe College.

In the fall of 1896 he entered Harvard Medical School, the institution that became his home until his death. His physiology professor there was Henry Bowditch, a man who fostered Cannon's research and was encouraging at all times. Bowditch was probably the major influence in Cannon's career.

While still a Harvard medical student, Cannon began research on the swallowing mechanism. The German scientist Wilhelm Roentgen had invented a machine that could look into the inside of a person, and a primitive X-ray machine was available at Harvard. Cannon's first experiments on swallowing were later demonstrated at the annual meeting of the American Physiological Society in 1896. Cannon and his associate showed that during the act of swallowing, the esophagus (gullet) relaxed to allow passage of food. Up to this time it had been thought that the esophagus contracted and pushed the food farther along the alimentary canal. These first medical school experiments led to further and more complicated studies that Cannon pursued during his entire academic life.

Cannon graduated from Harvard Medical School in 1900. Several months before his graduation, he was offered the post of instructor of physiology there.

A year after graduation, he married a Radcliffe student, Cornelia James, a hometown friend from St. Paul. On their honeymoon Cornelia and Walter climbed a dangerous ten-thousand-foot mountain, then called Goat Mountain, which never before had been climbed. After some narrow escapes, they reached the summit. Several years later when the area became Glacier National Park, the mountain was renamed Cannon Mountain in honor of the first persons to climb it; that remains its official name.

The marriage, a happy one, produced a boy, Bradford, and later four girls, who managed, as in all families, to annoy and embarrass their brother from time to time. In a 1982 medical journal article, Bradford Cannon, a plastic surgeon, related highlights of his father's scientific career as well as examples of Walter Bradford Cannon's sense of humor:

> My father had a knack for turning a phrase and also delighted in those of others. For example, my mother was quick to get things done. Her carpentry (ours was a family of carpenters) was atrocious, but it was finished with dispatch and unabashed pride. She looked upon her work and made no bones about expressing that pride. Father commented about her: "With Cornelia it is no sooner done than said."

It is of interest that Bradford Cannon and his wife carried on the tradition of his father in not buying toys for their children. Instead they bought tools, which the children could use for their own development and enjoyment.

In 1906, a bare six years after graduation, Cannon was appointed to succeed his old chief and friend, Henry Bowditch, as chairman of the Department of Physiology at Harvard Medical School. He remained at that post for thirty-six years.

In 1911 Walter Cannon performed important experiments concerning emotional reactions and their effects on the body. He showed that strong emotion increased the amount of sugar in the blood and eventually concluded that the sugar (glucose) released provided the chief source of energy for the great muscular exertion needed during an emergency. He understood that both fear and anger were likely to be followed by actions that require massive muscular exertion. He also showed that when fatigue occurs, adrenaline from the adrenal glands is secreted. Adrenaline raises blood pressure and acts on the liver to release sugar. These effects are responsible for the "second wind" noted by exhausted athletes who suddenly find they have renewed energy. (Adrenals are paired glands located above the kidneys. They control the salt and water balance of the body, produce hormones that control inflammation—cortisone, for example—and secrete adrenaline.)

In a quick moment of insight, Cannon formulated his famous fight-or-flight theory. He suddenly understood that in dangerous situations, changes in the body—rise in sugar, blood pressure, and adrenaline—prepared both humans and animals to either fight or flee impending danger.

Cannon was a great believer in the power of the unconscious mind to work out difficult problems. Frequently he would wake up with the solution to a problem that had seemed impossible to solve at the time he went to sleep for the night.

Cannon noted that amazing feats of strength are demonstrated when fear or anger or both are present. He told the true story of one John Colter, who, along with a companion, was seized by Indians in Montana and stripped naked. His companion resisted and was hacked to death, but the chief made signs for Colter to head across the prairie. When Colter looked back, he saw the younger warriors grabbing their spears, and he knew that he was being released, not to go free, but rather to be chased, caught, and scalped. He started to run even before he heard the war whoops. "Fear and hope lent a supernatural vigor to his limbs," Cannon reported, "and the rapidity of his flight astonished himself." After three miles his strength began to wane, but only one pursuer was still after him. The Indian tried to kill Colter but fell, and Colter grabbed the Indian's spear, killed him, and began to run again, his strength renewed. He told a friend later that after the struggle he felt that he hadn't even run a mile.

Later, in 1927, Cannon put to rest a theory of emotions that had been proposed by Harvard physiologist William James and had never been challenged. James stated that the strong emotions felt in connection with grief, fear, rage, and love really resulted from physiological changes in the viscera (large internal organs such as the stomach,

Dr. Walter B. Cannon. *National Library of Medicine, Bethesda, Maryland.*

intestines, spleen, and so forth). He believed that we feel sorry because we cry, are afraid because we tremble, and so on, and not the reverse.

Cannon's beautiful experiments provided a victory for common sense and an end to James's theory. They clearly showed that visceral perception is much slower than brain perception and could not possibly be the initiating factor of an emotion. Cannon performed experiments with cats, severing all nerve connections between the brain and organs like the heart, lungs, stomach, and bowels—all the visceral organs in which James believed feelings resided. He found that the emotional responses of the animals were *unchanged*. Cannon showed that the brain perception was the first step in the chain of emotional response. Thus, the brain, seemingly forgotten since the days of Hippocrates, assumed its rightful place in the origin of emotions.

Throughout his long tenure at Harvard, Cannon seemed to have time for much more than his beloved research and his beloved family and students. As professor of physiology, he had to make departmental decisions almost daily; as an investigator, he frequently testified against the false and outlandish claims of several New England antivivisection groups; as an authority on so much of his specialty, he had to travel in the United States and abroad giving scientific papers and exchanging views with fellow scientists. Perhaps the most important thing he did for young students was to point out the qualities important for a researcher.

1. An investigator must have a spirit of adventure. Cannon points out:

> Now that geographical boundaries in our own and civilized lands have been determined, the pioneering spirit finds in scientific research enticing vistas for adventure. The twilight zone between what we know and the vast unlimited range of what we do not know presents us with innumerable frontiers. In this zone the opportunities for novel experiences are immensely more abundant than they have ever been in the long explorations on land and sea. If anyone remains for a brief time in an active laboratory of experimental research he is sure soon to be shown phenomena never previously observed. Here again is true pioneering.

2. Fitness to be a researcher. Cannon mentions curiosity, imaginative insight, critical judgment, thorough honesty, a retentive memory, patience, and generosity.

Cannon liked students to learn material as they went along rather than cram at the last minute. He called crammers "long-distance putters" and illustrated this philosophy with a story of a complacent golfer:

[who] teed his ball, looked away to the next green, and declared confidently, "That's good for one long drive and a putt." He swung the driver, tore up a stretch of sod, and managed to move the ball a few feet off the tee. The caddy then stepped forward, handed him the putter, and suggested, "Now for a hell of a putt."

3. Ability to deal with uncomfortable circumstances. Cannon often was forced to defend his laboratory research, on which he commented:

> Within a half a day [after surgery] the animals were up and moving about and took their food as usual the next morning; thereafter, they wandered about the laboratory, rubbing their sides against table legs or coming to be petted, and exhibited no signs of discomfort. Yet in an antivivisection periodical they were described as "wretched animals," which had undergone a "frightful operation" and were subjected to "exquisitely contrived torture," suffering "agonies not to be described."

It is entirely accurate to state that every significant advance in the saving of life—from heart trouble to polio and cancer—is the result of prior research with animals. In every reputable institution, the animals' comfort and freedom from pain always are of primary concern to the investigator.

4. Hunches. Cannon strongly believed that a sudden hunch often led to successful research, although he cautioned that as much as one would like a favorite hunch to prove accurate, if experiments show that the hunch was wrong, it must be promptly discarded.

5. Serendipity. Cannon particularly enjoyed the results of serendipity, the discovery through luck of an important finding that one wasn't looking for originally.

When Joseph von Mehring and Oskar Minkowski were studying digestion, for example, they removed the pancreases from animals and for the first time accidently produced experimental diabetes. A lab assistant noted swarms of flies gathered around the urine of these animals, a fact he mentioned to the investigators. When the urine was analyzed, it was found to be loaded with sugar.

This and many other examples of serendipity prove Pasteur's dictum that "chance favors the prepared mind."

Cannon made scientific contributions in both World War I and World War II. He devised a substitute for blood loss in the treatment of septic shock. He also developed the concept of homeostasis, the effort of the body to maintain a stable environment despite changes in the outside environment; hormones, especially adrenaline, are mostly responsible for homeostasis.

When at age sixty-six Walter Cannon submitted a letter of resignation to Harvard, he was induced to remain for four more years. At age seventy-one he accepted an offer to be visiting professor at the New York University College of Medicine for three months and was very happy to be teaching again. He had always encouraged students to discuss and if necessary to dispute his findings, and he continued this method of teaching until the end of his life. He died in 1945 of a blood disease. A year or so before his death, sensing his decline, he quoted the famous neurologist and poet S. Weir Mitchell:

> I know the night is near at hand.
> The mists lie low on hill and bay,
> The Autumn sheaves are dewless, dry;
> But I have had the day.

Cannon's day had been long and fruitful. His scientific work was impeccable, but an equally valuable heritage was his autobiography, *The Way of an Investigator*. The book is a treasure chest of sound advice for anyone contemplating a career in research.

Charles Richard Drew

1904–1950 American blood researcher; eminent teacher

On June 3, 1904, a baby was born in Washington, D.C., at 1806 E Street, a three-story house across from a large park. In time this new arrival, Charles Richard Drew, would contribute significantly to the world of medicine. The house was located in an area of Washington known as Foggy Bottom, which today is home for the United States State Department. The neighborhood gets its name because of the morning and evening fog that drifts in from the Potomac River. In the early years of this century, the neighborhood was interracial, attractive, and middle class.

Despite the fact that blacks and whites lived side by side in that community, Washington, D.C., was segregated, so that one of the two public swimming pools in the park was for whites only and the other was used only by black children and adults. There were four elementary schools in the neighborhood, also segregated.

Drew's family was Negro. Today they would be called African Americans, but Charlie—he was always called Charlie by family and friends—as an adult always proudly referred to himself as a Negro, since he lived during those years when that word was used. His father, Richard Drew, was a carpet layer who had to drop out of high school so that he could earn money. Richard Drew was a popular and generous man who played the piano and guitar and was active in the Baptist Church.

His wife, Nora, was a Howard University graduate who, from the time of Charlie's birth, devoted her energies entirely to caring for her family. The Drew household grew to four with the births of Elsie, Joseph, and Nora, named for her mother. All of the Drew children were expected to do their best, and each was assigned responsibilities. Among other things, Charlie had to sew his own clothes when they needed repair, never imagining that he would later use this skill in surgery. He also was an enterprising paperboy at twelve; a few months after he started selling papers, he had six boys working for him.

In October 1920 the family moved across the Potomac to Arlington, where the last of the children, Eva, was born in 1921. Charlie went to Dunbar High School in Washington. Although segregated, its high standards and classical system of education had made it one of the finest schools in the United States and an excellent college preparatory school. (He graduated from Dunbar in 1922, the year that the Lincoln Memorial, located close to where he lived, was dedicated.) While at home his parents emphasized the academic side of school life, Charlie concentrated on athletics. He became a four-letter man, winning a scholarship to distinguished Amherst College in Massachusetts.

By the time he arrived at Amherst, the boy Charlie had grown into a handsome young man approximately six feet tall and weighing close to two hundred pounds. Excelling at track and football, in 1925 he received honorable mention as an all-American halfback in the Eastern Division. His Amherst coach, D. O. (Tuss) McLaughry, remarked years after Drew's death that he had been a "great" football player. Fortunately for so many people, Drew chose medicine for a career and surgery as his specialty. (The death in 1920 of his thirteen-year-old sister, Elsie, probably contributed to his decision to study medicine; of all the siblings, she had been closest to him in age, and he had felt deep affection for her.)

He graduated from Amherst in 1926. In order to save money for medical school, he coached athletics and taught biology and chemistry for two years at Morgan College in Baltimore. Using discipline and example, he excelled at both posts, and the football and basketball teams he produced were outstanding.

His first choice for medical school had been Howard, but he was turned down because he lacked two hours of English credits. Angered, he told his brother, Joe: "Someday I'll come back here and run this damned place." Eventually Howard Medical School and its affiliated hospital, Freedman's, did become home for him; there he would train young black men to become superb surgeons. It was McGill University in Montreal that accepted him in its highly rated medical school. Another bonus: Graduate students were allowed to participate in athletics, and Drew became Canadian champion in four track-and-field events. Over ten years after his graduation, he returned to watch a football game at McGill, and when it was announced over the public address system that Charlie Drew was in the stands, the place exploded with cheering. It was Drew the athlete they were yelling for, even though by that time he had achieved fame as a physician.

While Charlie was at Amherst and later at McGill, his father helped him as much as he could. Each week Richard Drew would cash his paycheck and immediately send a money order (colored blue) to his son. Then he would bring the remaining money home to support his wife and other children. Charles always wrote back immediately: "I received the blue. Thank you." Despite this help, along with a loan he received from Amherst classmates and extra money he earned waiting on tables, he was still short. In a letter to himself on New Year's Day 1930, he sounded discouraged.

What a hell of a New Year! As the year entered, I was paying the cashier at the Northeastern Lunch. Ten cents for tea and toast. . . . I never ask favors. That is one of the things I am proud of. Rightly or wrongly proud, I don't know. This I know—that this pride sustains me when otherwise I would sink. . . .

But in the fall he received a wonderful surprise that allowed him to finish medical school without further worry—a one thousand dollar scholarship from the Rosenwald Foundation. In his senior year he was awarded the Williams Prize for academic excellence. Earlier he had been elected to Alpha Omega Alpha, the honorary scholastic fraternity for every medical college, an achievement highly valued by medical students everywhere. During the course of his short lifetime, Charles Drew received medals and other awards too numerous to list, but it was not the awards themselves but the excellent work that prompted them that Drew valued most.

At McGill Drew became friends with a young instructor from England, Dr. John Beattie. It probably was Beatty who stimulated Drew's interest in blood research. Later during World War II, they would play important parts in each other's lives.

In 1933 Drew graduated from McGill with the M.D.C.M. degree (Doctor of Medicine and Master of Chirurgie, or Surgery). He did postgraduate training at Royal Victoria Hospital and Montreal General Hospital, staying on at the latter in 1934–1935 as a resident in medicine.

After the completion of his residency in 1935, two events led Drew to apply for an appointment to the medical faculty of Howard University: He wanted to return home following the death of his father, and he wanted "to help his people." This time Howard accepted him, appointing him to a routine position—instructor in pathology.

Howard University, founded in 1867, and its affiliated hospital, Freedman's, founded five years earlier, had risen from low to high stature primarily because of two factors. Howard's first black president, Mordecai Johnson, and the medical school's first black dean, Numa P. G. Adams, raised the academic standards. At the same time improvements to the facilities were made possible by the generosity of the university's principal financial benefactor, the Rockefeller Foundation.

Adams, a gentle man, had wanted to appoint black men as heads of the departments of medicine and surgery, but vague political considerations led him to choose two white men instead. One of these on loan from Yale was Chief of Surgery Edward Lee Howes, only one year older than Drew. Howes quickly recognized two unusual qualities in the man who would become his first resident and later succeed him as chief of surgery—leadership and skill. Accordingly, in early 1938, he recommended Drew for advanced training; Drew would be awarded one of the first two-year fellowships at Columbia University in New York City, and this would lead to a rare advanced degree.

At Columbia and its affiliated Presbyterian Medical Center (PMC), Chief of Surgery Allen O. Whipple assigned Drew to a laboratory under the direction of Dr. John Scudder. Scudder's interest in fluid balance, blood chemistry, and blood transfusion fitted exactly with Drew's primary research aims, previously fostered at McGill by John Beattie. Halfway through the year, a surgical residency became vacant, and Drew was appointed to fill it. As a result, for the remaining year and a half of the fellowship, Drew had teaching duties added to his research projects.

Since blood figures so prominently in Drew's career, its makeup is important to discuss. Blood is the red fluid that is pumped to all parts of the body by the heart, carrying nourishment and oxygen to the tissues. An average ten-year-old has about four quarts of blood in circulation while an average adult has about six quarts. Blood consists of red cells (erythrocytes) that carry oxygen and white cells (leucocytes) whose primary function is to fight infection. These cells are suspended in a yellowish

Photograph of an oil painting of Dr. Charles Drew completed around 1953. *National Portrait Gallery, Washington, D.C./Art Resource, New York.*

protein-filled liquid called plasma. Plasma accounts for about 60 percent of blood volume and contains, among other proteins and nutrients, fibrinogen, which is important in the clotting process.

A blood transfusion is the giving of one person's blood to another. It can be dangerous unless substances known as blood groups and Rh factors are compatible. The first successful transfusion of blood (between animals only) was performed in 1665 by an English physiologist, Richard Lower. Two years later, in France, Jean Baptiste Denis tried the first transfusion into a human using lamb's blood. The patient died. Transfusions were not safe and rarely successful until 1900, when Karl Landsteiner discovered the first red-cell blood groups, for which discovery he received the Nobel Prize in 1930. By 1902 he had discovered all four major blood groups, A, B, AB, and O; A and B are specific substances; AB blood type contains both A and B substances; O is the type free of any specific substance. Later Landsteiner was co-discoverer of another factor first discovered in rhesus monkeys and named the Rh factor. Each of us has one of the above types of blood and the presence or absence of an Rh factor. Those people with O type blood who are Rh negative can donate blood to anyone since no incompatible substances are present.

Successful storage of blood—at first whole blood from donors—in the United States was begun at Cook County Hospital by Dr. Bernard Fantus. He coined the term *blood bank*, which quickly came into general use. But Drew noted many years later that to the Russians "must go the credit for supplying the early work, most of the fundamental knowledge, and the impetus which has to a large degree been responsible for the widespread creation of the blood and plasma banks. . . ."

Despite all of his duties, Drew managed to find a beautiful, bright, and devoted wife during his stay at Columbia. In the early spring of 1939, he had been invited to take part in the annual clinic at the John A. Andrew Memorial Hospital in Tuskegee, Alabama. He first visited with his family in Arlington and then set out by auto with three other Howard University physicians. (Ironically, a similar trip to the same conference would result in his tragic death in 1950.) When they stopped at Atlanta, Drew was introduced to Minnie Lenore Robbins, a home economics teacher at Spelman College. It was love at first sight for Drew and probably for Lenore as well. On his return from the clinic, he left his companions and took the train to Atlanta. At 1:00 A.M., he went to the dormitory where Lenore resided and woke the matron in charge. He demanded to speak to Lenore who, though surprised, came downstairs to see this insistent young man. She was even more astonished when instead of just talking, he proposed. She finally agreed that if all went well, they would marry in the fall. All did go well, and they were wed on September 23, 1939.

Earlier that month Hitler had invaded Poland, which action was the start of World War II. Scudder and Drew's involvement with blood and its products would greatly aid the Allies in that terrible struggle. Before the war the two men had been involved in studying the preservation of whole blood—mostly work with sodium citrate (the most widely used preservative) and refrigeration; the research on the production of blood plasma came later, close to the time that Drew completed his dissertation "Banked Blood" in April 1940. To allow research on blood and its products to advance more quickly, Presbyterian Hospital opened its own blood bank on August 9, 1939. Excess blood was not wasted but sent over to Karl Landsteiner for his use in research.

In June 1940 Columbia awarded the degree Doctor of Science in Medicine to Drew, who prepared then to return to Howard. This was an advanced degree, a step above the usual M.D. given after graduation from medical school. Drew wanted to train other black surgeons and wrote to a friend:

> . . . in so far as the men who count know, all Negro doctors are just country practitioners, capable of sitting with the poor and the sick of their race but not given to too much intellectual activity and not particularly interested in advancing medicine. This attitude I should like to change.

Drew did return to Howard in June 1940, but a few months later he was given leave to go back to New York to become medical supervisor of a new program, Blood for Britain, proposed at the New York Academy of Medicine by the Blood Transfusion Association. Since he knew as much as anyone in the world about blood preservation and had kept current on all work with plasma, he was the ideal choice to head this program.

The early research with plasma as a substitute for whole blood had been led by Dr. John R. Elliott of North Carolina. He had issued his report on this new method of blood transfusion in September 1936. Plasma was badly needed when, in 1940, Hitler tried to bomb Britain into submission, and battlefield action against Britain was intensified in North Africa.

It was because whole blood could not

be preserved for very long that Dr. Drew concentrated on sending plasma overseas in the Blood-for-Britain program. Eight New York hospitals joined in the program. It was important to avoid processing blood containing the hepatitis virus and other contaminants, and here is where the genius of Drew came into play. He established uniform standards for the collection of blood and for its processing into plasma (by separating the cellular elements from the blood, leaving the plasma). He insisted that, for quality control, all blood collected should be processed in one central laboratory, and he also devised mobile blood collecting units supplied with refrigeration facilities. Now plasma sent to Britain was uniformly sterile. The program continued until Britain had facilities of its own and no longer needed American plasma. It became apparent then that the United States should prepare for its own defense and for plasma collection. The same rigorous standards were applied by the Blood Transfusion Association. (Later dried plasma that could be easily shipped and reconstituted on the battlefield was developed.)

Drew left the national blood program in April 1941 and returned to Howard. He justifiably was angered by the irony of the unscientific and bigoted armed forces policy of accepting blood from white donors only. (To make matters worse, the armed services remained strictly segregated throughout World War II.) But those issues weren't responsible for Drew's return to Howard. His primary reasons were that he had completed his assignment and now he wanted to return to teaching duties.

In April 1941 Drew took the examination for the American Board of Surgery, an exam that consisted of written and oral portions. It was while Drew was taking the oral examination that an incident occurred that became well known among all his colleagues. A distinguished Johns Hopkins professor was questioning Drew about fluid balance in the human body. Drew's answers were so thorough and advanced that the questioner sought help from other examiners. But having done research on the subject while at Presbyterian Medical Center, Drew knew even more than did the auxiliary examiners. Such a situation practically never happens, so it is not surprising that six months later Drew himself was appointed as an examiner for the American Board of Surgery, the first black surgeon to achieve that distinction.

It was only natural, after such an appointment was made, that Drew be promoted, and he was, almost immediately. In October he was named a full professor of surgery at Howard

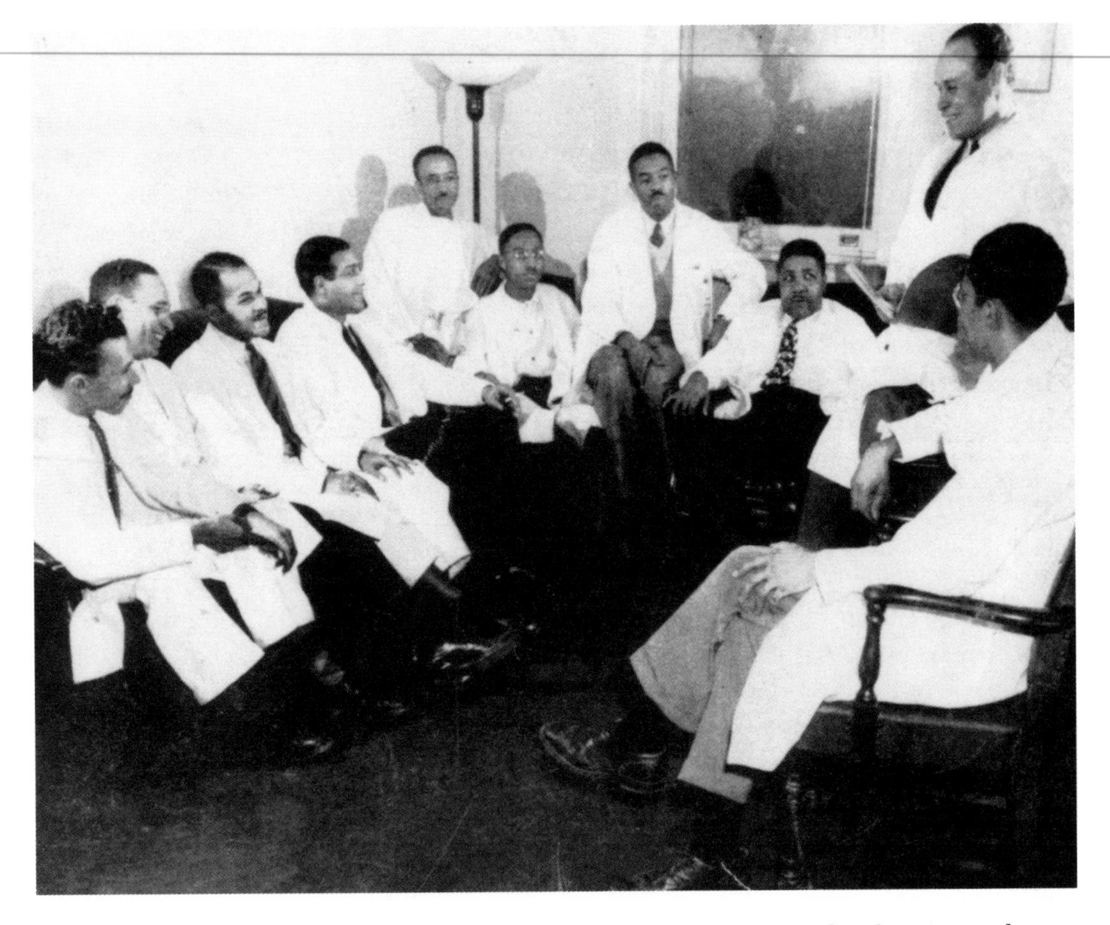

Dr. Charles Drew as chief of surgery at Howard University. He is said to have trained more black surgeons than any other physician. *Ebony,* February 1974.

and chief surgeon at Freedman's. He remained at Howard until his death nine years later. He was unique and had a magical presence. Adhering to his high standards, the young black surgeons he trained passed their specialty exams with high grades. At his insistence they were, in their own words, "sold down the river." What that meant was that whether they liked it or not, he had them placed in high-ranking medical institutions throughout the United States because it was important that their talents be used nationwide. Although gentle with his patients, Drew was strict with medical students and house staff (interns and residents who had already graduated from medical school). Once when an unkempt-appearing student, on being criticized, complained that he had "no time" and offered other excuses, Drew replied:

"Well, *I'll* wash your clothes; *I'll* darn your socks; *I'll* clean your shoes. . . ." That was sufficient to remedy the situation.

Drew fought prejudice wherever he found it and had a long battle with the American Medical Association (AMA), which in those days did not admit blacks, pleading that local southern societies were responsible, not the national AMA. Drew replied ". . . if a small minority of . . . chapters . . . persist in wagging the whole body . . . then it must be considered a body without true strength and purpose. . . ." He had an equally frustrating battle with the American College of Surgeons. Today qualified men and women of all races are accepted in all medical associations. The emphatic protests of men of the stature of Charles Drew certainly contributed to the destruction of such racist barriers. His feelings about overcoming discrimination were perhaps best expressed in a letter he wrote to a Texas schoolteacher who had organized an entire school program to honor Drew's achievements:

So much of our energy is spent in overcoming the constricting environment in which we live that little energy is left for creating new ideas or things. Whenever, however, one breaks out of this rather high-walled prison of the "Negro problem" by virtue of some worthwhile contribution, not only is he himself allowed more freedom, but part of the wall crumbles. And so it should be the aim of every student in science to knock down at least one or two bricks of that wall by virtue of his own accomplishment.

On April 1, 1950, Drew and three colleagues were on their way to teach an annual seminar at Tuskegee, Alabama. At Haw River near Burlington, North Carolina, Drew, who was driving and was exhausted from his operating schedule the previous day, fell asleep. According to Dr. Ford, one of the passengers, Drew initially was half thrown out of the car, and when the car overturned a second time, Drew's body was crushed. Taken by ambulance to the Alamance County General Hospital, he was given emergency treatment for almost three hours to no avail. The doctors at Alamance consulted by telephone with Duke University Medical Center, but after hearing the description of Drew's injuries, Duke concluded that transfer to their facility would be useless. Drew had sustained a broken neck, and the two largest veins in the body, the venae cavae, had been ruptured, completely blocking return blood flow to the heart.

Sadly a myth has persisted that Drew died of neglect—that he was "allowed to bleed to death" outside a whites-only hospital. Dr. Ford, twenty-one years later in 1971, emphasized that "the statement about his bleeding to death because of refusal of treatment is utterly false. . . . I have issued this statement all over the country, but 'nobody' wants to believe the truth about the matter." Even a letter to the hospital from Lenore Drew stating that ". . . there is much comfort derived in knowing that everything was done in his fight for life" failed to erase the myth of inadequate care; it was repeated in *Time* magazine in its March 29, 1968, issue, by the *New York Times* on June 14, 1981, and on a TV documentary in 1990. It is a falsehood that Charles Drew, above all, would have hated.

There is great sadness in the premature death of someone who had saved thousands of lives and who, had he lived the expected many years longer, would have done so much more for mankind. But we can be thankful for the tremendous productivity of those years given to him, for Charles Drew's accomplishments live on and, as is true in all scientific progress, leave a more secure foundation for those doing research in the same field. And so, too, do those traits of character live on in all those he taught and who, in turn, are teaching others indestructible values.

Marie Curie

1867–1934 French chemist; codiscoverer of radium

On November 7, 1867, in Warsaw, Poland, a baby was born into the household of Professor and Mme Sklodovski. This youngest addition to the family had four older siblings: Sophie (Zosia), age six, Joseph, age four, Bronya, age three, and Hela, age one and a half. Baby Marya received the most nicknames of all—Anciupecia, Manyusya, and the one she came to be known by, Manya. In later years when she went to Paris to study, she would register as Marie.

Professor Sklodovski taught physics and mathematics while his beautiful wife ran a boarding school. But with five children to raise, Mme Sklodovski, an accomplished musician, had to give up running the boarding school. As she grew a bit older, Manya noticed that her mother never kissed her but would affectionately caress her hair. The reason for this was that Mme Sklodovski had tuberculosis, and intimate contact with her children was not possible.

Manya was a fine student at an early age. Once when her sister Bronya was having difficulty reading, four-year-old Manya took the book and began to read fluently. Her parents looked so astonished that Manya, who had been taught the alphabet by Bronya and who had an amazing memory, began to cry, feeling that she had done something wrong.

In those years Poland was under the rule of the czar of Russia, and schoolchildren were not taught in their native language but were required to learn from Russian texts. In school Manya, who spoke Russian fluently, was usually called to recite each time a surprise visit by an inspector occurred. She would have to reel off in Russian the names of all the czars who had ruled Russia from Catherine II on. (When inspectors were not around, the teachers would hand out Polish books and teach their students Polish history; Manya thus became proud of her heritage.) Though two years younger than her classmates, Manya spoke German and French as well and excelled at mathematics, history, and literature.

In 1873, when the family returned from summer vacation, Professor Sklodovski was informed that his salary had been severely cut by the tyrant school principal Ivanov. The family was forced to move several times and tried to meet expenses by taking in boys as boarding students of Professor Sklodovski. They were already in severe financial straits—Mme Sklodovski made the shoes the children wore—and then a poor investment worsened their situation.

The children, usually happy despite the poverty, experienced unbelievable sadness when in January 1876 the two older sisters contracted typhus from one of the boarders. Zosia died while Bronya was convalescing. Two years later Mme Sklodovski died from tuberculosis. The loss of her sister and mother caused Manya to become less devout than she had been, although she always remained a Catholic. Later her daughter Eve was to write of Manya:

> She no longer invoked with the same love that God who had unjustly inflicted such terrible blows, who had slain what was gay or fanciful or sweet around her.

By 1882 life had improved for the Sklodovski family. Bronya, now a young lady, had taken charge of the house, watching over not only her family but also the boarders. When she finished high school, she had been awarded a gold medal, as had Joseph before her. Joseph now was at the University of Warsaw studying at the Faculty of Medicine. No women were allowed to enter this "czar's university," which had Russian teachers, and Polish students were forced to be subservient. On graduation from the gymnasium (high school), Manya, too, was awarded the gold medal, and her father decided she should have a year off.

For the first time Manya became lazy, enjoying the luxury of outdoor games, walks in the woods, and hunting for strawberries. With relatives all over Poland, she had many places to visit. She developed an attachment to rural life that never left her.

She shared the dream of most Polish youths that their country would one day be free. She joined with other young people who believed that the best way to reach that goal was to build up a superb intellectual storehouse and to educate the poor, whom the authorities deliberately kept ignorant. She felt that science was the most promising way to achieve the goal of freedom.

Manya's interest in science dated back to a childhood incident. She had been continuously staring at a glass case where her father kept tubes, scales, minerals, and the like. Finally she was satisfied by his two-word explanation—"physics apparatus." They were a harbinger of her future life. She attended a secret "university" where science, sociology, and other subjects were taught to bright Polish students who were expected to pass along to others what they had learned.

At seventeen Manya was ablaze with the spirit of her country. She became a voracious reader of complex fiction and nonfiction, adding immensely to the education her schooling and her father had given her.

Then she worked out an incredibly unselfish plan. She would work as a governess and save money to send to Paris where her sister Bronya would be studying medicine. Bronya tearfully protested, but Manya insisted. She promised that in a few years she would follow her twenty-year-old sister to Paris and medical school.

In 1888, Professor Sklodovski, having secured his pension, found a supplementary source of income directing a reform school. Manya continued to teach as a governess. Bronya insisted that her sister stop sending money and told her father to put away eight of the forty rubles he sent her each month so she could repay Manya. Bronya was doing well in her academic work and had fallen in love with a fellow medical student, Casimir Dluski, whom she would later marry.

In March 1890 Bronya urged Manya to come to Paris and live with her. Both she and her husband were almost ready to practice, and she felt her debt to her younger sister was overdue. But Manya declined. She wanted to stay another year with her lonely father and find a job for her sister Hela. In Warsaw Manya was finally exposed to scientific experimental work. A friend ran a lab that he called a museum to deceive the Russian authorities. Manya found that "even though I learned to my cost that progress in these matters is neither rapid nor easy, I developed my taste for experimental research during these first trials."

Finally, on September 23, 1891, Manya wrote Bronya that she had saved enough money to come to Paris. Not yet twenty-four, she tearfully bade good-bye to her father. Then this beautiful young woman with a high forehead, ash blond hair, and gray eyes began the most important journey of her life.

What struck Manya the most about Paris was freedom, the first freedom she had really enjoyed. People were allowed to speak their native language, and booksellers sold works from all over the world. From the first, she was enchanted by the ambience of the great city. On rue Saint-Jacques in the Latin Quarter she read the poster again and again.

FRENCH REPUBLIC
Faculty of Science—First Quarter
Courses will begin at the
Sorbonne on November 3, 1891.

She registered as Marie Sklodovski, but in 1895 she would become Marie Curie, and soon after that she would be the *celebrated* Marie Curie. She left Drs. Bronya and Casimir Dluski's lodging for her own in the Latin Quarter near the Sorbonne. She lived in a sixth-floor garret on only forty francs a month. She half starved herself as she studied, cooked her own meals, and froze, often forgetting to light her little stove. What little companionship she had was with fellow Polish students.

The brilliance of Marie Sklodovski was obvious to all. She received a master's degree in physics in 1893 and a master's in mathematics the following year. But her finances were almost exhausted when she won an award of six hundred rubles, the Alexandrovitch Scholarship. (Later when she earned money for a technical study, she returned the six hundred rubles to the Alexandrovitch Foundation so some other poor girl could advance her career.)

In 1894 Marie met the brilliant, thirty-five-year-old physicist Pierre Curie. A Polish friend, M. Kovalsky, a professor of physics, thought that Curie would be able to help Marie work out some details she had been unable to solve in the course of completing a research project. This tall, modest (he would refuse almost all decorations offered to him), bearded scientist immediately appealed to Marie, and he was absolutely fascinated by the serious and lovely young Polish woman. Pierre had made significant discoveries in physics and yet was practically unknown in Paris.

A few months after their first meeting, he asked if he might visit her. Her acceptance marked the first of many visits. Marie did not appear to be at all interested in marriage. Finally Pierre induced her to visit his father—a kindly physician—and his mother in Sceaux. The warmth of the Curie household was so similar to that of her own family that Marie immediately felt at ease. Still she turned down Pierre's pro-

Pierre and Marie Curie in 1896. *Roger-Viollet*.

posal, promising only that the two would remain good friends. He went so far as to tell her he would leave France and live in Poland with her. Still she refused. Pierre even brought Bronya to Sceaux. Mme Curie begged her to intercede for Pierre with Marie. Finally Marie realized that she was in love. She wrote her girlhood friend Kazia:

When you receive this letter your Manya will have changed her name. I am about to marry the man I told you about last year in Warsaw. It is a sorrow for me to have to stay forever in Paris, but what am I to do? Fate has made us deeply attached to each other and we cannot endure the idea of separating.

They were married on July 26, 1895, and since both loved bicycling, the summer was marked by relaxing bicycle trips all over France. In the fall Marie passed her examination for a fellowship in secondary education. In September 1897 Pierre's father, old Dr. Curie, was the obstetrician when Marie gave birth to Irène, the first of their two children, both daughters. (Irène with her husband, Frédéric Joliot-Curie, would win the 1935 Nobel Prize in chemistry for synthesis of new radioactive elements.) Pierre's father loved the new baby and became her first teacher and best friend.

The observation that led to the Curies' fame was made by the physicist Henri Becquerel. In 1896 he discovered, while working with *uranium* salts, that at ordinary temperatures invisible rays similar to Roentgen's X rays were emitted and, like them, could penetrate metal and act on a photographic plate. Also, gases such as air struck by these rays could become electrified. This was radioactivity (later named by Marie Curie), which would be of so much value in medical diagnosis and treatment. Marie Curie decided that it was possible that the uranium phenomenon might apply to other substances and that this would be a good subject for her doctoral thesis. Pierre worked with her. They were given only a damp ground-floor storeroom for their laboratory. On February 6, 1898, Marie noted the temperature—six degrees—and added six exclamation points in protest.

Marie Curie felt that these uranium rays emanated from the nucleus of the uranium atom, but it was not until 1905, when Einstein showed that mass could be converted to energy, that the process was understood. Soon, using equipment invented by her husband and his brother Jacques, she found that this type of radiation was not confined to uranium. Compounds of another element, thorium, emitted similar rays. Next she examined all known elements, followed by hundreds of other minerals.

Then came the great surprise! Pitchblende, an ore of uranium, produced much stronger radiation than could be accounted for by uranium. There must be one or more new radioactive elements. Her discovery of radium had begun! In the damp little workroom shed in the rue Lhomond (south of the Pantheon, a short distance from the Sorbonne), beginning in the summer of 1898, Marie and Pierre would collaborate for eight years.

The first discovery was a new element, which Pierre asked his wife to name. She called it polonium, "from the name of the original country of one of us." But there was a much stronger radioactive element than polonium hidden in the pitchblende ore. The Curies and an associate, G. Bémont, announced on December 26, 1898, the discovery of this powerful new element. They named it radium (from the Latin *radius*, meaning "ray.") They worked for four years refining pitchblende ore from the St. Joachimsthal Mine and were helped when the Austrian government gave them a ton of it. They were able to chemically separate polonium from radium. In 1902 Marie succeeded in purifying a small amount of radium and determining its atomic weight—225. One night, as they walked to their shed, Marie asked Pierre not to light the lamps. He had once said that he wished radium to be a beautiful color. Now they noted that it was more than a beautiful color. Radium was luminous, gleaming in the darkened workshop. It was a magical night to remember.

The biblical adage "A prophet is not without honor, save in his own country" certainly proved true for Pierre Curie. Repeatedly he was turned down for appointments. In 1898 the chair of physical chemistry fell vacant, but it was awarded to a less capable man; instead of ten thousand francs per year, Pierre had to manage on five hundred. Marie added to the family income by teaching at a school in nearby Sèvres while her husband taught at an annex of the Sorbonne. In 1902 Pierre failed to receive a deserved appointment to the Academy of Science. When proposed for the Legion of Honor, Pierre wrote: "Please be so kind as to thank the minister and to inform him that I do not feel the slightest need of being decorated, but I am in the greatest need of a laboratory."

Radium, whose chloride salt looked like common kitchen salt, proved to be two million times stronger than uranium. Radium also produced radioactive gases, gave off heat, made an impression on photographic plates, colored its glass containers mauve and violet, and could make diamonds, unlike paste imitations, luminous. It also could make the air or the clothes one wore radioactive. The dangers of this radioactivity were not recognized early enough. Becquerel, carrying some radium around, was the first to notice that his skin became burned. He hurried to tell this effect to the Curies. Pierre purposely placed a tiny amount of radium on his skin and was delighted to see that a lesion appeared. The Curies, understanding radium's potential for good, collaborated with others. Radium was found to cure certain kinds of cancer, particularly those cancers of the tongue, head, and neck. The therapeutic method became known as Curietherapy. As a result, the radium industry was born, and Pierre and Marie were consulted frequently during its beginnings.

A gram, just a pinchful, of radium was one of the most expensive items in the world. In the early years it was worth $150,000. The Curies, had they taken out a patent, could have become multimillionaires, but they never once considered making a profit. Their gift belonged to the world.

On June 25, 1903, Marie took the oral exam at the Sorbonne in front of a group of admirers, including her sister Bronya, her father-in-law, and Pierre. The examiners, some of whom were her early teachers, were delighted to announce her new title of doctor with the special distinction of "very honorable."

At the same time, the Curies were awarded the Davy Medal by the Royal Society, traveling to London to receive the honor. They were now celebrities, and everyone wanted to see these famous parents of radium. On November 14, 1903, they shared the Nobel Prize in physics with Henri Becquerel for the discovery of radioactivity. Now fame really became their enemy. They had always managed to avoid the spotlight, but no escape was possible now. Incredibly, France was always the last to recognize their achievements, and any honors given the Curies in France always followed an award from some foreign country. The Curies' daughter Eve was born on December 6, 1904, and although Marie always was a devoted mother, she never stopped her scientific experimentation.

On a rainy afternoon, April 19, 1906, Pierre was killed instantly when he was run over by a horse-drawn wagon. Marie was devastated. She had lost her beloved husband, her scientific collaborator, and her best friend all in one horrible instant. During all the years of their collaboration, there never had been a question of primary credit for any discovery. Always it was *we* observed this or *we* found that. Marie was bitter that her husband never lived to

Marie Curie with President Warren G. Harding during her tour of the United States in 1921. She is holding a gram of radium presented to her by the president. *Musée Curie, Paris.*

see the many modern radium institutes that were built in several countries.

After Pierre's death Marie was granted his chair of physics at the Sorbonne, the first time a position in French higher education had been given to a woman. Marie, at age thirty-eight, found herself head of her family. Although she never really recovered from Pierre's death, she had flashes of humor. Once she asked a class how they would keep the liquid in a jug hot. After several suggestions she simply smiled and said: "Well, if I were doing it, I should start by putting the lid on."

In 1911 Marie Curie received her second Nobel Prize for her work in isolating pure radium. When World War I broke out, she understood that X-ray equipment would be extremely important in diagnosing battle wounds. She created a radiological car, which she drove from hospital to hospital. Eventually she fitted out twenty motorcars with radiological equipment and established two hundred radiological rooms. Over one million soldiers were X-rayed in one of the Renault radiological cars or in one of the rooms. She herself became a skilled radiologist.

After the war she lectured all over the world. When a drive started by one Mrs. William Meloney produced donations from the women of America to purchase a gram of the precious radium, in 1921 Marie traveled to the United States, where the radium was presented to her by President Warren Harding. Back in France she was elected to the prestigious Academy of Medicine of Paris.

Finally the years of exposure to radium caused Marie Curie's illness and death. She was diagnosed as having grippe and bronchitis. Her daughter Eve sensed that the situation was far more serious than it was believed to be. Mme Curie was moved to a sanitarium, but on July 4, 1934, four months short of her eighty-eighth birthday, she died of leukemia, the white-blood-cell disease that can be the result of those same penetrating radium rays that can cure cancer. She was mourned by family and friends. The scientists at the Radium Institute in Paris sobbed as they stared at the apparatus that looked so forlorn without the presence of its creator. She was buried at Sceaux, home of the Curie family.

Albert Einstein had been a friend and admirer of Marie Sklodovski Curie. He once made an unusual and insightful statement about her: "Marie Curie is, of all celebrated beings, the only one whom fame has not corrupted."

William Osler

1849–1919 American physician; first professor of medicine at Johns Hopkins University; renowned teacher

The dedication in famed neurosurgeon Harvey Cushing's monumental biography *The Life of Sir William Osler* reads as follows:

TO MEDICAL STUDENTS in the hope that something of Osler's spirit may be conveyed to those of a generation that has not known him; and particularly to those in America, lest it be forgotten who it was that made it possible for them to work at the bedside in the wards.

Spirit is the key word in the above dedication. Osler's primary contribution to medicine was not in the laboratory; it was his dedication to the practice of good clinical medicine. He accomplished this through his teaching, through his writings, and through his successful efforts to establish high standards for his profession. His humane personality, combined with a capacity for hard work, allowed him to attain this goal.

William Osler was born on July 12, 1849, at Bond Head, Canada, a small wilderness town north of Toronto, the youngest son in a family of nine. His father was a minister who expected William to follow in his footsteps. The boy briefly considered becoming a clergyman and so attended Trinity College in Toronto. But his interest in natural science decided him on a medical career, and in 1872 he received his medical degree from McGill University in Montreal. The bedside teaching there was excellent and provided an influence for his later work.

In medicine William Osler's primary love remained his teaching on the medical wards, at every hospital he attended. His kindly presence gave reassurance to the patients. He was optimistic and never lost sight of the healing power of hope; his students at the bedside learned from his diagnostic skills and remembered his wise and pithy statements. Teaching at the bedside—that was always Osler's most enjoyable and profitable time.

In those years it was customary for medical school graduates to do postgraduate work abroad. Accordingly Willie (as he was called by his family) stayed two years in Europe, studying in Ireland, England, Scotland, Germany, and Austria. (Older brother Edmund gave him one thousand dollars, which covered all his expenses, including travel, during his time abroad!) An informal young man, Osler was somewhat startled in Germany, where he found the politeness overwhelming. ". . . they bow you in and out and seem in agony until you are seated, while in meeting hats come wholly off."

He was greatly impressed by Rudolph Virchow, from whom he learned much pathology. He also expressed great admiration for Robert Koch who, as a small-town physician, still managed to do brilliant research. During Osler's European stay, he also became proficient in all the other basic sciences—bacteriology, physiology, pharmacology, and so on—which provided an excellent background for his first love, the diagnosis and treatment of disease at the bedside. (Years later he noted that "Minerva Medica" [medicine] never retained its foremost position in any one country for more than a generation or two; for a while Italy was the leading light, then Holland, then England, followed by France, Austria, and Germany. Soon, he correctly guessed, during his overseas years, it would be North America's turn—Canada and the United States.)

Osler read the classics during those years, and that was the start of another great love, the collection of rare and important books, many but by no means all medical. For the rest of his life, he would love to browse in bookstores all over the world.

During his time overseas, Osler became proficient with the microscope, and in June 1873, in London, he made his most important scientific discovery; he provided the first description of blood platelets, the unnucleated third element of blood (which he called *discs*); red and white blood cells are the other two components. Platelets play an essential role in blood clotting.

Osler's reputation was spreading, and he received several offers to teach at his alma mater as soon as his overseas studies were completed. On his return to Canada, he accepted a position at McGill as lecturer in the Institutes of Medicine. His duties were to deliver "four systematic lectures a week for the winter session, from which period dates my ingrained hostility to this type of teaching."

In the manner of Vesalius, he preferred hands-on work to lectures. Soon Osler was appointed professor of medicine, a post he was to hold in four universities: McGill University, 1875–1884; University of Pennsylvania, 1884–1889; Johns Hopkins University, 1889–1905; and Oxford University, 1905 until his death on December 29, 1919.

Shortly after Osler's arrival at McGill, there was a particularly malignant smallpox epidemic. He volunteered to serve for three months on the smallpox ward of Montreal General Hospital. Although he had been vaccinated several times, none of these vaccinations took, and Osler contracted smallpox; luckily he had only a mild case of the disease.

Osler gave courses in physiology and pathology in 1876 but was much concerned over the lack of high standards in the United States, with the notable exception of Harvard under President Charles Eliot.

All his medical life Osler worked successfully to improve the character of medical practice. His ideas were partly expressed in the voluminous letters he wrote almost daily, always signing them W. O. except those to family, which he signed Willie.

Osler's next post as professor of medicine at the University of Pennsylvania in Philadelphia was secured through the efforts of several supporters but nailed down in an interesting way. He was invited to dinner by the esteemed neurologist S. Weir Mitchell and was given cherry pie for dessert, mostly so the Mitchells could observe his table manners. It was a question of what Osler would do about the pits. He reported later that he "had read of the trick before, and disposed of them genteelly in my spoon—and got the Chair."

Although Osler wanted the appointment as professor at the University of Pennsylvania, he had mixed feelings about leaving McGill. His mentor there, Professor Palmer Howard, did not: ". . . the thought of losing you stuns us, and we feel anxious to do all that we can to keep you amongst us. . . ."

But Osler had the capacity of keeping his friends, and all his life he continued to visit frequently and participate in the academic affairs of those institutions where he had formerly taught.

When Osler arrived at the University of Pennsylvania, the students were disappointed in him at first. This swarthy man with drooping mustache and halt-

John Singer Sargent's portrait of the first medical faculty of Johns Hopkins University. Dr. William Osler is second from right. *Johns Hopkins University Medical School.*

ing speech arrived by streetcar instead of by carriage. He was completely unlike his predecessor, whose manner was flamboyant and speech oratorical. But within a few weeks, they worshipped Osler and followed him around in order to catch his every word.

Osler immediately put some of his ideas to work, and soon he had set up a small laboratory so the medical students could start their own research projects. Instead of having the customary general practice to supplement his university salary, Osler limited his outside work to consultations. Thus he was able to spend more time with medical students at the Blockley, the oldest hospital in the United States. Osler also disagreed with the current practice of prescribing many drugs for an illness; he avoided the use of every drug unless he was convinced of its efficacy. An outstanding clinician, he already was regarded as a world expert on malaria, tuberculosis, and typhoid fever. But Osler had another side to him—practical joker—and he frequently wrote hilarious letters, one of which claimed he had seen an identical case to one written up by a pompous physician; this physician proudly showed the letter confirming his absurd findings. Osler had signed the letter with a name he relished—Egerton Yorrick Davis, M.D.—the name of an obscure drunken Canadian physician Osler once had met.

By 1889 almost every institution would have liked to have William Osler on board, but it was the yet-to-be-built Johns Hopkins Hospital that succeeded in getting him. The eminent Dr. John S. Billings came to Osler's rooms in Philadelphia. Osler reported:

> Without sitting down, he asked me abruptly: "Will you take charge of the Medical Department of the Johns Hopkins Hospital?" Without a moment's hesitation I answered: Yes. "See Welch about the details; we are to open very soon. I am very busy today, good morning," and he was off, having been in my room not more than a couple of minutes.

When the hospital opened in 1889 (an 1873 bequest from wealthy merchant Johns Hopkins had provided the funds), it was a unique place, purely because of its organization. The president of Johns Hopkins University noted that "for the first time in an English-speaking country a hospital was organized in units," a chief in charge of each one. Later, when the medical school was built, it, too, was preeminent with its famous "big four" professors: William S. Halsted (surgery); Howard A. Kelly (gynecology and obstetrics); William Osler (medicine); and William H. Welch (pathology).

Osler told his students (who always referred to him as the Chief) that three things were essential for maintaining their education: a library, constant note taking, and a brain-dusting vacation in a different setting every five years. He himself carried a notebook at all times and constantly wrote down items that interested him; despite an amazing memory, he was afraid that otherwise he would forget some gem of information.

Osler devoted most of 1891 to writing his famous textbook, *The Principles and Practice of Medicine*. Work on the proposed new medical school was postponed because the railroad bonds with which the university was endowed had depreciated. The delay gave Osler the opportunity to complete the work, which soon became the most widely used medical textbook (translated into French, German, Chinese, and Spanish) and which he revised every three years. One who read it was an employee of John D. Rockefeller. Fascinated by the straightforward and honest writing, this employee understood the need for a research center in the United States; he convinced his boss, and the result was the founding of the Rockefeller Institute (now Rockefeller University) and later the formation of the broader-based philanthropic Rockefeller Foundation.

During his Philadelphia years, Osler had become friendly with Dr. Samuel W. Gross and his wife. Gross died in 1889, and on May 7, 1892, Osler married his widow, Grace Revere Gross, who was the great-granddaughter of Paul Revere. Their Baltimore house on West Franklin Street remained for fourteen years the gathering place of friends and students. The junior house staff at Johns Hopkins were known as the latch-keyers, since each had been given a key and had free access to the house. Osler, no matter how busy, never minded being interrupted by his friends.

During that same year a woman named Mary Garrett offered to give badly needed funds for the building of the new medical school. She included three conditions, but the most important proviso was that women be admitted on the same basis as men. Accordingly, in the first class of fall 1893, three of the eighteen students were women.

At that time Osler wrote a sharp criticism of Baltimore's poor sanitation practices. He was particularly disturbed by the prevalence of pneumonia, typhoid fever, and tuberculosis. By 1902, when the situation hadn't improved, during a public meeting he shook his finger at the mayor while discussing the incidence of tuberculosis. "This is the whole matter in a nutshell, Mr. Mayor and fellow citizens," Osler reprimanded. "Now what are you going to do about it? Nothing." Dr. Bowditch, present that evening, thought a duel might result but was surprised, later that night, to see the mayor with his arm around Osler. "Osler was nothing if not frank," Bowditch said, "and the curious thing about it is that no one seemed to take offense." (As a result of that meeting, a Maryland Tuberculosis Commission was formed, and finally good public health measures were instituted.)

On December 28, 1895, a son, Edward Revere, was born to the Oslers. (Two years earlier they had lost an infant boy.) Revere, as he was called, was nicknamed Ike after Isaak Walton; as he grew he loved reading Walton's *The Compleat Angler*, and he loved to fish, especially with his father. Revere never liked classic languages nor did he want to become a physician. However, he shared his father's love of books, and this gave Osler much pleasure.

It is almost impossible to imagine a

typical day in Osler's life. The typical day, in fact, would seem to be comprised of a month's worth of the average person's activities. He seemed simultaneously to be teaching; writing textbooks and articles; entertaining along with Grace innumerable friends; traveling by train to conventions, meetings, or to testify before Congress; playing on the floor with small children, who shrieked with delight as he amused them with games he'd invent; traveling by ship abroad to lecture at an international meeting; vacationing (but, because he had become "the doctor's doctor," seeing physicians and other patients in consultation between periods of relaxation); and so on and so on. Despite all this activity, his health remained excellent except that he was subject to respiratory infections. However, he never was out of action for very long.

Osler received one of the greatest of his many honors when he was formally elected to the Royal Society of London. Like Benjamin Franklin, he was one of the few Americans entitled to write FRS (Fellow of the Royal Society) after his name.

He was generous in all matters. He never refused to give money to a beggar on the street, for example, and when head of an examining board, he always urged the junior examiners to be lenient with the medical students. Actually, he had complete faith in his ability to tell which student would become a good doctor by observing students as they worked with patients on the wards. Nor did he believe in unwarranted recognition. While he was at Johns Hopkins, a man named William Pepper came to observe a laboratory Osler had set up. Pepper wanted to set up a similar one at the University of Pennsylvania in honor of his father who had been a professor there. He questioned Osler about possible discoveries in the laboratory:

"Osler, if discoveries are made in such a laboratory as this, does the Director get the credit?" The answer came immediately: "Why, Pepper, no; the worker of course! Suppose we go to lunch."

Probably Osler's advice to students concerning his personal philosophy had at least some influence. Osler told them to work hard during the day and not bother about tomorrow, to follow the golden rule toward patients committed to one's care and toward professional brethren, and to maintain as much as possible an equally even disposition during times of triumph or despair. These precepts, he told them, had helped him immensely.

Osler was always being offered professorships. McGill and Pennsylvania wanted him back, and Harvard and Edinburgh offered him chairs of medicine, but he wanted to take life easier. At fifty-five he was offered, and finally after much soul-searching accepted, the post of the Regius professor of medicine at Oxford University. This was one of five royal professorships founded by King Henry VIII in 1546.

Before Osler left for England, he gave a farewell speech at Johns Hopkins, which got him into trouble. Actually, he was speaking humorously and considering his own age; his remarks weren't meant to be taken seriously but they were. He observed that practically all great achievement in science, art, and literature was accomplished by men forty years old or younger. Then he said: "Whether Anthony Trollope's suggestion of a college and chloroform should be carried out or not I have become a little dubious, as my own time is getting so short."

The following day newspaper headlines screamed: OSLER RECOMMENDS CHLOROFORM AT SIXTY. For a time *to Oslerize* became a verb of outrage, but in a few months the fuss died down. Osler did indeed believe that the greatest achievements were made by younger men and women, but he was certainly joking about euthanasia for those sixty and older. Perhaps he took consolation from one of his epigrams recorded years earlier by a student:

> Believe nothing that you see in the newspapers—they have done more to create dissatisfaction than all other agencies. If you see anything in them that you know is true, begin to doubt it at once.

His years at Oxford were happy ones from 1905 until the outbreak of World War I in 1914. One of his most pleasant duties was that of curator of the famous Bodleian Library, a place that he visited daily. And as always, his home was open to friends; 13 Norham Gardens, Oxford, became known to all as the Open Arms. Since he was incapable of inactivity, his pace never slowed. He taught, traveled, lectured, entertained, corresponded voluminously, and headed committees as he always had done. In 1907 his remarks at a Dublin international conference on tuberculosis, a disease then ravaging Ireland, launched a crusade that eventually greatly reduced the incidence of that deadly disease.

On June 11, 1911, as part of the coronation ceremonies for King George V, Osler was made a baronet. Thenceforth he and his wife were known formally as Sir William Osler and Lady Grace Osler.

Three years later, at Sarajevo, Yugoslavia, a fanatic Serbian student threw a bomb that killed Archduke Ferdinand of Austria and his wife. An involved set of alliances soon led to World

Dr. William Osler seven years before his death. *Culver Pictures.*

War I. Osler, in addition to his Oxford duties, took an active role in all Canadian and British medical matters concerning the war. It is clear from his letters of that period that the safety of his son, Lt. Revere Osler, was continuously on his mind.

World War I took a terrible toll. A former McGill house officer of Osler's, John McRae, stayed for a few days with the Oslers and then returned to the front, where in 1915 he wrote the touching poem "In Flanders Field." McRae died of pneumonia two years later.

The most devastating episode in the Oslers' life took place on August 29, 1917, when their beloved only son Revere, age twenty-one, was hit by artillery fire. He died the next morning. A soldier's diary contained words about his funeral:

A soggy Flanders Field . . . the boy wrapped in an army blanket, carried by four slipping stretcher-bearers. A strange scene—the great-great-grandson of Paul Revere under a British flag, and awaiting him a group of some six or eight American Army medical officers—saddened with thoughts of his father.

A few years earlier, when Revere had volunteered to enter the army, Osler had written of him: "His heart is not much set on the military life. Literature, books & art. He and I are so congenial mentally."

As desperately wounded as Osler was by Revere's death, he carried on, mentioning his loss briefly although frequently in his correspondence. He consoled others who had lost loved ones—few European families were spared similar tragedies—and continued working actively, remaining confident that the Allies would triumph. After they did in 1918, Osler with characteristic humanity worked to get famine relief for his former enemies; this was no easy task considering how much bitter feeling toward Austria and Germany remained.

Only months after a huge celebration of his seventieth birthday in 1919, Osler became bedridden with influenza and the pneumonia and other pulmonary complications that followed. Always the clinician, he kept an accurate daily account of his illness in his letters to friends.

Shortly before his death on December 29, 1919, he wrote out his wishes concerning the donation of his collection of rare and extremely valuable books. The British Museum, the Bodleian Library, the Royal College of Physicians, the Faculté de Médecine de Paris, the Royal Society of Medicine, the University of Leyden, Bibliotheca Lanciana in Rome, and the Surgeon General's Library in Washington all received books. Many other institutions and friends previously had received similar first editions or equally rare manuscripts.

No detail was omitted in this will, including who should conduct the postmortem examination of his body and directions concerning the disposition of his ashes after cremation. A funeral service was held on January 1, 1920, in the chapel of Christ Church College.

At a memorial service on March 22, 1920, at Johns Hopkins University, his former colleague William H. Welch delivered a stirring tribute:

> At the time of his death, he was probably the greatest figure in the medical world; the best known, the most influential, the most beloved. . . . I doubt whether the history of medicine records a man who had greater influence upon the students that came under his teaching. He inspired them with a remarkable devotion and loyal affection. He was their example. His life embodied his precepts, and his students cherished his words.

Osler's place in medical history results primarily from his extraordinary personality. His intelligence, supplemented by his unique warmth, gave him an aura that survives his death over seventy years ago. But above all, he wanted his own epitaph to read: "Here lies the man who admitted students to the ward."

James D. Watson (1928–)
Francis H. C. Crick (1916–)

Discoverers of the structure of DNA

Francis Crick and James Watson were key figures in the race to find the geometric structure of DNA. Essentially three laboratories were involved in the race, two in England and one in the United States. In England there was the Cavendish Laboratory at the University of Cambridge, where Crick and Watson won the very close race. Also involved was the laboratory at King's College, London, where Maurice Wilkins and his associate Rosalind Franklin were working on DNA, hating each other all the time. And in the United States, Linus Pauling in his laboratory at the California Institute of Technology was trying to win the race that certainly would yield one or more Nobel Prizes. (Pauling already had won two Nobel Prizes.)

What is DNA? The letters stand for a very large molecule chemically named *d*eoxyribo*n*ucleic *a*cid. DNA is the stuff of life that passes hereditary information from one generation to the next. Whether we are tall or short, brown eyed or blue, what kind of skin pigmentation we have, and so on depends on DNA located in the chromosomes we inherit from our parents.

Before telling the Watson-Crick story, it is essential to present some basic facts about chemistry, cellular structure, and genetics. The world, including our bodies, is comprised of matter and energy. Matter can be converted to energy, the fuel that keeps engines—including our body engines—running. Matter and energy are interchangeable, simply forms of the same universal quantity that can neither be created nor destroyed. Matter is made of solid, liquid, and gaseous states; sometimes a substance can exist in all three forms depending on the temperature. Water, usually liquid, can be frozen solid or become gaseous water vapor.

How the human body handles matter and energy is controlled by coded information in the chromosomes of the cells —the DNA, which contains the genes. The smallest unit of life is the cell, and now with more powerful microscopes, we can see details of the structures within the cells. (Leeuwenhoek's microscopes magnified 200X, modern light microscopes magnify 2000X, and the electron microscope magnifies 1,000,000X.)

In or near the center of the cell is the nucleus, which is round and usually protected by a circular double membrane. The nucleus contains the chromosomes—hence the *nucleic* of nucleic acids. The most important part—the hereditary portion—of the chromosomes are strands of DNA. And each strand of DNA is comprised of from 10,000 to 100,000 genes. (Chromosomes are comprised of 26–40 percent DNA, the remainder being protein.)

Surrounding the nucleus (as the white of an egg surrounds the yolk) is the cytoplasm of the cell. The cytoplasm contains many structures like mitochondria (the energy factories) and ribosomes (which manufacture proteins). The cell itself is kept intact by a cell membrane that encloses everything in the cell, the nucleus and the cytoplasm.

The matter of the human body is comprised of organic substances—proteins, fats, and carbohydrates—and inorganic substances called minerals.

The simplest and smallest unit of every chemical substance is the atom, and hydrogen is the smallest atom. (An element is a substance containing only one kind of atom.) There are 105 known natural or man-made different atoms of which—in living things—four are the most important; C (carbon); O (oxygen); H (hydrogen); and N (nitrogen).

Atoms combine to form more complex structures called molecules, which usually are comprised of several different atoms. DNA is a huge molecule.

The search for the structure of DNA never could have been started had it not been for earlier fundamental studies by an Austrian monk, Gregor Johann Mendel. Born in 1822, in what now is Czechoslovakia, he was the son of a father skilled in growing fruit. His twin loves—religion and botany—were combined when Gregor entered a monastery and was assigned a small plot of land to do his work. He began experimenting with the ordinary garden pea and the flowers it produced. By careful study and record keeping, he was able to grow some pea plants that had tall stems, some that had short, or dwarf, stems, some that produced purple flowers, and some that produced white flowers. Later he was able to produce hybrids, mixing tall-stemmed plants with the dwarf stemmed and purple blossoms with white.

In 1866 he published a paper showing that an inherited characteristic from one of the two "parent" pea plants was inherited as a complete "unit." He also showed that certain units were dominant and therefore more likely to occur than the weaker, or recessive, units. He found there were no halfway measures; plants were either tall or dwarf, and a dwarf "grandchild" that had skipped a generation and had tall parents was the same size dwarf as its grandparent.

When Mendel died in 1884, his work was unrecognized. In 1900 it was rediscovered, and interest in genetics quickly was aroused. It was proved that each species has a different number of chromosomes in the nuclei of its cells. The pea plants Mendel studied have fourteen chromosomes. Humans have forty-six in every cell. The male sperm and female egg each have twenty-three chromosomes. When these two cells combine in the process of fertilization, the new cell formed, and every subsequent cell, has forty-six chromosomes.

A baby is born with billions of cells, and an adult has 100 trillion cells. Each of these cells has forty-six chromosomes in its nucleus. And each chromosome (comprised of protein along with the all-important DNA) has at least 10,000 and as many as 50,000 or 75,000 or 100,000 genes. The exact number at either end of the scale is not known. In time a cell is altered to become whatever it was intended to be. Thus a heart-muscle cell will look different from a skin cell.

A strand of human DNA is extremely thin and long; stretched out and looking beaded, it would be about three feet in length and contain about six billion "steps." When Mendel's genetic theory was rediscovered, the entire field concerning heredity came to be known as genetics.

Much progress was made in the study of genetics during the twentieth century, and especially during the 1940s and 1950s. Thus the stage was set for the major discovery of James Dewey Watson and Francis H. C. Crick.

James Dewey Watson was born in Chicago in 1928. He was a radio "quiz kid," graduated from the University of Chicago at age nineteen, and received his doctorate at Indiana University at the age of twenty-two. Then he received a postdoctoral fellowship to study the biochemistry of DNA in Copenhagen.

Watson was not stimulated by his Copenhagen professor, but during a stint at the Zoological Station in Naples, Italy, in April and May of 1951, he heard Maurice Wilkins speak. Wilkins had been working on DNA at King's College in London and during his talk showed an X-ray diffraction picture of DNA. Wilkins felt that the X-ray photo showed that DNA existed in crystalline form and that when the structure of DNA was known, investigators would be in a better position to understand how genes work. Watson recalled:

> Suddenly I was excited about chemistry. Before Maurice's talk I had worried about the possibility that the gene might be fantastically irregular. Now, however, I knew that genes could crystallize; hence they must have a regular structure that could be solved in a straightforward fashion.

But although he wanted to, Watson did not work with Wilkins in London in this new field of molecular biology, which combined the sciences of physics, chemistry, and biology. In August 1951 he obtained a fellowship to work in the University of Cambridge's eminent Cavendish Laboratory. Originally Watson was assigned to work in the laboratory of Max Perutz and John Kendrew, but once he met Francis Crick, he was destined to work with Crick:

> From my first day in the lab I knew I would not leave Cambridge for a long time. Departing would be idiocy, for I had immediately discovered the fun of talking to Francis Crick. . . . Our lunch conversations quickly centered on how genes were put together. Within a few days after my arrival, we knew what to do: imitate Linus Pauling and beat him at his own game.

Francis H. C. Crick was born at Northhampton, England, in 1916 and was educated at University College, London. His first interest was physics. During World War II he was involved in radar research and also did some excellent work on magnetic mine development. When Watson arrived at the Cavendish, Crick was thirty-five years old and almost unheard of. He spoke quickly in a loud voice, laughed boisterously, was never modest, lectured to anyone available on whatever brilliant theory occurred to him, and was trying to get a Ph.D., like Watson, under the tutelage of Max Perutz and John Kendrew. But like his associate-to-be James Watson, Crick wasn't really excited as he halfheartedly worked on the structure of the hemoglobin molecule. It was when Crick and Watson realized that only DNA was vital to the interests of both that the inevitability of their collaboration became a fact.

The director of the Cavendish was Sir Lawrence Bragg, one of the founders of crystallography, a Nobel Prize winner, who for forty years had been following and solving X-ray diffraction structural puzzles. He seemed to have two major dislikes. The first was Crick, whose loud voice and relaxed attitude toward experimental work greatly annoyed the older man.

Sir Lawrence's second annoyance was the fact that, over a twenty-five-year period, Linus Pauling of the California Institute of Technology had often beaten the English labs to the punch. He had won almost every scientific race to date, and Bragg wanted his laboratory to be the first to determine the structure of DNA. This discovery would prove to be one of the most important scientific breakthroughs of all time. Although at first forbidding Crick to work on DNA, Sir Lawrence eventually decided not to impede the research of the team of Crick and Watson.

There was an ethical consideration in this race, which Watson points out in his book *The Double Helix*, probably the freshest and most honest account ever related concerning all aspects, human and scientific, of a monumental investigation. It concerned mainly the relationship of Watson and Crick with Maurice Wilkins who, with Rosalind Franklin, was working on DNA in London. Watson remarks:

> It would have been much easier if they had been living in different countries. The combination of England's coziness—all the important people, if not related by marriage, seemed to know one another—plus the English sense of fair play would not allow Francis to move in on Maurice's problem. . . . One would not expect someone at Berkeley to ignore a first-rate problem merely because someone at Cal Tech had started first. In England, however, it simply would not look right.

As we will see later, ethics faded a bit as the race heated up.

Another problem was the real conflict between Wilkins and Rosalind Franklin. Maurice Wilkins, a beginner at X-ray diffraction work, needed an expert crystallographer to study DNA. Franklin was an expert and, from the start of her work at King's, did not consider herself to be Wilkins's assistant. It was her understanding that she had been given DNA as her own problem. Adding to her difficulties was the fact that the scientific world often undervalued the intellectual achievements of women.

From the fall of 1951, when Watson arrived at the Cavendish, until April 1953, there were repeated highs and lows in the research. Both Watson and Crick had decided that, in light of Pauling's helix protein structure, the likeliest structure of DNA would also prove to be helical—a single, double, or triple chain. Compounds called bases, since they were known to exist in the DNA molecule, might extend outward at right angles to the chain or chains. (A base is the nonacid part of a salt.)

Rosalind Franklin, whose X-ray diffraction photograph of crystalline DNA was the clearest, never believed that the structure was even a helix, let alone a double helix (two chains) as it proved to be. (She did, however, correctly insist that the probably straight chain or chains were comprised of alternating sugar and phosphate molecules.) Maurice Wilkins, on the other hand, did feel that a helical configuration was probable.

The actual structure built by Watson and Crick was a double helix. It can be compared to a twisted ladder or to a spiral staircase. The rails of the ladder are the two chains, and the rungs are the combinations of the four bases, adenine (A) and thymine (T), cytosine (C) and guanine (G). It turned out that these rungs didn't extend outward—rungs don't; they were connected to the twisted rails of the mythical ladder. But it was the spiral staircase analogy that appealed to Watson. In 1952, while temporarily working on the structure of the tobacco mosaic virus (TMV), he spent a weekend at Oxford. "Every helical staircase I saw that weekend . . . made me more confident that other biological structures would also have helical symmetry." (The steps of this staircase, as mythical as the twisted ladder, would be paired bases, and the banisters, the sugar and phosphate chains.)

During these fruitful years of collaboration (1951–1953), Watson, who had decided that he would look English if he let his hair grow, which he did, was often interested in other activities that mildly annoyed Crick. For example, the older man couldn't understand why Watson often would want to take off afternoons to play tennis. But Crick, although happily married, shared Watson's enthusiasm for the young girls, usually "au pair," who frequently appeared at parties. Watson's interest in sex also extended to bacteria. He was intrigued to learn that bacteria, like humans, were comprised of males and females who mated.

Linus Pauling's son Peter, who was a research student of John Kendrew's, shared office space with Watson and Crick. Watson liked Peter, partly because they could discuss the comparative virtues of girls from England, the Continent, and California. But Peter

James D. Watson (*left*) and Francis H. C. Crick, photographed during the time of their collaboration. *UPI/Bettmann.*

would give both investigators a few impressive scares when, from time to time, he would appear with a letter from his father in California; the letter would announce that Pauling had solved the structure puzzle of DNA. Luckily for Watson and Crick, Linus Pauling had made a few mistakes each time so the solution remained up for grabs. But one letter in February 1953 showed that Pauling was so close that a window of only some six weeks was available before he would discover his error and return to full pursuit.

Maurice Wilkins luckily was in no hurry to build models. Watson was pleased about that. He said:

> Francis seized the occasion to ask Maurice whether he would mind if we started to play with DNA models. When Maurice's slow answer emerged as no, he wouldn't mind, my pulse rate returned to normal. For even if the answer had been yes, our model building would have gone ahead.

Finally it was James Watson who became obsessed with making the model, initially playing with cardboard cutouts. Pauling had said that models were needed to find out "which atoms like to sit next to each other." Watson and Crick had come to realize that two sets of paired bases could form the rungs of the ladder. Adenine was attached to thymine and cytosine to guanine. Hydrogen atoms bonded the bases together. Adenine and guanine are double-ringed structures called *purines*. Cytosine and thymine are single-ringed structures called *pyrimidines*. Thus the correct bonding of each rung was like to unlike (purine to pyrimidine), and the rungs connected at right angles to the backbones of the structure, the twin helical chains. Watson had a false start but was set straight by Jerry Donohue, an American crystallographer; he correctly showed how the hydrogen atoms that bonded the bases could shift position.

Now it worked! A machine shop manufactured the parts, flat metallic bases and the twin helices of alternating sugar and phosphate molecules. After days of intensive playing with the structural elements, the investigators connected all the pieces the right way and the model was complete. Very important to the process was that the connections be stereochemically correct. (Atoms and molecules join up at specific angles in space so the model had to be three-dimensionally accurate.) The model also had to satisfy the X-ray data.

As soon as the model was complete, everyone came to see it. Bragg had his first look late in the morning of the day the model was produced. He was satisfied but wanted the chemist Alexander Todd to check the model's accuracy. Watson and Crick agreed, and Watson, the tension now gone, went off to play tennis.

Watson and Crick were lucky that they hadn't wasted time. Earlier in that critical day, Crick had received a note from Maurice Wilkins mentioning that he, Wilkins, was ready to go ahead full steam on DNA with emphasis on model building.

Everybody was gracious about Crick and Watson's success. Maurice Wilkins, though he had lost the race, was excited, in Watson's words, "that the structure would prove of great value to biology." Fortunately he shared in the Nobel Prize.

Instead of reacting with the hostility her fellow workers expected, Rosalind Franklin showed genuine delight. Her beautiful X-ray photographs had convinced Watson and Crick (although not herself) that the structure was a double helix and had proved that the two helices—the backbones—were located on the outside of the molecule. Franklin had always maintained that the sugar-phosphate backbone would be located on the outside.

Peter Pauling was also enthusiastic about this success, and he did not give the slightest impression that "he

Watson and Crick with their DNA model. *The Bettmann Archive.*

minded the possibility of his father's first real scientific defeat." The reaction of Linus Pauling himself was "one of genuine thrill."

The final draft of the Crick and Watson paper was mailed to the prestigious journal *Nature* on April 2, 1953.

Linus Pauling arrived in Cambridge two days later to visit his son and to see the model. Watson pointed out that both he and Crick had learned much during the race from Pauling's book *The Nature of the Chemical Bond*. It should be noted, too, that Pauling's passport was taken away by the State Department in 1952; he was considered too liberal to be allowed to roam free. He might have had a better chance at the prize had he been allowed to go to England and see Rosalind Franklin's photographs at an earlier stage.

Pauling and his son, along with Watson and his sister, had dinner at Odile and Francis Crick's home that evening. It was evident that Pauling could lose an exceptionally important race with style and warmth.

In his epilogue to *The Double Helix*, Watson points out that everybody involved was still alive at publication time with one exception. Rosalind Franklin had died at the age of thirty-seven. He goes on to state that his impressions of her were entirely wrong and to detail her remarkable achievements, concluding:

> Rosalind's exemplary courage and integrity were apparent to all when, knowing that she was mortally ill, she did not complain but continued working on a high level until a few weeks before her death.

(Many believe that Rosalind Franklin should have shared in the Nobel Prize.)

The confirmation of the structure of DNA led to an explosion of scientific discoveries that continue to grow. A small part of one chain of the unwound double helix makes three different types of another nucleic acid, RNA (*r*ibo*n*ucleic *a*cid). RNA molecules are smaller and can escape from the nucleus to enter the cytoplasm of the cell, where they proceed, using three-letter *codons* in their structure, to make essential amino acids that combine to form proteins. During his research with Crick, Watson came to believe that DNA was the template upon which RNA was made. He felt that DNA made RNA and that RNA made proteins. This theory proved to be true.

A *Genome Project* (headed by James Watson) is under way to map and sequence all human genes. This project should make major contributions to human health. DNA "fingerprints" are now used in courts to exonerate innocent people and to convict guilty ones.

By a complex process DNA from the blood, semen, flesh, and so forth of an individual can identify that person as unique. The final step is an X ray, which shows a pattern of DNA bands resembling the bar code seen on supermarket products.

Most important of all, recombinant DNA is a scientific development that makes new forms of DNA using genetic material from two different organisms and combining them. This process, called genetic engineering, has already spliced the DNA portion of the human gene that directs the formation of insulin and combined it with bacterial DNA. This has resulted in the formation of bacterial "factories" that produce large amounts of human insulin. Allergic reaction to foreign protein is thus avoided.

Recombinant DNA, which has also proved valuable in agriculture, is already used in the treatment of several genetic diseases, and someday it undoubtedly will find use in the treatment of complex diseases like cancer.

When Watson and Crick built their model, they knew that important scientific advances would result from their work. It is clear that their dreams of the future are coming true each day with increasing frequency.

PART VII
Mental Health

Philippe Pinel

1745–1826 French physician; pioneer in providing humane care for the mentally ill

Of all the kinds of illnesses recognized since ancient times, none have been more misunderstood or more cruelly treated than mental disorders. People suffering from severe mental disturbances were labeled crazy, or insane, or mad, or lunatic. (*Lunatic* comes from the Middle English word for moon, the belief being that the moon was the cause of some kind of madness. Even today peculiar behavior is sometimes blamed on the influence of a full moon, and mentally disturbed persons are referred to as being loonies, or moonstruck.) Those words no longer are part of medical terminology, although *insanity* is a recognized legal term.

In prehistoric times mental illnesses were thought to be caused by evil spirits residing inside the heads of afflicted persons. The obvious cure for these disorders was to drill holes in the skulls to let these evil spirits escape, a procedure known as trephining.

During the Middle Ages the feeling persisted that devils were the cause of mental illness. Patients were prayed over, starved, beaten, and tortured in attempts to expel these devils. Sometimes these unfortunate victims were thought to be witches and burned at the stake, a practice that continued through the early seventeenth century.

Today we use the word *bedlam* to describe situations where there is uncontrolled disorder. That word relates directly to the treatment of mental illness. In 1247 a hospital was established in London that, from 1377 on, specialized in the treatment of lunatics. Origi-

A fifteenth-century woodcut showing early treatment of the insane. *Germanisches National-museum.*

nally known as the Priory of the Order of the Star of Bethlehem, it soon became known as Bethlem, which name in turn became Bedlam. This Royal Bethlem Hospital became the site of favorite entertainment for onlookers, who found the scene of chained and violent patients amusing.

The man who bravely started a reversal of all these inhumane practices was a French physician who didn't begin medical studies until the age of thirty. Philippe Pinel was the son of a country doctor, but instead of following his father's profession, he first became a divinity student and later studied philosophy. Eventually he turned to medicine, graduating with an M.D. from the University of Toulouse in 1773. Five years later Pinel moved to Paris, and like Linnaeus, the famous botanist-physician who classified plants and flowers, Pinel felt that descriptions and classifications of diseases were needed. He wrote a book on the subject, which, although not too enlightening, went through six editions and brought him some degree of fame.

Pinel's interest in treatment of the mentally ill began later when one of his friends became psychotic and was locked up, chained, and, as was the custom, treated like a wild animal. The man escaped and hid in the woods but was attacked by wolves and devoured. Pinel, horrified by this series of events, turned his interest toward treatment of the mentally ill. It was the dangerous time of the French Revolution, and Pinel risked his life by fighting for permission to begin reforms in the treatment of mental illness.

The year was 1793, and Pinel was appointed by the existing French government to be chief physician at the Bicêtre, part prison, part hospital, part home for the aged poor. The Reign of Terror was then at its height. This was the year that both King Louis XVI and his queen, Marie Antoinette, were guillotined. This was the year when the fictional Mme Defarge sat knitting in the Place de la Concorde as not only royal heads but any head that had displeased the commune fell into a basket next to the guillotine.

During these frightening times, Philippe Pinel, described as frail and timid, had the courage to ask to be allowed to speak for the rights of mentally ill patients. He appeared not once but several times before Georges Couthon, a member of the Committee on Public Safety. Each time he was dismissed without being allowed to plead his cause, but finally Couthon, a burly but basically humane man, consented to hear Pinel's views. Pinel had a good argument. Since the revolution had declared all men to be free and equal brothers, he told Couthon, patients at the Bicêtre should be allowed to share some of this freedom and not continue to be chained in filthy dungeons. Finally and amazingly, Pinel induced Couthon to accompany him to the Bicêtre to see for himself. The horrified Couthon warned Pinel that if he freed these "beasts," he would face real personal danger. Pinel's earlier pleas had elicited ominous threats, and once he had been told that if the experiment failed, he would be guillotined. This was no idle threat. Men of science and all intellectuals, as happens in many revolutions, were the objects of distrust. Couthon himself was later guillotined as was Antoine Lavoisier, one of the greatest chemists of all time. Pinel was almost hanged by a mob in the street when he was suspected of hiding "enemies of the Revolution" at the Bicêtre. Probably he had been doing just that, but his life was saved by an ex-patient who served as his bodyguard and who succeeded in dispersing the crowd.

After receiving Couthon's permission, Pinel began his own revolution of freedom by approaching a patient, an English captain, who forty years earlier had been manacled and chained after killing an attendant. Pinel walked alone into the man's cell and talked quietly to him. He told the patient that he would be allowed to walk in the

An early-nineteenth-century lithograph of Philippe Pinel. *Bibliothèque Nationale, Paris.*

prison yard if he promised to behave "like a gentleman." The man promised, and the chains were cut off. Since the patient had had no opportunity to exercise for so many years, he couldn't walk at first. Finally he was able to crawl to the door, and at the sight of the trees and the sky, he wept with joy.

Within a few days more than fifty men who had been declared violent were, at Pinel's order, released from their chains. An amazing change in their behavior occurred. No longer in chains and now treated with firm kindness, they became gentle. Fortunately, not a single violent incident marred Pinel's experiment.

Pinel's action was the turning point in the treatment of mental illness. He was the first to show that kindness, not cruelty, was the way to help patients with mental disorders. Two years later Pinel was appointed director of the Salpêtrière, an institution similar to the Bicêtre. There he carried out similar reforms, as well as adding new ones. He trained competent nurses, he separated new patients from those considered to be incurable, and he insisted that convalescing patients be paid for their work so that they would have money when they reentered society. Also, Pinel was the first to see the importance of keeping careful psychiatric case records and actually to do so. In 1809 a treatise he published based on observations made in both hospitals had great influence in changing older and more primitive ways of treating the mentally ill.

Pinel taught medicine in addition to his administrative duties and was on the faculty of the École de Médecine. In 1822 this college was closed briefly because of anticlerical disturbances; when it reopened, some of the faculty were not reappointed. Among those rejected was Pinel. He died four years later.

In England a merchant named William Tuke (1732–1822), possibly unaware of Pinel's work, succeeded in founding in 1796 a humane hospital for treatment of mental illness. At this hospital, the Retreat, which still is in existence, a minimum amount of restraint replaced the chains of other English institutions. And later an English physician, John Conolly (1794–1866), worked in the largest mental hospital in England. There, his accomplishments paralleled those of Pinel. He abolished most restraints on patients.

Today, while some restraint still is required to control violence, the use of safe and calming drugs has almost eliminated the use of physical restraints. When restraints must be temporarily used, sheets, not chains, keep the patient from hurting himself or herself or others.

In the United States Dorothea Lynde Dix (1802–1887) pioneered in the reform of treatment of the institutionalized. She was shocked by the conditions she noted when, as a Boston schoolteacher, she had been asked to give instruction to the inmates of an East Cambridge house of correction. As a result she began a two-year tour of other institutions in Massachusetts—prisons and almshouses. When she had completed her inspection, she wrote her famous *Memorial to the Legislature of Massachusetts*, in which she declared: "Violence and severity do but exasperate the Insane: the only availing influence is kindness and firmness. It is amazing what these will produce."

For the next forty years she visited every state in the Union as well as Europe to stimulate further reforms. In the United States she was responsible for the founding of thirty-two new state institutions. Just as important, her eloquence changed the thinking of the American and European public about the treatment of mental illness.

What Philippe Pinel initiated was improved upon and enlarged by others working in the mental health field—nurses, teachers, social workers, physicians. It is difficult to realize that less than two hundred years have passed since Pinel freed men and women suffering with mental disease from their chains.

Sigmund Freud

1856–1939 Austrian psychiatrist; developer of psychoanalysis

During the mid-nineteenth century to the early twentieth, very little attention was paid to the mind. When mental disturbances became obvious, their cause was ascribed to organic problems, some abnormality of the physical body such as a brain tumor. While many emotional problems did have an organic basis, most did not. And for the treatment of mental disease, very little had been done since Philippe Pinel had released the chains that had hobbled the criminally insane up to that time.

With the birth of Sigmund Freud on May 6, 1856, a new era in understanding both the disturbed and the healthy mind was about to begin. Freud's birthplace was Freiberg, Austria, but his father, a wool merchant, was having business reverses, and the family moved to Vienna in 1860. The family was Jewish, and Freud always retained his cultural ties as a Jew, but he never became a religious man in any sense. He could not, in fact, stand ceremonies of any sort, religious or otherwise. But anti-Semitism always figured heavily in his career, and he stood up to it admirably. Freud's pioneering studies formed the basis of modern psychology and psychiatry. He is known principally as the founder of psychoanalysis. This is one of the techniques of helping people with serious mental disorders (psychoses) or more common and less serious disturbances (neuroses) through the process of psychotherapy (talking with someone trained in the treatment of mental illness).

Freud was the oldest child of his parents' marriage. He had two brothers and five sisters. His father had been married before, and his grown son from the previous marriage had a small son and daughter of his own at the time of Freud's birth, making baby Sigmund an uncle before he was born. Freud was close to his nephew, John, and they were playmates growing up, being only a year apart.

As a young man Freud enjoyed reading (he started to read Shakespeare at age eight) and was at home with classical languages, Latin, Greek, and Hebrew. Besides his native German, he taught himself Italian, Spanish, and English. At age nineteen he visited his half-brother in England and loved the country, which would give him refuge in the last year of his life. "Neither at that time, nor indeed in my later life, did I feel any predilection for the career of a physician," Freud later recalled, but the theories of Darwin "strongly attracted me, for they held out hopes of an extraordinary advance in our understanding of the world." Finally it was Goethe's "beautiful essay on Nature" that decided him on medicine.

Freud entered the University of Vienna in 1873 and graduated as a physician in 1881. While still a student, he worked in Professor Ernst Brücke's physiology laboratory, performing important studies on nerve cell structure. His work in the laboratory continued after graduation, and his neurology articles remain today as important original work. (A year's military service added to his research work made his stay at the medical school three years longer than the usual time.) It was his need to make a living after falling in love with young Martha Bernays that made him decide to enter private practice.

Because of finances, he couldn't afford to marry at once—they were engaged for four and a half years—and even after marriage, they remained poor for years.

Freud worked in the General Hospital for three years after graduation, receiving a small salary. For a time he did some experiments with cocaine, trying it himself and then prescribing it for a friend who was addicted to morphine. The friend quickly shifted his addiction to cocaine. Seeing the results, Freud quit taking the drug himself. (Luckily he did not have an addictive personality, and during his last years, a fifteen-year struggle with a painful cancer, he refused all pain medication except aspirin.) He had noted during his studies that cocaine had the ability to anesthetize the tongue and thought it could be used in eye surgery. He suggested its use to a friend, Dr. Karl Koller, who thereby became the discoverer of local anesthesia by cocaine.

Sigmund Freud with his fiancée, Martha Bernays, around 1885. *Freud Museum, London.*

During his courtship, when Martha commented that she didn't think she was good-looking (she was), Freud responded in a way that hardly would make a young woman of twenty-two feel ecstatic. "I know," Freud replied in a letter, "that you are not beautiful in a painter's or sculptor's sense; if you insist on strict correctness in the use of words, then I must confess you are not beautiful." He went on to say "how much there is visible in your appearance that reveals how sweet, generous, and reasonable you are. . . . I will not conceal from you that some people declare you to be beautiful, even strikingly so. I have no opinion on the matter."

Despite Freud's bouts of jealousy and inability to flatter, Martha saw in him qualities of tenderness, integrity, and caring. They were married on September 13, 1886, after a courtship that had produced over nine hundred handwritten letters. (Some of Freud's were ten to twelve tightly written pages long.) They remained happily married for fifty-three years and produced three sons and three daughters.

"They must have been a good-looking couple," Ernest Jones, the famed English psychoanalyst and Freud's definitive biographer, commented. "Freud was a handsome man, slender but sturdy, with his well-shaped head, regular features, and dark, flashing eyes. He was five feet seven inches tall and weighed just over 126 pounds."

In 1891 the family (which included Martha's sister Minna) moved to 19 Bergasse, an address that became famous; it's a museum today. Freud lived there for forty-seven years. Freud was very fond of Minna but, contrary to rumors, had no romantic interest in her. (Of his children, the best known was Anna. She became a famous psychoanalyst and was his constant companion and nurse during his last painful years.)

Freud's interest in psychiatry began before his marriage. An older friend, Dr. Josef Breuer, related to Freud the case of Anna O., a young woman whom he had successfully treated with hypnosis over a two-year period. She had several physical disorders, including paralyses, which disappeared when talking about troubling thoughts while she was hypnotized. Breuer called his form of treatment *catharsis*, or the *talking cure*, because when disturbing thoughts were brought to the surface, the symptoms disappeared.

Shortly after hearing about Breuer's case, Freud traveled to Paris to study with the famed neurologist Jean Charcot, who was successfully treating cases of hysterical paralysis (paralysis due to an emotional cause) with hypnosis. He found Charcot an inspiring teacher, and he loved Paris, especially Notre Dame

Cathedral, which he visited at every opportunity. On his return to Vienna, he translated Charcot's books and in 1891 published his own first book, *On the Aphasias.* (The inability to speak is called motor aphasia; the inability to understand speech is sensory aphasia.)

Freud began to use hypnosis with his own patients—Dr. Breuer had withdrawn from the field—but found that some patients could not be hypnotized. As a result, during the years between 1892 and 1895, he gradually developed the *free association* method of treatment. He would ask a patient to relate whatever thoughts came into his or her head. He learned that these thoughts were not really "free" at all but were bound to buried thoughts. These buried thoughts were held in an area of the mind Freud termed the *unconscious.*

Patients often had difficulty in continuing with a train of free associations. Freud called the process of keeping these painful thoughts buried *repression.* He termed the patient's attempt to keep these thoughts from reaching the surface *resistance.* Freud also found that unconscious thoughts and feelings could be revealed in dreams. The free association and the dreams patients told about required analysis and interpretation before cures could be obtained; therefore, Freud called his new technique *psychoanalysis.*

From 1895 to 1899 he worked on his most important and influential book, *The Interpretation of Dreams.* Published on November 4, 1899, it received poor reviews or was ignored. Freud was paid $209 for the book, and it took eight years to sell the six hundred copies printed. Ten years later, however, when Freud's work was beginning to receive recognition, a second edition was printed. During Freud's lifetime eight editions were printed, and the work was translated into eight languages.

From all these studies Freud formulated the idea that there are three aspects of personality. He named them the *id,* the *ego,* and the *superego.* The id is the uninhibited part of the personality appearing at birth. It is concerned only with self-gratification. Later the child learns that to live in society, other people must be considered, and the id must be controlled. This learned part of the personality that includes putting a brake on the id is called the ego. Finally the superego develops from morals and ideals presented by parents and other authority figures. Essentially the superego is *conscience.*

Another Freudian concept is the *libido.* Initially considered to be energy of the sexual instinct directed to an outside object, the libido has acquired a broader meaning and applies to several kinds of love including love for parents and friends. It is a difficult concept to understand since, as is the case with all of psychiatry, exact measurement is not possible. In studies of the mind too many variables are involved to perform the exact kinds of controlled experiments that are used for proof in other fields of science.

Gradually Freud attracted a small number of practicing physicians to his method, and in 1902 they formed the early core of psychoanalysts. For a time they met weekly in his home and called themselves the Wednesday Psychological Society. Important early guests included Carl Jung, Karl Abraham, A. A. Brill (who introduced psychoanalysis to the United States), and Ernest Jones (who introduced it to England).

In 1897 Freud had begun his own self-analysis, a momentous achievement. Others had tried and failed. Freud endured the pain of uncovering his unconscious and succeeded.

In 1904 Freud heard from Eugen Bleuler, professor of psychiatry in Zurich, that he and his staff, including his chief assistant Jung, were using psychoanalysis. Thus, with this Swiss beginning, international recognition was on its way. Jung first visited Freud in 1907 and talked excitedly to the discoverer of psychoanalysis for three hours steadily. Freud was impressed with his young admirer and soon after designated him "son and heir." It was at Freud's insistence that Jung in 1910 was named president of the first international society of psychoanalysis. But by 1912 Jung had begun to withdraw from Freud's views. He despised the idea of infantile sexuality, and by 1914 the break was complete; Jung resigned from the International Psychoanalytic Association. Jung's defection, and his secrecy preceding it, hurt Freud enormously. Because of defections like Jung's, Ernest Jones proposed the formation of The Committee, a group of loyal followers. The Committee, whose function was to preserve Freud's concepts from being destroyed by dissension, began to function before the outbreak of World War I.

Freud's international reputation was enhanced in 1908 by an invitation from Stanley Hall, the president of Clark University in Massachusetts, to give a series of lectures. As usual, Freud spoke brilliantly without notes and made lifelong friends, one of whom was the esteemed Harvard professor of neurology J. J. Putnam.

Although psychoanalysis dominated his life, Freud enjoyed many things. He regularly played tarok, a four-handed Viennese card game, smoked at least twenty cigars daily, collected antiquities, attended the theater, and

This photograph of Freud's study in Vienna shows his couch and a small portion of his collection of antiquities. *Freud Museum, London.*

was especially fond of Mozart operas. He had many women friends and always respected women, believing them to be "finer and ethically nobler than men." Although continually short of money—it did not seem important to him—and borrowing frequently, he never economized on health, education, or travel. He especially loved Italy and visited Rome seven times. He was generous to all in need, even when he couldn't afford to give.

The Austrian government in 1913 wrote to him on the subject of his income tax, expressing their surprise that his income wasn't larger "since everyone knows that his reputation extends far beyond the frontier of Austria." Freud's caustic reply: "Prof. Freud is very honored at receiving a communication from the Government. It is the first time the Government has taken any notice of him and he acknowledges it. There is one point on which he cannot agree with the communication: that his reputation extends far beyond the frontier of Austria. It begins at the frontier."

World War I saddened him. He missed seeing friends and colleagues like Princess Marie Bonaparte, Lou Andreas-Salomé, and Ernest Jones, and worried about his sons Ernst and Martin, who were soldiers in the Austrian army. Fortunately they both survived the war. Through the gift of a dying friend, Dr. P. Anton von Freund, Freud was able to found his own publishing company; the freedom to publish his own work gave Freud much happiness. Curiously, despite worldwide recognition as a result of his published work, he had a modest opinion of himself. "I have very restricted capacities or talents," he once wrote. "None at all for the natural sciences; nothing for mathematics; nothing for anything quantitative. But what I have, of a very restricted nature, was probably very intensive."

When Jones asked Anna Freud to state her father's most distinctive characteristic, she replied immediately (as did several others): "his simplicity." Perhaps this impression was due in part to the fact that he owned few clothes and that he traveled lightly and so could pack quickly and without fuss. But a woman friend who was being analyzed said the simplicity extended to his psychoanalysis. His own self seemed to disappear, and his interest was concentrated solely on listening to his patient and sorting out the patient's important thoughts from the less important. In any case, the matter of his simplicity doesn't seem simple at all.

The years after World War I were generally painful ones, emotionally and physically, for Freud. His major work had been completed, and although he remained active, three events began to take their toll. Tragedy struck first in January 1920, when his beautiful daughter Sophie at age twenty-six died of pneumonia following influenza. Possibly she was his favorite child—the Freuds referred to her as their "Sunday's child"—and she left two small children. He grieved stoically and silently. His professional life continued to be active, however, and he was pleased when a psychoanalytic clinic was opened in Berlin. He testified strongly against the way victims of shell shock and other war-trauma related illnesses were treated. Generally regarded with disapproval, they usually had been subjected to strong electric shock and then sent back to the front. Even the Viennese psychoanalysts sided against Freud's humane ideas; he found their attitude hateful.

The second blow came in February 1923, when, probably as a result of his years of cigar smoking, he developed cancer of the right side of his jaw and palate. The first operation was botched.

As a result his mouth contracted from scar tissue and forever after caused him trouble. This was the first of thirty-three operations Freud would undergo until his life ended in 1939. Second and third operations excised half his upper jaw and palate. From that time on, Freud had to wear a painful prothesis in order to talk and eat. For a time he had been deceived and told the growth was not cancerous. When he found out the truth, he was furious, mostly at the untrue assumption that he would be unable to take the bad news, although he had suspected cancer from the start.

The third tragedy, around the same time as the appearance of the cancer, was one that Freud said permanently killed something in him. His favorite grandchild, Heinz Rudolph Halberstadt (Heinele), Sophie's younger child, died of an aggravation of preexisting tuberculosis following a routine tonsillectomy. In one of his letters Freud confessed that he was suffering from the first depression of his life. This loss was undoubtedly the reason.

Albert Einstein visited Freud in 1926, and the two men talked for two hours. "He is cheerful, sure of himself and agreeable," Freud wrote. "He understands about as much about psychology as I do about physics, so we had a very pleasant talk."

Freud doubted that the Nazi movement in Germany would ever affect his Vienna life, but he should have known better. In 1933 Jung became coeditor of an international psychoanalytic journal under Nazi control; the other coeditor was Hermann Göring, Reichsführer of Germany. The function of the journal was to show the advantages of Aryan psychology. A Swiss psychiatrist resigned, declaring that science should be neutral, and Jung has been criticized ever since.

Finally, in 1938, Austria was invaded by Germany, and Freud was induced to seek refuge in England. Despite his professed dislike for Vienna, he wanted to stay. It was only for the sake of his wife and daughter Anna that he consented to leave. (His other children had already left for sanctuary abroad.) Although he loved the freedom in England, he wrote that he "always loved the prison from which I have been released." His departure was effected through the efforts of Marie Bonaparte, princess of Denmark and Greece, along with Ambassador W. C. Bullitt, via the efforts of President Franklin D. Roosevelt.

During Freud's last days in Vienna, he was questioned by the Gestapo, who made him sign a release stating that he had been well treated. He could not resist adding a sarcastic note: "I can heartily recommend the Gestapo to anyone." Had the Gestapo understood its tone, Freud undoubtedly would have been executed.

He arrived in England on June 6, 1938, stopping first for a few hours at Marie Bonaparte's beautiful Paris home. Freud received a heartfelt welcome in London and actually practiced some psychoanalysis during this final year. On September 22, 1939, he was granted a long-promised request. If the suffering became too great, he would be given medication to die peacefully. Compassionate Dr. Max Schur honored Freud's feeling and administered a small dose of morphine. Freud slept and died just before midnight the following day. (He was spared the pain of learning about the later deaths of his four sisters in a concentration camp.)

Freud's legacy is as simple as it is powerful. He unlocked the door to the mind and revealed its complexity for the world to see and to learn what was inside.

PART VIII

Modern Times and Cures

Jonas Edward Salk (1914–)
Albert Bruce Sabin (1906–)

Conquerors of poliomyelitis

Today, when science is in the news, attention is focused on scientists, and the rivalries among them often are apparent. (Such rivalry is evident in the continuing controversy over who discovered HIV, the virus that causes AIDS.) No battle was fought more publicly than that involving poliomyelitis, the paralyzing viral disease. (The name of this viral disease was originally *infantile paralysis* and was shortened to *polio* after World War II.)

First, a few basic facts about viruses. The idea of filtration probably began when Louis Pasteur had the idea that bacteria could be filtered out—held in a kind of strainer. He had noted that water filtered through soil with a lot of sand in it was free of germs. An associate, Charles Édouard Chamberland, constructed a porcelain, candle-shaped filter whose fine pores did trap bacteria. Viruses are microorganisms much smaller than bacteria. Because of their minute size, they can pass through the finest pores of filtering devices and are called therefore filterable viruses. There are many viral-caused diseases—rabies, smallpox, influenza, AIDS, and the common childhood diseases measles, German measles, mumps, and chicken pox.

In the first half of this century, it was none of these viruses that caused nations, especially the United States, to panic each summer. It was the polio virus. Parents, grandparents, aunts, uncles, and friends were terrified that children would contract the crippling and often fatal disease it caused. Adults were attacked also, but in much smaller numbers. In the United States summer seemed to be the epidemic time. Swimming pools and drinking fountains were avoided, and those who could afford it took their children to the country, away from crowded cities where epidemics were more likely to occur. (During a severe New York City epidemic in 1916, some fleeing the city were refused lodging, sometimes at gunpoint, by equally terrified rural hotel owners.)

Summertime produced terror because, despite all precautions, no one really knew when or where the virus would strike. The virus is transmitted through pharyngeal (back-of-throat) secretions or by fecal matter. As happens in the transmission of many cases of infectious hepatitis, infected people may not wash their hands thoroughly enough and pass along the disease by handshake or food handling. (Actually, the blessings of sanitary advances like indoor plumbing were no boon to polio victims; in earlier days outhouses and other unsanitary places gave early exposure to the virus and resulted in lifelong immunity to babies and toddlers, a group always less likely to develop paralytic polio.)

The virus in food or water was swallowed or breathed in by droplet infection. The virus next moved to the intestinal tract, usually producing a mild flulike illness with sore throat, headache, aches and pains, and a high temperature. In almost all instances that was the end of the disease. The patient was now immune, his or her body having produced protective antibodies during the course of the mild illness. But in those unfortunate enough to get paralytic polio, the virus moved into the bloodstream and from there traveled to the spinal cord, where it destroyed motor nerve cells (those cells that direct muscles to move) and resulted in paralysis of arms and legs in any combination (sometimes one arm, sometimes both legs, and so forth). This kind is called spinal paralytic polio.

In other cases the virus traveled to the "bulb" of the brain, the medulla oblongata, where the respiratory center is located, and caused bulbar polio. Breathing muscles couldn't work, and patients were kept alive by metal mechanical breathing devices dubbed iron lungs.

What was hoped for was a vaccine that would eliminate this dreadful disease. This hope had a serious setback in 1935. In that year two separate polio vaccine trials were held, one using killed virus and the other live virus. Both were unsuccessful, resulting in several deaths. Obviously, more investigation was needed before it would be possible to produce and test a safe vaccine.

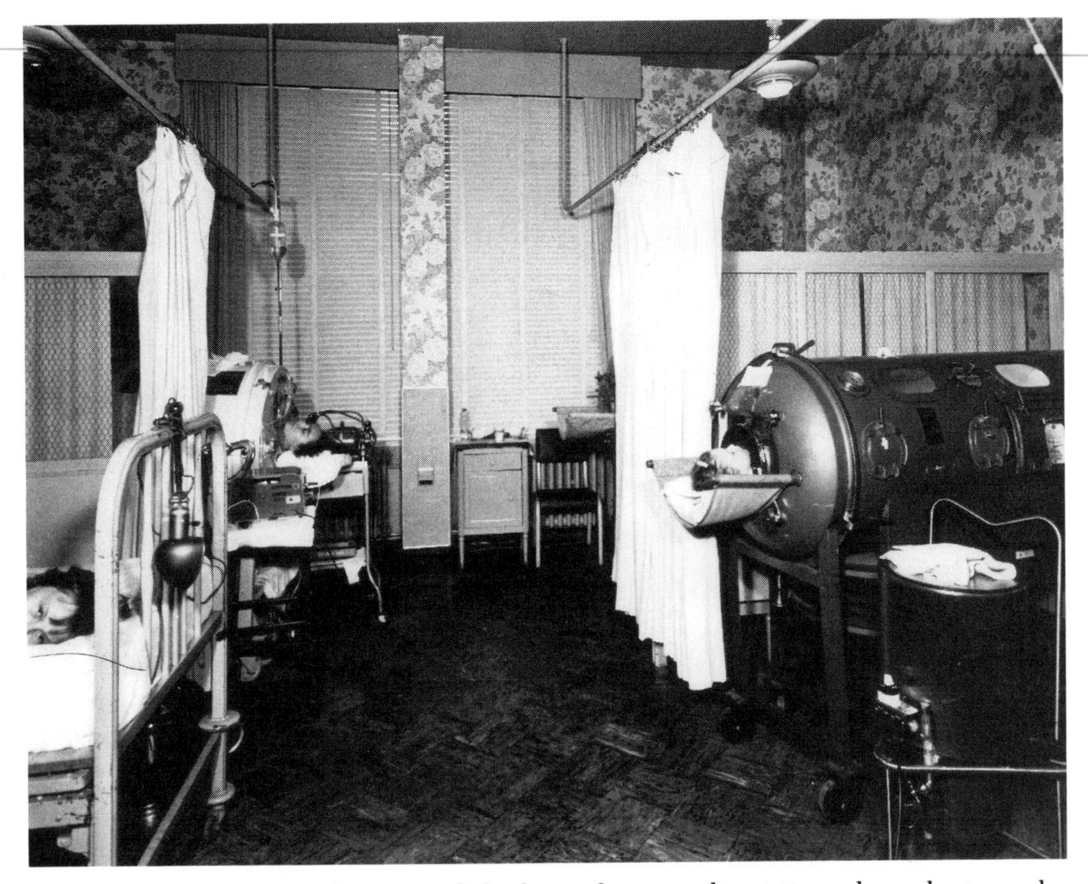

Respirators known as iron lungs saved the lives of many polio victims whose chest muscles had been paralyzed by the disease. *National Library of Medicine, Bethesda, Maryland.*

Then, like a miracle, in the mid-1950s, a very effective vaccine made from killed virus was given by a series of three injections. Later in 1961 an oral vaccine made from live but attenuated (weakened, or "tamed") polio virus was given by means of a few drops dissolved in a sugar cube and swallowed. The killed vaccine was developed by Jonas Salk and the oral vaccine by Albert Sabin. The widespread administration of these vaccines within thirty-five years completely eliminated polio from the Western Hemisphere.

The first use of microorganisms to prevent disease occurred in 1796, when Edward Jenner used harmless material from harmless cowpox disease pustules to prevent a similar but much more deadly disease, smallpox. A hundred years later Louis Pasteur called his method of preventing the disease anthrax in animals vaccination. Thus, *vaccination* became the word always used when live or dead microorganisms are injected into the muscle or are taken by mouth.

Neither Jenner nor Pasteur knew that they were injecting viruses, microorganisms so small that in only a few cases are they visible with the light microscope. Usually the powerful electron microscope is required to see viruses. (To this day, no one knows whether viruses are living organisms or not. They cannot reproduce by themselves like bacteria; however, they are able to use materials inside plant or animal cells to reproduce.)

Polio has been known to exist since ancient times. Mummies with withered legs have been found along with ancient drawings depicting withered arms and legs. The disease was first described in detail by a German orthopedist, Jacob Heine, who called it "spinal infantile paralysis," a name that remained in use until replaced by the term *polio*. When in 1898 Martinus Beijernck discovered something smaller than bacteria that caused disease in tobacco plants, he coined the word *virus*, derived from Latin and meaning "poisonous slime." In 1935 Wendell Stanley at the Rockefeller Institute was the first to isolate a pure virus. (He obtained the crystalline protein virus from the sap of infected plants.) Karl Landsteiner and Erwin Popper produced polio in monkeys from material taken from the spine of a human killed by the disease. Although the infectious nature of the disease had long been suspected, this work proved it.

No effective vaccine could be made until the polio virus could be grown in large quantities. This step was accomplished in 1949, when John Enders and his associates, Thomas H. Weller and Frederick C. Robbins, using human embryonic tissue, succeeded in growing the polio virus. This tissue could be kept alive in incubated test tubes for generations, thus eliminating the need to kill an infected monkey and grind up its spinal cord to get viruses for a possible vaccine. Theirs was a monumental achievement and one that earned them a Nobel Prize in 1954.

Another of the many critical discoveries leading to a successful polio vaccine was the confirmation of Sir Macfarlane Burnet's 1931 discovery in Australia that more than one type of polio virus existed. This was accomplished at Johns Hopkins by David Bodian, Howard Howe, and Isabel Morgan, who found that there were three—and only three—types of poliovirus; an effective vaccine had to immunize against all three types.

Finally, in 1952, David Bodian and Dorothy Horstmann of Yale proved that the polio virus circulated in the blood of animals and humans before it traveled to the nervous system. Therefore a vaccine could prevent paralysis by creating antibodies to attack the polio virus before it could do any damage.

After the Enders work, Jonas Salk started serious efforts to create an effective killed-virus vaccine. Salk, born on October 28, 1914, in New York City, graduated from City College and New York University Medical School, following which he had a two-year internship at Mount Sinai Hospital in New York. He had already decided on a research career and was accepted into the University of Michigan laboratory, at Ann Arbor, of Dr. Thomas Francis, Jr., one of his former medical school teachers. Salk arrived at Ann Arbor in 1942. War having broken out, he began working toward a vaccine against the influenza virus. (Every older military man remembered the terrible toll of flu on World War I soldiers.)

But when five years had passed and he had a wife and two sons, Salk felt he had to have a laboratory of his own. Through the efforts of William S. McEllroy, dean of the University of Pittsburgh Medical School, Salk was induced to move to Pittsburgh. There he became involved in a project of typing different polio viruses, finding out to which of the three polio strains each belonged. This project was funded by the National Foundation for Infantile Paralysis, which played the major role in the funding of the many investigations (including those of Salk and Sabin) leading to the conquest of polio. The success of the foundation was primarily due to the efforts of two famous men, Basil O'Connor and President Franklin D. Roosevelt.

These two men had met briefly in 1920, when a healthy young Roosevelt was running on the Democratic ticket for vice president as James M. Cox's running mate. The following year tragedy struck Roosevelt and almost finished his first love—a political career. Vacationing at Campobello, an island off the coast of Maine, he came down with paralytic polio, which left his legs paralyzed. (He had come from crowded and hot Washington, D.C., and New York City a few days earlier.) To make certain that Roosevelt's political career would not be affected, the illness was kept secret at first. Later, when it was known that he had contracted polio, all photographs showed him as vigorous. Usually he used a wheelchair, but in 1924 he "walked," legs locked in knee braces that prevented his knees from bending and assisted by crutches and leaning on his son, to the podium at the Democratic National Convention. There he made his famous Happy Warrior speech, nominating Al Smith, the popular (but twice unsuccessful) candidate for president. In 1928, nominating Al Smith again, Roosevelt walked without crutches. He was crippled, but never would he allow anyone to portray him as less than a vigorous and forceful man.

Roosevelt, always seeking a cure for his paralysis, visited Warm Springs, Georgia, where hot baths relaxed muscles that no longer could function. (All sorts of treatments were suggested; a compassionate Australian nurse, Elizabeth Kenny, came to America to show that plaster casts and splints caused further damage to withered muscles. She used hot packs and massage to give relief.)

By 1924 Roosevelt and Basil O'Connor had become law partners. O'Connor, a much better businessman, rescued the Warm Springs resort, which Roosevelt had purchased and which had steadily lost money. (Roosevelt never had the heart to turn away polio victims who had come to Warm Springs for treatment but had run out of funds.) O'Connor, by this time appreciating how much Warm Springs meant to his partner, other polio victims, and to himself, solved the problem by turning it into a nonprofit organization that could raise funds. In 1938 the Georgia Warm Springs Foundation became the National Foundation for Infantile Paralysis. It would grow into a powerful organization that over the years raised a half billion dollars. Most funds went to help victims of the disease, but over forty million dollars supported the research that led to polio's eradication.

From the beginning the National Foundation for Infantile Paralysis went about collecting money in a much different way from other foundations. Instead of appealing for funds to wealthy socialites and industrialists, the appeals were made to all the people. First, there were the President's Birthday Balls. Then in 1938 the annual January fund-raising campaign was named by entertainer Eddie Cantor the March of Dimes; Cantor suggested that every listener to his radio program help fight polio by sending a dime directly to President Roosevelt at the White House. Each year the heartstrings of the country were touched when a child, usually wearing braces or sitting in a wheelchair, was photographed and became the March of Dimes poster child. The government was glad to cede massive polio fund-raising to this private foundation. U.S. health agencies were then free to concentrate on such badly needed research as that for cancer and heart disease.

The National Foundation grew, helped greatly by its Women's Division; under the direction of Elaine Whitelaw, countless volunteers moved the program forward. Dr. Harry Weaver, an immunologist who guided Salk toward polio investigation, was made director of research for the foundation. He in turn enlisted the help of medical experts; Dr. Thomas M. Rivers became an unpaid adviser to the foundation in 1946. (Ten years earlier Dr. Rivers possibly started virology as a science when he stated that viruses were parasitic and, unlike bacteria, were unable to reproduce themselves unless they entered a living cell. Rivers would become one of the most powerful supporters of the Salk vaccine.) Further medical expertise was enlisted, and in 1951 the Committee on Immunization was formed.

Two years later, however, the newly formed Vaccine Advisory Committee became the scene of bitter controversy.

As a trial of the new Salk vaccine became imminent, there were two opposing schools of thought—those favoring a trial of killed-virus vaccine and those believing that the only way of securing lifelong immunity was by using attenuated live virus vaccines. (A few favored the use of gamma globulin over vaccines, but this substance gave temporary immunity at best, was in short supply relative to the need, and had not proved successful in field trials.) For various reasons neither John Enders nor his associates wanted to get into the vaccine business, but John Paul and Joseph Melnick at Yale were working on a live-virus polio vaccine as was Hilary Koprowski at Lederle, a pharmaceutical company.

Salk, using the Enders tissue-culture technique along with several of his own, had developed a killed-virus vaccine. The three strains of live polio virus were killed primarily by a formalin solution. Then Salk found that, although after meticulous testing no live virus remained, still the dead virus vaccine could cause the body to make protective antibodies against polio. He had tested his vaccine on animals and had enough faith in it to inject it into himself, his family, and some friends. "Asked to comment on his actions thirty years later," wrote Jane Smith in *Patenting the Sun*, "Salk said, 'I look upon it as ritual and symbolic. You wouldn't do unto others that which you wouldn't do unto yourself.' "

In 1952 Salk conducted small but successful trials in two institutions, the Polk School and the D. T. Watson Home for Crippled Children. In all instances the antibody levels against the virus were significantly raised, but the difficulties of proving absolute safety using Salk's methods of meticulous supervision over vaccine production continued.

The opposition to an immense field

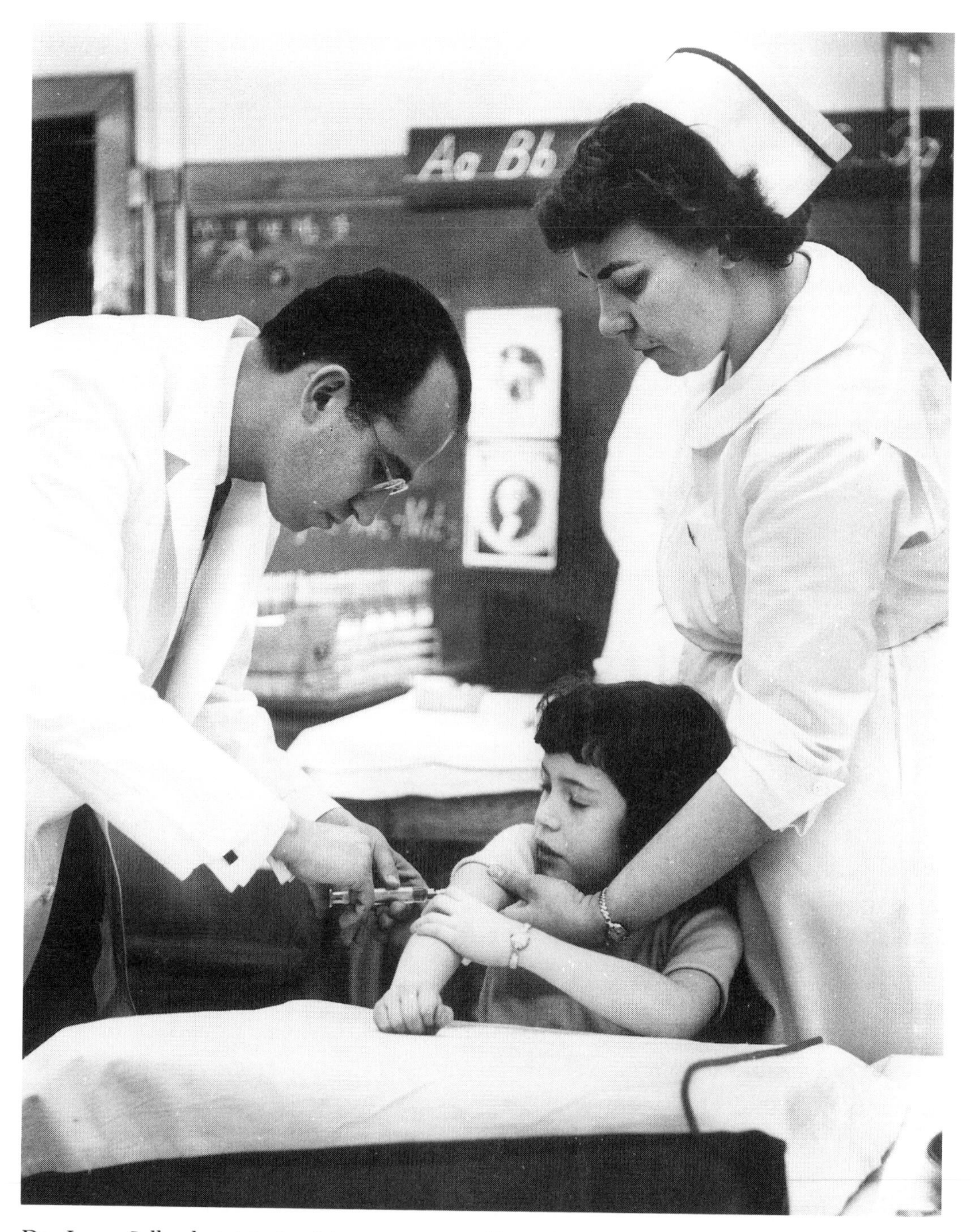

Dr. Jonas Salk administering his vaccine at Colfax School, Pittsburgh, Pennsylvania. *March of Dimes Birth Defects Foundation.*

trial was led by a man with impeccable credentials. Dr. Albert Sabin, professor of pediatrics at the University of Cincinnati since 1939 and eminent virologist, believed that lifelong immunity to polio could be achieved only by the use of a live-virus vaccine. This vaccine would be safe because it would be attenuated—tamed—by repeated passage through animals; with each passage the virus would become less deadly but would still be able to cause antibody production. (Attenuation had been successfully performed for years.) Sabin had been working on such a vaccine; it would be ready for use in a few years. In the meantime, he and several other distinguished virologists fought to delay the trial of the Salk vaccine tentatively scheduled to begin in the spring of 1954.

Albert Sabin was born in Bialystok, Russia, on August 26, 1906. He emigrated to the United States with his family in 1921. Sabin, as Salk did later, graduated from New York University Medical School, obtaining his degree in 1931. He first had leaned toward dentistry but fortunately became interested in microbiology and switched to medicine. Differing in their scientific belief concerning polio vaccine, Salk and Sabin also developed a personal animosity toward each other. Sabin thought Salk an upstart who courted publicity, and Salk resented the condescension with which the older man treated him.

On March 28, 1953, the *Journal of the American Medical Association* (*JAMA*) published Salk's article on his vaccine research titled "Studies in Human Subjects on Active Immunization Against Poliomyelitis." Salk had given his findings earlier to a foundation medical committee, and finally after weeks of bitter debate, the Vaccine Advisory Committee, guided by the firm practical advice of O'Connor, voted unanimously to proceed with the trial of the Salk vaccine.

The field trial was started on April 26, 1954. Because parents were anxious for their children to have protection against polio and through the efforts of thousands of volunteers, over 650,000 children in forty-four states received the three spaced injections of Salk vaccine.

Scrupulous records were kept and sent to Dr. Tom Francis at Ann Arbor. He had taken on the overwhelming and thankless job of evaluating the vaccine's effectiveness. He insisted on being allowed to work privately. Neither Salk nor anyone else was allowed to see preliminary results. Dr. Francis would do a thorough job of the evaluation and release his results only when he had completed his study.

On Tuesday, April 12, 1955, in beautiful Rackham Hall at the University of Michigan, Tom Francis delivered his report in the presence of five hundred invited guests. It was the date of the tenth anniversary of President Roosevelt's death. Reporters from all over North America waited for the press release, which would be handed out with the proviso (not observed) that the news not be released before Francis was finished reading his report. The meeting started at ten o'clock, and the excitement was almost unbearable when Francis began to talk. The result, screamed in headlines all over the world: The vaccine was safe and it worked! It was 60 to 70 percent effective against Type I paralysis and over 90 percent effective against Types II and III. Against the dreaded bulbar form, it was 94 percent effective; overall it was between 80 and 90 percent effective against paralytic polio. (Against Salk's wishes, merthiolate had been added in the production process. Salk claimed that without it the vaccine would have been 100 percent effective.) It was a triumph enjoyed by all. There was no inkling that day of the tragedy that would hit less than two weeks later.

On April 25, 1955, the first case of vaccine-induced paralytic polio was reported. The child had been injected with vaccine from Cutter Laboratories. Within days the cases began to mount up, all caused by the presence of live viruses in the Cutter vaccine. None of the six companies making the vaccine had followed the stringent Salk production specifications, but only the Cutter vaccine caused a total of 204 cases of polio. Of these, three-quarters were paralyzed, and there were eleven deaths. (Approximately 400,000 children had been vaccinated with Cutter vaccine.)

Surgeon General Leonard Scheele ordered a temporary halt to all vaccinations on May 7 in order to investigate what had gone wrong. Sabin felt that the Salk program should be abandoned, and Enders suggested a two-year delay to investigate a particularly virulent Type I strain. But the majority of a committee of experts voted to restart the program. (Enders and Sabin voted against, and Salk did not cast his vote.)

Vaccinations were resumed after several batches of vaccine from Parke, Davis had been inspected and found to be safe. Soon other companies were again in the vaccine business. The demand, since the polio season was approaching, was tremendous. Parents were understandably convinced that since all cases had come from the Cutter vaccine, it was safe to proceed with vaccine that had been cleared by the United States Public Health Service. In the ensuing years, there were no

Dr. Albert Sabin in his laboratory at the University of Cincinnati in 1959. *March of Dimes Birth Defects Foundation.*

more Salk vaccine polio cases. New standards for vaccine production and testing had been established. (The Cutter tragedy spelled the end of a privately run program. Government agencies would never again allow a private foundation to have such power.)

Over the next several years there was a remarkable decline in the number of polio cases. Whereas in 1952 a severe epidemic had caused 58,000 new cases of polio, the number of cases reported in 1962 had dropped to just over 900. Polio was on its way out.

By 1957 Sabin had developed a live-virus polio vaccine, and as Salk did, he first tried it on himself. He could not have a mass test in the United States, however, since so many children had received Salk vaccine. Accordingly, he had his live-virus vaccine tested in the Soviet Union in 1959 with great success. There was only a minimal possibility of paralytic polio—four cases per million oral vaccinations—and the Sabin vaccine was licensed for use in the United States in 1961. Because it is cheaper and easier to administer than the Salk vaccine, Sabin's vaccine is now almost exclusively used in America. However, it will never be known now whether, even without booster shots, the Salk vaccine could have provided lifelong immunity to polio.

Basil O'Connor lived to see his dream fulfilled. He died in 1972 at the age of eighty on his way to a National Foundation meeting, having outlived his wife and two grown daughters, one of whom had been a polio victim.

Neither Jonas Salk nor Albert Sabin ever received a Nobel Prize, probably because the Nobel committee considered its 1954 award to Enders, Weller, and Robbins proper acknowledgment of important and innovative polio research. In any event, it seems clear that Salk and Sabin did fulfill Alfred Nobel's criterion when he established the prize: that it be awarded for contributions to "the good of humanity." Today polio has disappeared from the Western Hemisphere, and the hope is that soon the entire world will be rid of this dread disease.

In 1963 Jonas Salk founded the Salk Institute for Biological Studies. The institute is still in operation, and scholars from all over the world pursue their studies alone or in collaboration with other researchers. Francis Crick is among the scholars working at the Salk Institute.

Albert Bruce Sabin, at the age of eighty-five, also continues an active research life. He has retired five times and in each instance, decided that he wanted to return to scientific studies. Currently he is working on the eradication of measles.

Helen Brooke Taussig

1898–1986 American pediatric cardiologist; discoverer of congenital heart disease repair

Helen Brooke Taussig, the first woman pediatric cardiologist, was born on May 24, 1898, in Cambridge, Massachusetts. She was the daughter of parents who instilled in her a sense of independence. Her father, Frank W. Taussig, was a professor of economics at Harvard. Helen began her undergraduate education at Radcliffe, Harvard's associate college, but although her relationship with her parents was close, she did not want to live in the shadow of her famous father. She moved to the West Coast and received her B.A. from the University of California, Berkeley.

When Helen Taussig told her father that she would like a career in medicine, he thought that she would have more success in the field of public health than in other areas of medicine. When the dean of Harvard's School of Public Health gave her permission to enroll in the four-year course, however, he informed her that no woman would be granted a degree. She learned also that she could not be admitted to Harvard Medical School, although she could take some courses there. (Women were not admitted to Harvard Medical School until 1945.) She enrolled in histology (microscopic study of tissues) and bacteriology classes and then transferred to Boston University's School of Medicine for a year of anatomy instruction. It was an important move, as she pointed out in an article in the February 1981 issue of the *Journal of the Ameri-*

can Medical Women's Association, "Little Choice and a Stimulating Environment":

> Dr. Alexander Begg, Professor of Anatomy and Dean of the Medical School, asked me to study the muscle bundles of an ox heart, saying it would do me no harm to be interested in one of the larger organs of the body as I went through medical school. That started my interest in cardiology. Later Dr. Begg urged me to go to Hopkins.

Dr. Taussig did go to Johns Hopkins, where during her medical school years she worked at the Heart Station (a division of the medical service) under the direction of Dr. Edward P. Carter. After graduation she was offered a fellowship by Dr. Carter. When Dr. Edwards Park arrived at Hopkins from Yale to become professor of pediatrics, he saw the need for a pediatric cardiac clinic. This decision was based mostly on the high incidence of rheumatic fever in children, a disease that often resulted in damage to heart valves. After postgraduate training at Johns Hopkins and then Boston, Dr. Taussig in 1930 was appointed director of the new Harriet Lane's Pediatric Cardiac Clinic for children. Her friends asked, "Why go into such a narrow field as pediatric cardiology?" Helen Taussig obviously did not view the study of heart disease in children as *narrow:*

> Dr. Park gave me the tools to work with: an electrocardiograph, a technician secretary and a social worker. All for $4,000, including my salary! He arranged to have x-rays taken without cost to the patient and installed a fluoroscope in Harriet Lane Home for the use of the pediatric staff. Dr. Park firmly believed that new tools brought new knowledge. In 1930 a fluoroscope was a new tool. It proved to be my most useful one.

The EKG and the fluoroscope were useful indeed, as was the sensitivity of Dr. Taussig's hands. The fluoroscope was especially valuable to her. It is essentially an X-ray machine. A person stands (or an infant is held) behind the screen. The motion of the heart and lungs can be seen. By repeatedly changing the position of the patient from front to back or halfway, one can observe the size of the heart chambers. What appears white on a developed X ray (bones, for example) appears dark on a fluoroscope screen and vice versa, the soft tissues appearing white.

Helen Taussig was hard of hearing, the result of a childhood attack of whooping cough, and also suffered in early years from dyslexia, a condition that makes learning to read most difficult. The stethoscope, so valuable to cardiologists, was of no use to her because she couldn't hear the heart murmurs. But she could feel the vibrations resulting from the turbulence caused by heart valve damage. In a 1981 article in *Medical Times,* she advised hard-of-hearing doctors how to "feel" heart murmurs: "The secret of palpation," she told them, "is gentle but close approximation of the sensitive part of your hand to the chest wall. Heavy pressure lessens the detection of the vibration."

When Dr. Taussig began her work at the Pediatric Cardiac Clinic, physicians in other pediatric areas were reluctant to refer their heart patients to her; they wanted the experience of learning about rheumatic heart disease themselves. But they were perfectly willing to send cyanotic infants ("blue babies"—those whose skin had a bluish tint because of lack of oxygen in their blood) to her. These babies were "gladly referred to me as nothing could be done for them," Dr. Taussig recalled. She was to change this hopeless situation and make medical history in the process.

Dr. Sherwin B. Nuland, in his book *Doctors,* explains that the disease originally was described in 1871 by a Dutch physician, Eduard Sandifort, who autopsied a blue baby who had reached the age of twelve before dying of his heart disease. But it was a French pathology professor who in 1888 recognized the four defects involved. His name was Étienne-Louis Fallot, and because of these four congenital (present at birth) anatomical defects, the disorder was named tetralogy of Fallot. It accounts for three-quarters of blue babies.

It is the oxygen supplied by the lungs to blood returning to the heart via the veins that gives blood its red color. Unoxygenated blood is darker, and when it predominates, it gives the skin a dusky or bluish color. The right side of the heart pumps blood returned by the veins to the lungs, and then this now oxygenated "red" blood returns from the lungs to the left side of the heart. The left ventricle pumps this aerated blood all over the body, leaving the heart through the largest artery in the body, the aorta.

The four major defects in tetralogy of Fallot are: (a) severe narrowing of the pulmonary artery, making it difficult for venous blood to get to the lungs and also raising the blood pressure inside the right side of the heart, normally lower than that in the left side; (b) an interventricular septal defect. This consists of a hole in the wall that separates the left side of the heart from the right. Because of the high pressure in the right ventricle, venous blood is forced into the left ventricle without ever having reached the lungs; (c) a thick-walled right ventricle caused by that chamber having to pump hard because of the obstruction above; and (d) an aorta displaced to the right side so that the unoxygenated blood from the right ventricle can flow into the aorta. As a baby with this disorder grows bigger, the body's need for oxygen is greater. The result is that these infants and children are not only blue in color but also very short of breath. Even slight exertion frequently causes them to lose consciousness.

Dr. Maude Abbott at McGill University in Toronto was at that time the world's expert on congenital heart disease. Author of *Atlas of Congenital Heart Disease,* she had acquired her knowledge by studying and classifying specimens of heart defects while she was unpaid curator of the McGill museum of pathology. In 1938 Helen Taussig traveled to McGill to consult with her. Taussig already had learned much by herself through the use of the fluoroscope and electrocardiogram and by being present at the autopsies of her young patients. She absorbed additional information from Maude Abbott.

Although Helen Taussig knew about the diagnosis of congenital heart disease, now she wanted to find a cure for her blue babies. She had been helpless to prevent their deaths. Based on all her experience, she had an idea. If a bypass could be surgically created that would bring the dark venous blood back to the lungs—it would connect *above* the narrowing obstruction in the pulmonary artery—then her patients could get enough oxygen in their blood to keep them reasonably healthy.

Dr. Taussig was thinking of the blood vessel called the persistent ductus, which shunts blood from the pulmonary artery to the aorta before birth. The unborn baby gets its oxygenated blood from its mother and its lungs are not used until the moment of birth. Sometimes this vessel (which almost always closes at birth since it no longer is needed) does not close but persists, and the blood flow through it causes heart damage. An operation had already been devised to tie off the ductus. But in the case of blue babies, she reasoned, why not create a ductus to reverse the procedure and get dusky blood to the lungs to be oxygenated?

Taussig traveled to Boston to persuade the surgeon who had devised the operation to consider her idea for the creation of a ductus.

He was not interested, but fortunately Dr. Alfred Blalock, chairman of the Johns Hopkins Department of Surgery, *was* interested in Dr. Taussig's idea when she presented it in the fall of 1943. Dr. Edwards Park, Taussig's mentor, remarked about that meeting that in Dr. Alfred Blalock she had at last found her "daring young man on

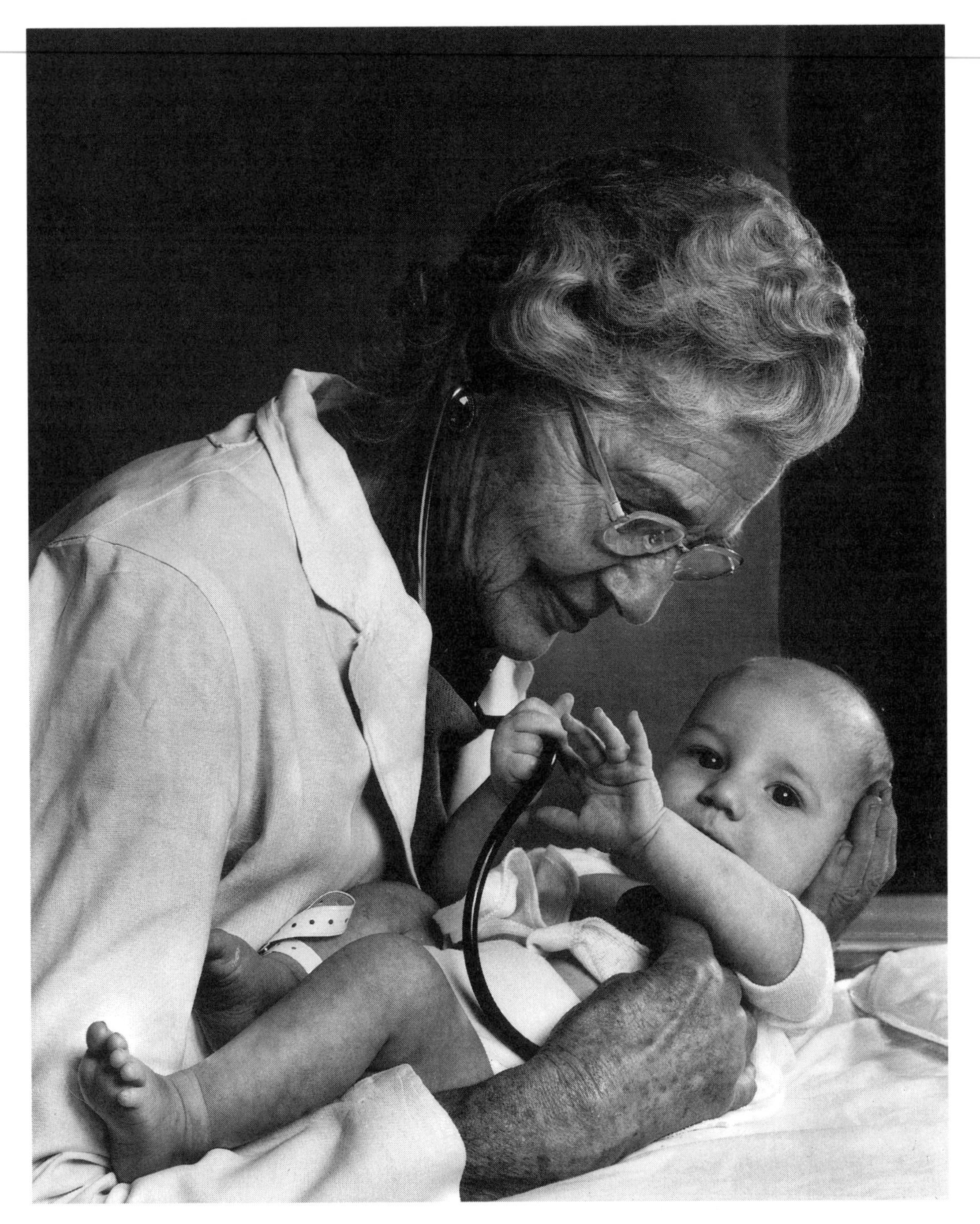

Yousuf Karsh's 1975 photograph of Dr. Helen Taussig. *Copyright © 1975, Yousuf Karsh/ Woodfin Camp & Associates.*

the flying trapeze!" Born in Georgia, Dr. Blalock was at Vanderbilt when, in 1930, he began working with a brilliant nineteen-year-old black man, Vivian Thomas, whose lack of funds prevented him from pursuing higher education. Blalock brought Thomas to Johns Hopkins with him since Thomas had, in the words of Dr. Nuland, "the hands of a master technician and the perceptive instincts of a born researcher." Thomas worked out the technical details of the proposed operation, using the subclavian artery in the foreleg of a dog to create a ductus. He operated on approximately two hundred dogs before he felt that the procedure was safe enough to try on a human. (The subclavian artery was used for the bypass in humans as well, without damage to circulation in the arm.)

The first patient was an eleven-month-old girl, Eileen Saxon, whose condition had deteriorated to the point that she could live only inside an oxygen tent. The first operation took place on November 29, 1944. During the course of the surgery Blalock had Thomas called to the operating room to advise on certain technical aspects of the surgery. Mary Allen Engle, later a well-known cardiologist, present at that first dramatic operation, recalled: "Little did I suspect, as a fourth year medical student and substitute intern on pediatric surgery, that I would witness history in the making."

The baby slowly improved. Dr. Taussig and one of her cardiology fellows stayed with her constantly, doing everything possible to insure that the baby would survive. And survive she did. The first time her mother was allowed to see her, she looked at her now pink baby and considered that a miracle had been performed, as indeed it had. Other successful blue-baby operations followed. In the next six years, Dr. Blalock and his associates performed surgery on over a thousand young patients. After the initial successes were heralded in the press, children with tetralogy of Fallot were brought to Johns Hopkins from all over the world. Many arrived unannounced, but through excellent organization not one child was neglected. (In later years with the development of open-heart surgery, pediatric surgery advanced to the point where it was possible to repair all of the defects of the tetralogy.)

Helen Taussig had been working for ten years on a book on pediatric cardiology, *Congenital Malformations of the Heart*. When it was published in 1947, she was able to report not only the surgical results of the Blalock-Taussig operation but also on surgical measures to correct other congenital heart abnormalities. Taussig recalled that some of her friends wondered why she would "waste her time" on "such a trivial subject." "I replied as I would today. 'If you stay in academic medicine and learn anything, you are morally obligated to make that knowledge available to others.'"

As a result of the research work preceding the successful Blalock-Taussig bypass, or shunt, antivivisectionists protested loudly against the laboratory personnel at Johns Hopkins and other institutions in the area. When hearings were held on the subject by the Baltimore City Council, Helen Taussig brought into the hearing room a group of smiling former blue babies whose cheeks were now healthily pink. Many of the children brought their own pet dogs to the hearing. The next day the newspapers carried the story along with photographs. When an antivivisection bill came to a vote, it was overwhelmingly defeated.

Alfred Blalock and Helen Taussig made several trips together to demonstrate their new procedure and in 1947 traveled to England, where Blalock performed his operation.

Taussig continued her heavy schedule through the years and in 1959 became professor of pediatrics at Johns Hopkins. By that time she was the most famous woman physician in the world. Despite her focus on heart disease, actually everything affecting the health of young people concerned her greatly. It was not surprising, therefore, that when a West German pharmaceutical firm marketed a drug called Contergan, Taussig became involved in the ensuing controversy. The drug, popular with pregnant women because it not only had sedative qualities but also prevented nausea, was sold over the counter. The William S. Merrell Company sought permission from the Food and Drug Administration (FDA) to market the drug in the United States under the name Thalidomide. Dr. Frances Kelsey, a physician administrator in the FDA, feeling its proof of safety was scientifically inadequate, denied Merrell's application, demanding that the company provide, via testing, better evidence that the drug was safe.

In January 1962 Dr. Taussig learned from one of her former German students that several babies of mothers in Germany who had taken Contergan had been born with a defect called *phocomelia.* They had abnormalities of the arms or legs and sometimes were missing almost all of their extremities; hands and feet seemed to emerge directly from their little bodies. Dr. Taussig wasted no time traveling to Germany to investigate the situation herself. She spent six weeks in visiting clinics, examining babies, questioning mothers. She noted

Dr. Taussig testifying before the Senate Committee on Drugs concerning the dangers of the drug thalidomide. *UPI/Bettmann.*

a curious fact: Phocomelia was absent among the newborn infants of American soldiers stationed in Germany with the exception of one case; there, the mother had obtained Contergan by buying it at a local pharmacy off the base. Dr. Kelsey was delighted to learn that Helen Taussig was conducting an independent investigation. Frances Kelsey's foresight and testimony combined with Taussig's resulted in the permanent United States ban on thalidomide. Fortunately only a small number of babies in the United States were born with phocomelia during the testing period.

Dr. Taussig retired as physician in charge of Harriet Lane's Pediatric Cardiac Clinic in 1963, but her research continued full speed. At the time of her death, she had published one hundred scientific articles, forty-one of them after her "retirement." In 1965, when she became the first woman president of the American Heart Association, she voiced her opinion that blood vessel disease began in infancy and childhood; the dietary modifications used in pediatric diets today—especially low fat—reflect her views.

It is interesting that a cardiologist friend, Carleton Chapman, wrote that "she never thought much of her own ability or intellect. I was astounded to learn this from her. She continually needed for her confidence to be built up and she was the last person to get into any priority battle." This quality is not unusual among those who have contributed mightily.

On May 21, 1986, only three days short of her eighty-eighth birthday, Helen Taussig's car was hit broadside by another car as she was backing out of her driveway, and she was killed instantly. It is typical of her public service that she had been about to drive some people to the polls to vote.

Helen Taussig's scientific contributions are only part of what she gave to medicine. Unlike some detached physicians, she never was afraid to show her emotions. She shed tears with parents when things went badly with their children, and she shared the parents' joy when results were successful. She was not only a brilliant, innovative physician, but just as important, she was at all times compassionate.

Joseph E. Murray

1919– American surgeon; initiated and advanced the surgical specialty of organ transplantation

From the beginnings of recorded medical history, all sorts of exciting advances continuously have been made. Several chapters in this volume have been devoted to the surgical area, and mention should also be made of Ephraim McDowell. In 1809 this Danville, Kentucky, backwoods doctor (educated at Edinburgh) did what had been considered impossible up to that time; he removed a twenty-pound ovarian tumor (before the days of anesthesia or antisepsis). McDowell must have had tremendous powers of concentration; a noisy lynch mob was waiting outside his cabin to hang him if his patient, one Jane Crawford, failed to survive. Luckily she lived for thirty more years. James Thomas Flexner reports:

> McDowell's operation was one of the most important in the history of surgery . . . his cure for this otherwise fatal condition was only the lesser part of his discovery. More significant still was his demonstration that the abdominal cavity could be cut into with impunity. . . . Every operation for appendicitis or gallstones is a lineal descendant of one daring experiment made in the wilderness of Kentucky.

This chapter tells the story of a surgeon, Joseph E. Murray, who was an equally daring pioneer in one of the exciting new surgical fields—organ transplantation—and of some other courageous contributors to that field. The scope of organ transplantation is widening every year, but the emphasis here will be on those early years when nobody could be certain that operations of this sort on humans would succeed. For his work in initiating and advancing the surgical specialty transplantation, Dr. Murray was awarded the 1990 Nobel Prize in physiology or medicine. (The cowinner was Dr. E. Donnall Thomas for his pioneering work in bone marrow transplantation.)

Joseph Murray was born on April 1, 1919, in Milford, Massachusetts, a town thirty miles southwest of Boston. His father's parents were of southern Irish and English extraction, and his mother had been born in Rhode Island, soon after her parents had emigrated to this country from Italy. Joseph Murray's father was a lawyer and a district court judge. His mother was a schoolteacher. Education and the need for service to others were emphasized by them, largely through use of example.

At Milford High, Murray was captain of the baseball team for two years, and although he batted .400 his senior year, he never considered an athletic career. Joseph Murray always wanted to become a surgeon. He chose a small liberal arts college, Holy Cross, concentrating there on Latin, Greek, philosophy, and English; he rightly assumed that medical school would provide ample science. Then he attended Harvard Medical School, which institution he thoroughly enjoyed. Aside from the stimulating classroom and clinical work, cultural centers were close by, and Murray appreciated Symphony Hall and the Gardner Museum. His interests during medical school (and thereafter) were multiple—he played tennis and squash, bicycled, joined a weekly singing group, and attended club dances.

"During the final few months of medical school," Joseph Murray recalls, "while attending a Boston Symphony Orchestra concert with several classmates and their dates, I noticed a lovely young lady 'far too nice' for the fellow she was with. At intermission I manipulated her towards the corridor and learned that she was Bobby Link, a music student concentrating on voice and piano. By the time the intermission had ended I realized that I had met the girl I would marry."

They were married in 1945 and have raised six children—three boys and three girls. "Each has contributed to society in her/his own way, in education, medicine, nursing, business and science," Dr. Murray states, adding that "Bobby's music, pursued professionally for fifteen years after marriage, continually adds to the richness and beauty of our family and social life."

After graduating from medical school in 1943, Dr. Murray began a surgical internship at Peter Bent Brigham Hospital (now the Brigham & Women's Hospital) in Boston. His training was interrupted by World War II. With only nine months of the internship behind him, he became a first lieutenant and was randomly assigned by the U.S. Army to Valley Forge General Hospital (VFGH) in Pennsylvania. His interest in the biology of tissue and organ transplantation originated with his military experience there. VFGH was a major plastic surgical center. The plastic surgical wards were jammed with hundreds of battle casualties. Dr. Murray enjoyed his time spent with the patients, and he had the opportunity to observe the results of the imaginative reconstructive surgical operations. Years later he learned that the chief of plastic surgery, Colonel James Barrett Brown, noticing the young lieutenant's day and night presence on the wards, asked that Dr. Murray remain at VFGH instead of being sent overseas. It was the world's good fortune that Dr. Brown's request was honored.

At VFGH Murray was influenced by several plastic surgeons including Dr. Bradford Cannon, son of the famous physiologist Walter Cannon. It was there that Dr. Murray's reflections about the treatment of burns led to his later work on transplantation. While scrubbing before operations, Dr. Murray would discuss skin graft rejection with his chief. Somehow the recipient's body recognized that the transplanted skin graft differed from its own skin—was foreign—and slowly reacted against it, eventually destroying it. The body's antibodies fought the foreign skin, resulting in an inflammatory reaction called an *immune response.* This host-versus-graft battle fascinated Dr. Murray. He knew that genetics were definitely involved, since Dr. Brown, in 1937, had experimentally and successfully cross skin-grafted a pair of identical twins. That operation became the impetus to Murray's study of organ transplantation.

The best candidates to be donors for a transplant (graft) are those people who are immunologically closest to the person who will receive the graft. For example, skin grafted from one part of our own body to cover a burn in another area is the very best match. This kind of graft is called an *autograft.* An *isograft* is a graft between individuals of the same species—for example, grafts within genetically pure strains of mice. Grafts between identical twins are properly termed *isografts.* An *allograft* is the term used to describe tissues or organs transplanted from a donor to a recipient of the same species where the donor and recipient are *not* immunologically alike. Cadaver donor grafts as well as all grafts from living donors (identical twins excluded) are allografts. *Xeno-*

grafts is the term used to describe transplants where the donor is a different species from the recipient. The most common xenografts are pig valves to replace damaged human heart valves.

After the war Dr. Murray completed his residency at the Brigham Hospital, and after working in head and neck surgery at Memorial Sloan-Kettering Hospital (now Cancer Center) in New York City and taking an additional half year in plastic surgery at New York Hospital, he returned to the Brigham to continue his monumental work on kidney (renal) transplantation. Beginning with the late 1940s, human organ transplantation was being attempted continuously but without good results. Curiously the basic scientists and immunologists were pessimistic that there ever could be success in this field while optimistic surgeons disagreed and pushed the program forward. The Brigham was an excellent place to work on transplantation because the surgical, medical, and pathology staffs were greatly interested in severe renal disease and in effecting permanent cures for it. A primitive artificial kidney was available, but this provided only temporary improvement for patients.

Dr. Murray was asked by Dr. David Hume to take over the experimental side of the renal transplant program and discovered at once that he was not satisfied with the surgical techniques used either in patients or in dogs. At that time there had been no successful long-term autografts in animals. One of Dr. Murray's first projects "was to devise a surgical operation which could produce long-term, normally functioning, renal autografts." This operation proved to be successful on dogs; then came a breakthrough case involving humans.

Identical twins, one with serious kidney failure and the other healthy, became the participants in the first successful organ transplant on December 23, 1954. A few months earlier Dr. Donald Miller of the United States Public Health Service referred the H. twins (Richard, the ill patient; Ronald, the prospective donor) to Dr. John P. Merrill, who headed the medical section of the Brigham's renal transplant program. Skin graft studies were done to prove that the twins were identical, and dialysis was used to bring Richard's renal disease under control. (Dialysis is the process of passing the blood through a machine, a method used to get rid of blood impurities that sick kidneys cannot excrete.) In his Nobel Prize lecture, Dr. Murray discussed the serious issue that had had to be addressed:

The only remaining problem was the ethical decision concerning the removal of a healthy organ from a normal person for the benefit of someone else. For the first

Dr. Joseph Murray with attendants and the dogs that successfully received kidney transplants. *Courtesy of Dr. Joseph E. Murray.*

time in medical history a normal healthy person was to be subjected to a major surgical operation not for his own benefit.

After many consultations with experienced physicians within and outside the Brigham and with the clergy of all denominations, we felt it reasonable to offer the operations to the recipient, the donor and their family. We discussed in detail the preparations, anesthesia, operations, possible complications and anticipated result.

The operations (removal of the donor kidney and its transplantation into the recipient) were completely successful. Dr. J. Hartwell Harrison removed the donor kidney—kidneys are paired organs, and a person can live a normal life with only one kidney—and Dr. Joseph Murray did the transplantation. The impact of this success was worldwide and stimulated research on how to overcome the immune response. If that could be accomplished, then transplantation operations of all kinds would not be restricted to identical twins. There would be an advantage to having as close as possible genetic similarity between donor and recipient,

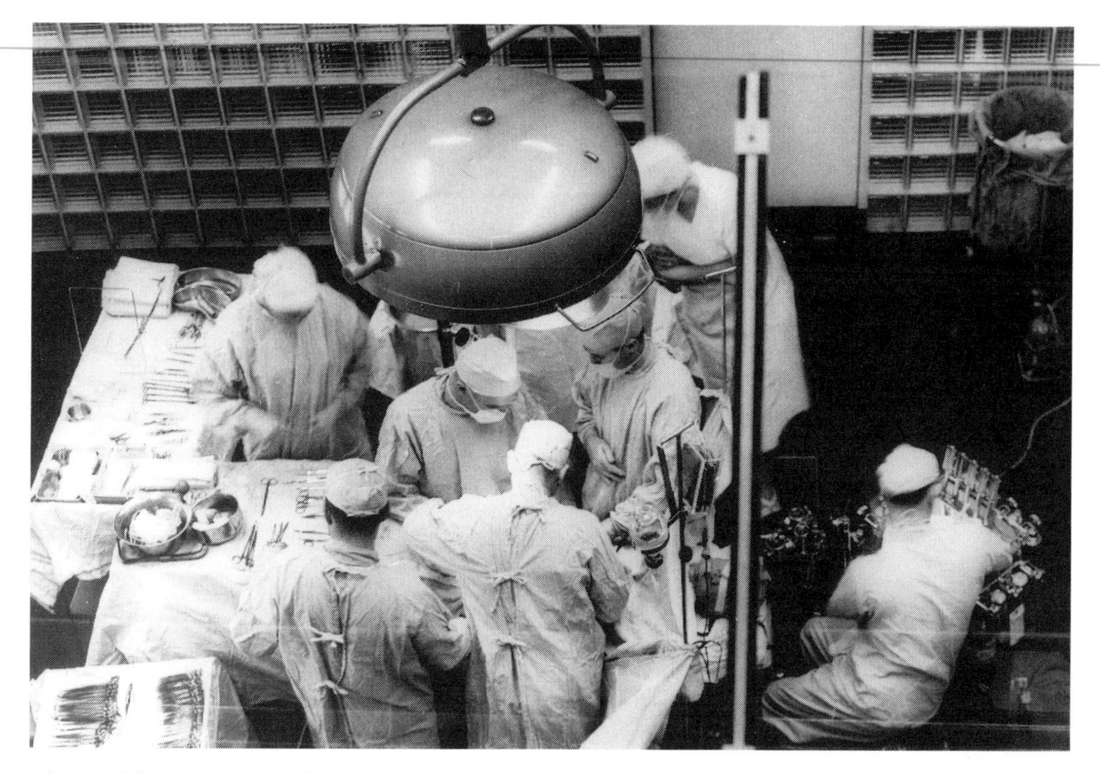

The world's first successful renal transplantation at Peter Bent Brigham Hospital, December 23, 1954. (*Dr. Murray is facing the camera under the lamp.*) *Courtesy of Dr. Joseph E. Murray.*

but if one or more drugs could suppress the immune response, then organs might be used for transplant surgery even after the donor's death (cadaver organs).

In the early 1950s, before that historic identical twin transplant, some human kidney allografts had been done at the Brigham, and one of them functioned for five months before it was rejected. These were the days when organ procurement was difficult because both the public and medical profession required education about the need for donating organs after death. The problems of organ preservation, formation of transplant banks, and tissue matching were profound; discussion of their solutions would be a book in itself.

The Murray operation created a tremendous stimulus to try to overcome the immune response. In the early 1940s, T. Gibson and Peter Medawar had shown that the rejection process was not necessarily uncontrollable; since a second allograft from the same donor was rejected more rapidly than the first, it became clear that the process was allergic or immunological and might be manipulated. It seemed that one could develop tolerance to foreign transplanted tissue. Instead of fighting this tissue, the body could be made to treat it as one of its own and not reject it. (Australian investigator Macfarlane Burnet formulated the theory of acquired immunity against foreign tissue, and Peter Medawar later confirmed it. The two shared the 1960 Nobel Prize in physiology or medicine.)

In 1959 the real breakthrough came when R. Schwartz and W. Dameshek published their report that the drug 6-Mercaptopurine (6-MP) could successfully suppress the immune reaction to foreign proteins—chemicals that constitute most body tissue. Since then many new drugs have been developed and when used continuously are effective in preventing graft rejection. Dr. Murray believes that in the future substances naturally produced by the body will be discovered and will eliminate the need for immunosuppressive drugs. He concluded his Nobel Prize lecture by stating that the outlook for that discovery "surely is as probable as the prospect of obtaining successful organ transplants was forty-five years ago."

Following the identical twin transplant, Dr. Murray and his team continued to try human kidney allografts using the drug Imuran (a derivative of 6-MP) to suppress rejection. Then in April 1962 they used a cadaver kidney for the human allograft and produced the world's first successful unrelated renal allograft. Kidney transplants now save innumerable lives. It is currently estimated that more than 200,000 human transplants have been performed worldwide.

For technical reasons, kidney transplants are placed low in the pelvis, not their usual location. This type of placement is called *heterotopic*. If possible, when a diseased organ is replaced with a healthy one, the new organ will be placed in the same area the old one occupied.

Renal allograft successes naturally led to attempts to transplant other organs. In 1968 Thomas Starzl and his team, using the surgical technique developed by Dr. Francis Moore, performed the first successful human liver transplant, replacing the damaged liver with a donor liver in the same location; this same-site operation is termed *orthotopic*. Today this operation performed all over the world is second in frequency only to kidney transplants. Heart transplantation followed. R. R. Lower and Norman E. Shumway had developed the technique in dogs in 1961 and were planning a careful program for cardiac transplantation in humans. But after Christiaan Barnard performed the first human cardiac transplant in 1967, a number of cardiac surgeons with little or no immunologic background jumped into the field. All of their patients died from tissue rejection within a few months, and Dr. Murray recalls that this period between 1968–1970 was "undoubtedly transplantation's darkest hour." But luckily Dr. Norman Shumway's careful work at Stanford University in California continued and by 1970 had achieved permanent success.

Early on Dr. Murray's work had pioneered the concept of brain death, but this didn't apply under California law. In 1973 Dr. Shumway, at great legal risk to himself, transplanted to dying patients the hearts of two young people, the first the victim of a shooting and the second the victim of a drunk driver. Both cases were tried in 1974, and the first became known as the "Heart Transplant Murder Case." In both trials the attorneys contended that their clients, the gunman and the drunk driver, respectively, were not responsible for the victims' deaths; they claimed that the deaths were caused by the transplant surgeon, despite the fact that both victims had suffered irreversible brain death and their hearts remained beating only because they were on respirators. (When the brain dies, other complications develop in the kidneys or lungs or elsewhere so that eventually the heart will stop beating even while that person is on the respirator.) These dramatic court trials resulted in a change in California's legal definition of death to include "total and irreversible cessation of brain function."

Dr. Joseph E. Murray in October 1990 after learning that he had won the Nobel Prize in medicine. *Reuters/Bettmann.*

Other single- and multiple-organ transplants have followed kidney, liver, and heart transplants. These include lung, combined heart-lung, pancreas, and multiple-organ transplants in combination with livers and parts of the intestinal tract.

Clinical transplantation required full-time commitment, and Dr. Murray's major commitment was to the repair of head and facial birth defects in children, so beginning in 1967 he gradually withdrew from the field. During the course of his subsequent travels, he spent time in India reconstructing the hands and faces of patients disfigured by leprosy.

Dr. Murray ended a short biographical note for the Nobel committee as follows:

For recreation, I have always been a physical enthusiast. As a family we have camped, hiked, trekked, or backpacked over portions of five continents. Competitive tennis remains fun. Our extended family, with 11 grandchildren, gets together frequently during the year, and always every summer on Martha's Vineyard Island in Massachusetts.

We have been blessed in our lives beyond my wildest dreams. My only wish would be to have ten more lives to live on this planet. If that were possible, I'd spend one lifetime each in embryology, genetics, physics, astronomy and geology. The other lifetimes would be as a pianist, backwoodsman, tennis player, or writer for the *National Geographic.* If anyone has bothered to read this far, you would note that I still have one future lifetime unaccounted for. That is because I'd like to keep open the option for another lifetime as a surgeon-scientist.

In an editorial in the November 1990 issue of the *Archives of Surgery,* Dr. Maurice J. Jurkiewicz points out that the combination of brilliant research ability, ability to inspire and teach, and outstanding clinical skills rarely occur in the same individual. "Individuals like Joseph Murray, pure gold, are uncommon." He concludes the editorial with these words:

His legacy to humankind: a definitive answer to end-stage renal disease, a powerful stimulus to basic immunologic research worldwide, craniofacial reconstruction, character, and kindness. His legacy to surgery: two entirely new fields of surgery, the stimulus and inspiration for numerous leaders of surgery not only in this country but throughout the world, and the model of an educated surgeon.

Further Reading

Titles marked by an asterisk are most suitable for young readers.

GENERAL

*Aaseng, Nathan. *The Disease Fighters, The Nobel Prize in Medicine.* Minneapolis: Lerner Publications Company, 1987.

Asimov, Isaac. *Asimov's Biographical Encyclopedia of Science and Technology.* New York: Doubleday, 1982.

Chandler, Caroline, M.D. *Famous Men of Medicine.* New York: Dodd, Mead, 1950.

*De Kruif, Paul. *Microbe Hunters.* New York: Harcourt, Brace, 1926.

Gibson, John, M.D. *Great Doctors and Medical Scientists.* London: Macmillan, 1967.

*Gibson, William L. *Young Endeavor.* Springfield, Ill.: Charles C. Thomas, 1958.

*Haggard, Howard W. *The Doctor in History.* New Haven: Yale University Press, 1934.

Lambert, Samuel W., M.D., and George M. Goodwin, M.D. *Minute Men of Life.* New York: Grosset & Dunlap, 1929.

*Lyons, Albert S. *Medicine, An Illustrated History.* New York: Harry N. Abrams, 1978.

Martin, Wayne. *Medical Heroes and Heretics.* Old Greenwich, Conn.: Devin-Adair Company.

*Nuland, Sherwin B. *Doctors.* New York: Alfred A. Knopf, 1988.

*Rapport, Samuel, and Helen Wright. *Great Adventures in Medicine.* New York: Dial Press, 1952.

*Riedman, Sarah R., and Elton T. Gustafson. *Portraits of Nobel Laureates in Medicine and Physiology.* London: Abelard-Schuman, 1963.

*Robbin, Irving, and Samuel Nisenson. *Giants of Medicine.* New York: Grosset & Dunlap, 1962.

*Sigerist, Henry E., M.D. *Great Doctors.* London: George Allen & Unwin, 1933.

Singer, Charles (updated by E. Ashworth Underwood). *A Short History of Medicine.* New York: Oxford University Press, 1962.

Wiglom, William H. *Discoverers for Medi-*

cine. Freeport, N.Y.: Books for Libraries Press, 1949 (reprinted 1971).

BANTING

Banting, F. G., and C. H. Best. "The Internal Secretion of the Pancreas." *The Journal of Laboratory and Clinical Medicine*. February 1922.

*Harris, Seale, M.D. *Banting's Miracle*. Philadelphia: J. B. Lippincott, 1946.

*Levine, I. E. *The Discoverer of Insulin, Dr. Frederick G. Banting*. New York: Julian Messner, 1959, 1968.

BLACKWELL

*Baker, Rachel. *The First Woman Doctor*. New York: Julian Messner, 1944.

Ross, Ishbel. *Child of Destiny*. New York: Harper and Brothers, 1949.

Wilson, Dorothy Clarke. *Lone Woman*. Boston: Little, Brown, 1970.

CANNON

Benison, Saul, A. Clifford Barger, and Elin Wolfe. *Walter B. Cannon: The Life and Times of a Young Scientist*. Cambridge: Harvard University Press, 1987.

*Cannon, Walter Bradford. *The Way of an Investigator*. New York: Hafner Publishing Company, 1965.

*Gibson, William L. *Young Endeavor*. Springfield, Ill.: Charles C. Thomas, 1958.

CURIE

Curie, Eve. *Madame Curie*. Translated by Vincent Sheean. New York: Doubleday, Doran, 1937.

DREW

*Wynes, Charles E. *Charles Richard Drew, The Man and the Myth*. Urbana: University of Illinois Press, 1988.

EHRLICH

*Marquardt, Martha. *Paul Ehrlich*. New York: Henry Schuman, 1951.

FLEMING, FLOREY, and CHAIN

Clark, Ronald W. *The Life of Ernst Chain*. New York: St. Martin's Press, 1985.

Maurois, André. *The Life of Sir Alexander Fleming*. New York: E. P. Dutton, 1959.

Bickel, Lennard. *Rise Up to Life—A Biography of Howard Walter Florey*. London: Angus and Robertson, 1972.

FREUD

*Curtis, Robert H., M.D. *Mind and Mood*. New York: Charles Scribner's Sons, 1986.

Gay, Peter. *Freud—A Life for Our Time*. New York: W. W. Norton, 1988.

Jones, Ernest. *The Life and Work of Sigmund Freud*. Abridged by L. Trilling and S. Marcus. New York: Basic Books, 1961.

GALEN

Sarton, George. *Galen of Pergamum*. Lawrence, Kan.: University of Kansas Press, 1954.

HARVEY

Keynes, Geoffrey, Kt. *The Life of William Harvey*. Oxford: Clarendon Press, 1966.

HIPPOCRATES

Levine, Edward B. *Hippocrates*. New York: Twayne Publishers, 1971.

Lloyd, G. E. R., ed. *Hippocratic Writings*. New York: Penguin Books, 1978.

JENNER

Fisk, Dorothy. *Doctor Jenner of Berkeley*. London: Heinemann, 1959.

KOCH

Brock, Thomas D. *Robert Koch.* Berlin: Springer-Verlag, 1988.

Koch, Robert. *Essays of Robert Koch.* Translated by K. Codell Carter. New York: Greenwood Press, 1987.

LAËNNEC

Kervran, Roger. *Laënnec—His Life and Times.* Translated by D. C. Abrahams-Curiel. Oxford: Pergamon Press, 1960.

*Webb, Gerald B. *René Théophile Hyacinthe Laënnec.* New York: Paul B. Hoeber, 1928.

LAVERAN and ROSS

Jaramillo-Arango, Dr. Jaime. *The Conquest of Malaria.* London: William Heinemann Medical Books Ltd., 1950.

LEEUWENHOEK

Nieuwkoop and De Graff. *Van Leeuwenhoek, Antoni—On the Circulation of the Blood.* Latin text of his 65th Letter to the Royal Society: Facsimile—Introduction by A. Schierbeek.

LISTER

Farmer, Laurence, M.D. *Master Surgeon; A Biography of Joseph Lister.* New York: Harper and Row, 1962.

Fisher, Richard B. *Joseph Lister.* New York: Stein and Day, 1977.

METCHNIKOFF

Mechnikov, Olga. *Life of Elie Metchnikoff.* Boston: Houghton Mifflin, 1921.

MURRAY

*Moore, F. D. *Transplant, The Give and Take of Tissue Transplantation.* New York: Simon and Schuster, 1972.

MORTON

*Baker, Rachel. *Dr. Morton—Pioneer in the Use of Ether.* New York: Julian Messner, 1946.

*Curtis, Robert H., M.D. *Triumph over Pain.* New York: David McKay, 1972.

*Woodward, Grace Steele. *The Man Who Conquered Pain.* Boston: Beacon Press, 1962.

OSLER

*Cushing, Harvey. *The Life of Sir William Osler.* London: Oxford University Press, 1940 (originally published 1925).

Howard, R. Palmer. *The Chief: Doctor William Osler.* Canton, Mass.: Watson Publishing International, 1983.

PARÉ

Paré, Ambroise. *Apologie and Treatise.* Edited and with an introduction by Geoffrey Keynes. New York: Dover Publications, 1968.

Paré, Ambroise. *Selections from the Works of Ambroise Paré.* London: John Bale Sons & Danielsson, Ltd., 1924.

PASTEUR

*Dubos, René. *Pasteur and Modern Science.* Berlin: Springer-Verlag, 1988.

Vallery-Radot, René. *The Life of Pasteur.* Translated by Mrs. R. L. Devonshire. New York: Doubleday, Doran, 1928.

PINEL

Gibson, John. *Great Doctors and Medical Scientists.* New York: St. Martin's Press, 1967.

*Haggard, Howard W. *The Doctor in History.* New Haven: Yale University Press, 1934.

ROENTGEN

*Ghent, Percy. *Roentgen—A Brief Biography.* Toronto: The Hunter-Rose Company, 1929.

Streller, Ernst, Rolf Winau, and Armin Hermann. *Wilhelm Conrad Roentgen.* Bonn-Bad Godesberg, Germany: Inter Nationes, 1973.

SALK and SABIN

Carter, Richard. *Breakthrough—The Saga of Jonas Salk.* New York: Trident Press, 1966.

Smith, Jane S. *Patenting the Sun—Polio and the Salk Vaccine.* New York: William Morrow, 1990.

Fisher, P. J. *The Polio Story.* London: Heinemann, 1967.

SCHWEITZER

*Marshall, G., and D. Poling. *Schweitzer.* New York: Doubleday, 1971.

SEMMELWEIS

*Slaughter, Frank G. *Immortal Magyar.* New York: Henry Schuman, 1950.

SERTÜRNER

Goodman, Louis S., and Alfred Gilman. *The Pharmacological Basis of Therapeutics.* New York: Macmillan, 1968.

TAUSSIG

McNamara, Dan G., J. A. Manning, M. A. Engle, R. Whittemore, C. A. Neill, and C. Ferenz. *Historical Milestones—Helen Brooke Taussig: 1898 to 1986.* New York: Elsevier, 1987.

*Nuland, Sherwin B. *Doctors.* New York: Alfred A. Knopf, 1988.

VESALIUS

Castiglioni, Arturo. *Andreas Vesalius.* Reprinted from *Bulletin of the New York Academy of Medicine,* November 1943.

O'Malley, C. D. *Andreas Vesalius of Brussels.* Berkeley: University of California Press, 1964.

*Tarshis, Jerome. *Andreas Vesalius.* New York: Dial Press, 1969.

VIRCHOW

*Haggard, Howard W. *The Doctor in History.* New Haven: Yale University Press, 1934.

*Nuland, Sherwin B. *Doctors.* New York: Alfred A. Knopf, 1988.

WATSON and CRICK

*Frankel, Edward. *DNA: The Ladder of Life.* New York: McGraw Hill, 1978.

Tiley, Nancy A. *Discovering DNA.* New York: Van Nostrand Reinhold, 1983.

Watson, James D. *The Double Helix.* New York: New American Library, 1968.

*Wilson, Frank H. *DNA: The Thread of Life.* Minneapolis: Lerner Publication Company, 1988.

Index